The Eupantophone

BY THE SAME AUTHOR

The Petitpaon Era
The Olotelepan

Henri Austruy

The Eupantophone
and Other stories

translated, annotated and introduced by
Brian Stableford

A Black Coat Press Book

ISBN 978-1-61227-293-1. First Printing. June 2014. Published by Black Coat Press, an imprint of Hollywood Comics.com, LLC, P.O. Box 17270, Encino, CA 91416. All rights reserved. Except for review purposes, no part of this book may be reproduced or transmitted in any form or by any means, electronic or mechanical, including photocopying, recording, or by any information storage and retrieval system, without permission in writing from the publisher. The stories and characters depicted in this novel are entirely fictional. Printed in the United States of America.

TABLE OF CONTENTS

Introduction

L'Eupantophone by Henri Austruy, here translated as *The Eupantophone*, was originally published as an eight-part serial in the fortnightly periodical *La Nouvelle Revue* between September and December 1904. It was reprinted in book form by Flammarion in 1905, and a second edition appeared in 1909. It was the author's first novel. The first of the three shorter works accompanying it here, "La Taverne," translated as "The Tavern," appeared in *L'Humanité Nouvelle* in 1899; the other two, "La Statue" and "Le Château," translated as "The Statue" and "The Castle" respectively, each appeared in two parts in the *Nouvelle Revue* in April-May and July 1901.

"Le Statue" and "Le Château" marked the beginning of a lifelong association between Henri Austruy and the *Nouvelle Revue*. The periodical had been founded in 1879 by Juliette Adam, a famous feminist and political activist who was close-ly associated with the left-wing Republican Léon Gambetta, and· whose second husband, the lawyer Edmond Adam, had also been very active in Republican politics. Although her name continued to appear on the periodical's masthead, proud-ly advertised as its founder, until it was finally killed off with-in weeks of the Germans occupying Paris in August 1940, she sold it in 1899 to Gambetta's distant cousin Pierre-Barthelémy Gheusi, a notable writer who had begun his career as a pub-lisher by helping Anatole Baju to found *Le Décadent*, one of the key pioneers of the literary Decadent Movement, in 1887, and had also edited the literary supplement of *Le Gaulois*.

It was Gheusi who hired Austruy as his "editorial secre-tary" in 1901, presumably making him responsible for much of the day-to-day running of the magazine. When Gheusi moved on in 1913, in his turn, in order to become the director of the Opéra-Comique, Austruy took over as "editor-in-chief," presumably having bought the periodical from Gheusi as

Gheusi had previously bought it from Juliette Adam, and he ran it until its demise, which was followed not long after by his own. The circumstances of his death are unrecorded, but it could well have been the case that the Nazis felt that stifling a potentially-troublemaking voice with a long and proud history of left wing agitation required more strenuous action than merely shutting down its printing press. Austruy had written and signed a long-running series of articles on foreign affairs under the general heading "L'Organisation de le Paix" [The Organization of Peace], explicitly representing European politics between the wars as a long struggle to stave off the threat of a second world war; understandably, his treatment of Adolf Hitler had been consistently scathing.

Little biographical information is available regarding Henri Austruy, most of it derived from the brief information he provided to the 1924 edition of the short-lived French equivalent of *Who's Who, Qui êtes-vous?* It is recorded therein that he had been born on 5 July 1871, and that he was a former advocate in the Court of Appeal. Two published works are listed: *L'Eupantophone* and the author's second novel, *L'Ère "Petitpaon"* (1906;[1] the full title is *L'Ère "Petitpaon" ou La Paix universelle*), although a volume of works for the theater is advertised as "*en preparation*," with no title. One pseudonym is listed (Mgr—i.e. Monseigneur—Peilhagor) although he had certainly used several more on articles in the *Nouvelle Revue*. There is a slim possibility that "Henri Austruy" was itself a pseudonym; the dedication of *L'Ère "Petitpaon"*—to his editorial colleague at *La Nouvelle Revue*, Johannès Gravier—is signed A.H., although that is probably a simple misprint. When he was awarded the rank of Chevalier in the

---

[1] The date of publication of *L'Ère Petitpaon* indicated in the Bibliothèque Nationale Catalogue is 1908, but that is definitely mistaken. The book is undated, but it was reviewed in the *Mercure de France* in 1906 and the "latest titles" advertised by the publisher in the back of the book are all 1906 publications.

Légion d'honneur in 1907, the award was made in the name of Henri Austruy.

The preliminary material in *L'Ère "Petitpaon"* also lists a title in preparation, *Les Joies de la vie et de la mort*, but it never appeared, and Austruy's literary career following publication of *L'Ère "Petitpaon"* seems to have been entirely confined to the *Nouvelle Revue* and its associated press, except for the occasional review in the *Revue Hebdomadaire*. Under the auspices of the *Nouvelle Revue* he also issued a number of books in the mid-1920s, mostly consisting of collections of his articles, although some include scripts for plays, at least two of which were staged, and a collection of five novelettes, headed by "La Statue." That tends to be cited in bibliographies as the title of the book, although it actually has none apart from a list of the five items it contains; the others are "Le Château," "Le Pays d'Humanie" (1902), "Miellune" (1908) and "La Jungle républicaine" (1919). Google Books gives the date of that collection as 1901, having copied that date from the capsule reference in the Bibliothèque Nationale catalogue, although the expanded reference makes it clear that that was the publication date of the first story in the collection and that the collection itself is of much later provenance. Although undated, the collection began to be advertised in the pages of the *Nouvelle Revue* in 1925, and that is presumably its real publication date.

The fact that another title had been listed as forthcoming in the Louis Michaud edition of *L'Ère "Petitpaon"* implies that Austruy had definitely hoped to continue his career on a broader front at that point, but that he ran into difficulties, perhaps caused by the controversial aspects of the novel, a combative satire which might well have caused considerable offence in some quarters, especially to religious believers. How long those struggles continued it is difficult to judge, but he certainly seems to have given up trying by 1913, when the option of exclusive self-publication became available to him. He did, however, continue to write fiction in addition to his articles and reviews, and although he never published another novel in book form after *L'Ère "Petitpaon,"* he did serialize three further novels in the pages of the *Nouvelle Revue*, "L'Olotélépan" (1925), "Un Samsâra" (1932) and "Antoine et Sidonie" (1940). It seems probable that he did not originally intend "L'Olotélépan" to appear only as a serial, as it was advertised in the pages of the *Nouvelle Revue* as a book "*en preparation*" in 1923, but no book version was released, and it seems likely that he was no longer in a financial position by 1925 to indulge in further adventures of that kind, even though the periodical was obviously still viable, and remained so until it was murdered.

At any rate, the shape of Austruy's career did not exactly pave the way for further remembrance, and he has, in fact, been almost completely forgotten; unlike his predecessors as proprietors of the *Nouvelle Revue*, he has no Wikipedia entry, and he has no entry in Pierre Versins' *Encyclopédie de l'utopie, des voyages extraordinaires et de la science-fiction* (1972), in spite of the fact that four of his five novels contain significant elements of scientific, technological or political speculation, as do three of his six novelettes; after "L'Eupantophone," in fact, all of his fiction contained at least a fugitive component of scientific speculation, although it is very marginal in "Antoine et Sidonie," a melodrama of tangled family relationships whose main characters include a veterinary surgeon and a physician.

The remainder of Austruy's shorter works are fantastic to varying degrees, often being set in fictitious worlds, although such supernatural elements as they contain tend to be surreal rather than magical, deployed in the interests of allegory or satire. All of his fiction is eccentric and highly idiosyncratic, bearing little resemblance to anything else published in the French genres of *roman scientifique* and even less to the genre of the *fantastique* as normally understood in France, but given the essential eccentricity of the genres in question, that would normally be regarded as an advantage, and the very peculiarity of the works in question adds a further dimension of interest to them within the context of the history of fantastic fiction.

This volume is the first of three collecting Austruy's work in those genres, which makes them available as an ensemble for the first time. The second volume, *The Petitpaon Era and Other Stories*, will include a translation of *L'Ère "Petitpaon,"* entitled "The Petitpaon Era; or, World Peace" plus translations of "Le Pays d'Humanie," "Miellune," and "La Jungle Républicaine," as "The Land of Humania," "Miellune" and "The Republican Jungle" respectively. The third volume, *The Olotelepan and Other Stories* will include, along with the title story, a translation of "Un Samsâra," as "A Samsara" and a translation of "La Révélation de Maître Flaver" (1939) as "Master Flaver's Revelation." Apart from "Antoine et Sidonie" and the short story "Ange Devermeil" (1902 in *La Rue Hebdomadaire*) the set contains all the fiction by Austruy currently available on *gallica*, which is probably all that he ever published.

Like P.-B. Gheusi, Austruy obviously started out his writing career under the aegis of the Decadent wing of the Symbolist movement, but apart from "La Taverne" and an incomplete short story read aloud by the eupantophone in "L'Eupantophone" he does not seem to have published much work that is entirely confined to that tradition. There are significant elements of Symbolist fantasy in both "Le Statue" and "Le Château," but there are other aspects to each story, which make them much more distinctive—a process of evolution clearly continue in "Le Pays d'Humanie," which I have placed in the second volume of the series in order to even out the wordage of the three volumes a little more, although it was originally published before "L'Eupantophone," and is thus out of chronological sequence.

The Decadent Movement effectively ended with the century, and although many of the leading figures involved in the Symbolist Movement continued to publish long after that, they no longer constituted a movement and their work usually diversified considerably. Austruy was by no means the only one who became a satirist, nor was he the only one to develop an interest in scientific and technological speculation. The same was true of the two writers who became the most significant forerunners of surrealism, Alfred Jarry and Guillaume Apollinaire, and there is certainly an element of surrealism in Austruy's work, although it is only given completely free rein in "La Révélation de Maître Flaver." He had more in common with Frédéric Boutet and Gabriel de Lautrec, both of whom started off with a similar interest in earnest allegory and dabbled briefly in proto-surrealist absurdism before going on to develop a career more fully adapted to popular taste—but Austruy, in command of his own marketplace, never felt the need to adapt his work more narrowly to public taste, and remained defiantly quirky until the end.

Although both Juliette Adam and P.-B. Gheusi had published a reasonably wide range of fiction while they were in control of the *Nouvelle Revue*, with a distinct preference for Symbolists, Austruy published relatively little fiction except for his own, mostly filling its pages with political, historical and critical articles, although he did run occasional serials by other hands and he also introduced a regular feature on "Le Sport hippique" (horse-racing). Most of the work he published was produced by a regular stable of commentators.

Austruy's pacifism, evident in his articles on foreign affairs, is only obliquely represented in his fiction, with a sarcasm that harks back to the satirical method of Albert Robida, another writer of imaginative fiction with whom he has a certain affinity—although his politics were a long way to the left of Robida's—and his later fiction gives the impression of being mainly for amusement, by way of relaxation from more earnest analyses of the way the world was going. The early stories contained in the present volume, however, illustrate the author's relatively tentative attempts to find a method and a purpose, and can all be regarded as experimental, although "L'Eupantophone" shows very obvious signs of relaxation and sheer self-indulgence.

The imagery of the three shorter stories is often striking without its import being abundantly clear. "La Taverne" and

"La Statue" are distinctly gnomic, refusing to draw explicit morals from their substance, although the latter does displays a marked antipathy to religion that was to become sharper and more explicit in later works. Both items give the impression that they might have been based on dreams—a source of inspiration deliberately deployed by several writers affiliated to the Decadent Movement, including Gabriel de Lautrec, and later taken up by the Surrealists. "Le Château" is considerably more disciplined in its capsule analysis of the manner in which history transforms the relics of the past, and the paradoxical way in which antiquaries preserve the fantastic aspects of legendry even while trying to deny or expel them. Although by no means overstated, its basic moral thrust is clearly perceptible

L'Eupantophone obviously marked a drastic change of direction by the author, moving his setting to the contemporary world, and involving a good deal of conventional satirization of both Parisian and Provincial mores, with considerable affection as well as a certain acidity. Although it takes its title from one of its protagonist's inventions—a machine for reading text aloud—it is actually the more basic invention from with that device is spun off that provides the plot with its impetus and direction. What makes the novel so very different from other contemporary works of fiction featuring new inventions is the manner in which it is deployed. The fiction of the period is by no means short of hypothetical scientists who keep their inventions secret, employing them privately rather than making them available to their fellows, but very few go to such extremes of secrecy as Victor Blancadet, or direct their purpose toward such an odd objective, toward with the narrative moves at an unusually relaxed pace, unafraid to digress in various seemingly-random directions—until it undergoes an abrupt change of direction that alters its nature, tone and satirical targeting drastically.

It is difficult to believe that the plot of *L'Eupantophone* was planned in advance, and its remarkable conclusion was probably a result of belated improvisation, but it is certainly an intriguing development, and it works to the story's advantage, at least from the viewpoint of readers fond of the eccentric and the unusual. It is not surprising that it was the most successful of his novels, in terms of its critical reception and its sales, although many of its readers probably thought it a promising work rather than one fully achieved.

The career for which it eventually turned out to have laid the most significant foundation-stone is not exactly the one toward which it seemed at first to be preparing, and it remains a trifle isolated in Austruy's canon, not merely as his longest and most detailed work, but the one that strives hardest to cultivate what were seen at the time as orthodox literary virtues. It did, however, lay significant foundations, not merely for Austruy's future dabblings with eccentric pseudoscientific theory and gadgets enhancing the human sensorium, but also for the determined unorthodoxy of his plotting. It is perhaps the least strange of all his works, but it nevertheless contains and nurtures the seeds of strangeness that were subsequently to see further cultivation in the curious hothouse of his creativity.

As a contribution to the evolution of *roman scientifique* in the years when French writers took significant inspiration from translations of the early works of H. G. Wells, *L'Eupantophone* was by no means as crucial as the works of writers like Maurice Renard and J.-H. Rosny Aîné; its narrative range is much more limited, and the novel with which he followed it up, although considerably more melodramatic, demonstrated that his personal interests were more political than technological, but it certainly helped to pave the way for "L'Olotélépan," in which the eponymous invention can be regarded as a further development of the underlying principle of the eupantophone, and whose further-reaching consequences are explored with a remarkable anticipatory acumen. Had either novel been more widely read and more widely inspirational, their influence could only have been benign, and all of Austruy's work still warrant reading today—perhaps more so than ever, now that the ingenuity of his thinking can be better appreciated than it could at the time when he was active.

All the translations herein were made from the copies of the relevant periodicals reproduced on the Bibliothèque Nationale's *gallica* website. One page of the *gallica* version of volume XXXI of the *Nouvelle Revue*, containing part of the serial version of "L'Eupantophone," is partially blacked out, but I was able to recover the relevant text from the London Library's copy of that volume.

Brian Stableford

THE TAVERN

The realization of a great event, the dawn was soon to rise over the city on the day appointed for the opening of the Tavern, unknown beneath its garment of mystery, which animated the spirit of its inhabitants.

One day, a ship had entered the port; no one knew where it had come from, and no one recognized the sky-blue flag that flew upon its mast; a man had disembarked, who simply said that his homeland was a distant country on the far side of the world, which was called Humanity. It was from there that he had come to build the city a Tavern, which his promise made unique in richness and splendor.

A few merchants, fearing an inconvenient rivalry, tried to oppose the Stranger's project, but when the latter had declared that on his death the Tavern would become the property of the city, general interest was finally won over.

Ruins stood in the central quarter; only fragments of walls remained standing, which must have vanquished many years, to judge by their enormous stones, blackened as if by the flames of a volcano, in which the rain had hollowed out deep grooves. They were the vestiges of a very ancient temple to a divinity worshiped many centuries ago; a sacred statue had been preciously guarded there, the possession of which was the pledge of the existence of the city. Speaking in the name of verity against the old superstitions, however, a new God had come; his devotees had broken the henceforth-unnecessary palladium; they had constructed another dwelling to their idol and that of the defunct divinity had become a lair of nocturnal birds, whose cries were used by mothers to frighten disobedient children.

The site of the temple was the location chosen by the stranger to build the Tavern. One of the city's administrators had advocated respect for that corner of ground, where the altar to the goddess protecting the city had been raised, adding that selling the ruins was trafficking the very soul of the ancestors, but so enormous was the sum offered that the majority, for fear of discontenting the people, dared not refuse the money, which would serve to construct schools for children and barracks for soldiers.

Several ships bearing the same sky-blue flag came to drop anchor alongside the first; they brought workmen and materials. Attentive to the enormous blocks of unusual substance, to which the oldest scholars could not put a name, but the value of which must have been very great to judge by the care with which they were disembarked, a crowd gathered in the harbor, vaguely oppressed by the mystery. People tried to question the workmen, but they did not appear to understand the words that were addressed to them; as for their master, his weary azure eyes, in which gleams floated like pale reflections of the flag of his ship, deterred the most audacious.

As the work advanced, unanimous anxiety increased, and when the solemn moment finally came, an anxious and fatal crowd, intimately moved by the new thing that was in birth, hastened toward the attractive edifice, the roof of which, as flat as the terrace of the royal palace, was higher that the tallest monuments of the city.

A peristyle with a triple row of violet columns preceded the high-ceilinged hall in which echoes vibrated as if in an immense bronze bell. In the silence of Erebus the walls rose up, high and implacable, without the slightest ornament. Sustaining the hyaline ceiling, like an immense blue cloud, though which light filtered, gigantic caryatids were standing, their arms in the arc of a circle above their heads; they were made of a kind of marble with the pale hue of the complexion of brunette women, and over their surface, which had the warmth of the human body, blue threads traced a network of veins. Beneath the weight of the ceiling, apparently as light as the air whose troubling transparency it had, the muscles of the giantesses bulged, and on the ground, their feet clenched their toes as if to dig their nails into the hard substance, of a motionless and profound black, without any gleam, which muffled the sound of footsteps.

Immaculate doves struck by sudden death and falling in the absolute darkness, came into the infinite void of the ground and the walls to bury their palpitating souls, which shivered in that funereal frame. There were sculpted cathedras of ivory and gold, the backs of which were illuminated by dazzling adamantine stones and blazing rubies. Minuscule lakes of light, turquoise tables and stellate aventurines stood out from the somber silver cradling their drowsy sparkle, like captive stars whose delicate and slender rays, having exhausted their uncertain life, sought rebirth in the flamboyant life of the cathedras. Cups of topaz and onyx, decorated with unknown gems, glistened softly. Then there were the discreet gleams of tender opals, the virginal breath of which was softly exhaled, sage amethysts advising against drunkenness, pious and placid sapphires and green heliotropes, which tinted the radiant daylight with blood.

It was a whole supreme world for which the early morning hour would come as a bright baptism of luminous glory, and even eyes accustomed to the most incomparable solemnities were dazzled, humiliated by those miraculous splendors. Probing the reality, hands advanced, fearful of killing the triumphant vision, and yet, no covetousness for the proffered riches was ignited in hearts, so monstrous and inconceivable did their personal possession seem, akin to that of the sun.

Perhaps there were a few among the inhabitants who calculated the profits they might extract from the travelers that the Tavern could not fail to attract, but the majority, ashamed under the gaze of the Stranger standing at the entrance to the Tavern, who fixed them with his pale eyes, imprinted with a vague merciful scorn, did not linger on the idea of lucre.

It also seemed to them that with that luminous palace, the soul of a previously-obscure and very distant past had emerged from the shadows, where it had been buried for a long time, surging forth into that dazzling present. They felt their being giving birth to a soul of light and life, with which they would live henceforth, and it was not without a great anguish that they thought about the imminent departure of the Stranger.

Perhaps he was quitting them to go to construct a similar Tavern in another city, and the tortuous desire obsessed them to know whether he had ever accomplished such a work before.

With an immense interior joy that not everyone could master, they saw the ship that was carrying the stranger and his workmen away sink as soon as it had left the harbor. Assuredly, it was some benevolent god who had caused that disaster, for the sea was strangely calm, and no one knew of any reef at the site of the catastrophe.

At the same instant, a mute chorus of unanimous gratitude rose up toward the heavens. Henceforth, the Tavern was theirs, and theirs alone, and they no longer feared a dispossession or any sharing of profit with allies or enemies, known or unknown.

Every day, the inhabitants came to the Tavern. While drinking and smoking their long porcelain pipes, they chatted about their affairs, and those of the city. Scholars had given names to the precious unknown substances, which had thus become less strange to them and had acquired an existence of absolute reality in their eyes.

No one seemed to be able to believe in a different state of affairs, and the quietude was general and perfect. One day, however, a young man who had studied theology and ancient philosophy, said in a loud voice, among a circle of friends, that although the Tavern was a monument of an incomparable and an inimitable beauty, the ceiling was gradually lowering, very slowly but with a regular and inexorable progress. It was, he explained, the sun's rays, the breath of respiration and the smoke of pipes that, in being gradually incorporated into the substance of the ceiling, were increasing its weight and its opacity. He added that day would come when darkness would be complete within the Tavern and the ceiling would reach the floor, forming a single sold block with it.

A shrugging of shoulders and loud laughter greeted the crazy assertion, and one old the oldest and richest merchants, constraining his smile into a pitying and mocking grimace, asked: "Is that what your philosophy teaches you, young man?"

Without another word or gesture, the young man, who perceived that no one was paying any heed to what he said, went away.

In spite of the ridicule and the insanity of what the young man had said, on the advice of the most prudent, who were able to find a reasonable motive—just as they would have summoned a physician to see themselves or someone dear to them, even in the case of an inoffensive malady—they asked the most skillful architect in the city, who had already received many honorifics and rare distinctions, to examine the Tavern.

After a mature and very conscientious examination, the architect declared that he was able to affirm the unparalleled solidity of the edifice and to offer a guarantee of its eternal duration.

Minds resumed the absolute quietude that the young man had ruffled momentarily with his folly, and all dread disappeared. Certain of their future, as they were of their present, joyful and proud, the inhabitants came to spend their time in that world of light and life.

"Down here nothing is perfect, and all happiness has its miseries," said the most illustrious philosophers of the city, so it was only with a very limited surprise that the inhabitants of the city who came to the Tavern related the dreams with which their sleep had been haunted. They had, indeed, seen that platform of the Tavern progressively sinking, the caryatids stiffening their muscles and flexing their backs and shoulders in vain beneath the crushing burden, to fall thereafter on to their knees in a definitive defeat one after another, their vertebrae cracking with a noise like broken seashells, and brains like their own spurting from their skull; and they were unable to escape from the tavern themselves, their breathless chests heaving, anguished by a few bubbles of air, until the enormous weight finally descended upon them for the most horrible of deaths.

The inhabitants laughed among themselves at atrocious unreality of their dreams—which were, after all, only vain terrors, perhaps caused by an excess of drink or brought on by evil spirits—and they made fun of the unfortunate visionaries, who, bravely and skeptically, also laughed at the terrors of their nights when they beheld the comforting sight of the Tavern, which still shone, in their eyes, with the same splendid brightness.

In solitude, however, hiding it as if it were an evil action, some of them secretly trembled with fear, and the most heroic consoled themselves with the thought that the ceiling was descending so slowly that the time of danger was very distant, and that only the generations of the far future would have to suffer it.

For some, that idea was a very real consolation, for after all, once their own task was complete and their life elapsed, it was up to their descendants to accomplish their tasks and arrange their lives; perhaps for them the labor would be hard and life difficult, but with the courageous will that the new generations would inherit from their ancestors, their victory was certain, and was not, in sum, a very admirable merit.

Happy and sure of their happiness and their life, the inhabitants were in the Tavern when, all of a sudden, a loud cry cut through the air.

All eyes looked upwards, and the transparency of the ceiling revealed a giant bird, whose flight had suddenly stopped above their heads. From its beak and its claws, human bones escaped: enormous femurs and tibias, perhaps whitened by some centuries-long flight through space, which fell through the ceiling, coming to smash up the whole interior and the resplendent life blossoming there. Under the impacts, the fulgurance of the diamonds was abruptly extinguished, and the pale frightened souls of agonizing gemstones expired in silent dread.

Changed into bleak and motionless statues, the inhabitants stopped, nailed by terror; and on their knees, with their heads lowered, they waited for death—which did not come for them all, however, at that moment...but forever and ever, night and silence enveloped the city like a black and lugubrious shroud, which was never lifted again.

THE STATUE

The sun had just risen over the waves when the man on watch identified a confused form that broke the monotonous line of the horizon. It was doubtless a ship, since the captain, an old mariner as familiar with the sea as an inhabitant of the city where he had spent his life could be, had said the day before that they would not encounter any land for a week.

The sailors were preparing the salute that they would exchange, in accordance with the invariable and courteous custom, with the as-yet-unknown vessel. If she was bound for the land that the *Vulture*, a naval vessel of the king of Ergastulia,[2] had just quit, she would carry good news to the wives and children left behind.

From the top of the mast, however, the man shouted that the distant blur did not seem to be a ship, and after having scrutinized the horizon for a little while longer he uttered the traditional cry: "Land ho! Land ho!"

The captain shrugged his shoulders and, with a loud burst of laughter, exclaimed: "If Heaven or Hell has placed an island out there, I shall be its king, and you, my lads, shall all be ministers!"

The crew, amused by the captain's quip, started replying with gibes to the watchman, who was still repeating his cry of: "Land ho! Land ho!"

Impatiently, the captain shouted to him: "Have you quite finished with your land, you blind fool! Wait, and I'll tell you the colors of her flag and her tonnage!"

And he aimed his telescope in an easterly direction.

---

[2] I have anglicized *Ergastulie*, as the story is set in an alternative world, which shares aspects of our legendry but not our history; it is, however, relevant that in French, an *ergastule* is a cell where convicts are kept.

"Why, that's odd," he murmured, with a vexed expression, wiping the lenses of his instrument. "But...yes...one might well think...but it's impossible: an island doesn't emerge like that in the middle of the ocean like a mushroom in a meadow! No matter...by all the devils, I intend to have a clear heart!"

He ordered that a course be set directly for the annoying blue patch that permitted itself to resemble an island unknown to him, Captain Hercule Cabanas.

The coast became clearer, interrupting the blue expanse of the sea with a somber line; gradually, all the anfractuosities emerged blackly from the gray background. The *Vulture* was now only advancing cautiously, for the captain had growled: "The devil's capable of having made reefs grow, since he's made an island grow!"

A few cables from the shore, as they were beginning to run out of depth, a launch was put to sea, in which ten sailors took their paces with the captain, who intended to set his own feet on the inadmissible land.

With a few strokes of the oars, the boat reached the beach—a beach of fine sand; true sand, its grains similar to those that Captain Cabanas had encountered in all the beaches in the world.

"It's strange, all the same," he murmured. "Land here, in the Ocean—a land I don't know. Oh, my lads, it's the first time that Neptune has given me that surprise! No matter: the inhabitants, if there are any, must be perfect savages, cannibals at least, who won't be unflattered to have the title of subjects of His Highly Exalted Majesty King Tyran I, whom we'll impose by consent or by force on these islanders, who belong to no one since their fatherland doesn't figure on any map. Come on, my lads, a triple hurrah in honor of our very powerful king His Majesty Tyran I! And you, Gaspard, hoist the national flag in order to proceed immediately with the baptism of our new colony. Now, you'll help me...what name should we give it?"

"The Island of Chance?" proposed one sailor.

"Imbecile! You know very well that there's no such thing as chance."

"Morning Island," suggested another.

"Why Morning Island? Because I discovered it as dawn was breaking? That's a reason! In faith, my lads, I believe that the God of the earth, the sky and the ocean simply wanted the name of the brave old mariner that your captain is not to be lost to posterity! So we'll offer to His Majesty Tyran I Hercule Cabanas Island!"

And the sailors, in chorus, replied: "Long live Tyran I, King of Ergastulia, and Hercule Cabanas Island!"

"Thanks, my lads, thanks. Oh, I'd never have dreamed of such glory. It's a matter now of conquering this land and taking possession of it in the name of our king. But before all, it's necessary to proceed with the greatest prudence. Gaspard, you go back to the *Vulture* with three comrades, and fetch arms and ammunition for everyone. Go, and be quick, because our thirst for conquest is ardent!"

The launch returned to the shore, and the little troop of reinforcements for which the captain had sent disembarked with weapons, which the sailors distributed. The captain gave a few further instructions, and the column marched off.

The sun had now dissipated the last morning mists, and they were beginning to perceive the distant trees of the forest, which extended in a verdant mass about an hour's march away, in the captain's estimation.

The latter, in fact, was not mistaken, for after that exact lapse of time, the Ergastulian sailors went into the tall trees.

The most profound calm reigned there; birds were fluttering in the foliage without calling out, with a dull rustle of wings, and the men, strangely impressed, fell silent too, pushing aside the low branches with their hands to avoid making the slightest sound.

The forest became so dense that the sky was no longer visible through the somber vault of interlaced branches. From time to time, the captain consulted his compass, muttering against the forest, which seemed never-ending. He was about to give the order to turn back, in fact, when a bright mass appeared through the curtain formed by the final trees, standing out against the backcloth of the sky.

Instinctively, the men inspected their weapons and Captain Cabanas, who was marching a few paces ahead, fell back to the right flank of the column.

The white mass was a huge stone construction, several stories high, with an almost-flat slate roof; large bays opened in the walls of the edifice, whose sculpted portal was hermetically sealed.

After having circled around the building in the most complete silence, so as not to awaken anyone, Hercule Cabanas decided to take advantage of the early hour to go into the city, from which a hundred paces still separated them.

The little troop advanced into a long avenue planted with trees of various rare species; branches doubtless broken by a recent storm hung down along the trunks or littered the ground, hindering the sailors' march. Suddenly, the foot of one of them collided with a mass buried beneath a pile of withered leaves. The man stumbled and, on getting up again, sought to discover what had caused his fall. To his great amazement, on parting the thickness of the branches, he discovered a cadaver lying on its back. The body was almost entirely naked, and the face almost completely crushed; nothing could any longer be distinguished but a long beard mingled with shreds of flesh.

The sailor could not suppress an exclamation, and Captain Cabanas, approaching, went pale at the sight of the corpse. Suddenly, danger loomed up, immediate and terrible. Understanding the folly of going into a city at the head of twenty men, keeping his voice low, as if he were now afraid of seeing someone surge forth at the end of the avenue, who might raise the alarm, he ordered a retreat. The troop made a detour to avoid the large white house, the sculpted portal of which might perhaps open, and rapidly returned to the shore at the place where the launch was still moored.

The boat returned to the *Vulture*, which raised her anchors shortly thereafter. The captain wanted to make a tour of the island, hoping to be able to discover the mysterious city, hidden to the east of the thick forest, from another direction.

A few hours later, the *Vulture* had terminated her voyage of exploration, which had not provided any result. Along every coast, about a mile and a half from the sea, the impenetrable forest loomed up, in which the city was buried.

Hercule Cabanas railed against the island, whose definitive conquest he planned to attempt the following day immediately after daybreak. The entire crew of the *Vulture* would be disembarked, with the exception of a few sailors indispensable to the maneuvering of the ship.

The night was spent preparing the weapons, and from dusk onwards, the launches transported two hundred men to the shore, who had made a solemn oath not to recoil before any danger and to die, if necessary, for the glory and honor of Ergastulia, their proud fatherland.

Sword in hand, the Captain reviewed his little army before following the same route as the day before, which did not seem as long because they all knew that they might find death at its end. Some would doubtless have liked to march for longer, or even to march forever, without reaching the perhaps-redoubtable goal.

They soon reached the large white house, which was silently surrounded. Rifle-butts hammered in vain on the portal, still closed, and all efforts to stave in the heavy oak panels remained futile. Breaking the glass, one sailor got into the mysterious house through a window; it was empty, but everything was in order, seemingly ready to receive guests who were temporarily absent.

The troop resumed its march, and arrived a few minutes later at the place where the mutilated cadaver had been found. The body was still there, more hideous than the day before, the insects and worms having continued the horrible task of eating through the green-tinted already-putrefying flesh to the bone.

They advanced further to the end of the avenue; a winding street commenced, bordered with houses with closed doors and shutters. The street made an abrupt turn, and an unexpected spectacle was offered to the dazed eyes of Captain Cabanas and his men. Cadavers were lying to the ground, pell-mell, with swords, spears and weapons of every sort.

With piercing cries, frightened birds of prey flew away, withdrawing their bloody beaks from ripped bellies, and the Ergastulians shivered, wondering how the silent and deserted city came to be populated solely by cadavers.

At every step now they encountered nothing but corpses, and a large square suddenly opened, which resembled a battlefield the day after a furious combat; heaps of cadavers rose up on ground greasy with blood and almost covered with frightfully mutilated bodies. A gigantic statue was lying there, with its head on the lowest steps of a broad marble stairway leading to an immense terrace, preceding the bronze doors of a palace. There were also corpses lying on the terrace, and blood had flowed down the steps, covering them with a blackened carpet.

The sailors uttered a cry of horror, forgetting momentarily that it was better for them to encounter dead men than living ones.

Then, through that city, transformed, for some unknown reason, into an immense charnel-house, there was a slow and funereal exploration, during which new scenes of horror surged forth at every step: old men snatched by the massacre from the imminent terminus of their lives and women with their throats cut, holding children in their arms. The houses were searched, the remotest corners of grain-lofts investigated; they descended into the depths of the darkest cellars, but it was impossible to discover a single living being.

That search went on for several days, but nothing was found to provide the key to the bloody mystery. A frightful calm reigned everywhere, and the Ergastulians were beginning to fear that they might be victims of an atrocious nightmare, when one of the sailors claimed to have heard a slight sound inside the gigantic statue lying in the large square at the foot of the stairway to the palace.

Captain Cabanas came to listen himself, and realized that the sailor was not mistaken. Several times, he struck repeated blows on the bronze, to which an equal number responded from inside the statue. Then he had the cadavers overlaying it removed, and the rhythmic noises continued, increasingly sonorous—but no trace of any opening appeared, although there was no doubt that a human being was enclosed in the flanks of the bonze colossus.

Hercule Cabanas thought that there might be a door on the dorsal surface that was set against the ground, and set about having the statue rolled over. It was a difficult task because of the formidable weight to be shifted, and it was only after several hours of effort that the two hundred mariners succeeded in changing the position of the enormous mass.

Abruptly, with a sound like that of a released spring, the bronze wall opened and the head of a man appeared. The Ergastulians recoiled from the fantastic apparition, and before they had had time to recover from their emotion, the man had already slithered down the side of the statue, which was as high as the hull of a ship. He stood there, motionless, without saying a word.

He was a man, similar in every respect to other men, except that he appeared to have pushed back the limits of old age indefinitely. His stature was neither tall not shot, and warranted perfectly the qualification of average. His hair, which he wore very long, was white, with the slightly jaundiced tint of linen that has been left too long folded in a cupboard. In sum, at first sight, he was an ordinary man: an old man, so remarkable well conserved that he still seemed to be endowed with the suppleness and agility of youth. On a more severe examination, however, it was apparent that the facial features and the entire person of the old man had arrived at a conclusive condition that time could no longer alter.

The strange individual did not raise his eyes, and the cadavers by which his feet were embarrassed did not appear to disturb or astonish him.

In a dull voice, he pronounced words that all the mariners heard.

"On my shoulders the years are heaped; in spite of their crushing weight, I who know the past, marched before you to light your path into the future...but the children are dead...shed my blood! Perhaps it will extinguish the gleam of the standards you follow!"

Taking off his black velvet cap, he knelt down before the gigantic status, murmuring "Poor, poor children!"

If one of the cadavers from whose bellies the entrails were spilling, excavated by the beaks of the birds of prey, had suddenly stood up, the amazement of Captain Cabanas and his crew could not have been greater. All the men whom death had not yet caused to go pale stood there with their feet nailed to the ground and their throats breathless before that fantastic creature, suddenly emerged from the bronze colossus, the sole living person in the city where death had spared no one else.

With a supreme effort, the Captain overcame his terror and, putting his hands together, he prayed in a strident and halting voice: "O charitable mother of the Omnipotent God, save us from Satan! On your altar, if I see our homeland of Ergastulia again, I shall burn a thousand wax candles!"

The old man shivered violently, as if awakening from some profound dream, and fixed the strangers with a blazing stare. A terrible cry escaped from his throat, which the frightened birds of prey soaring in the clouds repeated.

"Ah! The Land is no longer invisible, then? Who among you has torn away its veil? Brothers, brothers, what have you done?"

"To what brothers are you speaking? In the entire island you are the only living person...cadavers everywhere!" Hercule Cabanas articulated, with difficulty.

"Cadavers everywhere? In the entire island, I am the only man alive? Oh, death has fulfilled its mission! For you, poor

31

children, eternity was finally about to begin, but you have departed! Now there is unfathomable total darkness!"

And the strange individual's pupils dilated and retracted, like those of a man whose eyes really are seeking to pierce thick darkness.

Suddenly, his gaze was arrested, and, as if he were spelling out the words that he might have read in the frightened eyes of Captain Cabanas and his companions, he said in a slow and hesitant voice: "With the breath of souls flying toward the ethereal spaces, over the shores of distant countries, the breeze has lifted, inflating the sail that has brought you here to reforge the broken link..."

With a finger on his temple guiding the uncertain march of words, which emerged one by one from the silent shroud of his thought, he continued to speak, and at each phrase, each word he pronounced, his person shed something of its frightening aspect; the features of his face, as rigid as those of death, relaxed to melt into a human expression; the gleam of his eyes gradually faded, as the light of a star is extinguished at the approach of daylight, and it was merely an old man that was talking to the mariners, about their homeland Ergastulia.

"Strangers, I heard just now the name of Ergastulia...I know that country. I don't know whether I was born there, but I spend several obscure years of my distant infancy there; it's a very large country, so large that the sea cannot surround it, so large that the sun cannot illuminate it in its entirety!"

"Who are you, then?" interrogated Captain Cabanas, recovering his composure in the presence of a man who was familiar with his native land.

"Who am I? I was the adoptive father of two young children, who are dead now—and now I am only an old man, too old to live alone."

"What are the frightful events that have made this city a field of universal death? How have you, alone, survived the massacre?"

"You're asking me why the ground is strewn with cadavers? Why universal death reigns over this city and how I come to be the only living being therein? Oh, stranger, it's a somber story, such a somber story that the simple telling would seem to be madness. The city that sleeps today beneath the calm wing of death was a great city, whose flanks were agitated by luxuriant life...but men savagely and relentlessly, strove to destroy that life, and for many years, floods of blood in which the last combatants died flowed in the streets. One night, I took my children in my arms and went into the giant statue, of which I alone knew the secret issue. Hateful of every human form, the men tipped our bronze prison over, and the children perished in its fall..."

While the old man was speaking, a sailor had climbed up on the stature; he reappeared carrying the corpses of two children in his arms.

"You see! They're dead!" cried the old man, perceiving them. "But I have their white souls in my bosom, which I have taken, and I shall give them to two children of Ergastulia."

Captain Cabanas was anxious, because the city had undoubtedly been attacked and sacked by invaders from some neighboring land, and it was only too evident that the man speaking bizarre words had been driven mad by terror and fright. It was therefore prudent to return to Ergastulia as soon as possible, where scholars would take charge of interrogating the poor madman, and perhaps return his reason to him.

The captain ordered his sailors to collect some of the most precious objects, in order to make an offering to their sovereign. They were already all thinking about the recompenses they would be granted as they went joyfully back to the *Vulture*, which immediately set sail for the Ergastulian homeland.

In the joy of solemn festivals, Doulia,[3] the capital of the kingdom of Ergastulia, was preparing to celebrate Captain Cabanas' discovery, so profitable to the national patrimony.

---

[3] *Doulia* is a Greek term meaning reverence, in a religious context.

Grateful to the fortunate mariner, the king was to bestow upon him the insignia of the highest distinction with which an Ergastulian citizen could be invested. Indeed, only the sovereign's heirs wore the Great Regal Chain; on the day of his baptism the golden collar formed in a single piece, with the accompanying chain of the same metal, was placed around the newborn's neck. In no circumstance was the child ever to take off his collar, under penalty of losing all the privileges of his birth; he was expelled from the place, and as it was forbidden to give him shelter or to aid him, he did not take long to die of poverty and hunger.

The king himself could not elude that pitiless rule, nor accord any mercy in favor of his son, so the princesses of the royal blood watched over their children's collars with the same care as their own lives. That terrible danger remained a menace weighing relentlessly upon the frail slaves of their native grandeur, and the dread only ceased with adolescence because, at that age, the golden circle that had once been too large began to tighten around the neck, soon to become the definitive imprisoner of the shoulders and the head, which growth developed.

During his entire life it was impossible for the king to create more than six bearers of the Great Chain, so that honor was reserved as recompense for inestimable services rendered to the fatherland; for only the second time, Tyran I was about to use his right, having already accorded the Great Chain, since the beginning of his reign, to a man who had almost saved his life in a fire.

The ceremony of investiture demanded a pomp equal to that of the coronation of kings, so, for the people, it was one of the most early-anticipated spectacles as well as one of the rarest.

Before the entire Court, assembled in the chapel of the palace, the king closed the golden collar with his own hands, by means of a little lock in the form of a medallion, around his subject's neck, and then threw the little key into an ardent furnace, where it melted into a few formless droplets—which meant that the golden chain could never be unlocked again.

Afterwards, the popular rejoicing commenced; in the streets decorated with flowers of every sort and decked with flags in the national colors, preceded and followed by heralds and men-at-arms, the sumptuous cortege of the Court dignitaries advanced. They were placed in carriages with golden grilles, to remind them of the prohibition imposed on the great men of Ergastulia forbidding them to quit the territory of heir fatherland.

The inhabitants of Doulia had competed in zeal in making preparations for the festival; gigantic triumphal arches rose up everywhere, espoused by countless garlands, but as the spring was yet too young, only the rich had been able to procure natural flowers brought at great expense from a distant Ergastulian province where the hotter sun caused the first buds to bloom. In the poorer quarters, the hands of women and children had cut out artificial flowers from cloth and paper, larger and perhaps more beautiful than the veritable flowers; jealously ornamented, the humble streets seemed chimerical roads of dreams, timidly followed by unfortunates doubtless fearful of discovering behind the magical veil, at every heartbeat, the ordinary reality of their troubles and miseries.

Was it the ignorance of happiness that gave sight an unknown penetration, which made future events legible, as if in an open book, or did those fortunate on earth prevent those who suffered from losing a single minute of their dolor in an illusion or a lie? Either way, the poor people of Doulia were not deceived—and their dread was not in vain, for their dazzled eyes were to open again, with their dream barely commenced.

On the eve of the solemn day, the steward of the Court visited the city, and, doubtless judging unnecessary and superfluous that which his master would not see, he gave orders to take everything away, in order to add it to the ornamentation of the streets that the cortege would follow. Brutal hands took possession of the garlands whose multicolored flowers had been made with so much love that they no longer seemed to be inanimate flowers, and all the humble fruits of laborious and devoted hours went to mingle with the facile tribute of the rich and the aristocracy.

Sadly, the poor people saw their houses stripped of their festival garments, and in the shadows of the evening, furtive tears flowed before the lamentable black carcasses of crowns and trophies.

Leaving the suburbs of Doulia and the neighboring countryside, an enormous crowd invaded the great arteries of the capital.

After several hours of waiting among the enervating exhalations of flowers, from which a few petals were sometimes detached and flew over the triumphal arches, the blare of fanfares resounding in the distance announced the advent of the cortege and the first carriage came forward; it was the king of Ergastulia, holding in his left hand the chain attached to the neck of Captain Cabanas, who was sitting by his side beneath the gilded grille.

As they passed by, the people, frightened by the noise of trumpets and drums, exulted in frenetic acclamations; the same enthusiasm greeted the carriages that followed, and then the crowd became merely curious, impatient for the second spectacle they had been promised.

In one of the immense halls of the palace, Hercule Cabanas, Grandee of Ergastulia, was to bring before His Majesty Tyran I the unique subject discovered on the distant island, his conquest.

In spite of the prohibition of their captain, the sailors of the *Vulture* had talked about the man who had emerged, no one knew how, from a gigantic statue fallen among the heaped-up cadavers; some of them had repeated the enigmatic words than he had pronounced, which they had not understood. They had also said that, during the crossing, the strange old man had remained silent, after having declared that he would only speak before the Ergastulian people.

Legends were already circulating about the unknown man imprisoned in the fortress of the castle. When they spoke about him, men shook their heads or shrugged their shoulders, saying that he must be some madman, and women, as they passed before the barred windows of his cell, made the sign of the cross, as if in the vicinity of the demon. Everyone wondered what the things might be that until now he had not wanted to say.

The immense hall of the palace and the vast public square were, however, too small to contain the multitude that the attraction of mystery had added to the natural curiosity of the crowd. Many of the people heaped up there were too far away from the extremity of the hall where the stranger was to speak for any of his words to reach them, but they were resigned simply to look, and if it were even impossible to catch a glimpse of him, they would still be happy to be in the company of those who could hear and could see.

, A herald announced: "His Majesty the King!" and in the midst of the most profound silence, Tyran I made his entrance, followed by the royal family and the great dignitaries, among whom was Captain Cabanas, whose sparkling collar attracted the gaze.

At a gesture from the king, a door opened and four straight and rigid colossi wearing the uniform of royal guards came in, whose tall stature made the person of the old man seem even more paltry. All eyes were fixed upon him, without being able to extract a blink from him.

Slowly he advanced, and he passed in front of the king without bending his knee, without taking off his black velvet cap, his head upright, without a gesture.

As if petrified by the horror of the sacrilege, the courtiers did not budge, and only Hercule Cabanas had the presence of mind to hurl himself upon the old man in order to tear off his cap—but the latter had been warned and before he could seize it, calmly, the old man had thrown it over the ranks of the soldiers who were holding back the crowd.

The old man arrived at the foot of the red velvet stage that had been prepared in front of the throne; he stopped and turned his head, seeing Captain Cabanas depositing at the king's feet the cap that a soldier had brought from the place where it had fallen. Imperceptibly, his shoulders rose, a smile creased his lips, and he climbed the steps of the stage.

Upright, his black silhouette standing out against the red background of the drapes, he folded his arms over his chest, threw back his long white hair with an abrupt movement if his head, and the ardent pupils of his eyes drilled into the crowd as if searching for someone. Some people felt a sharp burning sensation in their hearts, reviving the obscure memory of a vanished past, revived by the strange man with whom it seemed to them that they had once lived.

The king, whose surprise impeded his anger, made a sign and Hercule Cabanas, his neck tight in his collar, bowed profoundly, low enough for the little sphere of ivory hanging from the end of his chain to touch the ground, as the rule required.

Turning toward the stage, he said, with a solemn stiffness: "His Majesty deigns to hear."

"To hear or to listen? What does it matter...?" said the old man—and, in a voice so clear that it seemed luminous, he began: "Powerful King, your realm is so large that men cannot be born outside its bounds..."

The courtiers, divining the delicate flattery hidden beneath these hyperbolic words, nodded their heads as a sign of affirmation.

"Your realm, O King, is as large as Hell, of which Heaven is the only rival. Like all men, therefore, I was born in Ergastulian territory; I can no longer count the time that I spent here, and my youth would be entirely foreign to me if, familiar in my dreams of infancy, my mother did not often come to caress my sleep. During my abandoned nights, clad in black, with eyes full of tears, she was close to me, and stayed there, inclining over my forehead until a sudden light was born in the shadows of her veils; my mother shuddered with a dolorous sob and her eyes closed in order no longer to see the accursed golden chain that trailed on the ground like a sparkling reptile; but the odious daylight became more powerful and my mother fled, her arms extended toward me, and I never knew why that accursed golden chain separated the mother from her child...

"Then there was a long voyage, the memory of which was buried in the creases of the white sails of the ship that carried me away to the unknown land where my adolescence lived its solitary years. I constructed a cabin of branches on the shore; the sea nourished me with shellfish, and at night, I captured weary birds that came to land on the sand...

"Thus, many days passed, monotonous and calm, accompanied by dull nights oppressed by the quivering dawn, one of which came preceding a woman whose white feet were pearled with delicate drops of dew. Harmoniously, with a slow tread, weighed down by her sodden robe, on which bright crystals scintillated, she came to my threshold, and rhythmic, starry words took flight from her lips: 'The tempest had swelled the waves and the light boat, passing over the summits of the silver mountains, came to lie upon the soft bed of sand...like a weary bird, my gondola has gone to sleep on the sand...like her, I am weary and would like to sleep...'

"We slept for a long time in one another's arms; less radiant than the auroras of our amour, long sequences of radiant dawns rose...until the sad morning when I woke up alone beneath my thatched roof. I ran to the boat asleep on the sand...the boat had gone, and lying in its place was a cradle in which two children were asleep...

"Before my eyes, which wept for the vanished mother, the two children grew, the brother loving the sister, the sister loving the brother, but, like birds that have a horror the nest in which their youth trembles, scorning my tenderness, the ingrates disappeared.

"For me, then, time no longer marched; the future was bound to the past in a perpetual present, and, as my eyes never closed, the days and nights melted into one another in identical, indiscernible hours, so I no longer know the number of years during which, always wearied by the road traveled, my feet trod the eternal forest whose shadows hid the stray children.

"On one dark night, I was walking sadly, when a faint light shimmered through the obscure mantle thrown over the crowns of the trees, and a few paces further on, my head bumped into a high wall, at the top of which a torch was burning. A cry rang out, followed by a sound of chains, and a blinding bay opened at the bottom of the high, dark wall. Men clad in somber iron threw themselves upon me and dragged me away brutally. Behind us, with a sharp screech, the door closed on the profound darkness of the forest.

"After advancing between several rows of torches that cast a harsh light of liquid metal, I was brought into the presence of a man clad in golden armor, whose hoarse voice rose up, saying: 'What were you doing outside the city? You know, however, that wandering in the forest is a crime punishable by death by the sword? How long ago did you cross the boundary wall?'

"When I replied that I did not know of any city and that I had left the shore in order to search the forest for my lost children, the man clad in gold stood up and remained immobile, with only the flicker of pale torchlight on his person; then his hand extended and, at a sign, two men bound my wrists with an iron chain, and the leader approached me in order to cover my eyes with an exceedingly thick black cloth. Afterwards I heard him give the order to follow him, and those surrounding me shoved me forward, holding me by the hands to direct me steps.

"In a profound silence, only troubled by the clink of weapons, I marched for a long time, until it seemed to me that our footsteps, now sounding on stone slabs, caused muffled echoes to rumble. 'Halt!' said a voice, which added: 'Untie him and make him kneel down.' The chain released my wrists while four hands weighed upon my shoulders, which forced me to fall to my knees.

"Abruptly, the blindfold slid from my eyes. It seemed to me that the harsh glare of liquid metal, put to sleep and muffled by the blindfold, awoke, and was liberated, springing forth in an immense flamboyance, which gradually eased into a soft light in which my eyes, momentarily dazzled, were able to recover their sight.

"I was beside the gold-armored chief, whose knees were also bent on the marble slabs paving an immense hall walled with silver, and in front of us, under a vault constructed of precious stones, on a throne richer than yours, O powerful King of Ergastulia, sat a statue of a woman, who was holding a sword in one hand and a long black veil in the other, which was hanging over a man prostrate at its feet.

"'Look,' said the gold-clad chief, getting to his feet, his right hand pointing at the statue. 'Swear love, obedience and fidelity.'"

The King, who had had seemed very interested in the story, burst out into sonorous laughter, which the echoes of the vast hall repeated; then the echo of the royal laughter was followed by the laughter of the courtiers, accompanied in its turn by multiple echoes that died away in the silent crowd, gravely stirred by the old man's strange words.

The latter, bowing his head, as if gripped by a kind of shame, turned to the King's throne, and continued:

"And from my lips fell those inert words: 'Love, obedience and fidelity.'

"'That is good; stand up,' the chief said to me, 'and never forget the oath that makes you a child of the city. Follow me,'

"The four men who had accompanied us inclined the heads of their spears toward the ground and marched behind us. After having passed through corridors and halls where guards stood motionless, who raised their right hands as we passed with an incomprehensible gesture of the index finger, to which my guide replied with a similar gesture, we arrived on a terrace of white marble that the rising sun was beginning to tint with rosy gleams

41

"At our feet an immense square extended, and my guide, his two hands resting on the large cross that formed the hilt of his sword, paused for a moment, and his eyes, full of protective tenderness, remained fixed on the compact crowd that was agitating, with shrill exclamations piercing the dull continuous murmur. Then his gaze turned toward me, and his voice, which now seemed to be the pure sound of his golden armor, said to me in a one of proud mercy: 'Old man, you cannot be a soldier. Down there are artisans, traders...you will find your place in their ranks...'

"Almost immediately, however, he went on: 'Your age might perhaps merit respect; I will have you taken to the house where old age has the right to shelter its final years.'

"One of the men who had accompanied us came forward and beckoned me to follow him; on his heels I went down the marble steps, and the crowd parted before his spear as before something menacing. At the opposite extremity of the square a long avenue opened, at the end of which I perceived a house with walls of white stone.

"With the shaft of his spear, the man struck three raps on a copper plate fitted into the walls of the portal, the enormous sculpted battens of which parted almost immediately, revealed the white silhouette of a man wrapped in a large cloak.

"'The chief has sent him,' said the soldier, turning the point of his spear toward me.

"The man held out his arms and his large floating sleeves looked like two great birds advancing toward me. 'Enter and be welcome, my white-haired brother; the duration of the city's happiness is augmented by the number of years by which your head is ornamented. How old are you, my brother?'

"'When the somber forest took my dear children,' I replied, taking the trembling hand that the old man offered me to help me cross the hospitable threshold, 'the waves had already given me the silver of their foam.'

"In a hall, men whose necks were curbed beneath the weight of time were walking with the uncertain gait of infants, holding on to heavy armchairs in which, their eyes still partly open to that life, other old men were following their ancient dreams motionlessly.

"When I came in, the heads inclined toward the floor straightened up slightly; the half-closed eyes raised their heavy eyelids to become animated with a fugitive gaze, and several voices quavered obscure questions. 'They are my elder brothers,' said the man who had introduced me, smiling. 'Our youth still loves the great trees and birdsong.'

"And together, the two of us went down into a vast garden whose laws softened with their verdant tints the shade of the dense foliage. As I often had in the forest, when my tired knees buckled under the weight of my body, I stopped at the foot of a tree, trying to give the soft clay the features of my children, and sat down on the bank of a stream whose clear water was gliding soundlessly by; and all day long I sought to revive the dear forms whose memory my eyes retained. Always, though, the obsessive image kept reappearing of the old men, who were stammering the vacillating detritus of their expiring lives in the hall above.

"Night had fallen and the moon was extending its pale silvery caress over the calm stream; my unskillful fingers had interrupted their impossible task, and he dolorous succession of my dreams had absorbed my thoughts entirely when my companion came back. 'Do you know,' I asked him, 'why knees bend before the statue sitting on the throne that sparkles out there between the silver walls of the mysterious palace? What do the words, *love, obedience and fidelity* symbolize that are murmured at its feet'

"'Lower your voice, my brother,' the old man replied, putting the imperious finger of silence over his lips. 'What, your white hairs have not informed you? Then content yourself with the three words, and combine with them, if you wish, all the human syllables affirmative of humility and adoration, and then pray, until the still-distant night when the new lustral star will rise; in the morning of that night, we shall go to the place to prostrate ourselves before the one of whom you speak, and on that day, perhaps you will understand.'

"Later a brilliant star appeared in the sky; immediately, all the old men added a ring to the necklaces that hung around their necks; the next day, at dawn, the stronger guiding the steps of the most debilitated, in a slow procession, we all went through the large doors of the palace.

"The statue of the woman who was holding a blade in her right hand and a dark veil in her left, suspended over the head of a prostrate man, was still sitting on the throne, under the vault of precious stones, at the back of an immense hall with a floor of marble slabs and walls of silver, but a large reliquary of fine crystal enveloped it entirely with its rigid shroud, as if they were afraid to let the slightest breeze reach it, and faithful soldiers were watching without pause, charged with putting to death anyone whose raised voice might impart the danger of the slightest vibration to the air. Even the lamps had muted their overly sharp rays and softened their discreet gleams, with which the shadows mingled, in a mild atmosphere of perpetual repose.

The crowd, in a silent flood, approached, kneeling down devotedly, and then, without topping on the marble terrace, went back down to the vast square, where men and women in compact groups were whispering and lowering their eyes; only bolder adolescents were talking in loud voices. 'Old age is fragile,' one of them said. 'It's for that reason that the ancient statue up there is surrounded by so many precautions—but all is vain against death, which comes to us all when the hour sounds!'

"One old man, his eyes fixed on his distant past, sang bitter words of regret in his tremulous voice: 'Once, in the times of my youth, as today, signs of weakness had appeared; as today, the young people proclaimed that everything was about to end, but they took possession of all those whose voices had spoken too loudly; then the white statue was bathed with their crimson blood, and the generous blood returned the statue to its primal firmness; but as it had taken on a red tint, a light delusory azure veil concealed the unusual color for many years for the people, who, their nostrils quivering at the odor of blood that it exhaled, bowed their heads very low before the somber and redoubtable mystery. Today the veil has disappeared and the statue has resumed its antique whiteness; as before, in my youth, her candid pallor is thirsty for the crimson blood of those who do not believe in her!'

"The old man continued, amid laughter and cries, and drew away, shaking his head.

"The lustral star was shining its final hours when, one morning, a great noise erupted in our silent abode; soldiers were coming, it was said, in search of a hundred of the oldest men, and one of them revealed the frightful secret that the palace still kept. In its reliquary of transparent crystal, the statue had vanished, and at the foot of the throne, lying on the marble slabs edged with gold, was a thick layer of gray dust. The guards, still standing at the posts they had occupied the previous day, had collapsed heavily on to the ground at a simple handclap, with a sinister sound, in the terrifying silence.

"At this story the old men went frightfully pale, for all of them had understood the soldiers' mission, and when the soldiers asked for the man whose age reserved him the honor of marching at the head, no one spoke. It was necessary then to seize the necklaces and count the years whose number, until then, had been a grave subject of legitimate pride.

"And those old men who were incapable of quitting their armchairs clung to them with all the energy of their last remaining strength, shreds of torn cloth remaining in their clutching fingers. The others tried to flee, but their tottering limbs betrayed them and they fell, with cried of impotent rage.

"When the soldiers had gone, the great hall was almost deserted, and on the faces of the old men who had been spared, anguish had imprinted something akin to the mark of a willful and supreme desire to go to living. They looked at one another, their eyes filled with tears, all thinking about the bloody sacrifice of which they were about to be the victims.

"The doors of the palace had been hermetically sealed, and under the blades of the chiefs, into the ancient brass vessel in which the impalpable dust fallen at the foot of the throne had been gathered, the blood of the old men had run, and the vigorous fingers of the soldiers were kneading the inanimate gray matter in the lukewarm crimson liquid.

"For long hours, by the light of lamps decked with mourning veils, the sinister work continued, but the audacious form stubbornly refused to be born of that bloody mud with somber gleams.

"Then the soldiers threw themselves at the knees of their chief, begging him to mingle their own blood with the willful blood of the old men, and the brass vessel could not contain all of the red tide that extended over the slabs in a sticky sheet, all the way to the massive close doors and beyond.

"Exasperated by anguish at the sight of the blood that was soiling the once-immaculate marble terrace, the young people rushed into the palace to seek liberation there from the pressing nightmare—the obsession of which disappeared before the horror suddenly surging before them.

"Empty of its statue, beneath the sparkling vault, the throne rose up, and in front of it an enormous basin was half-tipped over beneath the weight of a human body buried to the shoulders in the thick liquid still remaining in its bottom. All around the hall, leaning against the silver walls, decapitated bodies were sitting, some enveloped by the white vestments of old men and other tightly contained in the still breastplates of warriors.

"The adolescents remained nonplussed momentarily; then the youngest among them advanced and seized the belt of the man leaning over the brass bowl. With a great effort, weakened by the horror of his task, he pulled the cadaver out of its bloody tomb. First the head appeared, coiffed in a large helmet terminated by a long plume, then the hands came free, weighed down by two severed heads, held by the hair clutched in clenched fingers. From the upright body, sliding from the helmet and the shoulders, thick bloody clots reddened the pale hands that surrounded his waist. A cry escaped from all the contracted throats.

"'It's the chief of the soldiers!'

"At the same instant, the lamps veiled with mourning went out; the cadaver collapsed heavily on the damp ground, raising heavy splashes, and a voice rose up gravely in the silent shadows:

"'Floods of blood have dragged into eternal night our terrors and our dread; let us steep in this crimson our hands of liberated slaves and run outside to bring to our brethren the pious initiating embrace of nascent liberty! Let the doors of bronze be closed forever on this sepulchral darkness, and let a joyous sun rise, in that aurora of radiant light, into eternal space!'

"One by one the quivering juvenile hands plunged into the gaping vessel; then the heavy panels of the doors were carefully closed, with their powerful and solid bolts and their complicated and clever locks, of which they swore an oath to forget the secret, and the adolescents reappeared on the terrace, uttering loud cries, which joined in with those of the impatient crowd, and mothers and fathers held in their arms the children miraculously escaped from the terrible edifice.

"The emotion with which those individuals, who loved one another, was palpitating, attained the entire people, like a breath of wind running through the trees of a dense forest. Attracted to one another by a mysterious force, their hands gripped one another in embraces that became dolorous, and their eyes, seeking in other eyes the cause of that indescribable and triumphant joy, moistened with warm and tender tears.

"No question was born on the lips, extended in order better to respire and taste, it seemed, the profound joy that was floating, as if blossoming, in that radiant atmosphere of pure bliss, from flowers circling all foreheads with their perfumed adornment. Stunned in a calm and serene intoxication, all of them were contemplating one another with gazes overflowing with mute and reciprocal gratitude, and, scarcely emerged from their ecstasy, the adolescents came into our house to bring us the odorous offering of jasmines and roses.

"'We are your children,' they said, 'let our hands, trembling with tenderness, present you with these messengers awakened on this morning of immortal hope; like us, the odorous caress of perpetual roses will give you the ineffable joy that swells souls eternally.'

"'Have your children, then, no longer a place in your hearts, in which forgetfulness has frozen your memory?' asked one frail blonde young woman, softly, approaching me, her hand in the hand of a young man; then, their knees flexed, they both addressed to me their unique and common prayer: 'Father, bless the love of your children, and for your happiness, take all their joys with all their hopes!'

"My indefatigable fingers, vainly occupied in the impossible task, came to an abrupt stop in the soft clay from which human features were beginning to emerge, and from the eyes of the prostrate children sprang into my obscure memory the clear and warm fame of the renascent past. My arms opened to the adored heads, whose silky hair moistened with my tears, and, releasing their gentle embrace, the children took me to their dwelling, joyous with youth and love; and all the old men, surrounded by their relatives, who swore never to leave them again, went through the large sculpted doorway after us.

"Night did not dare to cast its veil over the expanded joy, and the sun, as if to reheat the hearth of pure love with its bright radiance, did not quit the sky, but continued shining with its powerful glare, until the time when my children knelt before me and I read the thought of a desire in their eyes.

"Anticipating their prayer, I asked if any cloud had come to tarnish the splendor of their days. 'No,' they replied, raising their foreheads toward the limpid azure, 'our happiness magnifies the severe light still blossoming without the palest stain, and yet we are trembling for its frail existence; we are afraid that one day, some doubt might come, in our souls, to brush it. Father, our eyes would like to see it, and our hands to touch it.

Father, do you remember the white statue that once stood in the palace?"

"But they stopped immediately, confused by having spoken of what they believed to have been banished from their thoughts forever, and their features contracted horribly.

"At the same time, great cries rose up. 'Our brothers and sisters have just addressed their prayer to you too,' my children murmured. 'Oh, for love of us, don't reject them!'

"In a host, mean and women were running, and their voices were howling their various desires and their various determinations. 'You shall dress her with azure, like the sky, toward which her head with rise very high...we want her as pale as the dawns that is born in the bosom of light cloud...on to her you shall cast the black mantle of dusk...!'

"And there were recompenses offered to my zeal, threats of death to punish my refusal, while above that crowd, beyond the horizon, a great plain extended, where an immense motionless multitude was kneeling, arms crossed over breasts...they were human creatures who had died while awaiting the absent object of their adoration to appear. Further away, a man was gazing at children who were playing with baubles; in their ardor of their frolics, one toy broke, and the poor child wept at the emptiness of his hands, but the man picked up the shards scattered on the ground, and in a matter of moments remade the bauble, which he returned to the child, whose eyes dried up immediately...

"I had them bring me all the bronze weapons and armor that there was in the city, and that same evening, I began my formidable task.

"After extraordinary efforts to dress my thought with the desired form, in the great square, at the foot of the marble stairway, the giant statue stood; the sun's rays sparkled over its bronze, and it was reminiscent of a cloud of arrows launched into space.

"A furious madness of kneeling, and humble oaths of obedience, took possession of the entire people, and even I was constrained to prostrate myself before the work emerged from the vigil of my hands. The hours of fervor ran into the past, heavy with vows and prayers; then, timidly, the people raised their heads to interrogate the rediscovered idol and to know whether it really was the dream of their hearts.

"The sunlight was plunging vertically in an incandescent column, which had just broken over the resplendent statue, spreading out around it in a rain of droplets of dazzling light.

"Immediately, hands raised their protective ramparts before the wounded eyes, over which the eyelids had suddenly closed, and all heads bowed to the point of touching the ground, in a similar terror of blindness.

"Slowly, the sun descended along the slope that incessantly draws it toward the horizon, and under the invisible blows of shadow, its rays were extinguished one by one in the night.

"Over the paled bronze, the moon developed its silvery network and its soft light seemed to be bandaging the wounds inflicted on its carcass by the cruel sun.

"In the mild night, my voice tried tenderly to awaken the kneeling creatures from their prostrate terror, but their ears remained deaf, and it was necessary for me to tear away by force the hands stuck to their faces and lift the eyelids screwed up over eyes filled with fear.

"Then long moans sprang forth, hands lost in tremors took possession of mine to make them touch the eyes burned in dolorous orbits. Then there were heart-rending supplications, and, slightly reanimated by the hope of a consoling word, the people asked whether care might ever render their gazes their former light—but immediately, fear of the imminent dolor shook them with fearful hiccups, because, they said, dawn would appear in a few hours' time, soon followed by the injurious flames.

"I told them that their eyes would become accustomed to that now-redoubtable glare; I told them that soon, in the radiant light, their gazes would rise up to the heavens, but the obsession of their suffering gripped them entirely, and suddenly, having become humans rendered to their strength and their will, all of them, with a cry of certain victory, accused me of treason and ordered me to hide that bronze, which, under the gold of the sun, caught fire furiously in a giant blaze of annihilation.

"'Take from your blue vault a shred of tutelary azure; in its limpid wave, our faraway eyes will allow themselves to be lulled, scorning the wounding reflections of the fire…the dark forgetfulness of profound nights will be an inviolable refuge for us against which the blinding assaults of vanquished day will contend in vain…'

"And, rising above the tumultuous crowd, one man hoisted up his tall stature and cried: 'Gather around me, you who fear that the perfidious waves of the blue sky might flow over you; come, somber warriors to deliver the supreme battle, in which the night, the eternal pledge of untroubled sleep, will emerge victorious!'

"That appeal sounded like a funeral knell, to which multiple challenges responded, unchaining a horrible melee; bones cracked in mortal grips; red flesh hung down over faces torn by teeth, and until the stars faded one by one in the whitening sky feet marched over quivering bodies to new destructions.

"At daybreak, the frightful rage eased; bruised by the blows struck, hands opened and exhausted arms fell inert alongside bodies; in the pallor of the dawn, red with the blood of the corpses heaped around it, the statue loomed up slowly, and, the first to overflow from the glorious cup of light, a ray of sunlight ran over it, immediately to sink into its somber redness; in a host, other rays raced to liberate their brother, but they all disappeared, and the entire sun seemed to entire into a tomb whose pitiless door closed upon it.

"The combatants had recovered their strength and the bloody fists, raised again, crushed limbs and skulls. Furious and terrible, the battle continued around the statue, without a moment's respite, and the number of the dead increased frightfully. I thought about the fatal moment when I would hear the death-rattle of the last of the living.

"One night, calm descended, and only distant cries testified that the work of extermination was not entirely complete. Two children advanced on to the great square; their little feet stumbled against cadavers that their short legs could not step over and their innocent gazes, unable to understand the horrors of death, searched for their parents, whom their voices demanded in pitiful tones.

"Poor children! You who still wanted to live, I took you in my arms for the salvation of hope; with you I climbed the horrible steps made of corpses heaped up around the statue, the bronze of which was pierced between the shoulders by an opening through which I had made my exit from the flanks when my work was finished. The secret door obeyed my fingers and the inviolable refuge opened to guard the children until the awakening of peace promised after the death of hatreds.

"The men worked furiously at the bloody task, and the dying exhaled breaths of the devouring flame, the burn of which reanimated fading ardor.

"Soon, of all the combatants, one alone remained standing, and, upright in the pride of triumph, he marched over the cadavers with a heavy tread; his heels crushed the faces in which a few features were still recognizable; sometimes he stopped, his nostrils flaring, and suddenly pounced on a cadaver from which an imperceptible gasp seemed to have been exhaled.

"Finally, to enjoy his victory, he sat down; but his eyes encountered the statue and that human form, still standing before him, tore a wild cry from his throat and, head first, he launched himself forward to attack it; at the impact, the bronze trembled, and the frightened children huddled against me, listening to the song of deliverance that, alas, proclaimed their agony. Under the furious assaults the statue tottered and fell, crushing its vanquisher in its fall.

"Poor children! Your fragile bodies could not resist, and your two lives flew away together to the radiant exile free of all servitude; but I have your liberated white souls in my bosom, and I have come to give them to two children of Ergastulia.

"Royal children curbed in the darkness, the hour has sounded to raise your heads charge with diadems! The dark cloud is overflowing with sovereign light! The golden chains are relaxing their grip! Sing, sing with all the might of your lungs the hymn of liberty! See, see the statues that flee in the thickness of clouds the powerful floods of the victorious day!"

And with an imperious finger, the old man, whose words burst forth in fulgurant lightning-bolts, indicated to the people the King of Ergastulia, who sat immobile, his face invaded by a mortal pallor.

"The statues have fled! The statues are dead!" cried the terrible voice, bearing anguish into every breast, and the old man, whose eyes seemed to be stars illuminated by unknown radiance, doubtless in order to head toward the shivering crowd, came down from the red-draped stage.

Then the king stood up, and his garments seemed to be covering a body stiffened by death. Slowly, he walked toward the old man; his hand touched his shoulder and, in the midst of the mortal silence that gripped the crowd, his sepulchral voice proclaimed:

"Madness is an insult to God, my master! The blasphemer must die! Your eyes will expiate the vision of forbidden gleams; your hands, for having dared to try to embrace infinity, will be separated from the rest of your body, and your culpable head will fall upon the ground that your unhealthy thoughts threaten to destroy. Executioner, do your duty!"

The executioner took a step forward, but Hercule Cabanas advanced and, bowing very low before the King, asked as a sign of favor to execute the criminal old man himself.

"He belongs to you," said the King, simply, making a sign of acquiescence with his right hand.

Hercule Cabanas took the executioner's blade and rushed upon the old man; twice he sank its point into the orbits from whose shiny globes a flood of blood escaped; the wrists cut, the hand fell away; and in its turn, the head rolled upon the ground, almost immediately joined by the body, which stained the viscous soil crimson.

Not a single cry departed from the oppressed crowd; slowly, like a funeral procession, its members flowed outside the palace, and, as if rays strayed from the agonizing eyes of the mysterious old man had entered into their own eyes, several felt their gazes penetrated by strange reflections.

THE CASTLE

In the heart of the land of Azure, about two leagues from the city of Lys, on a solitary crag overlooking three profound valleys, the gigantic ruins of an ancient castle lie dormant under their mantle of ivy.

It was on that grim crag that the castle of the Counts of Markor, whose lineage extended back to the dawn of the heroic nation of Azure, had once raised its invincible strength. Maternally, the valiant Azurean race had watched its valiant sons grow, and the glory of the land, linked to the glory of the noble family, had become a royal crown on the head of the Count of Markor, the seventh of that name.

As the centuries went by, time had veiled the sumptuous brightness of the luminous past with its implacable shadow; stone by stone, the Manor of Markor had fallen, and the illustrious house had been extinguished, as if some inviolable and secret law had forbidden life to the descendants of the powerful Counts as well as their ancestral dwelling.

Nothing any longer remained of the glorious race than the memory, and of the famous castle, a single keep, standing among the ruined towers like a warrior, the sole survivor of all the companions fallen around him.

From the city of Lys and further still, people came to admire the celebrated ruins; in the autumn especially, when the pale specter of winter was already threatening the remaining warmth of the days through the chill of the lengthening nights, joyful visitors profiting from the last fine weather arrived in interminable caravans.

Proud and bleak, the old keep loomed protectively over the summit of the scattered walls, veiled by their green shroud of ivy, and a gaze as mute as the blind eyes of its deserted battlements seemed to have dressed the trees of the surrounding forest, along with the empty fear of their complete silence, with foliage in mourning for the season of death.

Among the visitors, very rare were those whose souls quivered at the bewildered sadness exhaled by these witnesses of vanished life. The majority came with hearts carefully shielded from any tyrannical impression. Admiration, grave on the part of some and meditative on the part of others, accompanied by enthusiastic exclamations, lasted for the few moments indispensable to safeguard the celebrity of the goal of the expedition.

More often than not, only the young people climbed up to the castle to sing in the ruins a few baroque refrains imposed by fashion, which astonished the ancient echoes. At a bend in some subterranean tunnel, or behind a fragment of a wall, fiancés sought a place propitious to troubling embraces and to swear eternal love, hand in hand before those heroic witnesses of human inconstancy.

Ordinarily, serious people did not risk the puerile dangers of the climb, preferring to remain tranquilly seated on the edge of the crystalline stream in which the bright dresses of the ladies were reflected; a circle would form and conversations rarely flagged, sufficiently alimented by the habitual and banal gossip that was, so to speak, obligatory. Frequently, one of the fine talkers of the society found in a more or less distant allusion an indirect plea to display his intelligence and knowledge by talking about the castle, veritably a little too forgotten.

Sometimes, there was an old scholar, glorious in the admiration of the city of Lys; in a slow voice, after having contemplated the mysterious debris for some time, as if to inspire himself, he began:

"Gentlemen—and you, Ladies, who will forgive me for only addressing you in the second place when it is a matter of things so serious and so old, while you are all delicate grace and youth—you know that I am one of the people who know the obscure history of the ancient land of Azure well. That study has occupied my life, since my most tender childhood, and I am pursuing it in my maturity, hoping that God still has long days in reserve for me, in order that I might continue it in old age.

"I have gathered, with regard to the family and castle of Markor, inestimable monuments, which I have collected in a very remarkable work, and which, in parentheses, has earned me this little ribbon, normally reserved for those who fight with the sword, but which is equally merited—I say without false modesty—by those who battle with the pen, for science and for thought.

"When I tell you that my work has attracted notice, I am employing what is known in rhetoric as a figure of speech. Certainly, the scholars of all lands draw inappreciable information from it, as from an inexhaustible source; they will find the solution there to all the historical problems that the discoveries of future centuries will throw up, if there is any further need—but the public, the great public, does not know my work, and scarcely suspects its existence. That should not astonish anyone; how, in fact, can you expect an ignorant person to read fruitfully a book that is composed of pure science and in which, as the adage puts it, the useful has never been sacrificed to the agreeable?

"No one but a scholar can plunge his eyes into the immense gulf of our past without experiencing some vertigo; personally, I descend into that abyss step by step and I must say that, in spite of many frissons, the thought has never occurred to me to recoil, for I know that courage and determination bring superhuman tasks to a conclusion! The vanquished monster has yielded its secrets to me! It is my turn to reveal to you that which can be revealed...

"The Castle of Markor, which, thanks to the obliging invitation of our dear and devoted Dr. Lancette, we are permitted to admire once again, certainly dates back to a very ancient epoch, but is nevertheless more recent that one might believe at first glance. In fact, I have discovered at the bottom of the well that lies to the left on entering the courtyard known as the court of honor, a certain number of medallions and coins, and neither can be any older than the fourth dynasty of the Red Kings. It is, therefore, in that epoch, or very nearly, that the foundations of the castle were laid—for you are not unaware that in the construction of ancient castles, digging the wells was always the work with which one commenced, probably because the lord wanted to be certain of finding water, which did not always happen.

"Here, for example, it was necessary to dig another well, the first one—the one in which I found the medallions—having been abandoned for reasons that I do not know exactly, but might well be because it no longer provided water, and that explanation appears at first sight to be quite plausible. At any rate, I can affirm—and I have no fear of contradiction on this point—that the well that I have discovered, and to which it has been proposed to give my name, really is the one that was dug first; there cannot be a shadow of doubt about it because, on the one hand, I have found the medallions and coins, and on the other hand, the ancients were accustomed to holding a ceremony analogous to the one we call placing the first stone; they put medallions and coins with effigies of the reigning king in the bottom of the well that was the primordial work in the construction of a strong castle. My discovery is there to affirm the exactitude of that assertion, a discovery all the more important because, thanks to the absence of water and damp, the medallions and coins have been found in a state of perfect conservation.

"We have, therefore, fixed with perfect certainty what we historians call the age of the castle; what we need to know now is by whom it was constructed and in what era its edification was completed.

"I said just now that the medallions and coins found in the 'Narrassol well'—since it is necessary to give it its historic name—bear the effigy of Red Kings of the fourth dynasty. One question arises, which it is necessary to elucidate right away: who were these Red Kings? You don't know? Console yourselves, because many other people don't know any more than you do.

"The Red Kings, Gentlemen, are so named because it is supposed that they reigned over people of the red race...I'm expressing myself badly...the skin color of those people was, in fact more coppery. A few authors, and not the least, allege that a few specimens of the red race still exist in various hyper-occidental islands, which might make one think that that was the cradle of the race with which we are concerned. That would be a grave error, for the beings that are alive now are savages of the most primitive order, and there is no example in the history of human migrations of savages inhabiting an island quitting their birthplace. A child could find the reason for that particularity: to cross the sea requires ships, even large ships, for whose movement steam is virtually indispensable. Now, savages do not know, any more than apes do, what steam is, so both are condemned to play no role in human evolution.

"The red people of whom we are speaking did live in the Occident, however, but only in the Middle-Occident, approximately in the region that we now call Astaria. I have demonstrated this is a work as well-documented as possible, which I only cite for the sake of memory.

"You can see clearly, then, that the founder of the castle came from the Occident and belonged to the red race. That is a fact well-established by the discovery of the medallions, and I am certain of not going too far in affirming that he was of royal blood and that his name was Markor—yes, Ladies, Markor the Short, according to the epithet with which we historians, avengers of defunct times, have crucified the memory of our last king, had a Red Man for an ancestor.

"That Markor was his name is indisputable, since in the land of Azure, names are transmitted in families indefinitely from male to male, and our last kings, as well as the first, were called Markor. He was, in consequence, also the son of a king. In any case, it is difficult to suppose that just anyone would have been able to deploy the immense number of workers required to complete a labor as gigantic. That number must have been considerable, for every day, one finds, buried by some miser of time past, quantities of coins with the same effigies of the Red Kings, which tends to prove that many of your ancestors worked on the construction of the castle, those coins having constituted their wages.

"In spite of everything, Gentlemen, this is only deduction, and a scholar cannot be content with deduction to establish a certainty, until it is corroborated by irrefutable evidence. This evidence, I have found, and here, I am delivering to you one of the secrets that I shall only unveil to the public in my next book.

"I learned, by chance, that mariners coming back from a distant voyage had anchored in Astaria and that they had taken on as ballast a certain quantity of stone blocks, bought at a very low price at the harbor entrance. I examined these stones very closely, for you know that a scholar is like a poet and that inspiration is often his guide. I did not, in fact, have any reason to hope that I might discover bizarre signs on these stones at the first glance—symbols that were nothing less than Astarian letters.

"After enormous effort and labor, I succeeded in forming an alphabet, by means of a method of which I am the inventor, and you can imagine my joy when I read, written in those strange characters, the story of a Red Prince who had left Astaria in the fourth dynasty! Well, that exile, that prince, was the founder of the castle himself, the ancestor of our kings, of heroes who long ago rendered the name of the land of Azure illustrious, and who, alas, were also the artisans of its defeat and ruination!"

"But in that case, Mr. Narrassol," exclaimed a lady, "you know everything! Will you be kind enough to tell us the story of that exile, which the stones taught you?"

"Gladly, Madam—all the more so because I'm certain that the story will interest you, since it's a love story."

And as a few young women stood up, doubtless to go elsewhere to talk about the same subject with the young men, he added: "Oh, it's a perfectly decent love story! In any case, scholars always exercise a perfect decency and restraint in their ideas, as in their language. So sit down, young maidens—you can confidently lend your ears to this story!"

The young women and young men, blushing like schoolchildren caught at fault, resumed their places with resigned expressions.

"So, this happened in Astaria under the third king of the fourth dynasty—which is to say, for the profane, that it was about five hundred and ninety years ago. The reigning king, Fiormal, had several children, and, following the custom of the land, the throne was reserved for the eldest son, whose name was Markor. That young prince was, it appears, remarkably handsome; scarcely had he emerged from adolescence than his father wanted him to choose a wife from among the heirs of neighboring kings. But Markor refused all the contenders, causing his father to fall out with his most powerful allies and risking unleashing horrible wars.

"Driven to the end of his tether, he ended up declaring that he wanted to marry a young woman that he often met while out walking; she was a foreigner whose birth was unknown and who, according to what was known about her, was only rich in her singular and hectic beauty. Young Markor was, however, so smitten with the young stranger, to whom he had never spoken a word, that his father believed that his son was the victim of some malevolent spell, and had the sorceress expelled from the kingdom.

"Far from weakening the tenderness of the lover for the object of his flame, that rigorous measure only exasperated it. Gathering together his numerous friends, Markor took folly so far as to dare to rebel against his father; a veritable battle took place in which numerous partisans of Markor were massacred and the royal heir would infallibly have perished himself if his father had not given a strict order to respect his life.

"Markor was captured and, after having stripped him of his weapons, with which he might have attempted suicide, he was taken to the king, who was waiting with anxiety for the outcome of the hectic conflict in which some badly-directed thrust might have struck his favorite son. He opened his arms

61

to him, begging him not to refuse his pardon, on which he only put the condition that he should accept the hand of Eliale, the only daughter of his neighbor, King Farmart...

"You can see, young people that, as today, paternal bounty is limitless, and that the ingratitude of children is nothing new, for Markor refused the mercy so generously offered. He invoked the names of those who had died for him, and proudly declared that he could not abandon his companions condemned to exile, simply demanding to go with them.

"Before the vanity of his pleas, the poor father bowed his head dolorously, because, through the generous words of the obstinate Markor, he divined the ardent hidden desire to flee to the land where the unknown woman dear to his heart had been exiled, and to wander there at hazard, driven by the hope of reaching her place of refuge some day.

"Then the unfortunate monarch felt his royal pride buckling beneath the ardent affection he nourished with regard to his son. He ordered that a search should be undertaken for the vanished young woman, and that she should be brought back, surrounded by all the honors due to the bride of the heir to the throne. At the same time, he pardoned all the rebels, and Markor, finally touched by such complete generosity, threw himself at the king's feet, before the courtiers, who loudly applauded that act of clemency while secretly criticizing its weakness.

"Many days passed during which the lover, anxiously, saw the king's envoys return, one by one, alone. None of them had been able to find the slightest trace of the exile, and when no hope any longer remained, Markor secretly gathered his companions all of whom had remained faithful to him, and fled the country whose crown ought to have adorned his head one day, taking with him three carts laden with gold.

"It was in vain that King Fiormal sent an entire army of cavalry mounted on fast horses in pursuit of the fugitives, of whom nothing further was ever heard.

"As if death itself had stolen the dear refugee from him, the unfortunate king put on mourning-dress and had heralds announce throughout the kingdom that a cruel destiny had just removed the heir to the throne from the love of the Astarian people. He ordered public prayers, and funeral ceremonies were celebrated everywhere. I shall not give you a long description of those very complicated ceremonies, certain details of which would make you smile, so little do they have in common with present-day customs. However, I do not think I should omit telling you about one bizarre practice that appeared to be necessary to the eternal happiness of the person that was being mourned.

"In the room where the person in question had rendered the last sigh or in the one he usually occupied, dogs, cats and other animals were locked up without nourishment, the number of which was proportional to the rank and wealth of the afflicted family. These unfortunate beasts, driven by hunger, devoured one another with cries of agony and distress, to which the soul of the deceased listened, it appears, with an infinite joy, from which it drew the strength necessary to overcome the dejection caused by the recent loss of its body. If the story of the anonymous and precious writer that I had the glory of discovering can be believed, King Formal acquitted his pious duty magnificently.

"In Prince Markor's immense palace a multitude of animals was imprisoned. All known species were represented; there were elephants and tigers, horses and wolves, and even eagles and vultures. For several weeks the entire city resounded with the frightful agony of those beasts, victims of a belief as absurd as it is barbaric. In that gigantic charnel house, the blood..."

"Oh, Mr. Narrassol, what you're telling us is horrible—you're making me shiver all over!" interjected a lady sitting beside a young man—and she took her neighbor's hand, which she applied to her cheek, in order to enable him to feel the intensity of her emotion.

"It's history, Ladies," Narrassol continued, with an indulgent dignity. "I confess that my author relates a few details that are a trifle painful to hear, for hearts as delicate and sensitive as yours, but the first duty of an archeologist who doubles as a historian and a philosopher is to treat texts with as great a respect as he has for himself! But don't worry, I've finished with Astaria and its sanguinary customs, for the author, after having waxed lyrical in bitter reflections on the love that he considers the obligatory accomplice of death, concludes by praising the floods of bliss in the bosom of which the soul of Markor ought to have been swimming, magnified by all the splendor of the funeral ceremonies consecrated to his felicity.

"Now, I shall try to recompense your attention by narrating the idyll, replete with florid poetry, which has for its hero the first of the Markors. This story, I am certain, will make you forget the barbarity of the Astarian rituals, the mere evocation of which, Ladies, was such a legitimate cause of alarm and terror!"

The emotion of the ladies was not completely calmed, for the young man's hand, emboldened by the vibrant contact with his neighbor's cheek, had slid to the nape of the neck; now, the fingers were interrogating the curls crazily twisted over the collar of the dress, and the sensitive woman, doubtless distressed by the cruel sacrifice of the poor Astarian animals, tilted her had backwards slightly in obsessive flight from horror, and perhaps also to sense against her flesh the excessively aerial caress of fingers surely guilty of a exaggerated discretion.

And Narrassol launched into his idyll, replete with florid poetry.

"Markor and his companions had, therefore, quit the skies of Astaria. From that moment on, in a sense, they belonged to our national history, for they are the ancestors of whom we have the right and the duty to be fervently proud.

"How did those men not perish of hunger in the immense forests through which they were obliged to go? How did they escape the cruel teeth of the ferocious beats that were then the undisputed tenants of those virgin expanses? That is an enigma to which I cannot give you the key. But they must certainly have endured atrocious suffering and run many terrible dangers, and one shudders when one compares their fate to the horrible fate of the unfortunates who go astray in our woods, infantile vestiges of those green and unfathomable oceans of vegetation, the inviolate lairs of gigantic carnivores of which today's tigers and wolves are merely a pale and derisory copy.

"It is to be assumed that an attentive and omnipotent star was watching over them until the day when they arrived in a rich and populous plain that was none other than the cradle in which the glorious and flourishing city of Lys would later be born.

"The charm of that country calmed the errant ardor of the fugitives; they begged their leader to stop. The women were beautiful, and you know, Ladies, that beauty is an infallible sign of good breeding! You will permit me to tell you that you have not let down your origin, and if the companions of the first of the Markors returned to earth, your grace, I am certain, would seduce them as the grace of your ancestors seduced them!

"Markor did not have the courage to resist those pleas, and he consented not to continue his journey. But as his soul was sad, and inconsolable for the absence of the woman he loved with a tyrannical adoration, he wanted to settle in a place where the severity of the landscape was in harmony with his thoughts, and it is probably for that reason that he chose the grim location that our eyes are contemplating at this moment.

"It is difficult to establish whether he occupied without other formalities the sheer crag that he chose to bear the foundations of his dwelling, or whether he acquired it as his legitimate property by means of a monetary payment, but in any case, the inhabitants appear to have given him an excellent welcome and it is certain that they aided him in constructing the keep that was the first-born of the constructions of that giant fortress, as it is today their last representative.

From that moment on, thanks to old writings recovered on parchments, we can follow—step by step, so to speak—the development of the Markor family as well as that of it cradle.

"As I had the honor of telling you at the beginning of this informal conversation, they began by digging a well, but that first attempt was sterile and had to be abandoned. However, in order to follow the ever-respected rule, a certain number of gold and silver coins were thrown into the bottom of the excavation to mark the fact that it was the first work that was carried out, and that is an undeniable fact, for, in the other well that you can see at the occidental angle of the court of honor, it has been impossible to discover a single medallion or coin...

"In any case, those things are only interesting to scholars, who eventually make all these tiny and negligible details into a powerful ensemble of indisputable and luminous truth, and it will be sufficient for me to tell you that many years were necessary to conclude that colossal endeavor, worthy in every respect of the time in which it was carried out.

"Over time, however, the population became more attached to Markor and his companions, and the newcomers, who were all in the flower of youth, did not take long to find their hearts moved with love for some beautiful local girl. Only Markor, his soul still full of his passion, remained insensible, and many beautiful eyes must have wept secretly over his indifference. Desirous of ensuring the happiness of those who had made sacrifices for him, however, he wanted to unite them by the sacred bonds of marriage with those they had chosen.

"The entire country took part in that solemnity, which was to see forty young women become the wives of forty of Markor's companions.

"In that obscure epoch, almost fabulous to all of those who have not scrutinized it in depth, the ceremony of marriage was not what it is today; it had an essentially rural character, for it seems that people took nature in its entirety as a witness for the oaths exchanged.

"To that effect, a kind of altar of verdure and flowers was set up in the middle of the forest, around which the relatives of the future spouses stood, surrounded by all the guests. Then, walking toward one another, the couples appeared, all dressed in white and carrying bouquets in their right hand, of various flowers, in which rose and jasmine were predominant.

"They had to meet directly in front of the altar; they stopped and exchanged their bouquets, and then, after taking turns to kneel down and, reaching out their hands to help one another up reciprocally, the man cut a small branch from a tree, which he broke into three pieces. Each of the two spouses kept one and the third was given to the most worthy person in the assembly, who was thus instituted as the depository of conjugal faith.

"Following the spouses, henceforth united by bonds as tender as they were indissoluble, the company headed for the place where, under some great tree, a copious meal had been set out. Around the table, the frankest gaiety must have reigned. I do not want to speak ill of our ancestors but it is believed that the usage of certain beverages, the coarseness and energy of which our delicate and refined palates could only support with difficulty, was not unconnected with the blossoming of the general delight, translated by songs and dances that went on for several weeks when a large number of relatives and friends took part in the festivities.

"This only gives you a very imperfect glimpse of the pomp deployed in the celebration of unions in the distant times in which our heroes lived, but you can now imagine the enthusiasm aroused by the marriage of forty young women belonging to the richest and best known families in the country.

"In accordance with the rite, to which the foreigners gallantly consented to submit, the neighboring forests were searched for a propitious location for the celebration of that ceremony, which one of my most illustrious predecessors, the knowledgeable master whose favorite disciple I was, has reconstituted with genius and infinite patience.

"As union makes for strength in archeology as well as other human endeavors, I shall summon to my aid, and cite almost textually, that which it would be unseemly not to consider as the bright torch of the thick darkness of our aurora."

.

This elegant and light-hearted periphrasis brought a few smiles to the lips of his listeners, and one young man, doubtless in order to show everyone a "bright torch," set fire to a piece of papers crumpled up in the form of a torch, which earned him a reprimand on the part of the orator.

"What you are doing there, young man, is very imprudent. Terrible fires have been known to be started by a single spark; at your age one ought to think about the sometimes-irreparable consequences of a childish prank!"

At the young man's feet the piece of paper finished consuming itself by curling up, while the "bright torch" had already begun speaking again via the authorized mouth of Narrassol.

"Decisive of the destiny of a long series of centuries, the day came, full of majesty, that was proud to bear the witness of its light to the glorious union from which was to emerge a new race, elected to strike the world with its imperishable effigy.

"Children of a people still as simple as the flowers of their hills, forty young women, gentle virgins untouched by any desire, went to offer their hearts, delighted by love, to the strangers resplendent with distant glory.

"In the bosom of the profound forest, under the double vault of verdure and sky, in the temple erected by God himself, in praise of his own glory, they were no longer men but supernatural beings, handsome and powerful heroes, who, were about to put into their hands enriched by unknown victories the slender and timid hands of blonde enchantresses, for the birth of incomparable splendors.

"As if he had sensed that heaven had reserved the prerogative of offering him a companion, however, one alone had not made the choice of a bride; that was Markor, the valiant chief whose azure banner, after having fluttered for a long time over this hospitable land, was one day to bring it the same name as its color.

"That, Gentlemen, glorified in an inimitable language, is the magnificent threshold of our history. However, in spite of all his genius, my Master was unable to divine the secret of the first of the Markors. Certainly, he gives a poetic explanation of that heart, closed to the love of the most beautiful of our gracious ancestress—but I alone have discovered the exact truth, and it is an incessantly new dolor for me to think that the illustrious scholar, toward whom I contracted a debt of eternal gratitude, was able to close his eyes without knowing about my discovery, which I would gladly have changed into a pious filial ray worthy of illuminating the last moments of his dear soul.

"But it is in vain that death, which respects nothing, has carried away in its dark claws the learned confidant of the past of our great nation; seated on the throne of our own grandeur, his work remains, and it is with a holy emotion that I borrow from him these solemn periods, the superhuman beauty of which my feeble voice can only make you sense imperfectly.

"Already regal in the crimson of his floating mantle, followed by the entire crowd of the relatives and friends of the young brides, Markor came to take his place before the large altar whose summit rivaled the crowns of the tallest trees.

"Silent and meditative, solemn minutes went by, and the hearts of the least sensible were beating more rapidly when, from the right and the left, white forms gliding slowly between the rigid trunks emerged one by one from the depths of the forest.

"Facing the gigantic altar and occupying with its bright band the somber thickness of the wood, a path opened as far as the eye could see between two rows of trees whose trunks and branches disappeared beneath garlands woven, to the right, where the men were advancing, of lilies reminiscent of the heads of lances wounding the green foliage, and to the left, from which the maidens were coming, of white roses whose timid pallor was enhanced by brittle gleams departing from grains of sand decorating the thick bunches of multicolored flowers covering the ground. At the ends of the pathway, at the foot of the two flowery walls, facing one another and holding bouquets of jasmines and roses in their right hands, the fiancés stopped and smiled through sunbeams in which fine pollen was trembling.

"Markor and all the witnesses bared their heads. Taking the few strides by which they were still separated, the couples came into the middle of the pathway and, in accordance with the ritual, they made the exchange of their bouquets. To symbolize the reciprocal assistance that the spouses owed to one another, the men knelt down, and their companions graciously extended a hand to help them up, and then, in their turn, the young women bent their knees and each took the hand of the man who was to defend and protect them.

"This became irrevocable the bonds that united the forty knights with the companions they had chosen, and in order to receive from Markor's own hands the wand that would be ceremoniously broken into three parts, the couples prostrated themselves on the two sides of the avenue.

"Eyes raised to the heaven, the young chief opened his large red cloak, and his hands slowly detached from his belt the light quiver of white cloth from which the forty twigs were taken, frail sacred witnesses of the consecrated unions...

"Suddenly, there was a long clatter, like the beating of wings in the distant air, and a crimson wave invaded the blue horizon enclosed in the narrowness of the long avenue.

"The noise grew louder, soon becoming clearer as the gallop of a horse, the silhouette of which emerged, drowned by waves of scarlet veils.

"Motionless, Markor stared, and the people, believing that the very genius of the mysterious race that was about to alloy its purest blood with theirs was about to appear, knelt down and placed their foreheads on the ground.

"The horse's hooves were impeded by the thickly-strewn flowers and, weighed down by the slowing of its pace, the red veils, now trailing among the flowers, completely enveloped a woman whose white hands held golden reins.

"The white charger streaming with red advanced between the prostrate couples to the foot of the altar and stopped in front of Markor, releasing the reins, which mingled with its long mane. The hands parted the veils, uncovered the dazzling visage of a radiant maiden, and from her lips, these simple words descended upon Markor, as pure as crystal tears: 'I am Zvelda, your bride!'

"And Markor repeated the harmonious syllables: 'Zvelda! Zvelda!' his ecstatic eyes looking into those of the celestial creature, who, sliding down the flank of her horse, tripping on the waves of her veils, on feet inexpert on the ground—and she resembled a great bloody flower, kneeling amid the scattered flowers.

"Her hands extended toward Markor, who took them gently in his own and drew the divine Zvelda's forehead all the way to his lips; then, in ardent adoration, he fell to his knees, and in their turn, the little hands that he still held in his own helped him to get up, and both of them, lips together, spoke the infinite caress of their names, and, at the same time, the eternal avowal of their love.

"Thus was accomplished the fecund union of the earth and the heavens, and soon, in their glorious cradle, the firstborns were wailing of the giant Azurean race, whose roars were to fill the most distant heavens with their echoes..."

"Long live Azure! Long live Azure!" cried voices proud to extol with their eruption the glamour of their fatherland.

"Thank you, Gentlemen, thank you, Ladies, for associating yourselves with the patriotic thought of the great Palaille, my venerated Master. He had a sincere and truly worthy soul, that scholar, for whom the mast was merely a lesson written by destiny for the edification of the present, and I see with tender emotion that his teaching has born remarkable fruit.

"However, and although my own words might risk seeming dull and prosaic to you, I owe it to myself and to you to redress certain errors that escaped even the brilliant perspicacity of Hector Palaille. Certainly, I would not like to diminish in any way the solemnity of the story that I have just had the honor or reviving before you, but in spite of everything, it is necessary to reestablish the truth on its throne of inviolable purity, and necessary to render to history that which belongs to history.

"I ought not to leave your ignorant of the fact that texts exist that fix in a peremptory and indisputable fashion all the details of the marriage ceremony in the times when we place the union of Markor and his companions. Thus, we can affirm that the husband ought to have cut the branch destined to serve as a witness himself; it is, therefore, a flagrant inexactitude on the part of Hector Palaille to show us Markor taking the forty consecrated wands from his quiver. It is possible, however, that an exception to the rule was made for once: an exception that, as you know, can only confirm it. On the other hand, no one—myself less than anyone else—dreams of harboring any rancor against our illustrious national bard for variations that it is praiseworthy for science eventually to remove from the long and grandiose epic whose sublime accents cause Azurean souls still worthy of the name to vibrate!

"Markor had, therefore, rediscovered the unknown woman for whom he had renounced the paternal throne; she had come to offer herself to her faithful lover, clad in the royal red, and her appearance at that solemn moment seemed to all the people to be a supernatural sign announcing the great destiny of the young prince and his descendants.

"I shall not describe the festivals that followed the great event; to describe all their splendor would require poetic speech, and in the mouth of a scholar the language of the poet loses all its savor and all the power of its caress. Nor will I try to celebrate the days of love that shone for the young couple; conjugal happiness is too banal a subject for science to pause upon it for an instant.

"Following the example of the forty knights subservient to the azure banner, the entire country considered Markor as the sole master worthy of command, and a veritable town soon grew at the foot of the crag supporting the keep, in which the subjects of the new chief had come to settle in a host.

"Heaven did not take long to bless the poetic union of Markor and the beautiful Zvelda; a son was born, and, for love of his august companion, the happy father gave his firstborn child the name of Zveldor, a name that he only abandoned on the death of the author of his days, in order to take that of Markor, at the same time as the parental heritage. He it was who constructed the first tower raised to the east of the keep, of which no trace any longer remains.

"Before the increase in the number of his subjects, henceforth too great to be accommodated in this narrow valley, the elder son of the latter laid the first foundations of the future and glorious city of Lys; but, in order not to betray the promise made at the death-bed of the second of the Markors, he endowed the familial keep with a second tower, reserving for his heir the task of edifying the third vassal of the cradle of the race, which thus found itself standing at the center of a geometrical figure what mathematicians call an equilateral triangle, the apices of which were formed by three constructions now completely destroyed.

"Meanwhile, in the bosom of the nascent city, enormous wealth accumulated, which soon excited the covetousness of neighboring peoples, and to the fifth Count of Markor fell the heavy task of supporting the initial impact of avaricious invaders.

"That was the baptism of blood for the azure banner—a glorious baptism, in which chiefs and soldiers competed with all the presumptuous impetuosity of their youthful courage. In spite of their experience and numbers, the foreigners were driven back, and the victors, in commemoration of that victory, all the honor of which, they said, reverted to their leader, raised for the exaltation of his name, to the north of the oriental tower, a high turret whose summit was covered with bronze shields taken from the vanquished. That is why, in the place where that monument stood, our scholarly society has discovered a bronze slab sealed in the unbreakable rock, the eloquent inscription of which is only understood by a few initiates.

"I have said somewhere in one of my books that examples are always a dead letter and that no light can illuminate blind eyes; thus, the lessons inflicted on rapacious monarchs

73

do not profit their successors, and the sons of 'Markor the Victorious,' with neither truce nor remission, fought to defend the existence and wealth of their faithful subjects. They did so with an ever-equal joy, and the lot of armed struggle favored them with an untiring constancy.

"In the final days of his life, after a great battle, he wanted to render to his soldiers what their fathers had given his own father, and opposite the tower erected by the people in honor of the fifth Markor he had another similar tower constructed, the walls of which bore, engraved on marble plaques, the names of the warriors killed for the salvation of the land of Azure.

"An authentic fatherland was, in fact, born of those men: a fatherland born in love and brought up in the fruitful endeavors of commerce and industry, endeavors only suspended for the accomplishment of inevitable defensive works, and destiny, like the irresistible breath of an impetuous wind, drove toward the immense horizons the omnipotence of the ship of glory flying the azure flag, of which the first Markor had been the simple and happy pilot, and which, for the seventh representative of the family was about to change into a royal vessel ready to sail to the conquest of the most distant seas.

"The thread of our history is about to be tied into a gigantic knot, a knot formed of the actions of seven generations, and which seven further generations only succeeded in slackening, without ever abolishing or untying it completely.

"The heirs of neighboring kings, humiliated by the defeats suffered by their predecessors and emboldened by the age of the young Count, whose, while almost still a child, had succeeded the one known in our annals under the name of the Master of Victory, gathered their soldiers into a single formidable army. Command of it was given to the bravest and most experienced of them all, and, this time certain of beating their rival, thus far unvanquished, they marched on the city of Lys.

"At the approach of the gigantic invasion, the stoutest and most valiant hearts could not suppress a frisson of anguish—an anguish quickly dissipated by the assurance of the young prince, who said to all of those who let their fear show, shaking his blond curls: 'Have you no confidence in me, then? You know, however, that the feet of a Markor only tread the glorious roads of triumph!'

"Like the goddess of love—and permit me also to add, like all pretty women—Fortune, in spite of her blindness, loves ardent young men, so she reserved her most entire favor for the worthy descendant of the man whose heart had expelled him from his native land.

"Under the walls of the city the gigantic collision occurred. For several days, only interrupted by the brief hours in which total darkness prevented the combatants from distinguishing the enemy from their brothers in arms, fate did not pronounce a decision; innumerable splendid actions were accomplished on either side, actions that remain obscure and known only to their authors, who fell on the ground reddened with their blood.

"Finally, the eagle of victory came to extend its wings over the warriors of Azure; the foreigners buckled, opened their ranks for hectic flight over the cadavers, abandoning their weapons, and the supreme leader, on seeing the disaster of his own side, went to Markor, and on his knees, before all the latter's soldiers, handed him his sword, imploring mercy for his life, in ransom of which he offered his throne and his estates.

"As magnanimous in victory as he had been courageous in battle, Markor raised the old man to his feet, returned his sword to him, and sent him back to his country, after having made him swear that he would never again take up arms against him.

"All the kings imitated the wisest and most powerful of their allies, and a long period of peace seemed to be in prospect when Markor received an ambassador who came on behalf of his neighbor to offer him presents and invite him to solemn fêtes that he intended to hold in his honor.

"Markor accepted the presents, the certain guarantee of a durable amity, and consented to go to the capital of his former enemy. He departed with an escort of nobles and faithful companions, and on the way, the peoples welcomed triumphantly the man who had spared their master, and whom they loved like a father. The king's daughter came in person to meet him, in order to testify her filial gratitude.

"The ideal beauty of the dark-haired young woman struck Markor's youth, not all of whose ardor had been absorbed by combats, and when the old man, emotional on seeing his conqueror again, begged him to choose from his kingdom or his palace whatever would complete his desires, Markor looked at the young princess and said: 'My happiness is in the frail fingers of the one whose hair is as somber as a starry night; I do not ask for anything, for love is not alms, and the richest of all kings cannot give it.'

"Then...but Ladies and Gentlemen, I perceive that my feet are entering into a domain that is forbidden to them! However, is it possible to evoke the marriage and the coronation of Markor without remembering, even against one's will, the immortal masterpiece of our great poet Clairon de Lyre, whose grandiose and delicate *Marriage of Markor* is present in all minds?

"I will only permit myself to deplore the fantasy with which Clairon de Lyre has developed that page of our national life; in doing that, he has only done what poets invariably do, who do not hesitate to fell with their powerful wings the most solid and sturdy monuments of history.

"Has not Clairon de Lyre, in fact, set his action in the fourth year of the fifty-sixth lustrum of the Azurean era, whereas it has been materially established that Markor's marriage and coronation took place on the same day in the city of Lys at the beginning of the first year of the fifty-seventh lustrum? It is a formal and formidable error, my excellent friend César Tabellot would say, with his habitual wit—whom I shall call upon to give you a few explanations on the subject of the blazon of the Markor family. The different transformations undergone by the armories of the house will clarify many points obscure to your eyes, the 'heroic science' being the younger sister of history, an eloquent and devoted sister, ever-ready to help her elder in difficult moments.

"I am glad to salute here the most authoritative representative of that science; the noble heraldic language, which so many scholars only succeed in stammering with difficulty, our dear César Tabellot speaks so fluently, and with such elegance that, in his mouth, it appears to be his mother tongue. In the name of the old friendship that unites us as much, I dare say, as our common passion for everything that can develop human knowledge, I implore the modesty of my savant colleague not to be wounded by the public testimony that I am happy to render to his merits.

"For myself, I will simply add that the twentieth day of the third month of the year one hundred and eighty-five was a memorable one, on which the throne of Azure beheld its steps solemnly climbed by Bolette, the daughter of Tartas, supported on the arm of Markor the Paramount, her husband and king. Consequently, and in order not to betray the aim of my discourse, which is merely to explain to you by what hands and in what times the different parts of the castle were built, I shall tell you that Markor the Paramount was the author of the final work that completed the ensemble of the fortress.

"Doubtless to attract to himself and his people the protection of the spirits that maintain peace, by means of a sixth tower with walls lined with gold and silver, he completed the formidable enclosure around the old keep, the only edifice respected by time.

"And now, permit me not to descend from the majestic summit that we have just climbed in the course of my story; if I did not want to have the pleasure of listening to my friend Tabellot, I would ask heaven to let me die at this moment, from which I would carry into my tomb the glorious vision with which my eyes are filled!"

The notary César Tabellot was the complete opposite of Narrassol.

If the vestments of the latter seemed to be suffering from the disdain proclaimed on their part by a tall and thin body that only consented to their contact at the shoulders and a few other points of his angular person, those of the notary, by contrast, were visibly suffering from the tension to which they were condemned by the flesh that their mission was to contain. The frock-coat, confident in the vigor of its buttons, was struggling valiantly against the enormous abdomen, and that effort ceased it beneath the thickly padded arms, which faded away into the vast rounded surface of the heavy back.[4]

With a smile full of gravity, of which it was possible to suspect the finesse and which visibly stirred the adipose waves that accompanied his indecisive chin above the false collar, the notary Tabellot, in a high-pitched voice muffled, it seemed, by the hilarious rotundity of his entire being, embarked upon the important question of the Markor coat-of-arms.

"Thank you, my dear Narrassol, for the flattering words that you have just pronounced with regard to my modest person. Yes, dear and illustrious scholar, you are right a thousand times over to say that the science of heraldry is the indispensable auxiliary of history; I would even say that it is its soul. With an unparalleled eloquence you have invoked the events of the past; you have shown us the gigantic skeleton of elapsed times. To live, however, the times have need of an immaterial principle; to say the word, they need a soul.

Is not the human soul, in fact, the admirable symbol of the very causality of life? In the same way, in a family, does not that immaterial principle reside in its coat-of-arms, the imperishable and formal symbol of its existence? As a respectful guest, I have lived with the great soul of our kings, who, so long ago, extended their protective wings over the conquering

---

[4] Given that he was a well-known expert on heraldry, who had published a book on the subject in 1896, P.-B. Gheusi might have taken offense at the unflattering portrait of Tabellot, but it did not prevent him from buying and publishing the story.

destiny of this land of Azure, today so detached, alas, from its glorious traditions!"

In the audience, discreet smiles were exchanged at these words, accompanied by a gesture full of melancholy and regret, because everyone knew the origin, as noble as it was distant, to which Tabellot laid claim. Thanks to very ancient parchments to be found in his study and elsewhere, that estimable man had been able to demonstrate that one of his ancestresses had had the signal honor of being dishonored by one of the sons of the last of the Markors, and it was rather amusing to see that ancient blood occupied in making its laborious way through the veins of the corpulent lawyer.

"You are familiar with the arms of the house of Azure, and I will not insult anyone by suspecting that they do not know that our royal family wears 'azure on a right arm, gauntleted in silver, moving to the left and holding a sword of the same, lowered over seven silver bezants posed in point.'[5]

"However, Ladies and Gentlemen, it is precisely because a blazon is a living symbol and because the arms of a family have frequently been called, justly 'speaking arms,' precisely because the arms have followed the evolution of their bearers exactly as if they were speaking various and successive languages...I'll explain what I mean...but before any preamble, I ought to put before your eyes the primitive blazon of the Markors, which is found in traces completely effaced on the stone that serves as a keystone of the arch of the principal door of the keep. The son of King Fiormal whose story my illustrious colleague has just told you bore 'azure on a right arm, gauntleted in silver, moving to the left and holding a sword of the same, rising over a septenary of golden stars shining in chief.'

"How was that septenary of golden stars shining in chief changed into seven silver bezants positioned in point? How did that sword with the point directed heavenwards descend at a later date toward the edge of the shield? Those are the deli-

---

[5] A bezant is a heraldic coin.

cate problems that we shall have the pleasure of examining, and which we shall, I hope, resolve without any difficulty.

"What it is necessary for us to consider first of all is that stars are the symbols of human aspiration; it is in them that live, as if in a world distant from ours, all the virtues and ideals of humankind.

"Given that, you can read, as if in a book written in henceforth-familiar characters, the speaking arms, such as they are, of the glorious sons of Fiormal.

"Is there any need, in fact, to tell you that Prince Markor bore in his generous heart all human ideals? That his soul was moved by all the human virtues? Is there any need to tell you that he, one of whose descendants was to wear the royal crown, had for his ambition the realization of all the dreams, the possession of all the moral treasures than, in filling the hearts of kings, make the pastors of people heroic figures truly worthy of causing the earth to bend beneath their scepter, which is merely the salutary and sacred reflection of the divine scepter?"

"And that, Ladies and Gentlemen, is why the shield of Prince Markor shines with the septenary of stars whose scintillation laurels the totality of terrestrial virtues; and it is to render the admirable symbol more eloquent that in a right hand— the knight's own hand—a sword was held with the point directed upwards toward the conquest of the stars that personify the goals sought.

"Oh, conquering virtues is more difficult for a man than conquering kingdoms, and it required the life and determination of even generations of princes for that conquest to become complete; each of those princes struggled with all his might to accomplish that endeavor, and each, on his deathbed, at the moment when God speaks through the mouths of those he is recalling to him, was able to repeat what the first of the Markors said to his son: 'My son, my task is over; it is your turn to swell the heritage that you will bequeath to my grandchildren…take in the sky of our shield the most distant star and change it, to mark its capture, into a silver bezant, which you will place on the pommel of your sword.'

"Thus, one by one, the light stars were changed into heavy bezants; crowning the familial edifice by mounting the throne of Azure, Markor the Great took the last, and for the protection of the vanquished stars materialized in disks similar to silver coins, he turned the point of the heraldic sword toward them, needlessly raised toward the sky where nothing more remained to conquer!

"Oh, Ladies and Gentlemen, every coat-of-arms is a vast poem in which the life of a family overflows like the waters of a torrent on the days of a great flood, and when that family is the most illustrious in a country, when that family is the royal family, the heraldic epic attains the grandiose proportions of the life of an entire people..."

And the excellent Tabellot, the most erudite of notaries, got his breath back, in order to continue his discourse on the noble science of heraldry in general and the arms of the Markor family in particular, so dear to the heart of an anonymous and obscure descendant consigned by the disrespect and ingratitude of men to the honorable but very humble functions of a ministerial officer.

Suddenly, the young people, with ill-disguised cries of relief, gave a noisy and joyful ovation to an old man dressed like a beggar, whose silhouette appeared at the edge of the forest at the very bottom of the steep hill.

And cries of: "Here comes the old man! Here comes the old man!" resounded through the applause, while the unfortunate heraldist, with a gesture full of disdainful nobility, tried to make his audience understand that, in the midst of such a racket, there was no longer any scope for the delicate demonstration he had reserved for the most exciting part of his lecture.

Without perceiving his distress at all, old and young, glad of the diversion brought to the learned and ponderous discourse, stood up, repeating: "Here comes the old man! Here comes the old man!"

The man whose sudden appearance provoked such enthusiastic acclamations was an old shepherd who had lived for no one knew how many years among the ruins of which he had, so to speak, become a part. The relative generosity of visitors assured his problematic existence, so, infallibly, they ended up perceiving him at a distance, leaning on his long curved staff, seemingly plunged in profound meditation.

As no excursion to the ruins of Markor was truly complete without the "old shepherd's tale," visitors never failed to offer him a few leftovers from the hampers of provisions. Slowly, with an evident preoccupation to preserve his primitive dignity, the old man ate and drank under the gaze of all those people, curious to examine at close range that bizarre individual, so different from the rest of the human species.

His meal terminated, the old man fell back into his original immobility, waiting for questions, to which he usually replied to give thanks for the alms received, and to merit the few silver coins that would presently be slipped into his hand.

As if to take his revenge for the lack of success of his discourse and to claim even so the preponderant place that he merited in society, with a deceptive expression of pity seemingly directed at the old man, whom he had known for a long time, the lawyer Tabellot asked: "Would you care to tell us your history, old man?"

"My history? You want me to tell you my history?" And the old man paraded a suspicious and wily gaze over the assembly.

"Yes, your history, since you only know one. Oh, that's because you're not a scholar! It's even said that you don't know who you are yourself," Tabellot went on, with a smile in which the imminent and certain victory was visible that he was about to win over the apparent ill-will of his unloquacious interlocutor—who seemed, however, gradually to become animated.

"Oh, you know, you others, who you are? So much the better! Me, I don't know who I am. I must be the 'old man,' since that's what you call me. But what importance does a name have in passing over the earth?"

Tabellot, who had assumed the full responsibility for the interrogation, cut the discussion short by means of the question that would infallibly lead to the response desired by the whole assembly: "Why are you seen perpetually roaming around the castle?"

"Oh, it's because the castle protects me, and I protect it. Oh, it's because you others don't know that old men need to live with people and things of their own age...unless it's with very small children and brand new things."

"Where do you come from?"

"I have no memory of those who were born at the same time as me! When I was born, my father was very old. It's said that the sons of old men don't know the infancy of life. Me, I don't remember having had a youth. Once...oh, in a very distant time, when, as today, my hair was white and my stature curbed, while grazing my sheep on the hill you see over there, I tried to approach a young shepherdess who was guarding her flock. The child, frightened by my appearance, fled screaming! I never saw her again. I seem to remember someone telling me once that she was dead..."

An explosion of laughter greeted the poor old man's love story. He continued, without seeming to take any offense.

"Then I understood that only the amity of these stones was good for me. One night, we exchanged a solemn oath to love one another forever, and I'm sure that neither my keep nor I will be perjured. Since then, we've watched over one another. Oh, you can look at it, my castle; I'm not jealous, for no eyes but mine can see its inaccessible towers; no feet but mine can tread the court of honor paved with marble that sounds beneath the hooves of horses; no one but me, in the room with high walls paneled with oak, can talk to the master sitting by the hearth, where a joyous fire is burning. I alone order the men at arms to watch night and day from the summit of the towers when a danger approaches that causes me to lower the portcullis over the entrance door..."

And Tabellot agreed, with a slow nod of the head, to show to everyone that the shepherd's words were expressing in a precise manner what he had wanted him to say, and, as if he were anticipating the extreme interest of what was about to follow, he raised the index-finger of his right hand to invite the listeners to redouble their attention.

"I've spent many nights watching over the sleep of those walls. Sometimes, malevolent beasts try to make those poor stones their prey, which flee under the bites all the way to the depths of the ravine, where my tremulous hands collect them, in order to bury them in the earth, under a soft bed of moss, to give them a safe refuge. Doesn't it seem to you that it's wrong to leave the remains of those one loves scattered to the four winds of heaven? They're my dead, for whom I pray, and sometimes, veiled by the dusk, their souls come to me..."

"My word, you're truly astonishing—you talk like a poet!" César Tabellot interjected, bursting out laughing. "Where the devil did you learn to lecture thus on the beauties of the night and dusks? Are you, by chance, in love with the moon? She's a lady who, according to the best authors, repays the zeal of her lovers very poorly, and I ought to tell you that none of those gallants has yet succeeded in triumphing over her coldness. Oh, it's because she's serious, you see, the queen of the blue sky, and to disturb her reason, apparently fortified by all the reason she steals from mortals infatuated with her, it requires seductive means more imperious than those that nature has deigned to put at your disposal!"

Nervous laughter sounded, stamped with discreet voluptuousness, and a lady who was less cold and less serious than pale Astarte remarked to her neighbors on the futility of her efforts to hide her legs, obstinate in raising up her skirts. With her fingers on the bright embroidery that coiled around the black silk covering her slender ankles, to rise up toward the knees in a serpent's head with a streak of silver for a tongue, she added: "Look at these wicked beasts, which want to go make mischief in the dry grass!"

Gallantly, the lady's neighbor replied: "Oh, Madame, is it possible that these beasts can think for single instant of fleeing the intoxication of such a divine caress? No, look! I assure you, on the contrary, that, serpent as it is, that one is swooning at the victorious scents it respires, and has a thousand reasons for that! It's happy…oh, why does Eve always allow herself to be tempted by the serpent?"

"But my dear," the lady interjected, laughing, "the serpent is a creature of man; it's the man who sends the serpent to poor women, and the serpent is so cunning that when, in his turn, the man arrives, we're already vanquished, and the man has only to collect the laurels of his victory!"

"Enchanting and delightful laurels, when hands like your deign to place them on our head!" declared the gallant young man.

And the florets of the amorous dialogue continued, covered by the voice of Tabellot, who addressed the shepherd, having allowed the legitimate hilarity aroused by his witty interruption a few minutes to expand.

"Oh, we don't want to violate the secrets of your heart, in any case. Tell us, rather, who constructed your castle, for it's understood that it's yours; the government, I hope, won't take umbrage at your seigneurial rights, and as for us, you can be sure that we haven't come to fight you for this nest of bats and owls—funereal creatures whose wings seem to me to have caressed your brain with a tenderness somewhat injurious to its good functioning."

The old man listened impassively to the irresistible facetiousness of his interlocutor, who added: "Come on! Tell us the history of your castle. Do you know where the man who built it came from?"

"From far away. He came here following a star whose golden light guided him through the profound forests. The star stopped, and Markor did likewise. Beneath the protective radiation of the guiding star the keep was raised, and in the serene sky, one by one, six new stars appeared one by one to escort their elder sister, followed by six towers, built one by one by each of the Markors. And from the height of the blue sky, the seven golden stars leaned over the castle born beneath their light, and their love for it drew them gradually down to earth. On the day that was sacred to the first to the Markors, they were so low that the king took them to ornament his crown. But the captive stars paled so much that they soon seemed to be mere silver...their gleam was drowned in the vices of kings...exceedingly precious stones sought in vain to replace the divine stars...the last king was a miser...he sold the saddened crown for a few coins, from which the star of the keep had escaped in order to rise back into the sky. But the people, seeing him without a crown, immediately thought they recognized in him a slave who had stolen their master's place, and expelled him shamefully...

"Oh, the kings are dead, are they not? The castle has crumbled under the excessively heavy weight of the stones of its walls? Oh, yes! Look! Only the body of the keep, like mine, is still standing, with difficulty—but its star, in the sky, looks down at both of us, and toward it, on clear nights, the tree grows..."

"What is this tree you're talking about?" Tabellot interrupted, still wanting to appear to be dominating the old man's thought. The judicious notary added: "If you know all the trees in the forest you ought not to lack confidants!"

"The trees of the forest also lift their heads toward the heavens! Oh, I love them dearly, the trees of forests! But the tree of the keep isn't one of their brothers. They go toward then sun in order to draw life therefrom, while the other rises toward its beloved in the silence of the night. It was my father who planted that tree in the keep, and long ago, he found the seed of it in the tomb of King Markor, one night when lightning had broken the sepulchral stone..."

"Excuse me!" cried Narrassol. "I forgot a little while ago a detail of which the shepherd's fable has reminded me: that detail has a certain interest, because it demonstrates peremptorily the theory that makes the ancestor of the royal family come from Astaria. The tree about which this ignorant man is talking belongs to the flora of Astaria, where it can still be found in our day. By whom was it brought here, if not by an inhabitant of Astaria? And it's true that seeds of that tree were found in Markor's tomb, put there, it seems, in order to offer the perspicacity of distant generations the possibility of discovering the land of origin of the kings of Azure. Which proves, Gentlemen, that sometimes, legend is not the opposite pole of science, and that the latter does not disdain, when the case warrants it, to shake the hand of its fantastic friend. Go on, shepherd, continue the naïve legend."

"The tree is growing. One day, it will expand from the summit of the keep, and its perfumed flowers will reanimate the slumbering valley. The stones will emerge from the tombs where I have laid them, one by one...they will go to retake their places in the walls, and when the castle lives again, King Markor will return, his head encircled by the crown with the seven golden stars...and like me, you will only have to come to prostrate yourselves at his feet!"

"Oh, old man, may you speak the truth!" cried Tabellot, in an emotional voice. "Oh, certainly, yes, it is with joy that my knees would bend before the august revenant! But a happiness so great is not one of those for which it is permissible to hope in our present decadence...here, old man, take this silver coin; I give it to you with great heart, for you have just filled my soul with the holiest of emotions!"

And the old man took the small silver coin so generously granted in payment for the holy emotion felt by the comfortable soul of the lawyer. A few other people imitated the latter's noble example, and the lady who was still displaying the serpents embroidered on her silk stockings called out to the shepherd:

"You must be a sorcerer! Here's my hand, tell me whether I'm loved?"

The old man leaned over the white hand, which he had taken in his own, and he examined it attentively, nodding his head. Under the pretext of following the delicate examination, the young man had drawn very close to his neighbor, to murmur in her ear: "But you know that you're loved! You know that I love you!"

"Well, prove it to me," breathed the lady, withdrawing the hand that the old man was still holding.

"Whenever you wish!" replied the young man, whose face had suddenly gone red under the gaze of his neighbor.

The amiable Dr. Lancette had stood up. In the name of science, he declared that the time to leave had come, and that to stay any longer in that damp valley would be an imprudence that his status as a physician made it a duty for him to point out to his guests.

The order to hitch up the carriages was given.

The lady made the young man sit beside her, and pressed herself hard against him in order not to let him forget the promise he had made to prove his love ardently.

Narrassol and César Tabellot climbed into Dr. Lancette's vehicle—a vehicle qualified by the witty notary as "the scholars' carriage," and the entire caravan moved off, waving adieu to the old shepherd—who, leaning on his long curved staff, watched the citizens go back to the city of Lys, the ancient capital of the land of Azure.

THE EUPANTOPHONE

I

On 31 December last, *L'Écho Plaintif*, a newspaper of social demands and political revenges, published in its famous Thursday personal advertisement section the following item:

Blind man aged thirty-five, having lost his sight in a laboratory accident and enjoying an annual income of fifty thousand francs, revertible to his widow, desires marriage with a young woman blind from birth. Address communications to M. Victor Blancadet, 14A, Rue du Sabre-de-l'Abbé, Paris.

Among women whose orbits were radiant with ocular globes in a perfect state, the majority pitied the fate of the unfortunate victim of the laboratory accident, and some, immediately tempted by the annual income of fifty thousand francs revertible to the window, and also by the liberty that was bound to be enjoyed by the companion of a man whose eyes had been materially closed by an accident, wrote to the indicated address.

Each one boasted of the physique and the qualities that fate had devolved upon her; each of them possessed the grace of Venus and the virtue of Penelope, and dreamed of becoming the conjugal Antigone of the modern Oedipus struck by the terrible sphinx of science.

One of them, borrowing a pen from her lover, a journalist known for the incomparable voluptuousness of his style, celebrated her own charms with expressions capable of warming the most reserved manes of the Sages of Greece; but, to the shame of the Muse dear to adolescents still only nourished on dreams, and old men still trying to whinny at the evocations of the combat of amour, the letter, overflowing with such alluring promises, received a reply that did not fail to surprise is author.

In her large double bed—her drill-field, as she called it—the blonde Virginie Lauria was asleep, with one arm passed under the head of her lover, Alcée Baillargal, the vigilant reporter whom she had stolen from a socialite in the wake of a resounding scandal, and whom she could no longer live without.

Virginie and Alcée loved one another passionately, with a love that, for all that it was one of the most illegitimate, was nonetheless one of the most sincere.

Although entirely theoretical, Virginie's fidelity was considered as perfectly sufficient by the jealousy of the journalist, who was too well versed in modern life to pretend to an exclusive monopoly on the favors of a woman whose material needs had always been completely foreign to him. Would not any attempt to subsidize them be a prostitution of his pen and his talent? It was also evidently equitable, just, and infinitely more natural, that his mistress, utilizing the gifts with which nature had endowed her, should not refuse the presents that a host of admirers took pleasure in laying at her feet. A more austere morality and principles would certainly have displeased the blonde Virginie, who, thanks to that fortunate state of affairs, had lost none of the relative luxury of her existence as a kept woman, and also enjoyed the heart of "the handsome Alcée," as her friends were pleased to call her lover.

The handsome Alcée was in a sticky situation. Several articles had earned him some rather severe criticism on the part of the editor of the *Écho Plaintif*, and he sensed that his star was declining by the day. Had not a colleague, redoubtable for the ever-exact cruelty of his words, nicknamed him the "shooting star"? His faith in himself was almost shattered, and he was not slow to blame Virginie for his failures as a writer.

"You're my Delilah," he said to her, in a reproachful tone. "Like Samson, I can feel the chill of your scissors in my hair."

Virginie, to whom the significance of the symbols of sacred history was less important than her passion, replied: "My darling Samson, I love your long curly locks too much to have any desire to cut them!"

"Before knowing you, I worked hard, I wrote fluently. Now..."

"You're going to talk to me about your socialite again, aren't you?" She added, in a jealous tone: "But don't you see that she was the one who was using you?"

The dialogue continued on that theme until the chronicler, stimulated by such assaults—in which he rarely had the last word—found the subject of an article. He sat down at the small drawing-room table.

Virginie, conscious of being a hindrance to her lover's painful parturition, kept quiet until Alcée, after having blackened five or six sheets of foolscap, got up, rubbing his hands, and exclaimed: "Oh, this time, if the Chilly Ape"—a nickname that the editor of the *Écho Plaintif* had earned by virtue of a bizarre tic that made him ask all his interlocutors, in summer as in winter, whether it was cold out—"isn't content, he's very difficult to please!"

To recompense himself for the task accomplished, he went to Virginie, kissed her neck and begged her pardon for the hurtful things he had said.

Peace was quickly made, and, as usual, Charlotte, the young maidservant, summoned to put the scarcely-dry copy in the post, found her mistress on "Monsieur's" knees. That spectacle had the gift of provoking nervous laughter in the pretty soubrette, which she could not suppress, and which earned her furious reprimands on Virginie's part.

"Well, Charlotte, when will you have stopped laughing like the little imbecile you are? Are you making fun of me, by chance?"

Between two fits of crazy laughter, Charlotte tried to exonerate herself. "Oh no Madame! But when I see Madame like that..."

"There's nothing for you to see here! I forbid you to look! What I do is none of your business!"

"I know that, Madame, but when I see Madame like that, happy, I'm so glad!"

"Come on! Hurry up and take this letter to the post—it's very urgent!" Virginie ordered, feeling disarmed by the candid sympathy of the young maid, whose sonorous laughter faded away in the antechamber.

"How old is Charlotte?" Alcée asked.

"Sixteen, I think. Why?"

"No reason. Hey—a nice title for a novel: *Charlotte, or the Schoolgirl of Love*. Do you think she's still virtuous?"

"What concern is that of yours? Her virtue is her own business. She either has deposited it or will deposit it at the feet of some handsome Republican Guard, who'll take possession of it without hesitation. Me, I lost mine in a painter's studio in the Rue Denfert-Rochereau, and..."

"And, that painter having a policy of not giving back objects left in his studio, you never saw it again!"

"Never. I haven't even looked for it."

"You've done well. To live, it's sometimes necessary to sacrifice one's capital."

"Oh, if I'd only known you in those days!"

"Thanks—but I'm very happy with the interest. Will any be collected today?"

"If you wish, my love!"

And the heavy door-curtain separating the drawing room from the bedroom fell back behind the two lovers.

Life was, however, becoming difficult. Alcée thought more and more about his socialite, whose solid situation had once ensured the journalist an existence exempt from worry.

So Virginie, having chanced to read the advertisement in the *Écho Plaintif*, said to herself that becoming the wife of that blind gentleman, with an annual income of fifty thousand francs, would be an excellent operation from all points of view. She would enjoy a considerable income, and it would be easy for her, by passing Alcée off as her brother or her cousin, to install her lover in the home of the blind man—who, naturally, would not be able to keep an eye on them.

After having ripened the project for a few days, she had talked about it to Baillargal, who replied, with a haughty dignity, that he did not have to get mixed up in her affairs and that she had a perfect right to act in her own best interests. She had then written a letter to Victor Blancadet, in which, in scarcely-disguised terms, she had caused the unfortunate man to glimpse paradisal horizons.

Naturally, Charlotte had been taken into the confidence of her mistress, whose prudence had also judged it wise to warn the concierge, in case the blind man took it into his head to have enquiries made regarding his passionate correspondent. The instruction was to reply that Virginie Lauria, a young woman of excellent family, the orphan of a father—a senior officer in the French army—who had died a long time ago, lived with her mother, who was away for the moment in one of her properties in the Midi.

Everything had therefore been anticipated, and several times a day, in order to manifest her zeal, the concierge came up to tell her tenant that the postman had just gone by without leaving anything for her.

Finally, one morning, by the first post, a letter was found bearing the inscription: *Mademoiselle Virginie Lauria, c/o her mother, 12 Rue des Hautes-Herbes, Paris.*

The concierge easily deduced that the envelope in question must contain the response so impatiently awaited, because letters to 12 Rue des Hautes-Herbes were usually addressed simply to "Mademoiselle Virginie," the surname Lauria only being employed by neophytes of Parisian life, and the addition of the maternal chaperone never reproduced, so far as the concierge could recall.

Without taking the time to lock the door of her lodge, the worthy concierge raced upstairs. Her violent agitation of the doorbell brought Charlotte running, still barefoot and in her underskirt, her hair virgin of any attempt at brushing, and the two women rushed into the room where Virginie was asleep, lying beside her lover.

"Madame! Madame! It's the reply!" cried the two voices, while the young maid drew the curtains from the window.

Woken with a start, Virginie freed her arm—a movement that caused Alcée to utter a dull groan. She took possession of the letter, which she swiftly unsealed, and, at the bottom of the last page, her eyes, still full of sleep, read the signature *Victor Blancadet* traced in large letters.

Then, with no hesitation, she shook her companion, who had automatically turned over in order to continue sleeping. Increasingly sonorous groans preceded Baillargal's awakening. Quite bewildered, he articulated with difficulty, in the midst of an enormous yawn: "What? What is it?"

"The response! It's the response!

"What response?" Alcée interrogated, negligently, his intelligence still obscured.

"*The* response—Victor Blancadet's response!" yelped the blonde Virginie, irritatedly, propping herself up on her elbow and exposing the upper part of her body, devoid of the most transparent night attire, without worrying about it unduly.

"Ah! And what does it say?" Baillargal asked, in a tone that he strove to render distracted.

Virginie began reading, while Charlotte and the concierge, side by side, awaited the great news that they would incontinently communicate to the entire house and much of the neighborhood.

"*Mademoiselle,*

"*The terms of your letter have touched me infinitely, and certain passages went straight to my heart. The delicacy of the sentiments that you express do the greatest honor to the sex to which you belong, and the grace with which nature has delighted in embellishing your person yields nothing to the precious moral qualities that fate has accorded you in surplus, to make you, it seems, a rare creature, an exceptional individual...*"

"He's going for it!" Alcée exclaimed, now sitting up beside his companion. "And what style!"

"Shut up, then—let me continue. *I have read and reread your letter...*"

"Not bad for a blind man!"

"Shut up! *I have weighed all its terms and I believe that I have penetrated your thought completely. Your ardent desire to consecrate your days to the poor invalid that I am, to be the light in his darkness, the eyes through which he will see, has made me weep tenderly—for I weep, alas, as other men do! Well, having reflected at length. I can only thank you for your spirit of sacrifice; your beauty is not made to be contemplated solely by blind eyes; perhaps I would see you poorly and you would, if you will pardon the expression, be like flowers that one places before animals that are unable to appreciate them...*"

"Oh, the imbecile!" Baillargal burst out, the irony of the last lines causing him to foresee eventual disaster.

Imperturbably, however, Virginie continued: "*So, I shall not be able to follow you into the heaven whose delights you paint for me; I shall continue to live with my cherished works of science and literature until the day when God permits me to unite my destiny with a blind woman, whose misery it will be given to me to soothe.*

"*Please accept, Mademoiselle, the homage of my respectful sympathy. Victor Blancadet.*

"That's a slap in the face, all the same," poor Virginia declared, in a disappointed tone.

"For sure," cried the maid and the concierge, in chorus—an exclamation that earned them a swift rebuke.

"What are you two doing here? I don't need you! Leave me alone and get out—you to your kitchen and you to your lodge, or the devil!"

The two women withdrew, their curiosity satisfied, while a suggestive dialogue commenced between Virginie and Alcée, the former occupied in turning Blancadet's letter over and over between her fingers as if, by examining it more closely, she retained the hope of discovering something other than it contained. In the meantime, Alcée scratched his torso energetically through the gap in his shirt.

"Always the same! I have no luck. One can say that I have no luck at all!"

"What do you want? It's isn't my fault," Virginia excused herself, humbly.

"Perhaps it's mine? What did you tell the imbecile? Obviously, things that immediately made him see what you are."

"For a start, he can't see, because he's blind."

"Go on! What did you write to him?"

"I told him that I'd be happy to become his wife...that his misfortune was one of those that only a woman's hands can soothe...that to love, there was no need to see...that he only had to place his ear on my breast to hear a heart that would only beat for him..."

"Oh, that's nice! And you wanted him to take you for something other than you are?"

"Oh, what I am...what I am! I know full well that I'm not as honest as your socialite...but one does what one can. For a start, I'm not deceiving anyone."

"Naturally."

"Of course, naturally! Do you think that if I didn't love you, I wouldn't have gone to Russia with that prince who wanted to take me away to marry me?"

To marry you? Oh la la! If he knew about me, your prince, he'd light a big candle to me for having kept you! Anyway, all things considered, I'm wondering why I'm arguing with you. You're perfectly free to do as you wish. You wanted

96

to attempt a marriage. That was your right. I don't see why I should get mixed up in things that don't concern me!"

"So, my love, you don't hold it against me?"

"Me? Not at all!"

"That's nice. Let me kiss you. So, if I wrote to him again…?"

"To whom? To that imbecile? To expose yourself again to his secretary's lack of gallantry and facile irony? Not on your life! Hang on, though…I've got an idea. I'll go see this cripple, whose eccentricity isn't devoid of a certain cachet—there's material there for a superb article. With the letter he's addressed to you, I already have a respectable number of lines, which I can frame with a description of his apartment and his entourage—things and people that are, I suppose, in harmony with his character."

About midday, Alcée decided to get up. When Virginie reminded him about the projected visit, he said: "It isn't worth the bother of dressing up for a blind man. A casual jacket will be perfectly sufficient."

After a sober lunch, as is appropriate for people who get up late and are saving themselves for dinner, Alcée Baillargal kissed Virginie, went down three flights of stairs, hurried past the concierge's lodge to avoid being interrupted, and went into the street in search of a cab.

II

On the stroke of three, Alcée Baillargal crossed the threshold of the house bearing the umber 140A in the Rue du Sabre-de-l'Abbé and asked the concierge for directions to Monsieur Victor Blancadet's apartment.

"Facing block. Ring loudly if you want Monsieur Célestin to come and open up!"

That remark, made in a very engaging tone, suggested clearly that the worthy concierge was disposed to chat a little. Baillargal did not want to let an opportunity escape to procure some information that was bound to be useful in presenting himself to Blancadet.

"Oh yes," he said, with his most gracious smile. "He's a trifle deaf, Monsieur Célestin!"

Slightly surprised at first, the concierge, concluding that her interlocutor was perfectly naïve, laughed as she replied: "Deaf, Monsieur Célestin? But he's no more deaf than you or me—he doesn't want to hear, that's all!"

"Oh, you think so?" said Baillargal, mechanically, primarily concerned not to let the conversation drop.

"Certainly!" As if seized by a sudden suspicion, she added: "You don't know him, then?"

"I confess to you that this is the first time I've come here," Baillargal replied, humbly.

"Oh, then it's not surprising! You don't know Monsieur Blancadet either?" the concierge asked, curious to know who the new visitor was.

"No, Madame, I don't know Monsieur Blancadet—so you could render me a great service by giving me a little information. I'm a journalist."

"Ah! Monsieur is a journalist? If you'd care to do me the honor of coming into my lodge for a moment, we could chat more easily. I like journalists. They often came, once, to see Monsieur Lézardot—you know, it's his son, Napoléon Lézardot who was eaten by the natives in Africa six years ago. Since that misfortune, Monsieur Lézardot did nothing but weep, and the grief ended up killing him. He was a very decent man, all the same. Look—he lived up there on the third floor; you can see his windows if you lean out a little."

In order to put a stop to that flow of useless words, Baillargal declared that the remembered Napoléon Lézardot perfectly; he addressed a sigh of dolorous sympathy to the manes of Monsieur Lézardot and abruptly reverted to the subject that interested him.

"So, Monsieur Blancadet is blind?"

"Yes, Monsieur—but between us, I think he can see regardless."

"What! Come on—if he's blind, he can't see; and if he can see, he's not blind."

"That was my reasoning, and that of all the people who don't know Monsieur Blancadet. What I'm sure of it is Monsieur Blancadet no longer has any eyes, but I've often had proof that he can still see, since his terrible accident."

"Ah! Monsieur Blancadet was the victim of an accident?"

"What? You don't remember the catastrophe at the Sorbonne? Wait…yes, it was ten years ago…exactly! It was eight years after the death of poor Benoît…"

"Who's Benoît?"

"My man, of course! Of, Monsieur, he was a hard worker. That one could say…in the quarter too. He left me a widow in 1877. So it was in 1885…you don't remember?"

"No, not at all. In that era I was doing my military service in Corsica."

"In the zouaves?"

"No, why?"

"Oh, no reason. Benoît did his service in the zouaves, in Algeria, and he told me extraordinary stories. He told me, for instance, that in Algeria, there are no concierges! It was to make me angry, you understand, that the poor dear man told me that. Can you imagine, a house in a city without a concierge? In the country, I don't mind, but in a city…"

"Obviously."

"It's astonishing, all the same, that you haven't heard talk of that accident. It made enough noise, though. The entire Sorbonne quarter had blown up!"

"Indeed."

"Oh, you've got it now? It was terrible. You could hear the explosion all the way to Orléans. Me, I was in my cellar, and at first I thought it was a truck that had crashed in the street. I ran upstairs—I was still nimble in those days. In the street I saw men, women and children running away as if the police were after them. Oh, my poor Monsieur…Monsieur?"

"Baillargal."

"It's difficult to say, that name. You're not French, for sure?"

"Yes—I'm from the Midi."

"Oh! Then it's possible, after all...what newspaper do you write for?"

"Several...mostly the *Écho Plaintif*."

"Hey, that's nice! I read it every day. I'll wager that you write the latest news?"

"Oh—no, actually."

"What do you do, then?"

"Articles...current affairs...the society column."

"Oh—it's you who's always talking about a heap of people that nobody knows? I don't understand why you, who seem intelligent, aren't writing the latest news! Perhaps it's difficult to do, but that's what's interesting."

"From now on, I'll try to do it, Madame."

"I'll read it with pleasure. But let's get back to the accident. Where was I? Oh yes...people shouting in the street—and, a few minutes later, they brought back that poor Monsieur Blancadet on a stretcher. They thought he was so completely dead that they'd covered him with a sheet that was already stained with blood. I'm so sensitive that I faint when I only see an animal suffering..."

"You fainted?"

"Me, Monsieur? What about my duty? I accompanied the porters to the apartment. Oh, if you'd seen the picture when they took off the sheet! Oh, my poor Monsieur...Monsieur?"

"Baillargal...Alcée Baillargal."

"Ah, Monsieur Alcée...if you'd seen poor Monsieur Blancadet! A veritable living dish-cloth."

"A dish-cloth?"

"That's not how you say it? What do you say?"

"A wreck?"

"Ah! Yes, a wreck...and for sure, he was one! Of, merciful Father in Heaven! One eye hanging down on his cheek...and blood everywhere! It was terrible!"

"And Monsieur Blancadet?"

100

"Well, Monsieur Alcée, can you believe that he was still breathing? Oh, not much, poor fellow. He hovered between life and death for three months, much closer to death than life. He was well cared for, though! I watched over him for several hours every day. And his mistress, a genteel little woman, spent days by his bedside. She was so tired, poor child, that she fell ill and died before Monsieur Blancadet was in a fit state to accompany her to the cemetery. Oh, merciful Father in Heaven! It's terrible, things like that! And if you'd seen poor Monsieur Blancadet cry with the one eye he still had…!"

"Ah! He still had one eye?"

"Yes, Monsieur Alcée; the other had been ripped out in the explosion by a shard of glass, because, I forgot to tell you, Monsieur Blancadet was working at the Sorbonne in Monsieur Lehargnol's laboratory—he was a famous scientist too…but he was blown to pieces. They didn't find anything but his watch, on the top deck of an omnibus that was going through the Place Saint-Michel. In the laboratory they were heating up a heap of stuff in big glass flasks. And when everything exploded, can you imagine the mess?"

"Yes I can. So, Monsieur Blancadet is a cyclops?"

"What do you mean?"

"That he only has one eye."

"Then Monsieur Blancadet isn't a cyclops."

"Why not?"

"Because he doesn't have any eyes! And even that's very curious: three months after his accident, the doctors tried to make him understand that it was necessary to take great precautions to save the eye that had only been slightly injured, but Monsieur Blancadet said that he had no need of that eye and that it would be better to take it out straight away. The doctors thought that the poor fellow had gone mad and every morning and night they put him in a cold bath, in spite of his protestations and screams. But he stuck to his idea, and one day, when a pair of scissors had been left within his reach, he picked them up and punctured the left eye, which the physicians had almost succeeded in curing. He had to undergo another operation, which he did without the slightest emotion, and when the last bandages were taken off he put a pair of spectacles on his nose that he'd made himself, and in the most natural fashion in the world, he declared that he'd never been able to see so well."

"Of course! He'd gone mad! And since then?"

"Since then? Well, it's still the same. One would think that he could see like you or me."

"Madame Benoît, you're making fun of me!"

"Me? Not at all. Anyway, go make your visit, and afterwards, tell me whether or not Monsieur Blancadet is blind!"

"The facing block, isn't it?"

"Exactly. Ring loudly because of Monsieur Célestin."

"Until later, Madame Benoît!"

"Until later, Monsieur Alcée."

III

Alcée Baillargal rapidly traversed the long courtyard, which the presence of a few stunted trees could, strictly speaking, have qualified as a garden. Following the directions given to him by Madame Benoît, who was watching him from the threshold of her lodge, he tugged forcefully on the ring of the bell-rope, and almost immediately, a clean-shaven man appeared in a narrow gap in the doorway, whose expression, simultaneously suspicious and protective, could only have belonged to a domestic.

Immediately, Baillargal understood that he was dealing with Monsieur Célestin, and without any hesitation he asked to speak to Monsieur Victor Blancadet.

"Monsieur is out," the domestic replied, in accordance with the consecrated formula, inspecting the visitor from head to toe.

"Come on, Monsieur Célestin...!"

"What? You know me?" said the pacified Cerberus, not without a certain contentment.

"But of course I know you! Such a worthy fellow! Oh, Monsieur Blancadet is lucky to have a man like you in his service!"

"You'd like to speak to Monsieur? Please come in, then. He's in his laboratory. If you'd care to give me your card?"

Baillargal was about to interrogate Monsieur Célestin, whom the flattering words he had just addressed to him had placed entirely at his disposal, when a large door-curtain rose and almost immediately fell at the far end of the hallway.

"It's Monsieur!" whispered Célestin, whom the summons of an electric bell decided to deposit the card that he had to present to his master on a small tray, not without having darted a preliminary glance at it.

A minute later, the domestic reappeared and, opening a door with sculpted panels, said: "If Monsieur would care to wait in the drawing room, Monsieur will be with him shortly."

The room into which Baillargal had just been introduced overlooked the garden through three large windows richly draped in red velvet trimmed with gold. On the walls, among paintings by old masters, were canvases by young artists, all chosen with a consummate artistry and revealing the most reliable and delicate taste. There were bathing scenes in which the transparency of the water added a voluptuous nacre to feminine bodies adorable in grace and suppleness, landscapes which inclined their gleams over display-cases filled with works of art of all sorts, while a bust, probably the portrait of the master of the house, exhibited on a pedestal covered in claret plush, decorated the middle of the mantelpiece.

Baillargal set about examining that bronze, to which an ancient patina gave a harsh and severe aspect: an enormous forehead, disengaged from back-combed hair, attracted the attention initially; the nose, a trifle forceful and slightly hooked, was in perfect harmony with the vigorous shape of the entire face; and as for the eyes, sheltered behind simple spectacles, they expressed absolutely nothing abnormal. It was evident that Blancadet had posed for the artist before his terrible accident.

Alcée Baillargal was indulging in conjectures of various sorts, while darting a distracted glance over a bookcase in which preciously-bound volumes were arranged with care, when a door opened and a man, still young in appearance, came in. Instantly, Baillargal established the resemblance between the bust and the model, who wore spectacles with thick lenses.

It really was the blind man with whom he was dealing, and he immediately posed the conventional interrogation: "Monsieur Victor Blancadet?"

"That's me," replied the unfortunate victim of the accident at the Sorbonne, who as holding the journalists card in his hand. In a soft and musical voice, he added: "Monsieur Alcée Baillargal, you're not unknown to me. I read your articles in the *Écho Plaintif* with great pleasure."

Baillargal bowed mechanically; then, reflecting that his interlocutor could not see his gesture, he stammered: "Thank you, Monsieur; you're too kind, and..."

"I'm one of your most fervent admirers. To what do I owe the pleasure—and, permit me to say, the honor—of your visit?"

Perhaps the poor fellow doesn't want people to perceive his infirmity, Baillargal thought, and, searching for a way to strike up a conversation, inevitably fell upon the banal formulae of politeness.

"I'm touched by your welcome, Monsieur. I've come to see..."

Indicating a seat to his visitor, Blancadet said down in an armchair, and said, while laughing: "To see a blind man, no?"

"Oh, Monsieur!" Baillargal protested.

"But yes, yes! You can admit it! What harm is there in that? Curiosity is one of the principle virtues of the journalist!"

"Oh, I beg you, Monsieur, to believe that it isn't only..."

"Not only because I'm a blind man?" Blancadet interrupted, with a sonorous burst of laughter. "I should hope so! Naturally, you wouldn't take the trouble to go to see just any blind man, and you'd be right. But I'm not a vulgar blind man!"

"Permit me to salute in your person a glorious victim of science..."

"Why victim? Why glorious victim?" After a pause, he went on: "Oh! Perhaps you want to talk about that explosion in which a few donkeys who spent their lives suspended from the empty teats of experimental science lost, some of them their lives—of which they were, in any case, only making mediocre usage—and others their sight, of which it wasn't proven that they had any imperious need."

"But you, yourself...?"

"Let's talk about the others first...it's more polite. Since the story seems to interest you, I'll tell you about it, if you'll permit. Don't worry—it won't take long. This is it: on the fifth of May 1885, according to his trilustral habit, to employ the language disencumbered of all simplicity that Jérôme Lehargnol affected—or, as you and I might say, a habit of fifteen years—the celebrated chemist was working in one of the famous laboratories that France is kind enough to place at the disposal of scientists, under the express condition that they do not violate or attempt to violate any of the supposed secrets of nature.

"Monsieur Lehargnol, having the reputation of being profoundly respectful of everything which, closely or distantly, might merit the pejorative epithet of the unknown, had obtained the enjoyment of one of those installations, so costly for the unfortunate taxpayer. The goal that Jérôme Lehargnol proposed to himself, recognized and consecrated by a solemn approval of tutelary councils of science, was to carry out a profound study of explosives through the ages.

"Indefatigably, for fifteen years, Lehargnol carried out experiments whose results would doubtless have been able to demonstrate that the qualification of explosive is quite mistakenly inflicted on certain substances that only ask, in reality, to live in peace, without smashing anything and without mani-

105

festing themselves in outbursts that are as noisy as they are inconvenient...

"Chance—and by chance I mean the crucible in which the destinies of human beings are elaborated—had served Jérôme Lehargnol marvelously. You have, of course, heard mention of Orpheus, whose lyre soothed the anger of ferocious beasts? Well, Monsieur, the mere presence of Jérôme Lehargnol reduced to absolute silence the explosives reputed to be the most terrible. In the course of his quotidian experiments, in spite of employing the most aggressive methods with regard to the least stable of mixtures, he never produced the slightest deflagration!

"I, who am speaking to you, have seen him take a red hot iron and bring it down with all his might on a mass of green powder without unleashing anything more than a cloud of dust; nitroglycerine and the most irritable picrates were as if domesticated! It's necessary to have seen such things to find them plausible!

"It's true that Lehargnol had been one of the most distinguished pupils of the School of Fuses and Capsules; he had passed through a host of Institutions of Detonation in France and abroad, and although his studies had been carried out in the utmost depth, he was almost shot by a firing squad for high treason perpetrated in the course of the last war. By reason of his education and his capacities, Lehargnol had been appointed as a captain in the artillery, and for the twelve hours that a battle in which his regiment took part, in spite of the most formal orders of his commanders, he was never able to obtain the consent of his cannons to separate themselves from their projectiles.

"The unfortunate captain was brought before a court martial and a sentence of capital punishment was about to be pronounced when his defending counsel asked the colonel presiding over the debate to order the experiment that would permit his client to prove that in his hands, a firearm lost all the properties that were obligingly attributed to it. The advocate was authorized to have him given a service revolver of the latest model, which was loaded before the tribunal by an expert amorer. Before anyone had thought to stop him, Lehargnol applied the barrel of the weapon to his chest and pressed the trigger five times in succession.

"Five times the hammer fell with a dry click, and, still very calm, Lehargnol said to his guards, who took the weapon from him: 'Gently! Gently! Be careful—it's loaded!' Which was so true that a shot departed, and a bullet broke the clerk's writing-desk of the clerk; his face was covered in splashed ink. That spectacle determined a sudden fit of madness among the members of the court martial, who were obliged to postpone the sentencing. Then the peace treaty was signed, there was a general amnesty and Jérôme Lehargnol took his place among the scientists upon whom France founded her best hopes.

"I'm not boring you, am I?"

"Oh no, Monsieur!" Baillargal protested, vigorously. "Your words are full of powerful interest."

"You're too kind," said Victor Blancadet, modestly. "To continue my story, since you judge it worthy of being heard...I was very young then—you're following me, aren't you? We're now in the period after the war...at that time, I was undertaking various studies of photographic reactions and sensitive substances in general. I had heard mention of Lehargnol and, still full of illusions with regard to many things, I imagined that I might obtain some benefit from working alongside and in accordance with the methods of such a renowned scientist.

"Thanks to particular circumstances that it would be pointless to expose to you, and above all thanks to the intervention of Madame Lehargnol, who happened to have been a cook in my parents' house, from which the distinguished chemist had removed her to make her progressively his housekeeper, his concubine and finally his legitimate wife, I was able to enter the Master's laboratory as an assistant."

"To your misfortune!" said Baillargal, troubled in spite of himself by this fantastic story."

"To my misfortune? To my good fortune, you mean. Remember that, but for the catastrophe of the fifth of May 1885, I might never have had the courage to carry out an experiment that was very dear to me. I was nearly killed, it's true, and against death, I haven't yet found a remedy!"

"But your eyes?"

"What do eyes matter, when one has spectacles?—my spectacles, of course! So, on the fifth of May 1885, Lehargnol and his aides were testing the passive obedience of cartridges of sublimated dynamite. In one corner, under the ironic eye of the Master, who exercised the causticity of his wit by nicknaming me 'the inventor,' I was carrying out experiments that had already allowed me to demonstrate, I won't say the uselessness, but at least the non-necessity of eyes in the matter of visual perception..."

"Now we're getting there!" murmured Alcée Baillargal, his attentiveness increasing.

"Suddenly, we were projected into the air, amid blocks of stone and fragments of timber torn away from the walls; it's impossible for me to describe the catastrophe in which we were playing too considerable a part for us to be able to witness it. At any rate, I no longer remembered anything when cares that were doubtless very enlightened and no less devoted brought me back to life after a few weeks of coma, during which I belonged, body and soul, to science. It is, therefore, to those representatives that you will need to address yourself if you feel any curiosity to know about what might be called the state of mind of a human being who has lost all contact with the external world.

"I ended up opening my eyes again—or, to be more exact, my eye; for one of my ocular globes had been so pressured in its orbital refuge by a hard body, qualified very accurately the scientists as a foreign body, that the surgeons had been obliged to proceed with its ablation."

"Oh, that's frightful!" cried the journalist, gripped by a veritable emotion. "That's atrocious. Why does humanity have to suffer such terrible evils?"

"In order better to enjoy life, a moralist would say, my boy," Blancadet went on, in a mocking tone. "You know that one only appreciates the wealth one has when one no longer has those that one has lost."

"Oh, you must have regretted your eye a great deal?"

"That's where you're mistaken, my dear Monsieur. Perhaps the precise moment when I was separated from it was painful, but thanks to the beneficent coma in which I remained plunged for three months, I did not retain any impression of it. Afterwards, only one thing troubled me, even causing me veritable suffering: my remaining eye, over which the physicians were exercising so much solicitude that, in order to avoid the unfortunate organ experiencing the slightest fatigue, they almost forbade me the use of it. The sympathy it had for its vanished companion might, it seemed, have stifled within it any will to 'persevere in being.'

"I accorded complete credence to what those scientists said, because I had had, some time previously, a striking example of that sympathy in a very banal but nevertheless quite peremptory fact. I, whom am speaking to you, possessed two canaries—I would say two lovely canaries if the color of the canaries had not shown the word love in a slightly unflattering light. My two pets formed what we humans call an ideal couple. One of them died, eaten by a cat, and the survivor, doubtless finding life intolerable, allowed itself to starve to death...

"That is the story of my eye, to which, I ought to say right away, I did not leave either the time or the trouble of committing suicide. As for the sympathy invoked by the scientists, it is merely the horror inspired by the widowhood of those of our organs known as twins, which, in reality, live in a state of marriage without ever knowing divorce or separation..."

"Are those unions always sterile?" Baillargal asked, glad to be able to indicate to his interlocutor, by means of a ludicrous question, that he had wit.

"My dear Monsieur," Blancadet went on, mildly, "your question evidently embodies a few seeds of the wisdom with which human brains are sown to varying extent. You doubtless mean, in voicing it, that you have never seen a couple of eyes, let us say for instance, have a child? First of all, how do you know that it doesn't happen?

"What happens to many people might happen to you: you will become an old client of a shop to which you have the custom of going several time a year. You see at the till a blonde lady elegantly clad in black. You murmur a 'Thank you, Madame,' to her in exchange to the change she hands you. One day, you go into the shop; when you have completed your purchases, the vendor, after having supplied all your needs and exploited all your weaknesses, murmurs in your ear: 'You know, Monsieur, we have a new cashier; Mademoiselle Jeanne has run off with a client.' Without that eminently confidential information you would have gone tranquilly to the till, you would have deposited your gold or silver coin on the little grooved copper plate and you would have collected your change, adding the usual 'Thank you, Madame,' without perceiving that the former lady elegantly clad in black had been replaced by another lady no less blonde and no less elegantly clad in black....

"Thus it is, in an entirely different order of ideas, Monsieur, with all our organs. How do you know that our orbits are not filled with globes whose substance is being renewed by a perpetual parturition?

"Anyway, I prefer to speak to you frankly; you seem intelligent and I like you. Yes, you were right to ask me just now that question, which, without having the slightest intention of wounding you, I shall permit myself to qualify as ironic..."

"Oh, Monsieur!"

"Don't defend yourself, I can see it clearly! Yes, some of your 'married' organs are sterile, but they have not always been; their prolific virtues have certainly equaled those which, even now, are exhibited, for instance, by our sanguinary corpuscles. Are our teeth not replaced spontaneously? It's true that human eyes, like several other organs of our machine, don't reproduce themselves in their entirety, as those of certain less perfected—or, to be more exact, less evolved—animal species do. With regard to us, the responsible cause is a senile impotence, perfectly admissible in view of the degree of evolutionary advancement of the human species. One day, if people ever decided to do veritable science, they will discover the reason for the peculiar and assuredly anomalous circumstance. But let's get back to our sheep...

"So, I had, therefore, one unique eye in my head..."

"Like Polyphemus," Baillargal put in, the tone of the conversation having driven him to the point of making merry quips.

"Like all cyclops!" Blancadet continued. "I had, therefore, no more to do than suppress the eye that remained to me—in which I was merely anticipating the work of the sympathy that we were talking about just now—in order to test for myself the certainty, theoretically acquired some time before, that the eyes are not indispensable to perceive in images the various phenomena of the external world. I therefore evaded the vigilance of my physicians and, with the sharp points of a pair of scissors, sent my remaining eye to join its companion in the other world..."

"Monsieur," said Baillargal, rising to his feet, "I don't wish to hear any more. My human dignity, combined with my self-respect as a journalist, commands me not to let you make fun of me any longer. I beg you to excuse me for having disturbed you. I have the honor of bidding you farewell..."

"What insect's biting you, Monsieur Journalist, Monsieur...Baillargal?" said Blancadet, after having picked up the card that he had put down on a table. "I thought you were an intelligent man, capable of resisting the surprise of the revelation of facts that could, strictly speaking, pass for new on a planet as banal as ours! I have allowed myself to impart confidences to you that, believe me, don't contain the slightest mockery..."

"But after all, Monsieur—that story of Lehargnol...?"

"Nothing but authentic and exact. You can, if you wish, refer to the newspapers of the day, the fifth of May 1885. People have tried to explain the catastrophe in various ways, and I don't know which one of them is true, but the one thing of which I'm absolutely certain is that Lehargnol was not the guilty party. In any case, that's relatively unimportant; the consequences are much more interesting, as you're about to be able to judge. Having lost my eyes, I'd evidently be blind if I hadn't solved the interesting problem..."

"But Monsieur, are you blind, yes or no?" Baillargal interjected, impatiently.

"My dear Monsieur Baillargal, that depends what you mean by it. In the etymological sense of the word, I'm incontestably 'blind'—which is to say, deprived of eyes. Look!"

And, as calmly as anything in the world, Blancadet lifted up the arms of his spectacles, whose lenses rose up over his forehead, and by means of a simple pressure of the thumb and index finger operated on his eyelids, he caused two glass globes, slightly flattened on one face, to emerge from his orbits, and held them out to his fearful interlocutor.

"You can touch them; they've very solid. They were supplied by an excellent manufacturer. Examine them carefully, True jewels—pure marvels...and so similar: two raindrops from the same shower! Imitating nature so closely, isn't the result already considerable? But that's where I find the absolute and radical impotence of science, which limits itself to mimicking its model. To give them life, to replace them, to create, in imitation of God or Nature—depending on whether you accept the yoke of Faith or Reason, those two inevitable females that humans always end up encountering on their path—to create, yes, create, Monsieur journalist, that's the goal, the sole *raison d'être* of human genius, and you'll agree that I haven't been too undeserving in being able to prove that eyes aren't indispensable to vision."

Alcée Baillargal held in his fingertips the little globes of glass that he had taken, automatically, from Blancadet's hands, while his eyes focused on the empty orbits of his fantastic interlocutor. The walls of the cavities in question, over which, by some inexplicable anomaly, the eyelids had not fallen back, seemed to be covered in a kind of white matter similar to rice powder. His gaze fixed, his mouth open and his hair stuck to his head by the cold sweat of fear, Baillargal remained petrified, while Blancadet, after having used his index finger to bring his lenses back down on to his nose, uttered a violent burst of laughter.

"Oh, my poor Monsieur Baillargal, what a face you're pulling! Oh, I beg you, look at yourself in a mirror—the spectacle's worth the trouble!"

With an automatic movement, as if acting under the influence of a magnetic pass, Baillargal stood up, and, perceiving his own image in the mirror over the mantelpiece, stammered: "It's me...it's really me!" And, to prove the reality of his own existence, he put both hands to his forehead. In the course of that movement he dropped the two glass eyes, which fell on to the carpet.

Judging it necessary to reassure his visitor, Blancadet had risen to his feet in his urn. "Come on, Monsieur Baillargal, come on my friend, pull yourself together, I beg you. I didn't think you were so impressionable. If I'd anticipated, for an instant..."

Alcée Baillargal, his nose against the mirror, continued making sure of his objectivity, and murmured: "No, I'm not mad. I'm not mad...no! No!"

"Evidently not—you're not mad," said Blancadet, taking the unfortunate journalist by the arm. "Confess, all the same, that you've been slightly distressed!"

"Oh yes!" sighed Baillargal, with undisguised conviction.

"It's the fault of your education again! Oh, that modern education! One thing that you're not accustomed to seeing, that hasn't been anticipated in the nonetheless-overloaded curricula with which your youth had been stuffed, appears to you, and rather than being obliged to admit to yourself that facts might exist with which you haven't been acquainted, you prefer to think that you've been afflicted with mental alienation!"

Mopping his forehead, which was streaming with sweat, Baillargal turned to his interlocutor and said, very humbly: "I beg your pardon, Monsieur. A hallucination..."

"Ah!"

"An accident happening to me for the first time...which I was unable to foresee. One of my great-great aunts was, it appears, afflicted by that disease. I'm a victim of heredity. You're a man of science, Monsieur, You understand..."

"I understand, my dear Baillargal, that you're one of the innumerable victims of the intransigent relativities of the word 'science,' which you articulate so ostentatiously. But take account, once and for all...oh, excuse me—what have you done with my eyes?"

"Your eyes?" queried Baillargal, lamentably.

"Yes my eyes! I confided them to you a moment ago. Oh, there they are!" He indicated a precious Persian rug that was ornamenting the front of the hearth. "My poor friend, you've dropped them!" And as Baillargal instinctively made as if to bend down, he added: "Don't trouble yourself!"

Victor Blancadet picked up the superior products of modern ocularistics, carefully dusted them with a pink silk handkerchief and set them down on the mantelpiece, in a crystal receptacle decorated with gold, saying to his visitor, who was now lending himself to the mystification in a joyous fashion: "I don't need them for the moment!"

"Fortunate blind man!"

"My God, don't feel sorry for me. I'm blind, it's true, but..."

"You can see!"

"Yes, exactly, I can see. And you'll admit that it's a consolation. But come on! Will you give me the pleasure of being reasonable? I'll explain the secret of my 'sighted blindness,' if you'll permit me that heteroclitic combination of words."

"Oh, I beg you, Monsieur. I wouldn't want to experience any shock in discussing your physiological theories, but..."

"My theories! My theories! And the practice, then—what do you make of that? Well, so be it; I won't insist. Let's talk about something else, and tomorrow you can tell your readers about your visit to a blind man whose glass eyes are a match for those of the lynx of such clear-sighted memory, and everyone will take you for a joker..."

"Oh, Monsieur...!" begged the journalist.

"I'm not the joker, though. And people will put forward hypotheses, all as preposterous as one another. I'll amuse myself reading those stories of brigands..."

Baillargal gradually recovered his professional poise. His gaze was scarcely astonished by the pieces of glass deposited in the receptacle; he was content now to recognize that Victor Blancadet was a master in the art of mystification, so opposed to the mediocre. The most elementary politeness commanded him not to seem to perceive anything—so, while according himself the secret credit of an ulterior revenge, he got ready to lend an attentive ear to the words that were about to flow from the bizarre being who had succeeded in making him believe, momentarily, that glass eyes might have replaced the natural organ of vision in him.

Victor Blancadet abruptly changed the subject of the conversation. "My dear Monsieur Baillargal, as you're 'on the inside,' can you tell me if many marriages are made as a result of advertisements inserted in the newspapers?"

"It depends," Baillargal prevaricated, immediately returned to thinking about Virginie Lauria and her inflamed epistle.

"On what does it depend?" Blancadet immediately reposed. "I ask because, I ought to tell you, last week I placed an advertisement...hold on, it was in the *Écho Plaintif*. It was thus composed: "*Blind man aged thirty-five, having lost his sight in a laboratory accident and enjoying an annual income of fifty thousand francs...*""

"*Revertible to his widow...*" Baillargal continued, his mind now completely taken over by the abortive projects of his mistress.

"You've read my advertisement!" Blancadet exclaimed, joyfully. "No need to tell you the rest, then. Oh, that's lucky! Well, what do you think of it?"

"Me? Nothing! I don't have anyone in my family to marry off…," the handsome Alcée replied, in a detached tone.

"That's a pity. If you had a sister or a cousin blind from birth, I'd gladly have become our relative, for I like you a lot…"

"Thank you! But will you permit me to ask a question?"

"Please do!"

"Why are you so essentially intent on marrying a blind woman?"

"Why do I want to marry a blind woman—and, let's be clear about it, one blind from birth? That's quite a question! But my dear Monsieur Baillargal, I'll wager that you've never asked why brunettes, blondes and redheads are the object of exclusive preferences, why corpulence and slimness find equally passionate admirers? A matter of taste, my dear friend! A simple matter of taste! Such reasons suffice to legitimate, after a fashion, the dream that I have of uniting a blind woman with my destiny. Believe, however, that it's not only the consideration, assuredly respectable but, it must be admitted, secondary, of epidermis, hair and silhouette that have determined my conjugal volition; I affirm to you that I'm absolutely convinced that only a blind woman is capable of providing what is conventionally called happiness!"

Involuntarily disturbed, Baillargal sketched a grimace.

"Oh, that makes you smile?" asked Blancadet, without any hint of bitterness.

"No, I assure you!" the journalist protested, weakly. "Like you, I think that blindness isn't an obstacle to happiness. Amour passes through life with a perpetual blindfold over the eyes…"

"You have intelligence, Monsieur Journalist. I prize that quality greatly. But to get back to what I was saying, I assure you, in all sincerity, that a blind woman is the ideal woman. Why, you ask me? Think about it for a minute, my poor friend. What does a man seek, in general, in marriage, if not a latent soul and a new body? Two equal illusions in different domains.

"By virtue of reasonings and inconsequences—hereditary or acquired—men are persuaded that they have some benefit in being the first to open the wings of a soul, which, for not having had occasion to manifest itself, nevertheless exists, sometimes even tyrannical and violent, while the unfortunate husband ordinarily has some experience. Furthermore, a pride that is in some sense constitutional—an entirely physical vanity—incites the male to believe that the redness of the virginal bouquet forms a magical principle that attaches a female to his heart forever. The man who has opened up the field of sensuality in his wife has the illusion of a perpetual debt of gratitude contracted by the neophyte.

"Husbands are numerous who content themselves with planting the flower of amour without worrying overmuch about the nature of the soil. Those reckless and incompetent gardeners are soon punished for their blindness and their ignorance, for the wife, only finding disappointments in the conjugal cultivation, sets out in quest of another gardener, whom a hope—very often illusory, alas—causes her to consider the proprietor of more sweetly-perfumed flowers.

"That is life, Monsieur Baillargal; that is what happens on a daily basis between people who see with the eyes that an imprudent creator has given them. I shall not linger over the chapter of frustrated amours and badly-matched couples, and will return to my proposition: only a woman blind from birth can provide happiness..."

"I'm beginning to believe that you're right," the journalist put in, by way of politeness. These unexpected observations regarding amour were opening the horizons of a sensational novel.

"Oh, you're beginning, are you?" mocked Blancadet. "Well, continue! In a little while, you'll be completely convinced. I therefore take a blind young woman—blind from birth, of course. The young woman in question has never had

117

contact with the external world except via hearing, touch, taste and smell—all secondary senses, which are, so to speak, the lieutenants of sight, the principal sense, which incontestably dominates its companions.

"Ignorant of the light, that young woman is as little 'affirmed' as possible—I mean by 'affirmed' the degree of crystallization of the self: a crystallization resulting from everything that can augment the consciousness of being. It is, in sum, the terrestrial paradise before the appearance of the serpent. I beg you not to lose sight of the fact that it is materially impossible for my descendant of Eve to head toward the famous apple-tree of her own accord.

"You understand, don't you, without my insisting, the abyss that separates the young woman of my dreams from numerous marriageable young women whose parents make much of their state of virginity, like those fairground horse-traders who signal to buyers the knees of their products, free of any rings. Well, yes, I know full well that that proves, up to a point, that those chargers have never bitten the dust by bending the articulation of their anterior limbs in a particularly harmful fashion, but can one deduce from that carpal integrity that the noble beasts have never fallen and are flowers of perfection, comparable to my blind girl, on whose nose I shall place, on our wedding day, a pair of spectacles like those I'm wearing myself at this moment?

"Suddenly, the brain of that disinherited child is invaded by a flood of light: for the first time, the blind woman, by virtue of that simple adjunction of optical accessories, can see like you and me. While she cries miracle and, in the effusion of her gratitude, bestows on me the capital epithet of 'God,' I gallantly take her by the hand and lead her, by the paths that tempt my fantasy, at a rapid or a slow pace, in accordance with the attraction of the place and the moment, to the famous apple tree, the most beautiful fruits of which we consume together!

"Agree, my dear Baillargal, that it's already not banal to be able to be the serpent to one's wife!"

"In spectacles?" said the journalist, ironically.

"In spectacles…or rattles, if you like the music," the obstinate mystificator acquiesced. "Do you understand now why I'm intent on marrying a blind woman?"

"I understand perfectly," Baillargal opined, without recrimination. "But you haven't found one?"

"My dear fellow believe it or not, but I must confess to you that, in fact, I haven't had the good fortune, thus far, of discovering that rare bird, a woman blind from birth. I have, however, received lots of letters. Think about it! Fifty thousand francs in annual income! Oh, I'm a good catch—all the more so because, after my death, my wife will have, as a thread of consolation, the total property of my fortune. If I were not endowed with a temperament inclined more to philosophy than indignation, you would see me, at this moment, expand into lamentations regarding the absence of moral sense that characterizes the feminine element, in the epoch that it has pleased destiny to make us live!"

"Oh, it's a very sad spectacle!" Baillargal declared.

"Not at all! You are again, on that point, a victim of the ridiculous psittacism that is the entire science of the sociologists! You'll never understand, therefore, that in the life of peoples as in the life of individuals, every age brings with it exactly what it requires: antidotes to the momentarily-dangerous poisons.

"For instance: the need for wealth that is the capital mark of this century. That need has become a contagious disease, which it is impossible to escape; but, thanks to the marvelous law of equilibrium that regulates time and space, human consciousness has adapted to that new state of affairs; the modern era no longer has the same conception of good and evil, those two essentially mobile poles of physical and mental activity.

"A weapon, once withered by the epithet of dishonesty, has become classic, and whoever hesitates to employ that weapon will reproach himself for his too-recent nobility, and will put himself in a state of marked inferiority. Believe me, those times that we are pleased to qualify as heroic were just as corrupt as ours, and, in the balance of the absolute, the virtues of our ancestors weighed, just as exactly as today, what their vices weighted!

"Then again, those words 'virtues' and 'vices,' so expressive in the mouths of our hypocritical moralists, do not signify anything essentially different. So, let us get to the bottom of things with what has happened to me in consequence of my advertisement in the *Écho Plaintif.* I told you that I'd received a multitude of letters, each more alluring than the last. Why should I pass upon my pretty correspondents a judgment not merely severe but unfair? Perhaps, in that number, there are some who acted in a spirit of sacrifice in offering to share my existence; to those I can bear no resentment and ought, in all justice, to content myself with feeling sorry for those victims of a heavy and absurd heredity of religion and moral law.

"With regard to the others, those who were primarily attracted by my fortune and the prospect of my inheritance, it's necessary to be equally just. In our manuals of morality, we can read that a woman has a right to give herself, but not to sell herself. That rule, to be sure, has been laid down by an ineffable philosophy, the enemy of economic perturbation, with doubtless thinks it simpler and more comfortable to open the heart than the purse-strings.

"Such as you see me, I haven't always been rich, and in the springtime of my life I've been loved for myself by a woman as opulent in form as in fortune; nevertheless, I deceived her at every opportunity—and, sincerely, I don't know why; perhaps to prove to myself a liberty of the heart, which I admit to being perfectly ridiculous. Of that amour I've conserved the best memory, and even, I dare say, some pride. Later, the roles were changed; I became infatuated with a she-devil who had nothing at all, whom I paid generously and who deceived me no less copiously—who treated me, in brief, as I had treated the other. Was that not what one calls a just compensation of earthly affairs?

"Believe me, my dear Baillargal: an admirable and indestructible harmony reigns over people and things. A pendulum cannot oscillate in only one direction, and what we call evil is the essential condition of what we call good. Thus, for instance, in the letter that I ask you permission to read to you, you will find pell-mell sentiments of a diversity that might appear disconcerting at first sight, but which, however, constitute the very substance of the human soul, masculine as well as feminine."

Victor Blancadet pushed back his chair in order to be able to pull out a large drawer stuffed with letters, which exhaled vague scents of perfumery. His hands rummaged in that mass of paper, of all colors and various formats.

Pensively, Alcée Baillargal watched him do it. He wondered whether it might not be the letter from his mistress that Blancadet was about to read to him—and the theory of admirable and indestructible harmony appeared to him to be irrefutable when Blancadet, after having carefully readjusted his spectacles, exclaimed:

"Ah! Here it is! My dear Baillargal, you will not hold it against me that I do not violate, to your benefit, what one might call professional confidentiality. I shall only tell you the forename of my correspondent; it's a pretty one: Virginie."

"A predestined name," Baillargal hastened to interject, in order to let nothing show of the slight shock he had just felt.

"It's an admirable epistle," Blancadet went on. "You'll find material for a dazzling article in it."

While speaking, Blancadet had risen to his feet and approached a kind of rotating bookcase surmounted by a copper box. Standing up, he seemed to scan the latter he held in his hand rapidly, as if to rememorize its terms and to prepare to read it aloud.

˙ "If you'd care to let me read it myself," Baillargal offered, "it would save you the trouble..."

"Oh, thank you, thank you—you're too kind! My eupantophone is here."

That unusual term had the effect, in the tranquilized play of Baillargal's faculties, of King Log falling into the frogpond, and he queried with an involuntary shudder: "Your...?"

"Eupantophone," the imperturbable Blancadet replied, and, as if perceiving that he had forgotten something, added: "Oh, forgive me! I haven't introduced you to it." Conscientiously, his right hand indicating the copper box set on top of the rotating bookcase, he went on: "My eupantophone, the most faithful and most precious of my collaborators."

"Delighted," said the journalist, mechanically, searching in vain to penetrate the new mystification that his redoubtable interlocutor was preparing for him.

"You will, in any case, make its more ample acquaintance," Blancadet continued, inserting Virginie's letter in a slot contained in the lid of the box.

Immediately, a loud voice emerged, proclaiming: "Love is to humans what Heaven is to God."

The first words of that picturesque aphorism were greeted by an enormous burst of laughter from Blancadet, who, placing the index finger of his right hand on one of the corners of the box, exclaimed: "My dear eupantophone, you're being facetious! Excuse me, Monsieur Journalist. I'd forgotten the tragic voice. My eupantophone imitates to perfection our illustrious tragedian Bouquet-Joly. I take advantage of it to offer myself an occasional tirade from *Les Burgraves*[6]—this very morning it declaimed for me the famous passage: 'Whoever you are, have you heard tell/That there is in the Taunus, between Cologne and Spire…?' That's not exactly the voice to suit the prose that I want you to appreciate. Let's see…the angelic? Yes, that's it: the angelic!"

At the same time, Blancadet turned a little key fitted into one of the side-walls of the box from left to right, and a feminine voice, musical and tender, repeated: "Love is to humans what Heaven is to God."

Again, Blancadet applied his index-finger to one of the corners of the container, and addressed the journalist—whose flair was not in default this time, and who had immediately discovered the phenomenon of ventriloquism, albeit manifest-

---

[6] The 1843 play by Victor Hugo.

ed with a rare perfection. "Isn't that the kind of voice best suited to a young woman?"

"Oh, marvelous!" Baillargal acquiesced. "Marvelous!"

"Oh, I had a lot of difficulty achieving that softness of tone."

"That doesn't astonish me," said Baillargal.

"Let's listen to Mademoiselle Virginie's prose!"

And, one of the corner of the box having been pressed again, while Blancadet came to sit down facing Baillargal again, the musical voice rose up again: "But if divine bliss has need of infinite azured space, human happiness cannot do without tenderness."

Baillargal watched Blancadet's lips attentively, with the hope of glimpsing a movement that he promised himself to point out in order to humiliate his mystifier, but not the slightest quiver was evident. That bizarre voice really seemed to be emerging from the copper box. Baillargal interrogated his memory in vain; he could not remember ever having seen such incomparable ventriloquism, and he had to suppress an impulse to clap his hands to testify to his enthusiasm, as he would have done at a theatrical performance. He desire to know the contents of his mistress' missive held him back, and, with his eyes riveted on the immobile face of the extraordinary individual in front of him, he listened.

"It is an insult that you have made to all women in thinking that not one among them would consent to unite her destiny with that of a man who, for not having received his wounds on a battlefield, is no less worthy of being loved. I am writing to you, Monsieur, in secret from my mother, and if certain things seem to you to be out of place under the pen of a young woman, you may blame the profound disturbance that I feel in opening wide my heart, which I would like you to be able to read as if it were a book in which there is nothing but love and tenderness.

"A young woman is like a rose which only opens when one breathes her in; under your kiss, I would bloom, and the wing of happiness, sheltering our two beings, huddled together against the cold, would give birth to perfumes so sweet that a divine scent of paradise would expand around us. In the evening, after having united our lips in order to empty to the last drop the thirst-slaking amphora of pleasure, you would rest your head upon my breast and you would listen to my heart beat for you, my gentle master, my beloved husband.

"I pray to the one on whom human destinies depend, who has made me blonde and pretty and who would be my God if you believe in him, to give these lines the eloquence that their emotion and sincerity requires from them. Believe in the imperishable love that you have awakened in the heart of one who would be proud and happy to call herself Madame Victor Blancadet, and who signs herself: Virginie..."

"And professional confidentiality!" exclaimed Blancadet, precipitating himself toward the rotating bookcase in order to place his index finger very ostentatiously on the copper box, which suddenly seemed to resume the mute function appropriate to that kind of object. "Well, what do you think of that?"

"You're an odd...I confess that I've never seen such an odd...specimen...!"

"A specimen, me? An odd specimen? That's a good one!" said Blancadet, joyously, in the satisfied tone of people conscious of having provoked some amazement in their neighbor and sense a vague sensual pleasure in consequence.

"Don't be offended, I beg you. Believe that I don't put into the term any unkind, or even ironic, intention."

"But Monsieur Alcée Baillargal, man of letters and journalist, why are you intent on seeing me as a phenomenon?"

"Well, that performance of ventriloquism authorizes me..."

"My poor eupantophone, you're calumniated again!" cried Blancadet, melodramatically, placing his right hand on the mysterious box.

"I agree that you're a master and...I bow down before your incontestable talent."

"Thank you," said Blancadet, sketching a reverence. "Well, since you don't want to let go...yes, exactly...I'm a ventriloquist. A ventriloquist! I only ask you not to publish my name. That might impede my matrimonial plans."

"Then you're authorizing me to publish?"

"Anything you wish! On condition of not putting my name, and not describing me too clearly. I want to live in peace, and glory is merely a vain word to me."

"That's a promise! Count on my discretion."

"Thank you. And by the way...the young woman..."

"What young woman?"

"Virginie! The young person who wrote the letter that my eupantophone just read to us..."

"Forgive me...allow me to write that name in my note-book. Eu-pan-to-phone...eupantophone!"

"It comes from the Greek."

"That doesn't surprise me."

"I assure you of it. What do you think?"

"It's very good."

"I'm not talking about that, but her...Virginie my correspondent."

"Oh! Well, what?"

"Well, do you, who know our young Parisiennes better than I do, believe that delightful stylist to be sincere?"

"I believe so."

"However, it seems to me that...for a young woman...?"

"Oh, today, young women, especially those who are somewhat literate, like to manifest themselves as amiable little monsters of perversity. Drive them into a corner, or to work, if you prefer, and they'll appear to you as ingenuous and as candid as the lily-white pupil of Madame de Maintenon..."

"We're in absolute agreement! You'll agree, however, that that inflamed literature..."

"Proves that no fire is brooding under the ashes! Believe me, there's nothing to fear in a flame that, free and unconstrained, is as resplendent as the sunshine!"

"All that glitters isn't gold! Then again, I'm sticking to my idea; I want a blind woman for a wife. That's what I replied to my amiable correspondent after here days of reflection, I confess. I was on the point of asking to meet her...and I'm not sure what would have happened if, as she says in her letter, this Virginie is blonde and pretty..."

"She is blonde and pretty!" Baillargal exclaimed.

"Do you know her?"

"Me? Not at all!" said the handsome Alcée, recalled to practicality. "But since she says so..."

"That's true. It's always necessary to believe a woman, especially when she affirms that she's pretty."

"Obviously."

A knock on the door preceded the entry of Célestin, who, bowing to his master, announced the arrival of the optician.

"That's good—show him into the laboratory. I'll be there in a moment. Excuse me, Monsieur Baillargal—it's a matter of an experiment whose results are imminent and which can't fail to interest you. Come back in a few days' time and bring me a few copies of the *Écho Plaintif* in which the article appears in which you talk about me...my eupantophone reads newspapers admirably. What about my eyes? I no longer have the habit...their absence causes me some slight fatigue...and then, one's no longer twenty!" Blancadet spoke cheerfully while taking the two globes of glass out of the crystal receptacle and replacing them in his orbits, pushing his spectacles up to his forehead and then readjusting them on his nose. "I'll see you soon, then, my dear Monsieur Baillargal. Show Monsieur out, Célestin. A blind ventriloquist, no? That would be very odd!"

The obstinate mystifier lifted up a door-curtain and disappeared.

"This way, Monsieur," said Célestin.

"Tell me, Monsieur, will you speak to me frankly?"

"I'm an old soldier!" said Célestin, indignantly.

"Is your master blind?"

"Monsieur is asking whether Monsieur is blind? I can only reply affirmatively to that question."

"Can he see?"

"As well as you and me."

"Ah! And is Monsieur Blancadet a ventriloquist?"

"A ventriloquist?"

"Yes, a ventriloquist. Can he speak without seeming to?"

"Not as far as I know!"

"His voice doesn't seem, sometimes to be emerging from somewhere other than his mouth? That copper box, for example?"

"The eupantophone?"

"You're familiar with it too?"

"Of course. I pass a chamois leather over it every morning. I care for it as if it were Monsieur's child."

"Célestin! Célestin!" shouted a voice.

"That's Monsieur calling me. If Monsieur will come..."

Célestin opened the door and the unfortunate journalist went out, wondering whether, in truth, he had not lost a little of the reason with which his fellows were kind enough to credit him.

Madame Benoît was on the lookout for him, and as he passed by, she invited him to resume their conversation, with all the grace in the world.

"Well, Monsieur Alcée, have you seen Monsieur Blancadet?"

"Yes, thank you, I've seen him," the journalist replied, curtly, adding, as he reached the door in order to rejoin his fiacre: "*Au revoir*, Madame Benoît."

He was beginning to curse his coachman, who was probably at table in some nearby wine-shop, when he discovered the automedon through the carriage window; he had installed himself inside his carriage, in order not to waste his time, and was sleeping peacefully, his varnished cap on his knees.

Baillargal woke the sleeper. "To the *Écho Plaintif*!" he ordered.

"Very good, Boss," said the coachman, climbing on to his seat.

"Stop when you go past the Bibliothèque Nationale," Baillargal added, as he ducked his head in order to get into the

127

vehicle, which drew way under the wrathful gaze of Madame Benoît.

IV

Huddled in a corner, in order better to resist the jolts of the carriage rebounding over the unequal crests of the cobblestones, Alcée Baillargal recalled the various incidents of his visit one by one, like a miser fondling his gold. In a kind of exaltation, compounded out of his professional vanity and the anticipation of serious material advantages, he saw himself once again as the king of news. The next day, under his signature—a banner covering for too long, according to Anacharsis Lacrimal, the editor of the *Écho Plaintif*, banal and uninteresting copy—the columns of the celebrated newspaper would inform the public of the improbable story of Victor Blancadet. The success of curiosity could only be enormous—but the prospect of that renewal of glory inevitable rendering the fiber of prudence in the journalist's heart more sensitive; so, before writing his article, Alcée Baillargal had decided to go to kneel at the altar of Our Lady of Documentation.

He had abandoned himself to his reverie when a shock produced by the sudden halt of the vehicle returned him to the perception of circumstances. A high, broad breach cut through the gray wall running along the sidewalk to the right. For Alcée Baillargal it would have been superfluous to read the inscription engraved in golden letters on the fronton of the monumental door, which declines to the profane the name of the Bibliothèque Nationale, to which the boulevardian fashion followed in all editorial offices referred as "Notre Dame du Document."

It is the obligatory place of pilgrimage for all people in the toils of intellectual production: the giant warehouse containing, in effect, almost in total, the artistic, literary and scientific life of humankind. Scholars, stubborn collectors of trivial facts parasitic on history, now promoted by virtue of antiquity to the first rank, come to draw from that well every day.

The great frescos of the past, epics and legends nourished by all the peoples of ages, unconscious of their brutal adolescence, lend debilitated imaginations the support of their heroic prestige. More humbly, the special collections, the encyclopedias and the gazettes, offer on the universality of subjects a banal rudiment capable of satisfying those who have no appetite for the dusty confidences of defunct epochs.

On the innumerable shelves of the enormous dormant hive, arranged like funerary urns in a columbarium, are scrolls, files and volumes of every form and color. It is the integral heritage of the speculative and practical genius of humankind, transmitted from the most distant eras by an incessant labor, which has become the formidable succession that a more or less distant catastrophe will hurl abruptly into oblivion, as if nature desired, from time to time, to affirm the inescapable law of the perpetual recommencement of all things.

Alcée Baillargal only possessed the most summary education, so every time he entered the immense reading room, as high-ceilinged as a basilica, he experienced the emotion of a neophyte about to penetrate the mysteries of his faith. His quality as a certified devotee gave him freedom of entry into the temple, and he limited himself to giving the clerk entrusted with examining credentials a brief nod, to which the other replied with a bow and the murmur of a familiar welcome. A handshake was often exchanged, because, by means of that politeness, the journalist ensured himself of the perfect complaisance of the humble employee, whose title as a functionary made it a strict duty for him to persecute the public in the name of the letter of some aggressive an obtuse regulation.

"Is Père Van here?" asked Baillargal, pressing the phalanges of the man in the silver-braided black coat.

"Indeed, Monsieur Baillargal; Monsieur Van Columelle is in service every day except for Saturday morning," the Cerberus replied, quite amiably, although he would have nailed an unknown or antipathetic silhouette to the threshold with a gesture of his free hand.

"Thanks, my dear...!" said Baillargal, garbling the incomprehensible syllables that represented the forgotten or never-learned name of his interlocutor.

"Père Van" was the familiar denomination, used by all the regulars, of the librarian Van Columelle. Several generations of readers had filed before the elevated desk at which he sat on a daily basis, flanked to the right and left by colleagues completing the redoubtable trinity charged with governing access to reading material. His particular function consisted of putting on a slip of green paper the visa authorizing the recipient to give chase to the ungraspable assistants forever in flight, who had to be cornered before they would consent to take the ticket and set off at the automatic pace of a somnambulist for the probable location of the requested volume.

Among the numerous staff of the Bibliothèque, Van Columelle constituted such a touching exception that his colleagues held him to be an abnormal creature, a sort of monster introduced by some unknown means into the bosom of the administration. Van Columelle was, in fact, kindness personified; he had a passion for rendering service to his fellows, devoting himself to it entirely, with a serenity of soul that seemed to provoke the muted jealousy of his two perpetually-preoccupied neighbors.

A shrug of the shoulders, corroborated by a scornful glance, habitually disapproved of the conduct of Père Columelle—who did not depart, for that, from his inalterable zeal, and continued to give out information and to brighten with his "feeble enlightenment," as he called it, the research of the numerous readers good enough to address themselves to him. Timidly, he indicated a source—"I believe that you wouldn't consult this volume without some profit... I believe that you might find material useful to your interesting research in this book... Excuse me for wanting to appear erudite...by dint of handling these books..."—and his eyes embraced the numerous shelves with a familiar gaze—"one ends up knowing a little of what they contain."

Unfortunately for him, Van Columelle did not emerge from one of the schools outside which, in many careers, there is only a relative salvation. Condemned and perfectly resigned to vegetate in subaltern employment, he had had, in the course of his long career, the exclusive ambition to do his duty punctiliously, sufficiently rewarded, he affirmed, by the marks of esteem and affection that all those who approached him strove to testify to him.

A few years before, Van Columelle had lost his wife; his dolor in consequence of that death, which, on the threshold of old age, had separated him brutally from the companion of his life, had been tragic. One afternoon, someone had come to look for him at the Bibliothèque; it was a neighbor sent, he had said initially, on behalf of Madame Van Columelle, who had been taken ill in the street.

"It's nothing serious, is it?" the poor man had asked, from his elevated station, on taking the hand that the messenger held out to him in both of his. The latter had lowered his head without replying.

Then, Van Columelle, leaning anxiously toward his interlocutor, brusquely pulled him toward him. "What is it? An accident? Speak! Tell me quickly. Oh my God, it's not serious, is it?"

"Monsieur Van Columelle, it's necessary for you to come with me. It's necessary for you to go home right away."

"It's only four o'clock!" cried the functionary, looking at the clock mechanically. "Oh my God! What's happened? Speak, I beg you."

"Come, Monsieur Van Columelle. They're waiting for you to..."

"I'll come with you, Monsieur Van Columelle; I might be of some use to you," offered an old physician, a regular at the Bibliothèque, who, with his green ticket in his hand, had followed the rapid dialogue, immediately divining the misfortune, the details of which were briefly recounted to him while Van Columelle went to inform the Curator. Madame Van

Columelle had collapsed in the street a few steps from home, because of a ruptured aneurism.

During the journey in the carriage the two men, taking turns, tried to prepare Van Columelle gently for the terrible news, but the latter was so far from suspecting the truth that he did not grasp any of the allusions made to a possible disaster, and when he arrived home he still knew nothing more.

As rapidly as his old legs permitted, he went up five flights of steps. On the threshold of his dwelling a man was standing, the local physician, whom he had known for a long time.

"Monsieur Van Columelle, I beg you…have courage…it's over. Madame Van Columelle is…"

"What? What are you saying?" snapped the poor man in a distraught voice, seizing the doctor by the lapel of his coat.

"Courage, my friend, I beg you; destiny…," the man of science tried to interject, searching for words capable of softening the blow of reality, but Van Columelle had already hurled himself into the bedroom where the inert body of his wife was lying on the bed.

Only then did he understand, and, without any apparent emotion, he approached slowly, planted a long kiss on the dead woman's forehead, and murmured in her ear the simple words: "*À bientôt! À bientôt!*" Then he had returned to the doctor and the two men who had brought him from the library. He had asked them a few questions about what had happened, and immediately begun talking about funeral arrangements.

The funeral took place the next day; the humble coffin was followed by all the staff of the Bibliothèque whose service was not strictly required that day, and by all the regulars, happy to make in that circumstance a gesture of sympathy for their old friend Van Columelle—and on emerging from the cemetery, having resisted without a tear the great grief that afflicted him, he could no longer contain his emotion before the touching manifestation of which he was the object.

The Curator had told him that three months' leave had been granted to him, but Van Columelle asked for the favor of resuming his functions immediately. In fact, the poor man could not live alone, and the Bibliothèque constituted, for him, a kind of second hearth from which he could not be separated, even temporarily. His occupations lightened his burden; he talked to everyone about his dead wife, and employed his leisure time reading the philosophers and scientists who had studied grief, as if he wanted to find in their books the sensation of a suffering more bitter than his own—but after every reading he confessed to a friend: "No, they don't know what desolation is! Perhaps it's impossible to express the void…and to lose someone that one loves is to sense that one is prey to the void."

Van Columelle's colleagues had ended up taking pity on him; his errors with regard to the fundamental principles of administrations were almost forgotten. A kind of custom was established at the Bibliothèque; within a fortnight of his installation, every new employee was invited to lunch by Van Columelle, and if, sometimes, slightly astonished by that unusual demonstration of amity, the guest sought information, he received the reply that it was a tradition and that it would be a grave fault to attempt to avoid it.

As the habits and customs of an institution are its principal and almost exclusive reason for being—its essence, in a way; the equivalent of the unexplained and inexplicable mysteries of any well-organized religion—the newcomer asked no more and prepared, not without a secret pride, to cross that step of the bureaucratic initiation.

One Sunday, therefore, on the stroke of noon, the guest went to number 3, Rue du Zèbre d'Or, climbed five flights of stairs, got his breath back momentarily before Van Columelle's visiting card, stuck to the door by a few copper pins, and, slightly emotional in spite of himself, pressed the doorbell. Van Columelle, clad in his eternal black frock-coat, whose buttonhole was ornamented by the ribbon of a Chevalier of the Order of the Celestial Papyrus, immediately appeared to receive his guest. The usual compliments were exchanged, after which the host declared that it was time to sit down at table. They went into the dining room; three places were set on the white tablecloth. Often, the guest begged Van Columelle to waste for the latecomer.

"Oh, pardon me, my young and dear guest; that's *her* setting. I haven't yet had the courage to dispense with it. Sit down here, to my left. You'd be on the right if she were still here, my poor dear wife..."

The guest gave his face the most consoling expression possible and listened to the touching narration of Van Columelle's misfortune.

Ordinarily, the young employees submitted to that ordeal with the greatest philosophy, and did not retain the slightest resentment against their elder. One of them, however, whose name remains mysterious, once played a practical a joke in extremely poor taste, very cruel to the old widower's dolor.

Invariably, in the course of the lunch, Van Columelle, after having spoken for some time about the qualities of his other half before the old housekeeper, who wiped away a tear on hearing mentioned of the mistress she had loved so much, said: "Oh yes, she was a unique individual. She even had little faults that made me cherish her even more. Would you believe it? She was distracted. For the sake of hr health, she went out every morning, only coming back for lunch, and sometimes even later. Three times out of four, she forgot her key. Naturally, I waited for her before sitting down at table. I waited behind the door, and scarcely had she pulled the bell-rope than I asked: 'Who's there?' The poor dear replied: 'It's me, Mademoiselle Eugénie!' That reminded us of our young days, when she was a milliner and came to see me in my mansard in the Latin quarter. I opened the door and my Eugénie fell into my arms. Oh, the joy! Sometimes, you know, when someone rings, it seems to me that she's come back. As before, I ask: 'Who's there?' but from outside, the placid voice of a delivery man breaks the dear echo of her voice, always alive in me, and recalls me brutally to reality."

For the anonymous author of the macabre joke, it was a matter of sending to Van Columelle's residence a woman answering to the name of Eugénie, one Sunday when he had a guest and, unfailingly, at about half past twelve, in the course of lunch, was explaining the relationship between his door and his conjugal love.

The sinister trickster's plan was easy to carry out. Like all well-brought-up people, who are in consequence somewhat ceremonious, Van Columelle issued his invitation several days in advance, which was naturally the object of conversation among the staff of the Bibliothèque. As for discovering one of those amiable individuals ever willing to hire out their worldliness to the advantage of an ephemeral benefactor, only the choice was delicate, and among many consulted, the selection, thanks to the forename Eugénie, received Van Columelle's visiting card—obtained by some ruse from its legitimate carrier—between two glasses of beer in a Montmartre café.

The most detailed instructions were furnished to the blonde Eugénie, who swore on a lock of hair taken from her first lover, to go on the following Sunday, at half past twelve, to number 3 Rue du Zèbre d'Or. To that rendezvous, the beauty, conquered by the promise of serious traveling expenses, only objected on account of the early hour. She was told that after having rung the bell, she was to announce herself through the door and that, very probably, a gentleman of slightly ancient appearance would come to open it: he was an uncle who had remained a bachelor and very Bohemian, bearing the same surname on Van Columelle, who loved to be treated as a young man and to be kissed by a pretty woman.

The scene, carefully scripted and conscientiously acted, caused the unfortunate librarian such emotion that he nearly dropped dead.

He was in the process of feeding his guest a very complicated dish whose recipe he had found in a manual of cuisine attributed by scholars to one of the best maîtres-d'hôtel of Lucullus, and he had just arrived at the "Who's there?" of his conjugal apology when the doorbell rang, accompanied by the prescribed declaration from without, which seemed to be the response to the interrogation uttered by Van Columelle.

The fellow went frightfully pale and repeated, as if in delight: "It's me, Mademoiselle Eugénie!" Then, leaving his bewildered guest, he raced to lift the latch of the door, which opened violently, giving passage to a young woman whose insouciant voice proclaimed, amid joyful laughter: "Bonjour, old man! Bonjour, my old Columelle!"

The librarian stood there petrified, allowing himself to be kissed on both cheeks by Mademoiselle Eugénie—who had not forgotten the old uncle's tastes—and listening to her recriminations against the concierge, who had made difficulties about letting her come up.

"She's annoying, that concierge! You know, my dear, I had to put her in her place. 'Where are you going, Mademoiselle,' she asked me. I replied—very politely, because, you know, I'm always polite to subalterns: 'To Monsieur Columelle's apartment." "You must be mistaken, Mademoiselle!" Finally, I argued. I explained that I'd been invited to launch. I showed her the visiting card. But where's your nephew?"

"My nephew?" stammered the old man.

"Of course, your nephew! Not mine, for sure! He invited me to lunch. He even instructed me to be nice to you...come here so I can kiss you!"

The warmth of lips on his forehead had the effect on Van Columelle of an electric shock, and, shoving the young woman away violently, he uttered a speech borrowed from some antique tragedy: "Back, you who would profane a hearth extinguished by the wing of misfortune! Back, creature devoid of soul and devoid of heart!"

Mademoiselle Eugénie, thinking that she was dealing with some old actor still infatuated with his métier, applauded him: "Bravo, old chap! That's good—very good!"

But Van Columelle's wrath was still rising.

"Oh, you laugh at my grief? You think that you can come with impunity to soil this dwelling, the chaste abode of the purest of women, with your presence? Get out! Get out! I'll have you arrested by the police!"

136

Van Columelle would have made good his threats if the guest, running into the antechamber, had not intervened, along with the old chambermaid, whose arms were taking heaven as her witness.

"Oh, my God! What a scandal! What a scandal! If it isn't shameful to see in the home of honest folk a kind of...a kind of..." But the worthy woman could not find a descriptive term sufficiently energetic to describe the blonde Eugénie, who, frightened by the threat of the police, protested her innocence in a tearful voice.

"But I didn't know, my good Monsieur! Forgive me! It's not my fault that an individual gave me this card and invited me to lunch! It was at the Café des Liserons, five days ago. I'm not suspicious, me... Oh, men! They're a villainous race! Oh, it's not about you that I'm saying that, my poor Monsieur! You must have suffered misfortune. I feel sorry for you, with all my heart...I've suffered too, you know...I can't show it every day, but I have, you know! Forgive me if I've reminded you of your grief...it's the fault of that wicked imbecile! Oh, if I run into him again, I'll teach him a lesson!"

Before this flood of evidently sincere words, which proved adequately that the visitor had been the victim of a practical joke, Van Columelle calmed down, apologized for his brutality, and, as he had a tender heart, he gave Mademoiselle Eugénie a gold coin, which she accepted, swearing that she would make use of it to find the client of the Café des Liserons.

Then next day, the entire Bibliothèque knew about the adventure. With one voice, everyone proclaimed that the author of the cruel trick was the worst of scoundrels. The guilty party presumably joined in the concert of imprecations, and the most scrupulous investigations failed to obtain any clarification. The good Van Columelle—who, in any case, only made weak demands for justice—was the object of an increased sympathy on the part of his colleagues and regular clients, Alcée Baillargal, in an article in the *Écho Plaintif*, held

137

up the anonymous artisan of the infernal joke to public execra-
tion, calling upon him—in vain—to reveal himself.

From that day on, a solid amity linked the journalist and
the librarian, the latter striving, by means of daily kindnesses,
to acquit the debt of gratitude contracted with regard to his
defender, and he would not have pardoned Baillargal for addressing himself to anyone else for any information of which
he might have need in his quests for documentary information.

"Père Van," from the height of his stage, perceived the
journalist advancing toward him between the two rows of tables, and addressed an amicable smile of welcome to him,
while wiping the chronically ink-stained fingers of his right
hand with a handkerchief.

"Are you well today, my dear friend?"

"Not too bad, thank you—and yourself?"

"Not bad! It's very good of you to pay us a little visit."

"An interested visit, my dear Van Columelle."

"So much the better! Oh, if I could be useful to you!
You've always been so good to me. What is it about?"

"You might perhaps be able to give me some information…"

"With pleasure!"

"Thank you! Have you heard mention of a laboratory accident that occurred at the Sorbonne some years ago? It was…"

"Might it be the catastrophe of the fifth of May 1885 to
which you're referring?"

"Yes, precisely!"

"Alas, I remember that horrible event perfectly, which
cost the life of one of my dearest comrades, Jérôme
Lehargnol, the head of the laboratory…"

"What? You knew Jérôme Lehargnol?"

"We were childhood friends. He was a worthy fellow.
His death caused me considerable grief."

"And Blancadet? Did you also know Blancadet—Victor
Blancadet?"

"Blancadet? Victor Blancadet? No… wait, though…
yes… I seem to have heard that name somewhere…"

"Blancadet was a pupil of Lehargnol's."

"Exactly! I have it now! He nearly perished in the catastrophe. I believe he recovered from his injuries..."

"It's a pity that you didn't know him. You could have given me some interesting information...."

"I regret it—but you'll find some in the newspapers of the epoch. I'll go and ask for them for you..."

The worthy Van Columelle traced a few lines on a slip of green paper and hailed an attendant with a wave of his hand. The latter, not daring to hide from an order given by his hierarchical superior, darted a slightly disdainful glance at the slip and set off in a resigned fashion for the section where the newspaper collections were held.

"You knew Jérôme Lehargnol, then?"

"Very well...a childhood friend!"

"What kind of man was he?"

"A scientist, my dear Baillargal, a great scientist. His death was a great loss for France and humankind."

"He studied explosives, didn't he?"

"Alas. If he hadn't been studying them, he wouldn't have been blown up. But his sights were set on higher things and his dream wasn't limited to the discovery of some new formula of powder or the improvement of the murderous engines that a few brains still laden with barbarity thought indispensable to the maintenance of peace between nations."

"Wasn't Jérôme Lehargnol the hero of an adventure, in the course of the last war, the epilogue of which was his appearance before a court martial?"

"Oh, you know about that? An infamy, my dear Baillargal, an infamy. To accuse Lehargnol, my old friend Lehargnol, of treason, is as if one were to accuse you, my dear Baillargal, of being kept by a woman!"

"That would be droll," said the journalist, with an expression of perfect detachment.

"Well, it was, nonetheless, of treason that Lehargnol was accused..."

"What happened, then?"

139

Ah! Battlefields, like *Enfers*,[7] guard their secrets jealously—but you can be sure that, like all his companions in arms, Jérôme Lehargnol conducted himself like a hero. Why would he have been an exception? Fatality determined that the powder had been forgotten in the cartridges destined for the mouths of the cannons of which he was in command. That negligence, as you'll understand, had grave consequences. In spite of his ballistic science—which was, believe me, indisputable, on the day of the battle the cannons remained mute and, to safeguard the principle of obedience, the principal force of armies, as they could not reasonably charge the rebellious cannons or the unknown workmen who had manufactured the cartridges, Lehargnol was dragged before a court martial. It was epic!"

"So it seems!"

"Oh, you know about the experiment of the revolver? Well, judge for yourself. To accuse of professional incapacity a man who can determine, at his whim, merely by virtue of the way he presses the trigger, whether a weapon fires or misfires, is evident madness..."

"Which struck one of the members of the Court Martial?"

"Exactly! An artillery commander was afflicted with mental alienation during the debates that I followed from the courtyard of the prison—for, as you can imagine, the most rigid closure was imposed on the session.

"And what do you know about the accident at the Sorbonne?"

"Nothing but what you'll be able to find in the newspapers that the attendant has just taken to your usual place—the fifth armchair in the third row on the right. I was in service here when the news of the accident arrived...it was from the

---

[7] As a librarian, Van Columelle is, of course, not referring to Hell but to the *Enfer* section of a library, where books are kept that are not made accessible to public consultation on the grounds of having been banned, usually for obscenity.

evening papers that I learned that my friend Jérôme Lehargnol had been killed in that horrible catastrophe. I went to his funeral, and I've often thought about him…that's virtually all I can tell you…"

"Thank you, my dear Van Columelle. I'll go ferret through the 1885 newspapers—perhaps I'll find something interesting there!"

"I hope with all my heart that you do."

"Thanks."

Alcée Baillargal went to his seat and started scanning the enormous volume under the hostile gazes of his neighbors, scholars who considered as a personal insult the action of coming to the Bibliothèque to read newspapers, when it is so easy to peruse them in any café.

First, Baillargal found the story of the catastrophe, with the list of the dead—Jérôme Lehargnol at the head—and that of the injured, including Victor Blancadet.

Every day for several weeks, under the rubric of "science in mourning," the papers extended an epilogue to the accident, the exact cause of which no one could explain. Almost unanimously, the experts attributed it to the count of fatality. Among the injured, about whom daily bulletins were issued, Baillargal was only interested in Victor Blancadet; he was able to ascertain that the fantastic tale he had just heard in the Rue du Sabre-de-l'Abbé was not an invention created in its entirety by its author. One of the first to be brought out of the smoking ruins, he had been carried to his home with the advice of the physicians that he would not survive his horrible wounds.

Baillargal followed all the phases of Blancadet's recovery, including the ablation of the eye and the crisis of madness in the course of which the unfortunate fellow, taking advantage of a moment of inattention on the part of his nurses, had destroyed the remaining eye. The demented words that he had uttered, by which he affirmed the non-indispensability of his eyes in the perception of external phenomena, were carefully reported.

Then, public curiosity having found its pasture in new events, the newspapers had made no further mention of the Sorbonne catastrophe.

The foundations of the adventure were, therefore, real. That was all that Alcée Baillargal needed. In that authentic frame, he was going to embroider the marvelous story of vision without eyes and the eupantophone, or perfected ventriloquism.

The journalist rubbed his palms together energetically in honor of his interior joy and left the Bibliothèque without having shaken the hand of his excellent friend Van Columelle. He reintroduced himself into his fiacre and reminded the coachman of the location of the next and last stop.

V

Night had fallen completely when Alcée Baillargal arrived at the offices of the *Écho Plaintif*, which an enormous luminous sign designated to the attention of the crowds.

"Is the Boss in?" he asked the office boy.

"Yes, Monsieur Baillargal. Monsieur the editor is in his office."

"Thanks, Auguste. Oh, by the way, Auguste, pay my coachman. They were journeys made for the newspaper...I hired him at two o'clock..."

And, in order not to endure the recriminations of the office boy, he hastened toward the editorial office, on the door of which he knocked discreetly.

"Oh, it's you Baillargal. Cold, isn't it, this evening?"

"Oh, my dear Editor, for the season the temperature is exceptional..."

"Exceptional! Exceptional! Like your copy! Come on, Baillargal, you're going to have to..."

"Oh, my dear Editor, you can scold me. You'll be forced to give me an apology."

"Impossible! Me, Anacharsis Lacrimal, editor of the *Écho Plaintif*, apologize to you? Know that I already had writer's cramp eighteen years ago. I'm about to see my forty-fifth spring; I no longer have cramp because I no longer write, but I still know what's what, and I've had enough of your stories that you ought to be telling in prison."

"Oh, Monsieur Lacrimal!"

"There's no Monsieur Lacrimal here! There's your editor, and he's furious, is your editor. Your copy is good, at the most, for the *Nouvel Ours*! Once and for all, Baillargal..."

"My dear editor, I'm bringing you a series of articles that will impassion Paris, the provinces and foreign lands."

"And the moon!"

"It's very serious, I assure you."

"Oh! And...what's it about?"

"You must, my dear editor, have heard mention of the accident at the Sorbonne?"

"Your editor has hard mention of everything! That's an elementary principle that I don't permit you to doubt..."

"It's the catastrophe of 1885 that I mean..."

"I know it, your catastrophe. Go on!"

"The catastrophe was terrible There were dead, injured..."

"Of course! Can you imagine a catastrophe without deaths and injuries? Don't you read the news sections?"

"I follow the one in the *Écho Plaintif* passionately."

"Very good! In that case...anyway, go on!"

"That catastrophe, however, spared a few lives..."

"Tell me, Baillargal, where did you spring from? A catastrophe, in a self-respecting paper—mine, for example—is always recounted by a witness. If that's your hook..."

"My dear editor, I'm bringing you something better than that. I've discovered a victim of the Sorbonne accident...."

"I repeat, it's of no interest, no interest at all. By the way, Baillargal, you know that the petty cash isn't making any more advances..."

"I can only congratulate you on it, my dear editor."

"I'll make a note of that."

"My dear editor, I've discovered a blind man—and what I mean by that term is a man deprived of eyes—who can see as well as you and me, and who, what's more, is an incomparable and amazing ventriloquist..."

"Baillargal, you'd do well to be kind enough to cancel the synallagmatic contract that we made last year..."

"You can't think so, my dear director? We're both parties—which is to say, the heroes—of a synallagmatic contract made in due form, and you'd like us, benevolently, to abolish that agreement—which perhaps contains, in embryo, the realization of great things—with a reciprocal and simultaneous gesture? Stamped papers, my dear editor, are our parchments, and we have a duty to defend them against all weakness and all whimsy; but it isn't the virtue of a rectangle of wrapping-paper on which the woman with the scales, clad in her toga, whom I want to invoke at this moment, stands. Tomorrow and the following days, the elite of the entire world, who draw from the columns of the *Écho Plaintif* the nourishment indispensable to its intellectual life..."

"That's right, what you say there. The clientele of the *Écho Plaintif* is, indeed, composed of all that can be found of the enlightened and the intelligent on the surface of the five continents, and it's profoundly regrettable that convenient communication can't be established between us and a few other planets, for that would be a new field of action for my paper, which is beginning to feel too narrowly confined by a world that one can go around in a few paltry weeks."

"I have the man you need to establish the postal service that you appear to desire: it's Victor Blancadet"

"Who's Victor Blancadet?"

"My blind man who can see, my distinguished ventriloquist, the extraordinary victim of the accident at the Sorbonne, whose acquaintance I had the advantage of making this afternoon."

"Let's be serious and take stock. What is it that you want to do?"

"I would like—under the reserve of your approval from above, of course—to write for the readers of the *Écho Plaintif* a faithful account of what I've just seen..."

"What have you just seen that's so extraordinary?"

"A blind man seeing—seeing, my dear director! Don't you find that astonishing?"

"Nothing astonishes me! In brief, you're going to tell a more or less fantastic story?"

"I can guarantee its authenticity."

"Polemics will follow. Épées will emerge from scabbards. It will be necessary to go to the dueling field!"

"I'm not on my first duel, my dear editor, and I won't tolerate anyone..."

"Go on, then! Go on! You'll kill our adversary, or you'll be killed by him. For me, it's the same thing: trouble. Nothing soils a day more disagreeably for me than being obliged to march behind a hearse, even if it's only for a few minutes!"

"The dead are so demanding today!"

"Especially in winter, in cold weather. And it saddens me to observe the fragility of life. It's very painful to die when one has achieved a certain situation!"

"Like yours, my dear editor!"

"Well, yes. I can't say that I'm the son of my endeavors, because I've never attached my name to anything in particular; I prefer to be universal. I believe I've succeeded. I am my paper, and my paper goes everywhere, even among the savages, who, not being able to penetrate its substance, make policemen's hats out of it."

"My dear editor, I swear to you that I won't attract any trouble. I won't be shedding my neighbor's blood, and all of mine will remain in my veins. My subject will excite curiosity to the highest degree, but won't bear any leaven of anger and hatred into souls. You won't have any death to deplore!"

"And canceled subscriptions, the scourge of journalism—will you take responsibility for them?"

"Absolutely! Anyway, my dear editor, I know that scruples are situated so deep in your conscience that they don't emerge easily; if you still have a few, or even one, I won't insist. Give me the authorization to take my copy to the *Nouvel Ours*..."

"Never! Not on your life! Our agreement forbids you to write for any other paper than the *Écho Plaintif*, and I'm not going to renounce my rights to a competitor like the *Nouvel Ours*."

"Just now you wanted to annul my agreement!"

"An editor's ruse, my dear Baillargal. I observe nevertheless, with certain pain, that your contributions are less brilliant than they once were. Sharpen your pen, damn it! And it's not on the day when you find something interesting..."

"It pleases you, then?"

"It's not a matter of pleasing me! What do you expect me to do? Literature, music, science, the arts—what people call the esthetic consolations of life—have the effect on me of a dish on which I'm obliged to nourish myself exclusively every day, year after year. The public still shows some appetite; that's entirely to the honor of its stomach—but make sure that the kitchen doesn't spare the spices!"

"I make a rather brisk habit..."

"I agree, loyally, as befits a newspaper editor. And I don't address any reproach to you on that subject; nevertheless, a trial that outrages good morals, even with a condemnation at the end, isn't to be disdained. You can offer it whenever you like—the expenses and compensations on my account, of course..."

"You're too kind. In this instance, I'm not saying..."

"The sooner the better..."

"Tomorrow, people will be snatching the *Écho Plaintif* from the vendors' hands."

"So much the better! But I warn you—if I get canceled subscriptions, we'll be tearing up our agreement. Is that agreed?"

"If you wish."

"Word of honor?"

"Word of honor."

"You have my word as an editor."

"That's amply sufficient. I'm going home to write my article. You'll have my copy at ten o'clock. Until tomorrow, my dear editor..."

"*Au revoir*, Baillargal. It's cold, isn't it?"

"Somewhat, my dear editor."

"Excessively. Much too cold! I detest winter, because of the temperature..."

"Winter is the ransom of summer! *Au revoir*, my dear editor!"

Alcée Baillargal emerged from the editorial office. His expression was so perfectly satisfied that a comrade, who passed him in the corridor, greeted him with the question: "Hey, Baillargal, have you just, by chance, just forced the pass at Thermopylae?"

"I haven't forced anything at all! You'll read it in tomorrow's paper!"

"Your article?"

"Exactly."

"The sequel to your article on the relationship between feminine undergarments and repopulation?"

"No, my dear chap, no! You're wide of the mark. You'll read it in the paper tomorrow. That's all I can tell you."

"*Au revoir*, Chevalier of Mystery!"

The two men shook hands and Alcée Baillargal went back to the extra-conjugal domicile where the love of the blonde Virginie assured him of a good supper, good shelter, and the rest.

VI

For reasons of delicacy, Alcée Baillargal refused to consider himself as being at home in his mistress' apartment, so he almost never made use of the key that Virginie had confided to him. The journalist preferred to ring and wait, just like Virginie's vulgar adorers, until young Charlotte came to open the door and introduce him discreetly to one room or another, according to the requirements of the moment.

Toward dinner time, there was no longer any risk of Baillargal bumping into some pilgrim of amour, but, ever respectful of protocol, he pressed the button of the electric bell, as usual.

"Oh, it's Monsieur!" Charlotte exclaimed, opening the door. "Madame has gone out, but she'll be back for dinner."

"I'll wait for her."

"Madame has gone out with Monsieur le Comte de Bigornot..."

"Very good, Charlotte, very good! I have a rather long article to write."

"Oh, Monsieur has a very difficult métier! Writing! That must be very difficult!"

"Yes, Charlotte, it's very difficult. No one will disturb me in the drawing room, will they?"

"Oh no! Monsieur can be tranquil. When Madame isn't here, it's as if there was no one, for they never come for Monsieur!" The maid burst out into shrill laughter, as if to reward her sagacity.

Alcée Baillargal installed himself in the drawing room, at a small table near the fire. Charlotte asked him if he needed anything, and, after receiving a negative response, retired to the kitchen to prepare Madame's favorite dish, with a strong reinforcement of spices.

"Ah! Now it's a matter of distinguishing oneself!" Baillargal said, looking anxiously at the sheets of foolscap paper carefully laid out on the table by Charlotte. "As a title: *Sight Without Eyes*. Yes, that's very good. Ah, the first idea, the first jet, the thunderclap of thought, there's nothing as true as that! *Sight Without Eyes*, then...."

And the pen began to scratch the paper resolutely, without a pause, without the slightest hesitation, recording the sentences that Baillargal articulated aloud, as if he were dictating them.

"The Sun King, at the zenith of his glare and his power, cried: *The Pyrenees are no more!* But, even if that that cry of legitimate pride had not been a simple figure of rhetorical speech designed to express the triumph of a politics of conquests and alliances, what would even the material suppression of a chain of mountains be by comparison with the pure and simple abolition of nature herself by the human will? That is, however, what is proclaimed today without false modesty by the man that has repudiated, as imperfect, obsolete and unworthy, the habit of seeing with eyes.

"Boldly, with the assurance that carrying off a resounding personal victory gives, one of our fellows has not feared to break with that routine, as old as the world, inaugurated by evil spirits to fill the brains of the blind with darkness. If I had not sworn an oath to keep silent, I would proclaim the name of that man, and tomorrow, it would be in every mouth, for it is the exact synonym of light. Thanks to him, henceforth, the adage that the sun shines for everyone will no longer be a vain and deceptive assertion; humanity has just taken a new and decisive step on the tortuous and thus-far deceptive path of equality.

"All seeing, and seeing clearly: such will be the motto of the present century, and the day is imminent when no one will any longer want to lend themselves to the caprices of those fragile and uncomfortable instruments of vision that are known as eyes. Human genius has just covered in ridicule the word 'blind,' pronounced with so much terror since the debut of our species on the terrestrial stage. Thus have disappeared, as the adaptation of the planet to our needs has progressed, those disproportionate and bizarre animals whose reason for existence probably resided in the future joys that their vestiges reserved for our present and exceedingly sympathetic curators of paleontological exhibits.

"It is to you, lovely female readers, that I would like to introduce my hero first of all. His original person seems scarcely to have attained the age of thirty-five. He is brown-haired, with a mat complexion and an essentially distinguished appearance. His voice is warm and admirable in its tone, and he cultivates therewith an incomparable talent for ventriloquism, which, without effort, he raises to the height of a veritable art under the harmonious appellation of eupantophony. Nevertheless, Mesdames et Mademoiselles, it is not the eupantophonist that I want to talk about today; it is merely the new Hercules who has slain the centuries-old Hydra of blindness. How many years of struggle and hard labor does that victory represent? We will never know; for that admirable man has the coquetry of mystery, like a god or one of his prophets.

"I would like to be able to offer a few refreshments here to the memories of my amiable readers with the aridity of a few dates, but I have sworn to allow the historic deeds from which my hero emerges float in the mist. It is, however permissible for me to recall, without being precise, a catastrophe that put all of science in mourning. Eyes in France were not sufficiently numerous to weep for the numerous victims of the holocaust on the bloody altar of experimentation. The man whose name is burning the nib of my pen, still at his post in the bitter battle fought on the limitless terrain of discovery, was among the number of the wounded; anyone but him would have lost his life in that rightful adventure; he was left with only one eye, but, far from complaining, he thanked his lucky star, which had marked out in such a precise fashion the route of his destiny.

"The unanimity of men would have guarded preciously, in the more or less avowed aim of giving you the eye, Mesdames et Mademoiselles, his remaining globe, but it would be to calumniate abominable the inventor of genius to suppose for a single instant that he was capable of renouncing the realization of his projects. Then, at the risk, if some unfortunate hazard had annihilated his hope of making simple spectacles play the role of eyes, of no longer savoring feminine beauty other than by touch, hearing, taste and smell, that superhumanly heroic man rendered himself completely blind—but it was in order to see better!"

The violent ringing of the doorbell caused the journalist to stop. A few moments later, Charlotte came in with a large cardboard box in her arms.

"It's a package! Madame's purchases! There's nothing to pay."

"I should hope so. Put it there, on the sofa."

The young maid had scarcely closed the door when Baillargal got to his feet, murmuring: "Let's see whether Virginie has thought about me!"

He set about untying the parcel, wrapped in thick yellow paper. First he took out a mauve skirt ornamented with lace; he examined it, and let a connoisseur's "Not bad!" escape. Then there were batiste bloomers, whose transparency the journalist checked, and chemises with odiously beribboned epaulettes that he judged hideous. A complete spectrum of silk blouses occupied the bottom of the box, which his finger explored scrupulously.

"Nothing for me! But Virginie promised me cravats, gloves, false collars and socks. Women's heads aren't worth two sous!"

He seemed genuinely disappointed, like a child expecting a gift that has not been brought for him. He left the items of clothing spread out on the sofa and was going back to sit at the table when Virginie Lauria, full of joy, irrupted into the drawing rom. With one hand in her sleeve and the other lifting her veil, she placed her lips on her lover's.

"Have I made you wait, my door dear? It's eight o'clock! But it's not my fault; the Comte never stops!" Turning to the sofa, she added: "Ah, you've unwrapped the parcel. How do you like the skirt?"

"Very nice! Very nice!" said the journalist, taking up his pen-holder again.

"And someone has forgotten her little Alcée!" said Virginie, ridding herself of her hat and jacket and wrapping her arms around her lover's neck teasingly.

"I have to finish my article!" the journalist protested, coldly.

"Let's eat first—you can work afterwards."

"If you wish," Baillargal acquiesced, unable to find his next line.

"Charlotte, you can serve!" Virginie shouted. "Do you like these chemises?" In response to his negative pout, she went on: "That's your surprise, my love! The Comte didn't leave my side for a minute. I couldn't choose your cravats, gloves and socks with him there—he might be stupid, but he'd have noticed!—so I bought a dozen of these chemises, which are hideous but expensive. Tomorrow, I'll go an exchange these articles that have ceased to please for beautiful cravats and socks, and all the beautiful things that I know my little Alcée loves!"

"You're an angel!" Baillargal declared, kissing his mistress.

"Madame is served!" Charlotte announced.

Arm in arm, they went into the dining room and sat down next to one another. While Alcée was blowing on a spoonful of soup to cool it, Virginie asked: "And your blind man?"

"Blancadet? Admirable! I'm still completely flabbergasted."

"It didn't go well, my poor dear?" said Virginie, compassionately.

"On the contrary, yes!"

"Then why are you completely…what was it?"

"Flabbergasted; it means that I'm still utterly amazed by what I saw," Baillargal explained, charitably.

"Oh, so much the better…so much the better, my poor dear. Kiss me!"

Their mouths came together and Virginie took advantage of it to share with her lover a piece of truffle she had collected from the *pâté de foie gras*.

"You'll read tomorrow's *Écho Plaintif*," the journalist said, solemnly.

"You're talking about Blancadet?"

"Naturally. He's very curious, that blind man—he can see!"

"Alcée, you know very well that it pains me when to make fun of me."

"I'm not making fun of you, my dear Virginie. I swear to you on what I hold most sacred—your golden hair—that Blancadet is blind, but can see all the same."

"Then, if he had married me…?"

"No means of deceiving him."

"My dear, you're not serious?"

"Yes, yes! Charlotte, give me a plate!"

The young maid hastened to clear the soup-dishes and deposited a dish on the table that Virginie pulled toward her in order to examine it.

"You put in the black pepper, the ginger and the pimento?" she asked.

"Oh, yes, Madame!" Charlotte affirmed.

"We'll see!" said Virginie severely, cutting a thin slice of bread, which she dipped in the sauce in order to taste it. "It's still too insipid. Do you hear, Charlotte?"

"Yes, Madame," murmured the cook who had been too miserly with the spices, as she drew away.

"Are you trying to kill me?" Alcée asked, in a tone of tender reproach.

"Oh, no, my love! Oh no! You won't take long to finish your article, will you? I'm sleepy…"

"Go to bed, little idler. In half an hour I'll have finished my article. Charlotte will take it…it has to be handed in at the paper by ten o'clock…"

"I don't much like Charlotte going out alone at night…but when there's a reason…"

The dinner was rapidly concluded, and while Virginie was giving instructions to Charlotte, Baillargal went back to his article, resuming where he had left off.

"That superhumanly heroic man rendered himself completely blind—but it was in order to see better! How was this lay miracle accomplished? I confess my inability to explain it

153

to you, but if I did not fear wounding respectable religious beliefs, I would say that God has just lost his monopoly on the supernatural and that man has become, in his turn, the master of a category of facts that thus far, only celestial intervention, which is very miserly in its manifestations, could realize.

"To see without eyes: is that not a magnificent and triumphant response to the challenge thrown down to humanity by nature on the terrain of vision? The horrible Fate of blindness is in her death-throes, carrying with her into her tomb the entire host of infections, even more ridiculous than they are cruel, which afflict our eyes and make them the victims of age or accident. My pen feels impotent and my ink pales before the luminous majesty of what might be called the apotheosis of vision!"

"Are you going to be much longer, darling?" Virginie enquired, in an impatiently coaxing voice. Her face, drowned in the blondeness of her loosened hair, appeared between the curtains separating the drawing room from the bedroom, which she drew together over her bosom to hide the complete nudity of her body.

"*Oof!* I've finished…and none too soon!" said Baillargal, adding his signature with a flourish of the pen. "Call Charlotte; it's ready to go to the *Écho Plaintif*."

Baillargal gathered together the white sheets striped with his large handwriting, numbered them, and, in order not to make Charlotte wait—she had come running at the first call—thought it unnecessary to reread what he had written. He slipped it all into an envelope, which he handed to the maidservant.

"Here, Charlotte. Hand this to the office boy, saying that it's on my behalf."

"Oh, Monsieur! Monsieur Auguste knows me well. He's always very nice to me."

"In that case, Charlotte, try not to be delayed," said Virginie, whose bare feet were protruding though the curtains, which were slightly raised above the carpet, "and if anyone speaks to you in the street, don't answer. I don't want anything to happen to you."

"Oh, Madame can be tranquil," Charlotte assured her, taking the envelope and going out, addressing the obligatory "goodnight" to Madame and Monsieur, which she accompanied with her usual nervous laughter.

Virginie was already on Baillargal's knees. Full of solicitude, he observed to his companion that her hair alone was an insufficient shield against the treachery of the air currents.

"Carry me to bed," the beauty implored, suspending herself around her lover's neck. He kissed her on the lips, and hugging her against him, carried her to the chamber of amour. Her hair, hanging down, formed a bright golden train on the carpet.

VII

"Midday already?" Virginie yawned, as Charlotte came in, as usual, to draw the thick curtains that made the room completely dark.

"Bonjour, Madame!" replied the maid, putting a packet of letters and newspapers on the bed.

"Thank you, Charlotte—and don't forget the pepper and spices!"

"Very good, Madame," said Charlotte, retiring.

Virginie used a hatpin to open the letters she thought capable of containing something interesting, and let them fall one after another over the edge of the bed after having scanned them rapidly.

The broad daylight had woken Baillargal. He stretched himself lazily, with a profound sigh.

Virginie seemed not to pay any attention to her companion, for the journalist did not always wake up very amiable, and the poor amorous woman had often seen her caresses and kindnesses brutally rejected: "In the morning I'm like the late Félix Faure: I don't like anyone to take the initiative of speaking to me."

155

Frightened by the evocation of the Louis-Quatorzian president, Virginie had therefore resigned herself to it, and unless the circumstances were grave, she waited for her love to want to communicate with her.

That day, the preliminaries were very brief; in spite of the frankness of numerous embraces, the journalist felt fresh, fit and glad to resume contact with life.

"Bonjour, darling!" he said, turning toward his mistress, who immediately took advantage of the inauguration of daily communication to kiss her lover and say, in a regretful tone: "You know, Alcée, it's already noon. Oh, the nights pass quickly when one's in love."

"Nights of amour fly by like rapid zebras."[8]

"Poets often say stupid things, but that one's right

"I'm glad to hear it—the line is mine. I just made it up."

"Make up some more, darling!"

"Yes, my muse! Soon. Look to see whether my article has appeared. With the Chilly Ape one is never sure of anything."

Virginie unfolded the *Écho Plaintif*. Immediately, following the first three columns of the paper with her finger, she said: "Yes, yes, my daring, your article's here. There it is! Three columns. Come here so I can kiss you."

The sound of voices in the antechamber suddenly froze Virginie's enthusiasm, and she listened, propped up on her elbow, while Alcée, uninterested in such things, buried himself under the bedclothes again.

Charlotte was arguing with a visitor whom she could not succeed in sending away.

"But I assure Monsieur le Comte that Madame has gone out!"

---

[8] This literal translation cannot take aboard the fact that French has a verb *zebrer* [to stripe], which allows a picturesque implication of flashes of lightning.

"My girl, know that I've been frequenting women for more than twenty-five years, so there's no point in telling me stories. Has your mistress gone out, yes or no?"

"Yes, Monsieur le Comte, Madame has gone out."

"Oh? At what time?"

"Noon was about to chime Monsieur le Comte."

"Noon was about to chime? Noon was about to chime!" the visitor repeated, angrily. "And that demoiselle arranged to meet me at eleven o'clock at my apartment. I've been waiting nearly an hour. More than an hour, do you hear."

"Madame will be desolate…," Charlotte hazarded.

"Tell me, wretched maid, you're not trying to put one over on me, are you? First, tell your mistress…then again, don't tell her anything…perhaps, in fact, she's at my place, waiting for me…"

"Probably," said Charlotte, supportively, in a convincing fashion.

"In any case, I'll know for sure! All the same, women are very annoying—and I've spent my time chasing after them for more than twenty-five years! *Au revoir*, my girl."

Charlotte accompanied the individual to the door, which she closed again firmly, in order to race to her mistress' bedroom.

"Madame! Madame! It's Monsieur le Comte de Bigornot!"

"Well, so what?" said Virginie, who was sitting on the edge of the bed. She had already slipped black silk stockings over her legs, which she extended toward Charlotte. "Put on my boots. Be quick—I'm in a hurry."

The young maid strove to make the numerous small buttons enter their buttonholes as swiftly as possible, and Virginie, having carefully put on her undergarments, started dressing rapidly.

"I haven't curled my hair. I'll still be pretty enough for that imbecile, won't I, darling?"

Alcée Baillargal, whose head had almost disappeared between the two pillows, must have gone back to sleep, because

157

he did not reply. In her bloomers and corset, Virginie leaned over him. "You won't hold it against me, darling? I can't have lunch with you."

"What? What's that?" Baillargal started. He rubbed his eyes. "What, you're ready already? You're going out?"

"Yes, my darling, I'm going out," Virginie said, kissing her lover, whom she knew to be grateful for her extreme discretion. "You'll be lunching alone, my poor darling, but I'll be back early." Seductively, she added: "We'll dine intimately, as we did yesterday evening."

"As you wish," the journalist acquiesced, as if he were condescending to a caprice on the part of his mistress.

In haste, Virginie pinned on her hat and went out, after having kissed Baillargal several times. He began whistling the Habanera from *Carmen*, which he concluded with the philosophical reflection: "Love, women—it's necessary to take a little and allow a lot!"

Young Charlotte had a veritable devotion for her mistress' lover; she lavished petty attentions upon him, attentive to his tastes, seeking to anticipate his least desires. "Oh, Monsieur Alcée, I haven't yet added the pepper and spices, and since Madame isn't here, I won't put them in today..."

"On behalf of my stomach, Charlotte, thank you," said Baillargal, touched that the maid had noticed his aversion for the ardent cuisine so dear to Virginie.

Over lunch, he reread his article, and classified it among his best; he discovered refinements and stylistic effects in it that he had certainly not premeditated.

"It's obvious," he thought aloud, "that there are days when one has genius."

"Does Monsieur desire something?" Charlotte asked.

"No thank you, my girl."

"Monsieur ought to eat a little more. There's no pepper or spices…"

"Thank you Charlotte, I've finished. Serve the coffee. I'll go get dressed..."

A few minutes later, Baillargal reappeared, his hat on his head, ready to go out. He drank the cup of fine mocha carefully prepared by Charlotte.

"I've made it very strong, the way Monsieur likes it."

"It's excellent, Charlotte—all my compliments!" Baillargal said, as he got up. "Tell Madame I'll be here at seven o'clock."

"Very well, Monsieur. *Au revoir*, Monsieur." Slowly, as if regretfully, Charlotte swung the apartment door shut.

In the street, Baillargal went to the nearest newsstand, chose three copies of the *Écho Plaintif* from the display, slipped them into his overcoat pocket and, as the weather was fine and he was not in any hurry, he set out on foot for Victor Blancadet's house.

Madame Benoît was at her post—which is to say, on sentry duty on the threshold of her lodge. She could not suppress a start of joy on seeing the journalist.

"Ah, there you are, Monsieur Alcée! Yesterday, I was almost annoyed with you."

"Why is that, Madame Benoît?"

"Well, you left without saying anything to me, and I don't much like that."

"Forgive me, Madame Benoît—I was pressed for time...."

"And do you think I'm not pressed for time? There's time for everything, damn it."

"You're right, Madame Benoît. Have you read my article?"

"Indeed. It's no good at all."

"What? The story of Monsieur Blancadet..."

"Oh, it's Monsieur Blancadet that you were talking about? You should have said so. One can't guess!"

"It seems to me that it's easy for those who, like you, know Monsieur Blancadet, to recognize..."

"One doesn't recognize anything at all. You're telling a story of brigands with grand phrases."

"My writing isn't good?"

159

"No, it isn't good. Oh, Monsieur Alcée, you can believe me…I've been reading newspapers for a long time, and I hear people around me talking. I can tell you what your article lacks…"

"Oh! Well, what does it lack?"

"First of all, you could have mentioned me at the beginning, said that you were greeted by a charming woman…"

"You?"

"Of course me! Then, you could also have talked about that poor Monsieur Blancadet."

"He forbade me to do so! But I beg your pardon, Madame Benoît; Monsieur Blancadet asked me to meet him at three o'clock; I ought not to keep him waiting."

"Oh, there's no risk of that. He left this morning on a voyage. He won't be back for three days."

"Oh," said Baillargal, disappointed. Recovering, he said: "Monsieur Célestin is there, isn't he? His master or him—it's all the same. Excuse me, Madame Benoît."

"Go, go, Monsieur Alcée. You don't have to worry about me—but remember the proverb: *Miserly with words, poor in ideas.*"

The overly sociable Madame Benoît's sally made the journalist smile as he summoned Célestin by ringing the bell repeatedly.

"Bonjour, my dear Monsieur Célestin. I didn't want to pass by without shaking your hand."

"You're too kind, Monsieur Baillargal," said the domestic, gripping the journalist's right hand. "Please come in."

"With pleasure. I won't ask you for news of Monsieur Blancadet; he's traveling, so he's in good health."

"Perfectly! He left suddenly."

"On business?"

"Evidently. He'll be back in three days. But sit down, I beg you. I was just reading your article in the *Écho Plaintif*…"

"How do you like it?"

160

"Very good, very good! You have very accurate ideas about God. I don't believe in him, myself, but if I did believe, I'd think exactly what you think..."

"I'm glad to hear it, Monsieur Célestin."

"What do you expect? In religion, I have very advanced ideas, and I'd like to be in parliament, in order to demand that a tax be put on the sacraments, to the advantage of people whom like me, have the civic courage not to use them..."

"With that tax on consumption, you'd add another string to the bow of indirect contributions," said Baillargal, nodding his head.

"I'm in favor of justice, me."

"I congratulate you for it, my dear Monsieur Célestin. You like my article, then?"

"A lot—but between us, it's Victor who gave you the idea, isn't it?"

"Victor?" Baillargal appeared to be searching his memory.

"Victor Blancadet, of course."

"Your master?"

"My master? My master? When he's here, obviously, I obey him, but I'm in favor of equality, me. By what right does he give me orders, Blancadet? What does he have that I don't?"

"Nothing, evidently. He even has two eyes fewer."

"Do you think that's just?"

"Oh, not at all. And it's doubtless in a spirit of equality that Monsieur Blancadet insists on seeing like everyone else."

"Oh, it's not that for which I'm reproaching him."

"What are you reproaching him for, then?"

"Nothing at all. It's a question of principles, and I'm in favor of principles, me. So it's Victor Blancadet that you're talking about in your article?"

"Of course! What—you didn't guess that, Monsieur Célestin? You, who are so intelligent!"

Leaning back in his master's armchair, in which he was siring to strike poses, citizen Célestin, presently in the service

161

of Victor Blancadet, approved without too much false modesty of the estimate that Baillargal had made of his intellectual faculties.

"Obviously, I understood right away, but I confess, my dear Baillargal, that a second reading was almost necessary to acquire the absolute certainty of the identity of your hero and my boss."

"He's a very curious fellow, all the same, your boss!"

"Oh, don't exaggerate, I beg you," the valet protested, with a gesture full of dignity.

"Exaggerate what?"

"My boss's talents, of course."

"You don't find it extraordinary, then, for a man to see without eyes?"

"Me? Oh, not at all. If Victor can see without eyes, it's because it's possible, that's all."

"You can give me some information, Monsieur Célestin. I'm not asking you to betray your master..."

"Betray? Oh, a vile word," the domestic opined, nobly. "Doesn't every man have the right to look at what another man does? What about liberty—what do you do with that?"

"I use it, being only too rarely able to abuse it. Tell me, Monsieur Célestin, can Monsieur Blancadet see?"

"As if he had eyes everywhere, alas."

"He lost them, didn't he?"

"Yes, so it appears. An accident...a long time ago. Ever since, Monsieur Blancadet has worn glass eyes, but it's not with them that he sees..."

"Ah! And how do you know that?"

"Oh, it's quite simple. Sometimes, the Boss takes them out to can them; He rubs them with a kind of whitening. While he's occupied in making the pupils shine, he can see, I can assure you. I know that all the better because he nearly sacked me the day after I entered into his service. I'd tried to drink from the jug of curaçao that was on the table. He made such a fuss! Since then, I'm wary of him. Between us, I think it's by means of his spectacles that he can see."

As on the previous day, Baillargal felt close to vertigo in that atmosphere of madness; a frisson ran over his epidermis; he wanted to react by interrupting his interlocutor, but his dry throat would not let any sound pass, so he continued to listen, while remembering that Blancadet had emptied his orbits while keeping his spectacles carefully perched on is nose.

"However, my dear Baillargal, I carried out an experiment that also made me doubt the virtue of the famous spectacles. Like all bourgeois, the Boss takes a siesta after lunch. He lies down on the divan and has the habit off taking off his spectacles, which he puts on the table, within easy reach. One day, he was snoring, fast asleep; I took advantage of it to try the glasses on. Well, I, who have such good eyes, couldn't see anything at all through them!"

"That's bizarre...quite bizarre," Baillargal sighed, thinking that the solemn Célestin might well be continuing the mystification commenced by his master. "But these spectacles don't have anything peculiar about them?" he hazarded.

"Absolutely not, apart from the form of the branches, which get thinner and terminate in a kind of wire that Blancadet winds round his ears. Oh, if the Boss loses his spectacles, I can assure you that it won't be his fault!"

Judging it appropriate to change the subject, Baillargal rewarded Célestin's story with a burst of laughter, and asked: "You're familiar with the eupantophone, you told me yesterday?"

"And how, my friend? I'm familiar with the whole family—for there are big ones and small ones—of those interesting instruments, which are Blancadet's pride and joy. Would you like to see one? I've just been polishing one; it shines as if it were made of gold..."

Célestin stood up, marched over to the rotating bookcase, and, lifting up a black velvet dust-cover, revealed the copper box. "There it is!"

Still suspicious, Baillargal looked at it.

"Oh, you can touch it—it doesn't bite!" sniggered the domestic.

The journalist moved closer, and, in order not to seem that he was duped by the trick, he hastened to appreciate the artistic value of the box. With an approving nod of the head, he said: "Nice work! Copper beaten in a single sheet, as in the Middle Ages." Not without a certain anxiety, his fingers brushed the walls of the box, in which a number of little steels buttons were inlaid.

"To think that the machine can read like a person," Célestin said, not without a pronounced hint of admiration.

"Is that possible?" said Baillargal, feigning profound astonishment.

"It's exactly as I tell you!"

"And may we have a specimen of Monsieur Eupantophone's talents?" the journalist enquired, ironically.

"Oh, as to that, no. I greatly regret it, but it only works with its master. One might say that it's faithful! I've tried hard, but I've never been able to get anything out of it. All that one can see, look, is this..."

Celestin pressed one of the steel buttons. One of the sides of the box swung open, uncovering a rectangular cavity formed of two compartments separated by a kind of articulated grille.

"Cigars must dry well in there!" Baillargal observed.

"Oh, I beg your pardon. Excuse me—I forgot to ask whether you smoke. Have a cigar, I beg you." Célestin picked up a box, which he held out to the journalist.

"No, thank you," Baillargal said.

"You're making a mistake—they're not bad! I'm going to light one anyway—the smoke won't bother you?"

"Oh, not at all! Besides, my dear Célestin, I'm going to ask you for permission to retire. It's already late and I need to call in at the paper. Monsieur Blancadet will be back the day after tomorrow, won't he?"

"Indeed. Come to lunch on Tuesday."

"But Monsieur Blancadet hasn't invited me."

"I'm inviting you! Isn't that sufficient? Informal, of course."

"I can see that. Until Tuesday, then, my dear Célestin."

"Until Tuesday, my dear friend." Célestin conducted the journalist to the door, while cursing the State monopoly, which, even for an exorbitant price, was incapable of furnishing a good cigar.

Escaping the vigilance of Madame Benoît, Baillargal transported himself by means of a democratic omnibus to the *Écho Plaintif*.

On the threshold of the editorial office he met Anacharsis Lacrimal, who was coming out.

"Ah, there you are, Baillargal! It's cold today, isn't it? By the way, tell me: your article is a hoax..."

"I assure you, my dear Editor..." Baillargal protested.

"Come in tomorrow at four o'clock; I need to have a serious talk with you. Someone's waiting for me; I'm in a hurry. It's cold, isn't it?" And without listening to Baillargal's protests, either on the subject of his article or the clemency of the weather, the editor of the *Écho Plaintif* turned up the collar of his overcoat and left for his meeting.

Baillargal went into the office of the editor's secretary, with whom he was on excellent terms; the latter did not hide the fact that the Chilly Ape was furious with him.

"Oh, I've had enough!" declared Victor Blancadet's unfortunate praise-singer. "It's not worth the trouble of writing sensational copy!"

"Between us, you'll admit that you're putting one over on the Chilly Ape."

"Me—never! What I've recounted, I've seen, you know—seen with my own eyes."

"You'll have to get yourself out of trouble. I'm your friend, but I can't do anything."

"You're offering me your condolences—so the Chilly Ape's going to show me the door, then?"

"I'm afraid so..."

"Well, I won't give him the pleasure. I'm going to hand in my resignation. I've finally had enough!"

"Calm down. Perhaps things will sort themselves out."

"No, no—I'd rather go. The *Écho Plaintif* isn't the only paper in the world. The *Nouvel Ours* will open its doors to me gladly!"

Baillargal scribbled a few lines on a large sheet of paper, which he held out to his comrade. "Here's my resignation. Give it to the Chilly Ape on my behalf. Naturally we'll remain good friends..."

"I hope so. *Au revoir*, my dear chap..."

"*Au revoir*, my dear chap..."

Baillargal quit the *Écho Plaintif*, counting on having a spectacular revenge by taking his precious collaboration to a rival paper. He went back to the Rue des Hautes-Herbes and showed a perfect tenderness to his mistress, whose love, in anticipation of possible bad days, would be indispensable to him. He did not make the slightest allusion to what had happened at the *Écho Plaintif*, only telling Virginie that Blancadet had gone away and that he would be lunching with him on the day after tomorrow.

Journalism and gallantry having left Alcée Baillargal and Virginie Lauria simultaneous leisure, they did not fail to devote them to their love, and for two days and two nights they only emerged from their bedroom to renew their vital energy with the flamboyant dishes prepared by Charlotte according to the instruction that her mistress had repeated a thousand times.

VIII

Smiling broadly, his eyes walled up by his thick lenses, Blancadet held out his hand to Alcée Baillargal, who had just been introduced, authoritatively, by his friend and protector Célestin.

"Forgive me, my dear Monsieur Baillargal; I left Paris in a hurry. My domestic tells me that you came the day before yesterday. I keenly regret...forgive me..."

"You're completely forgiven, my dear Monsieur Blancadet."

"Thank you. Sit down, I beg you."

"Should I set a place for Monsieur?" asked Célestin, indicating the journalist.

"Certainly, certainly! If you'd care to accept a place at my table, I have many things to tell you."

"I'm veritably confused in accepting thus..."

"It's understood, then—two places?" Célestin concluded.

"That's good—go!" Blancadet ordered—and Célestin, in spite of the egalitarian principles that he professed internally, bowed and went out, without deigning to notice Baillargal's grateful glance.

"You wouldn't believe, my dear Baillargal, with how much interest I read your article. It's fantastic!"

"Alas," sighed the journalist.

"You haven't received compliments? That astonishes me. It's written with an extraordinary verve."

"Why hasn't prevented my being obliged to quit the *Écho Plaintif*. The Chilly Ape thinks my article is a hoax. I believe you, but..."

"And you're right, a thousand times over, my dear Baillargal. But permit me one question. Who is it that claims that our article is a hoax?"

"The Chilly Ape, of course. Oh, pardon me, you don't know that that's the nickname of Anacharsis Lacrimal, the editor of the *Écho Plaintif*?"

"I confess that I did not. And it's the man with the regressive nickname, doubtless merited, who has accused you of mystification?"

"In person, my dear Monsieur Blancadet. And now I'm out on the street!"

"Under it would be sadder. I know what the life of men of letters is like. You've done what the grasshopper did—sung without putting anything aside! Don't worry about it. I'm rich, and if you'll permit me to help you..."

"You're very generous, Monsieur Blancadet."

"I'm something of a capitalist, that's all. Don't thank me, I beg you. I'll be only too happy to put my purse at your disposal. Let's get back to your article; it's very interesting. The title is perfect, but you refrain from explaining the phenomenon that you describe, if I might use the term, magisterially."

"How do you think I could have explained it?"

"You've represented me for the phenomenon. I almost have a right to that honor, I suppose, since no one in the world except me can thus far flatter themselves with conserving the exercise of the visual faculty while being blind On several occasions I've tried to enable my fellows to benefit from an invention whose utility is incontestable; I once published a little book entitled *The Unity of the Senses*, and do you know what that earned me?"

Baillargal made a gesture that abandoned any pretention to divine the recompense awarded to Victor Blancadet.

"A demand for the deprivation of my rights on the part of distant relatives, infatuated with the idea of obtaining power of administration over my wealth! The law rejected the claim in a judgment whose preamble did not fail to cause me a certain joy, in that it said that 'the facts articulated, while establishing grave presumptions of mental derangement, do not prove sufficiently that Monsieur Victor Blancadet is in the habitual state of imbecility, dementia or fury demanded by legislation to pronounce a legal deprivation... Oh, a masterpiece, that judgment, soon promised to the dignity of being overturned on the appeal of my over-attentive relatives. Anyway, although having saved the material integrity of my rights, I nevertheless submitted to a profound mental decline, which forced me to confine myself to the most absolute seclusion. In the meantime, the blind cannot see, the deaf cannot hear, the mute cannot speak—but official science only descends from its pedestal of stupidity and pretention to permit is disciples to hold some solemn ecumenical conference from time to time in which the articles of faith are renewed in order to obtain a harvest of prestige from the incurable credulity of society! Would you like, my dear Baillargal, to be my confidant?"

"It would be an honor, and also a great joy."

"Well then, in a quarter of an hour, you'll be a fervent apostle of 'sight without eyes,' to use the fortunate expression that you have employed. I only ask that you don't publish your impressions until few weeks hence, after my marriage."

"You're getting married?"

"Indeed, my dear Baillargal."

"But you were looking for someone blind from birth!"

"And I've found someone blind from birth! A rare bird, but I ended up finding one. Anyway, I need your help..."

"At your service, my dear Blancadet."

"Thank you. We'll talk about it over lunch. First, I'd like to prove to you that I'm not the hero of any imposture. Let's proceed in order. Give me your hand."

"Here!" said Alcée Baillargal, holding out his right hand to Blancadet—who, after having removed his spectacles in order to expel from his orbits the little globes of glass that filed them, took it in his own and directed the index finger between his gaping pupils all the way to the back of each ocular cavity.

"Can you put the finger into your own eye like that?"

"So it's true! You really are blind!" the unfortunate Baillargal could not help exclaiming.

"That point established, let's continue," Blancadet declared, tranquilly, refurnishing his orbits and replacing his spectacles on his nasal appendage. "Now write on a piece of paper any sentence that you please; by reading what you've written, I'll be able to convince you of the reality of my visual faculties."

With the hand that his interlocutor had just released, Alcée Baillargal traced a few words on a piece of paper, which he handed to Blancadet.

ꞏ "Oh, how you're trembling, my friend. You're difficult to read." But Blancadet, energetically scratching his right ear with the branch of his spectacles, deciphered: "'Death is a sleep with unknown dreams.' Your Alexandrine isn't very cheerful!"

"I didn't make it up expressly," the journalist apologized, his head beginning to swim.

"Involuntary servant of the muses, are you that convinced that I can see things? Good. Now, without giving you a lecture on physics, I'll permit myself to remind you of certain things that you doubtless know and will instantaneously clarify the explanation that I owe you. "

Baillargal retreated into the depths of his armchair, put his arms on his knees, and prepared to listen.

"As has been demonstrated, almost since Adam found in a fig-leaf the idea of a complete suit, all of nature only exists by virtue of motion. Everything down here, therefore, is to varying degrees, in motion, from the minerals that, by an inexplicable aberration, we describe as inert, to our own bodies, to which scientists have condescended to accord the epithet living, passing via the vegetables, which occupy a rather strange intermediate state that is neither entirely alive nor entirely its absence. In that incessant agitation, we occupy a very honorable place due to the molecular movements of the atoms that make up our bodies; and not one of the most wretched attributes of our superiority is our ability to observe the movements that are going on around us, which is what we designate by the name of perception. Are you following me, my dear Baillargal?"

Involuntarily, the journalist made a slight affirmative nod of the head, while Blancadet continued his explanation.

"Science, whose sovereign quality is the mania of always wanting to classify and catalogue the more or less notorious facts relating to people and things, has attributed to members of the human race five senses by means of which they communicate with the external world. There's no need to name them, is there?"

"Sight, hearing…," Alcée Baillargal began, as if at the examination for the baccalaureate that he had been refused.

"Let's stick, if you wish, to sight and hearing. Those two senses will sufficient to make apparent to you the infantile simplicity of what still seems to you, at the moment, so extraordinary. The men of science, who have elected to cut the world into five continents, have also had the ingenious idea of attributing a identity to each of our senses by specifying the strict role that it ought to play; they have made them into five agents operating in isolation for the benefit of the brain, which assumes the task of centralizing the labor of those subaltern intermediaries..."

"It seems to me that science has demonstrated sufficiently...," Baillargal protested, grasping, like a drowning man at a last spar of wreckage, at the reason that remained to him.

"But science has demonstrated nothing at all!" cried Blancadet, with a broad gesture. "What has it done? Oh, it's quite simple. It has observed that each of our senses plays a different role! A fine thing! Have you ever been to the Comédie-Française?"

"Often. I've even written a tragedy for it, which was refused by the reading committee."

"Perfect! Let's take your tragedy, which was surely a masterpiece, since those Messieurs did not want it. For the distribution of the principal roles, you would have been guided by the employ in which each artiste is specialized—but what would you have done if, for some reason, one of the actors was unable, at the last moment, to play the role confided to him? You would simply have asked one of his comrades to replace him, and the latter, combining conscience with zeal, although with less appropriate means, would win applause in the place of the absentee. Thus it is for the human organism, with the difference nevertheless that, for our senses, cumulation is not forbidden, and they can, without too much inconvenience, substitute for one another. I don't have to tell you that the various cerebral circumvolutions lend one another reciprocal aid, and can even replace one another completely when an accident or other circumstance puts one of them out of action. Why should it be any different for our organs of perception?"

"I'd like that!" Baillargal acquiesced warmly.

"Remember what I told you a moment ago: nothing can exist without movement. When I've told you that each of our senses having had, since the earliest days of human existence,

171

the idea of specializing, perhaps to acquire a greater perfection from that division of labor, you'll have the key to a problem as simple to solve as that of Columbus' egg. Each of our senses ended up by identifying itself so narrowly with its employment that they were rendered incapable of fulfilling another task. That's why we see exclusively with our eyes, to take but one example. To return our senses to the various utilizations that they doubtless once had, it would be necessary to subject them to a new and laborious education that would probably demand a long sequence of generations. So, rather than remaining blind after that adventure at the Sorbonne, I sought and found a means to force nature to employ a more rapid means than that of time..."

"Who eats his children...," recited Baillargal, his brain pricked by the distant memory of one of the old Greek myths.

"He has to live, like everyone else! But don't lose the thread of my reasoning. I would certainly be unjust to your scientific knowledge if I suspected you to be capable of not knowing that the senses we mentioned just now, sight and hearing, are indebted for their sensitivity to waves appropriate to two different milieux. The eye registers vibrations both and transmitted in the body of the eminently subtle fluid that fills celestial space as well as the interstices separating the atoms of mater: the ether, the lightness of which is so incredible that a volume of the gas in question equal to the volume of the Earth would not equilibrate a weight of a single milligram. The quasi-imponderability of the ether is not its only virtue; it has a fantastic elasticity, and the perturbations that are attributable to a given point of its mass are transmitted with a velocity of three hundred thousand kilometers per second..."

"What a record!" said the journalist admiringly, now haunted by sporting statistics.

"That is quite simple the speed of light, for light is nothing but a rapid sequence of vibrations produced by electricity, which propagate in the ether like the undulatory ripples on the surface of a tranquil pool after an impact. The number of these vibrations, for a given space of time, is essentially variable, and their effects upon us similarly have no fixity. If they are too rapid, they are not perceptible by any of our organs, and only very delicate instruments can reveal their existence. Is it necessary to tell you that these waves agitate at a speed of more than a thousand trillion periods per second—and I'm only talking, within that category, about those that move more leadenly."

Alcée Baillargal, his gaze fixed, seemed to be contemplating a rain of shooting stars.

"It's therefore necessary for us to descend along a long series of steps to enter into what can justly be called the zone appropriate to vision, and we thus arrive at the still-respectable figure of seven hundred and eight trillion vibrations a second. From then on, our retina commences to perceive something: what we qualify as the color violet. The virginity of our eyes once being lost, we make the successive acquaintance of indigo, with six hundred and sixty-nine trillion vibrations a second, blue, which represents six hundred and thirty trillion, green yellow and orange, respectively animated by five hundred and seventy-six, five hundred and forty-three and five hundred and thirteen trillions of vibrations a second. We make up the bouquet with the color red, which our retina perceives thanks to the four hundred and eighty-three trillion vibrations with which nature has endowed it..."

"A pretty gift to make to a child!" exclaimed Baillargal, slapping his thighs furiously.

"Calm down, my dear Baillargal, for here opens the abyss into which, emulating the astrologer of fable, all our scientists have let themselves fall."

"Poor fellows!" said the journalist, sympathetically.

"Oh yes, poor fellows who have fallen into the well hollowed out between the four hundred and eighty-three trillion vibrations a second, the lower limit of visual perception, and the seventy-five thousand that inaugurate auditory perception. They are so desperately slow, those poor sonorous waves, that they had been forced to change vehicle..."

"Like merchandise that is too heavy to travel at high speed!"

"Exactly! They take a slower train, but one that is no less sure. It is, in space, the atmospheric air—the air that one could breathe gratuitously before it became, in almost all latitudes, a national asset, which the public powers sell dearly to selected races, composed of individuals known as taxpayers..."

"It's ignoble! Hurrah for anarchy!" proclaimed Baillargal, who had often been wounded by blows of the fiscal rod.

"The term anarchy, my dear friend, is a human invention, and as such, capable of enclosing all lies and all hypocrisies. Be philosophical and satisfied with your lot, unless you prefer to back your bags and go to live beyond the limits of our atmosphere; you won't pay for your consumption of air, because there isn't any, but in those spaces, thus far inhabited only by angels, sonorous waves are afflicted with impotence; they die as soon as they are born; the silence is absolute."

"I was taught in my childhood that angels make music."

"You were deceived, but it doesn't matter. You've understood, haven't you, that our eyes are specialized in the perception of movements varying between seven hundred and eight trillion and four hundred and eighty-three trillion vibrations a second, and that our ears begin to give evidence of sensitivity below seventy-five thousand?"

"Perfectly!"

"It was, therefore, a matter of making a slight modification to the functioning of the human machine; when one thinks about it, one is astonished by the simplicity of the operation that consists of obtaining a considerable reduction in the rapidity of vibrations. It matters little, in fact, which medium transmits them, provided that they arrive endowed with the velocity corresponding to the sensitivity of the organs of perception. Having, as you now, lost my visual apparatus in the accident at the Sorbonne, it only remained for me to persuade my auditory apparatus to take over its role..."

"You've put your eyes in your ears?" queried Baillargal, extracted a further salvo of sonorous thuds from his thighs.

"Strictly speaking, no—for reasons of pure coquetry, for I insist on not seeing like a chicken or some unfortunate astigmatic. I preferred, and I think you'll approve..."

"Oh, with all my heart, my dear Blancadet!"

"Thank you. Yes, I preferred to resemble the most vulgar of sighted individuals—which is to say, to make use of the two sides of the summit of my nasal appendage to register images. You now, don't you, what an image is?"

"I know that they manufacture them in Épinal."

"That's exactly right," Blancadet agreed, smiling, "but scientifically, an image is the formation of a flat or curved surface of the ensemble of all the luminous points of the visual field, with their respective places and intensities. The ocular globes are indefatigable fabricators of images which they picture as they are presented, leaving the optical nerves the care of transmitting them to the brain, where perception takes place. I have, therefore, manufactured ocular globes with a special material whose formula you will permit me, for the moment, not to disclose..."

"Oh, certainly!"

"Merely imagine an extremely sensitive substance that can be indefinitely impressed, exactly like the erythropsin of living eyes. I therefore picture all the images offered to my objective..."

"But that's photography!" Baillargal exclaimed, finding his feet.

"You've said it: it's photography. Just like our eyes, mine are merely a photographic apparatus, except that I've been obliged to annex an objective represented by the lenses of my spectacles. As for the other parts of my visual material, they're identical to those with which the Creator had the generosity to endow human beings, and if my optical nerves had retained their virtues I would have been able, like everyone else, to communicate images to my brain by that route. My optical nerves having been abolished, I had a minor difficulty

175

to overcome; it was, in fact, necessary to transform the luminous vibrations into sonorous vibrations transmissible by the auditory nerves. For that, I only had to impede the vibrations in order to slow them down and conduct them to my tympanum at the regulation velocity..."

"It must have required a powerful brake!"

"Powerful is no exaggeration when one thinks that my change of velocity varies between seven hundred and eight trillion and thirty-two vibrations a second. I was constrained to discover a metal that was a sort of demultiplier; I've named it 'assagitator' and I've manufactured the frames of my spectacles with it—which, by simple contact, take possession of the luminous waves received by my ocular globes and transform them—conserving their elative intensity, of course—into sonorous waves, which impress my tympani, in contact with the flexible extremities of my spectacles. My auditory nerves take charge of the rest, since it's no longer only sound that they have the mission of conducting to my brain..."

"Which is to say that you hear what others see!" exclaimed Baillargal, triumphantly.

"Quite simply—but why, since you have grasped my explanation, do you persist in complicating with various appellations the unique phenomenon, always identical to itself, of perception? Seeing and hearing are merely two different modes of our relations with the external world, realized by our brain..."

"Lunch is served, Monsieur," Célestin announced, solemnly, his clean-shaven face appearing in the gap in the partly-open doorway.

"To table, then," said Blancadet, standing up. "Excuse me—I'll go in front of you in order to show you the way."

Following Blancadet, Alcée Baillargal went into a dining room of entirely bourgeois appearance: a square table with a white cloth, leather-clad chairs, a sculpted dresser and shelves, still life images and old faiences. At a sign from his host, the journalist sat down, and it was not without a certain emotion that he examined the tray that Célestin presented to him. He was instantly reassured on recognizing the classic *hors-d'oeuvres*: sausage, salted herrings, olives and other scouts of more serious gastronomic satisfactions. He helped himself copiously, at Blancadet's invitation.

"No need for formality, my dear friend—if you'll permit me to give you that title."

"I'm veritably confused, my dear Master. You're the greatest man of the century..."

"No, no! Don't diminish the epoch in which we live like that. I'm merely a humble adaptor, and all my knowledge consists of not mistaking the nature whose forces are infinite for whomever wants to make use of them without pride, and above all without authority or tyranny. Thus, the euphantophone..."

"What?" Baillargal queried, stopping the rhythmic working of his jaws.

"The eupantophone is an instrument of stupefying simplicity..."

"As long as you're a ventriloquist," quipped Baillargal, merrily.

Blancadet, his nose in his glass, could not suppress a violent burst of laughter, which scattered red droplets of wine on the tablecloth. "Ventriloquist! Ventriloquist!" he repeated, trying to subdue, by thumping himself on the back, the fit of coughing that as shaking his throat. "Why do you insist that I'm a ventriloquist? Célestin, bring me the small eupantophone."

The domestic went out, and came back shortly afterwards, carrying a black morocco traveling bag, which he placed on the table to his master's right.

"Prepare the *Nouvel Ours*," said Blancadet.

Célestin went in search of the *Écho's Plaintif*'s rival paper, and after having taken off the elastic band, folded it along the gaps separating the columns and introduced it into the unfastened traveling bag.

Good!" said Blancadet. "Have you read this morning's *Nouvel Ours*, my dear Baillargal?"

"I scanned it," the journalist confessed.

"Well, you're going to hear it."

He pressed a metal button scarcely visible in the grain of the morocco, and a voice rose up, which articulated the syllables with a clarity at least equal to that we admire among the Messieurs of the Conservatoire National de Musique et de Déclamation.

"Governors and governed!"

That's Thémistocle Iris's article," said Baillargal, whose trembling voice mingled with the voice reading the famous rabble-rouser's prose.

"Every people has the government it deserves! The French, therefore, have a right to this government, whose formula can be summed up in half a dozen words: *One for all; all for one!* The Republic, the sovereign of governmental forms through time and space, bears all benefits in the folds of its toga and gives body to all dreams of nobility..."

The most improbable figures of speech, the neighborhood of the most unexpected terms, which evoked the variegated display of a democratic bazaar continued in that vein until the name of Thémistocle Iris, the signatory of the article, was solemnly pronounced. With his index finger, Blancadet touched the side of the traveling bag and enquired as to the impression made on his guest.

"Do you suspect me of having learned that nonsensical prose by heart?"

"I wouldn't go that far," the visibly-troubled journalist admitted, in spite of a gesture of suspicion. "However..."

"However what? Do you want to listen to the latest news?"

"No thanks."

"I'll wager that you'd prefer to penetrate the mystery of the eupantophone. You're my universal confidant; I have, therefore, nothing to hide from you; I'd prefer, however, not to trouble your digestion. Have another piece of this tart—it's excellent!"

Mechanically, Baillargal stuck the tines of his fork into a piece of the recommended pastry and slid it on to his plate without paying any further heed to it, too intrigued by the secret of the eupantophone.

"You're familiar, my dear Baillargal, with the interesting family of phonographs, gramophones and all the more or less ingenious instruments that reproduce the human voice?"

"They were the joy of my childhood."

"And they would be the convenience of your entire life if they were worthy of the title of eupantophone! However, my eupantophone is merely an improved phonograph, of which the only merit is the ability to dispense with cylinders or disks of special manufacture. It reads any writing, from the masterpieces of print to the mot artistically-defective graphic manifestations."

"Which does it great honor, but to what is your eupantophone indebted for all its talents?" Baillargal asked, incited by the peremptory demonstration of "sight without eyes" to the most heroically eccentric propositions.

"To electricity, my dear friend—the electricity that the description of magical has not yet put in its veritable place, for it is energy in person, the source of movement—which is to say, the soul of the world and of life. We are merely a manifestation of it ourselves, and can you expect the cause to be incapable of that which one of its effects is already capable? It's necessary to be logical, damn it! But let's not take flight into the sometimes-unreasonable lofty realms of metaphysics, and let's not lose sight of our modest and precious auxiliary. Its mechanism is as simple as that of the vulgar phonograph; I've merely provided an improvement deduced from the principle of the rigorous identity that exists between luminous waves and sonorous waves; you've just followed an explanation of it."

"I've understood your explanation, but I don't see..."

"A quarter of a minute's reflection and you'll reach the conclusion yourself. What is writing if not, according to the expression of one of your illustrious colleagues, Voltaire,

179

'painting with the voice?' We'll focus, if you'll permit, on the kind of writing we use, known as alphabetic. The eupantophone that you have before your eyes only reads that kind of writing; the others—the phonetic, the hieroglyphic, the syllabic and the demotic—are absolutely dead letters so far as it is concerned..."

"As they are for me," declared the journalist, blushing.

"You can see that there are many points of resemblance between a human being and the eupantophone, which lacks consciousness..."

"There are people who also lack it—the Chilly Ape, to name but one!"

"Every sound being represented by a letter—which is to say, by an image, what was it necessary for me to do, if not the same operation that permits me to hear what you see? In the sides of that little box there is an electric source of very great energy, thousands of volts; it aliments a powerful lamp, because, in order to read, the first requirement is to see clearly."

"Evidently."

"And no less evidently, black isn't white and white isn't black; from which it results that the membrane, held on the face of a cylinder that passes the printed or manuscript page over it, vibrates in accordance with the impressions it receives, each of which is faithful to the representation of a letter—which is to say, a sound. That sound would require an unimaginable sensitivity of hearing if one had the pretention to perceive it directly, so I have been obliged to amplify it considerably by the adjunction of an apparatus analogous to the one employed by the telephones known as 'loud-speakers.' That was not, in any case, what gave me trouble in the construction of my perfected phonograph; it was, above all, the tones of the voices, which, by virtue of my research, I succeeded in varying at whim. The eupantophone that you have before your eyes is a traveling eupantophone, which I use to read newspapers or small booklets on trains and in hotels. The poor devil only possesses one voice..."

"Like a normally-constituted man or woman!"

"Absolutely. But my home eupantophone—the one you've seen in my drawing room—has half a dozen voices at its simultaneous disposal, which I can vary at whim, for I've found the means of photographing with perfect exactitude all those that I desire to employ, from the voice of the currently-fashionable tenor to that of the least of fairground buffoons. That eupantophone is also provided with a mechanism that permits it to cut and turn the pages of a volume..."

"Without leaving finger marks?"

"Naturally, but when I put in too much oil or grease, it stains the edges. I lost that way, a few days ago, a beautiful example on China paper of *The Memoirs of a Canteen Stewardess during the Hundred Years War*. That euphantophone model also has a whole range of variations of speed, which it adapts to all the movements of a piece, just like an intelligent reader. Anyway, if you would like to, let's go take coffee in its presence. You're not in a hurry?"

"I have absolutely nothing to do all day."

"Perfect—for I have to talk to you about my marriage plans, for which your advice and assistance will be very valuable to me."

"Use and abuse me, as you please!"

"Thank you."

The two men exchanged a vigorous handshake. Blancadet rang for Célestin and gave him the order to serve the coffee in the drawing room, adding that absolutely no one was to disturb him under any pretext.

Sitting by the fire with Baillargal, Blancadet began by taking out his eyes, which, while chatting, he wiped carefully with a silk handkerchief.

"My dear Baillargal, you're going to lose your cravat-pin."

Baillargal put his hands to his shirt-front and replaced the item of jewelry in question, a present from Virginie. "You can see that without eyes now?"

"Obviously. I see it poorly, but I can see it. Objects appear slightly deformed—your cravat-pin looks like a bean."

"It's a real diamond, though!"

"I don't doubt it for an instant; but that's to tell you that I only have approximate perceptions when, as at this moment, I'm cleaning my eyes. I am, in fact, obliged to clean them quite frequently, to get rid of the fatigued sensitive matter..."

While speaking, Blancadet had taken something akin to a box of rice powder from his pocket, and he carefully coated the ocular globes with the powder-puff before replacing them one by one in their respective locations.

"Now my eyes are as good as new, my dear Baillargal!" Blancadet said, wrapping his handkerchief around the little silver box before putting it back into his trouser pocket. "A little of that sensitive powder always remains on the back of my orbits; that's how I can still continue to distinguish something of the objects around me..."

"And without your spectacles?"

"Ah! Without my spectacles, I'm entirely parallel to Tobit before his son learned about the therapeutic virtues of fish bile from the archangel Raphael."[9]

"You believe in Holy Scripture?"

"It's a work that has a right to all our respect—but let's leave sacred prose for a more down-to-earth subject no less dear to my heart."

"Your marriage?"

"Exactly. I've told you that your friendship will be precious to me in that regard."

"I say again, use it and abuse it."

"Thanks! So, I ended up finding a young woman blind from birth susceptible of becoming the companion of my life. It was a provincial notary who revealed her existence to me. May that lawyer be blessed, to whom I reserve the honoraria of the contract relating to the happiness that it will perhaps procure for me. I received his letter three days ago; you had just left me. I left that same evening and..."

---

[9] In the Apocryphal *Book of Tobit.*

"And you came back affianced? You work quickly! All my compliments."

"Take them back. I have too much respect for love in general and marriage in particular to act thus without the slightest reflection. First I wanted to see the young woman whose native blindness permitted me to consider her as an eligible companion. I therefore took the train to Ilderon-sur-Noizette."

"But that's in the Midi!"

"What's astonishing about that? I carefully refrained, of course, from informing my honorable lawyer, much less the family of Mademoiselle Cécilia de La Moutardie..."

"Of the nobility!" observed Baillargal, admiringly.

"Very old, my dear friend! Utterly incognito, therefore, I disembarked the day before yesterday, in the morning, at Ilderon-sur-Noizette. I had even taken the precaution of donning blue-tinted lenses."

"To hide your eyes?"

"To hide my eyes? They resemble anyone else's! But you're not taking into consideration the fact that I'm going to return to Ilderon-sur-Noizette in a few days, as soon as possible, and I don't want to be recognized."

"Oh, of course!"

"I had myself taken, under the pretext of visiting, to a farm-school situated near the Château de La Moutardie. On the way I got my driver to talk about the local area and its people. The knight of the whip was loquacious and, I must admit, well documented about Ilderon and its surroundings. He cited the Château de La Moutardie as one of the principal curiosities of the region, and without my having to question him at all, I learned from him that the only daughter of Comte Noé de La Moutardie had been blind from birth.

"Between two strokes of the whip applied to the mare's bony back I discovered that Mademoiselle Cécilia was twenty-seven years old and that it was a great pity that she had been born blind, because, beautiful as she was, although not very rich, she would have made a fine marriage. The judgment, passed in crude terms by a man with the rubicund face on a young woman that I had not yet met but who might become my wife, caused me a veritable irritation..."

"Look out love—here comes jealousy!" said Baillargal.

"Don't mock, I beg you. I'm talking to you as a confidant and a friend, without searching for phrases or choosing my words. I know full well that it's only appropriate to be jealous of a material and palpable fact. There are, however, desires and covetous expressions that soil a beloved object more than physical dirt..."

"Forgive me."

"I believe that there are, down here, beings chosen for one another since very distant ages, and who always end up meeting. So, Mademoiselle Cécilia..."

"You've met her?"

"Yes! We were about to arrive at the farm-school. A short distance ahead of the carriage, which was climbing a rather steep slope, a white-haired old man with a young woman on his arm emerged from an avenue of cedars at right-angles to the road. 'That's Monsieur le Comte with his Demoiselle!' my coachman whispered. The man had had no need to speak; something, like a particular beat of my heart, had already told me that it was her.

"Entirely dressed in black, she was walking slightly behind her guide, with her head held high, her eyes, of a very pale blue, fixed upon a distant goal. The carriage went past them; the coachman took off his cap, shouting a respectful "Bonjour, Monsieur le Comte!" to which Monsieur de La Moutardie replied with a "Bonjour, my friend!" accompanied by a slight bow, probably addressed to me. I raised my hat, and while my driver tried to increase the speed of the vehicle I turned round to look at Mademoiselle Cécilia. I was able to examine her at my leisure.

"Tall and brown-haired, she was walking at the rhythmic pace that reveals a perfect harmony of the body. It seemed to me that she was definitely the companion of whom I had dreamed, and I was absorbed in my mute contemplation when my companion's voice asking me 'what I thought of Mademoiselle Cécilia' recalled me brutally to reality.

"I learned that the Comte de La Moutardie had spent almost all of his fortune in the attempt to render sight to his unfortunate child. The greatest physicians of Europe and America had been called in consultation, but all the efforts of science had been futile. Mademoiselle Cécilia could see no more at twenty-seven than at birth.

"While listening to the coachman I sensed something akin to a great flame of tender pride born in my heart; my love was going to render the divine light to that unfortunate woman. You'll help me, won't you, Baillargal?"

"What can I do? Speak, I beg you," said the journalist, whose sentimental fiber had been forcefully struck by Blancadet's story.

"Can you leave Paris at the moment?"

"I have absolutely nothing to keep me here."

"Marvelous! We'll leave for Ilderon-sur-Noizette tomorrow, then."

"With pleasure. But before then I'd like to consult my...wife." Baillargal had suddenly thought of Virginie, and wondered how she would react to that departure and the prospect of a few weeks' separation.

"How bizarre you are, my dear friend! Why didn't you say right away that you were married. Simply bring Madame Baillargal with you!"

"Perhaps she'll prefer to come to join me in a few days...," the journalist hazarded, foreseeing a professional impediment on the part of his mistress.

"Arrange things as you wish. In the meantime, here's a small viaticum—for I don't want to be the cause of any expense, however small."

Amid a flood of protestations, Alcée Baillargal pocketed the banknotes that Blancadet held out to him. "I'm entirely at your orders, my dear Blancadet."

"It's agreed then: we'll leave by the two o'clock express from Quai d'Orsay."

"Agreed."

"We'll have plenty of time to talk on the train; however, as chance might put us in the presence, as soon as the departure platform, of some inhabitant of Ilderon-sur-Noizette, remember that I'm blind—completely blind—and that I can't see. I'll explain to you later my reasons for acting thus.

Searching in his pocket to assure himself of the reality of the precious banknotes, Baillargal encountered his watch, which he pulled out mechanically.

"Oh! I beg your pardon, my dear Baillargal, for having kept you for such a long time. I'll return your liberty."

"I assure you that nothing urgent..."

"But yes! I don't want you to be inconvenienced because of me."

"Since you're throwing me out," said Baillargal, laughing, in a hurry to return as soon as possible to the Rue des Hautes-Herbes now that he had the means to offer Virginie dinner at a cabaret.

"Until tomorrow, my dear friend. Present me most respectful regards to Madame Baillargal, who is very welcome to come with us to Ilderon-sur-Noizette."

"I'll try to convince her," said Baillargal.

Blancadet escorted his guest to the door. The latter drew away after an exchange of multiple handshakes.

IX

Several times, in the fiacre that took him back to the Rue des Hautes-Herbes, Alcée Baillargal counted and recounted the soft blue banknotes so kindly offered by Blancadet. For the journalist, they not only represented the rather respectable sum of three thousand francs, but also the departure point of ulterior requests for funds that could not fail to be favorably welcomed.

As perspicacious as all amorous women, Virginie Lauria divined immediately, when she saw her lover come in, that something fortunate had happened to him.

The story of the visit to Victor Blancadet was punctuated by numerous kisses, and afterwards, the question was discussed as to whether Virginie would leave tomorrow for Ilderon-sur-Noizette. The reasons for and against were carefully weighed; Virginie ended up having the same opinion as her lover, who judged it more appropriate to let a few days pass between the introduction of his friend Blancadet to the woman who would acquire the title of legitimate wife and her arrival in Ilderon.

The prospect of a separation saddened the tender Virginie somewhat, but on reflection, she realized that a sudden departure would strongly resemble a flight in the eyes of her friends and protectors, who had a right to every consideration. She only asked her lover to renounce the trip to the cabaret, an intimate dinner having infinitely more charm, especially on the eve of the solitary nights that were to follow.

Little Charlotte was charged with going in search of the wherewithal to put together a succulent diner and to send a telegram to Victor Blancadet informing him that he would only have one traveling companion the next day.

On the pillow, nibbling the delicacies of the almost-neglected dessert, Alcée and Virginie confided their respective hopes and dreams to one another.

"You see, my darling, that there are still worthy men!" declared Virginie, tenderly. "You ought to found a newspaper—a great newspaper! Blancadet wouldn't refuse you the capital."

"You think so?" asked the journalist, in whom were born the editorial ambitions in embryo in every servant of the pen.

"Of course," said Virginie. "You'd be an excellent editor." Very seductively, she added: "We'd be able to get married," and then, more boldly: "We'd have to get married, because, you understand, in your position, the slightest grounds for criticism would be a danger..."

Both lulled by their dream, which was perhaps not absolutely common, Alcée and Virginie went to sleep, purified by their hopes. The fisherwoman told herself that she might be able to dispose of all her admirers and devote herself entirely to her love; the journalist anticipated being able finally to get down to the serious and definitive work that he believed that he owed to humankind.

The next morning was devoted to packing the bags of the "Monsieur," whom Charlotte could not help questioning about the duration of his absence. "Oh, Madame's going to be bored without Monsieur!"

Virginie put on a somber costume, whose sobriety would have done credit to the most honest woman, and, in order to prepare herself for the role she was about to play, renounced the habit she had of eating lunch on her lover's knees, sitting down ceremoniously facing him.

"You won't have to blush at your wife, you know; I can behave myself when necessary."

"All my compliments, Madame Baillargal," praised the journalist, with a smile, amused by the comedy. "Oh, I forgot—our Blancadet is blind. He can't see. You understand, don't you? He can't see!"

"What about your story in the *Écho Plaintif*?" asked Virginie.

In order to avoid further explanation, Alcée Baillargal contented himself with broadening his mouth in loud laughter.

"You're making fun of me, my love. I knew perfectly well that when one is blind, one can't see."

"Obviously," the journalist admitted, with perfect simplicity.

At half past one, Baillargal and his mistress got down from the fiacre that had brought them to the Gare du Quai d'Orsay. With a glance, the journalist searched the vast hall, and was about to head for the window reserved for the sale of tickets for the main lines when he perceived Victor Blancadet on the sidewalk, a traveling bag at his feet, in the process of searching his purse for the wherewithal to pay his coachman.

Baillargal joined him; he exchanged a few words with him and, taking him by the hand, led him over to Virginie in order to make the introductions. His hat in his hand, Victor

Blancadet bowed to the pseudo-Madame Baillargal, in accordance with the ritual commanded by the most puerile and honest civility, and having encountered, after some groping, the hand that the slightly-emotional Virginie held out to him, he raised it to his lips and kissed it as gallantly as could be. He formularized all his regrets at being deprived of such an agreeable traveling companions.

"My husband must have apologized to you, Monsieur," Virginie replied, in a tone of impeccable worldliness. "It's materially impossible for us both to leave Paris at the moment; we're expecting provincial relatives—my husband's relatives—who will be spending three or four days here. I'll come to join my husband as soon as possible. I don't like to be far away from him for long..."

"I can understand that, Madame!" said Blancadet, approvingly. Turning to Baillargal, he added: "Don't worry about the tickets, my friend. I had them purchased at the local office in my quarter."

Baillargal bowed, and proposed that they go on to the platform. The guard, incited to respect and complaisance by the exhibition of two first-class tickets, was perfectly willing to permit the "family member" to go through the access gate.

In order to give the impression that all the seats in the compartment were taken, the journalist scattered the meager luggage over the large white cushions, and Victor Blancadet began to chat with Virginie alongside the carriage.

"Monsieur Baillargal must have told you, Madame, the reasons for my—or rather our—journey to Ilderon-sur-Noizette. I hope that you, who have the good fortune to savor the joys of the conjugal hearth, will approve of my marriage plans. An accident has caused me to lose a precious possession: sight; so, you will understand that I have not dared to cast my eyes on a young woman who would only see me as an unfortunate invalid. In brief, I do not want to take more than I can give, and I said to myself: for a blind man, a blind woman!"

189

"Of course, of course!" Virginie acquiesced, visibly disconcerted by her interlocutor's matrimonial theories.

"Passengers for Orléans, Limoges and Toulouse board the train!" an employee began shouting, running along the train in order to give an example of haste to the belated.

Blancadet presented his compliments of Madame Baillargal and groped his way to the compartment, leaving his companion time to deposit a farewell kiss on his wife's cheeks.

A blast of a whistle, to which the locomotive's siren replied, and the train moved off. Baillargal leaned out of the window, waving his handkerchief, for as long as he thought that he was still visible to Virginie; then he raised the glass and sat down facing Blancadet, who observed with satisfaction that all the passengers in quest of a seat had been deterred by the clever arrangement of bags, walking sticks and umbrellas.

"What luck! We're alone! We can chat a little. You have a charming wife, my dear friend; I congratulate you."

"One does what one can," the fortunate Baillargal agreed, modestly.

"Evidently! Which doesn't alter the fact that having chosen a pretty woman for a wife is an irrefutable proof of good taste."

"You have only to do the same!"

"I shall try, and you'll aid me in that task. We'll arrive in Ilderon-sur-Noizette tonight; our first visit, tomorrow morning, will be to the notary Des Échinettes, to whom I owe the discovery of Mademoiselle de La Moutardie. I'll wager that you haven't understood why I desire to be an ordinary blind man—which is to say, a man incapable of dividing time into the usual two fractions of night and day?"

"I confess that I don't understand very well—but you're such an extraordinary man!"

"You do me too much honor in judging me thus—but don't think, however, that it's merely a joke on my part. My sole intention is not to bring disturbance into the heart of a young woman. Until the precise moment when we are united

190

before God and men, I only want to be her peer in misfortune. In brief, I'm reserving a surprise for her."

"Ah!" said the journalist.

"Yes, a surprise—you haven't guessed?"

"You're going to enable her to see!"

"You've got it! I believe I've made my confession of faith to you; I'm something of an atheist—which is to say that I only believe in God in the limits of his role as creator, and what is more I confess that it's by virtue of a kind of laziness, to avoid the difficulty of seeking the solution to a problem that cannot, all things considered, have the slightest practical utility. So, I consider God to be absolutely disinterested in his work, which he has abandoned to what might be called evolutionary hazard. My ambition is limited to correcting the whims of that evolution, and most of all, I don't want to wound the religious principles of the very Catholic Mademoiselle Cécilia.... However..."

"You'll only accept civil marriage? You'll refuse to go to the church?"

"Come on! Come on, my dear Baillargal. For men like us, exemplary slaves of the numerous subjections of modern life, is it not to show a very minuscule spirit to take exception, other than privately, to a ceremony in which everyone only plays the part that suits him? I shall leave that entirely to my wife, whom I shall oblige without making the slightest sacrifice. I've never thought of distinguishing myself by those exterior revolts that cause a sensation in political and electoral matters."

"I approve, although it seems to me that one ought to have the courage of one's opinions."

"And when one has no opinions, one keeps one's courage to oneself! One waits for a better occasion to display it. But this is taking us away from the surprise that I have in store for Mademoiselle Cécilia. The La Moutardie family is very devout; that tells you that the young woman who will become my bride attaches a capital importance to the nuptial benediction; I shall therefore choose the solemn moment when the priest puts the blessed rings symbolic of indissoluble union on our fingers to render my wife the usage of light."

"What a *coup de théâtre*!" said Baillargal, admiringly.

The wheels of the carriage, impeded in their movement by the brake-shoes, began to screech lamentably; the train came to a halt with a shock that precipitated Baillargal on to Blancadet's knees. On the platform, a voice howled the name of the station: "Les Aubrais! Les Aubrais!"

The door opened, allowing the passage of a head coiffed in a cap checkered with gray and black squares. The head turned to utter an exclamation of delight, and the compartment was immediately invaded by four bizarrely-clad individuals who, successively picking up all the objects disposed on the banquettes by Baillargal and his companion, placed them in the racks without addressing the slightest formula of politeness to their owners.

Baillargal felt a reflexive surge of anger against the casual attitude of the intruders, but then reminded himself that it was, after all, their right. As for Blancadet, he observed with a perfect calm that "*savoir voyager*" is a French art completely unknown elsewhere: a reflection undoubtedly suggested by the Englishmen who had just installed themselves.

The train moved off again and he compartment, previously so tranquil, resembled a travel agency box; each of the islanders started to read, in the kind of voice that seems to take pride in being shrill and bruising to foreign ears, passages from their guide-books relating to Orléans, Jeanne d'Arc and the region they were traversing. That fourfold yapping was beginning to exasperate Baillargal when Blancadet rose to his feet to take a morocco bag from the luggage-rack, which the journalist immediately recognized as the eupantophone.

Blancadet introduced into the slot a small book that he took from his pocket and replaced the whole in the rack above the heads of the English party. He had scarcely sat down again when a voice rose above the chatter, which stopped it almost instantly.

"Orléans, Aureliani in Latin, and previously Genabum, according to vulgar opinion, city in France, administrative center of the département of the Loiret on the right bank of the Loire, 120 kilometers from Paris. 70,000 inhabitants. Suffragan bishopric of the Archbishopric of Paris..."

All the qualities, particularities and specialties—the entire identity—of Orléans, was carefully related.

The Englishmen uttered "*Ohs*" on a chromatic scale, whose alarm made a comical contrast with the phlegmatic and dismal expression of the clean-shaven faces. Their eyes, similar to those of the horned beasts that watched the train pass by along the track, remained stupidly fixed on the morocco bag from which the voice was emerging, and as the least timid of the professional travelers got up, probably to take account of the cause of the phenomenon, Blancadet, in the most natural fashion in the world, set the eupantophone down on the banquette opposite, which continued to give details of the history and situation of Orléans.

"Orléans only became a city under Aurelian (270-275), who gave it its name. Attila, in 450, and the English, in 1428, laid siege to it, but all efforts were in vain against the valiant city; it will be necessary to follow Jeanne d'Arc step by step, who, with the aid of God, chased the invader away!"

"Ventriloquism," one of the Englishmen declared to his companions, who examined Blancadet carefully before taking from their pockets the notebooks in which they recorded the principal events of their peregrinations. One of them, who was particularly interested in ventriloquism, wrote for several minutes; then he stood up, and approached Blancadet, cap in hand, and held his notebook out to him.

"Please sign it, Monsieur Ventriloquist. Here's twenty francs!"

Without blinking, Blancadet took the notebook and the fountain pen; he traced a few letters, pocketed the louis and returned the notebook to the Englishman, who went back to his companions, as curious as he was to know the name of the phenomenon. They all uttered, in chorus, a quadruple: "Oh! Joe Chamberlain!"[10]

admirable in its unison and amazement. Baillargal burst into mad laughter, which only calmed down at the next station, where the Englishmen, understanding that they had been tricked, left the compartment.

Alone with Baillargal again, Blancadet resumed the explanation of his matrimonial plans; darkness fell; the train arrived in Limoges, where the travelers found a modest and unappetizing meal in the buffet; then they set off again, twenty-five minutes later, finally arriving, on the stroke of one o'clock in the morning, at Ilderon-sur-Noizette a small town whose geographical situation places it equidistant from Périgueux, the truffle town, and Agen, the fatherland of plums, which ought, in order to be authentically aristocratic, to deny with equal firmness Touraine and California.[11]

X

The Hôtel de l'Esturgeon occupies a privileged situation on the right bank of the Noizette, which, combined with the natural distinction of its owner, makes it an establishment unrivaled in Ilderon.

L'Esturgeon receives bishops, generals and great artists on their travels. On the occasion of an execution, which is still remembered in Ilderon, where crimes are rare, "Monsieur de Paris" and his assistants stayed at L'Esturgeon, where the maids still show bourgeois gentlemen whose opulence gives

---

[10] The Liberal statesman Joseph Chamberlain was still at the height of his fame in 1904; it is highly unlikely that the Englishmen could have been fooled for an instant by the false signature

[11] This places the imaginary town of Ilderon in the Périgord region, where much of "L'Olotélépan" and "Un Samsâra" are also set; Austruy was obviously fond of it and might well have been native to it.

rise to the hope of a good tip to "the executioner's room." A little frisson runs down the neck of those worthy visitors, whose snores, appropriate to tranquil consciences, trouble the repose of neighboring rooms not haunted by such bloody memories.

Without any possible hesitation, Blancadet had selected the Hôtel de l'Esturgeon; in accordance with his instructions, therefore, on disembarking, Baillargal had accepted the offer of the Automedon of the antique omnibus that had filled the badly-cobbled road leading from the station to L'Esturgeon with the noise of its shaking windows.

In order to avoid any indiscretion on the part of the hotel staff, Blancadet had decided to simulate the most complete blindness. It was, therefore, leaning on Baillargal's arm that he climbed into the omnibus and got down therefrom. At the reception desk, the journalist asked for two fine rooms with a communicating door, the infirmity of his "relative" requiring multiple services that it was is habit to render to him. The chamber of "Monsieur l'Inspecteur des Finances"—so called because that highly-placed functionary spent one or two nights there every year—was the only one with an internal connection, to "the other one." Without paying any heed to the denomination employed to designate the second room placed at their disposal, Baillargal asked the maid to show them the way. The young woman, coiffed in a pretty white bonnet, took two keys and, candle in hand, went along a corridor, followed by Blancadet, to whom Baillargal made recommendations regarding the danger of staircases to which one is unaccustomed.

When they arrived on the first floor, the maid turned to her clients. "This is it, Messieurs! Which Monsieur desires the chamber of Monsieur l'Inspecteur des Finances?"

"The larger one for Monsieur!" said Baillargal, indicating his companion.

"No, no!" Blancadet protested.

"Yes, yes!" Baillargal insisted.

"Then Monsieur will have 'the other one.' That one's very nice too, but..."

"But what?" Baillargal queried, intrigued.

"It's just that 'the other one'—I beg Monsieur not to say that I said so, because Madame will scold me—is the executioner's room."

"What executioner?" asked Baillargal.

"The one from Paris, of course! Doesn't Monsieur know that, twelve years ago, there was an execution in Ilderon? Monsieur de Paris slept in that room..."

"Well, so what?" said Baillargal, wanting an explanation of the mystery.

"It's because of the spirits," whispered the maid, with such a comically serious expression that Baillargal, very amused, took hold of her chin.

"And they frighten you, the spirits, lovely child?"

He was about to take the flirtation further when he remembered his status as a married man. He obtained from Blancadet the favor of staying in the executioner's room, and the maid withdrew, after wishing the Messieurs good night.

The next day, Blancadet came to wake his companion, who was not habitually an early riser. Once across the threshold of the room, the blind man resumed his role conscientiously, and it was under the curious gazes of the staff that he absorbed a cup of chocolate in the large dining room.

Baillargal asked for directions to the office of Maître Alcindor Des Échinettes, the notary who had had the fortunate initiative to alert Blancadet to the existence of Mademoiselle de La Moutardie, the first visit naturally being owed to him.

In the most placid street in Ilderon—which does not have a single one of those streets whose encumberment is a subject of pride for industrial and commercial towns—stood, to the modest height of two stories, the abode of the youngest and most brilliant lawyer in the region.

Placed as scouts on the spikes of the railings that left a narrow space between themselves and the house, brand new escutcheons signaled the presence of a ministerial officer, and a black marble plaque fixed to the door itself had the mission of revealing, in letters of gold, that the name of the ministerial officer in question was Maître Alcindor Des Échinettes.

Baillargal's ringing of the bell caused a young clerk to appear, who took charge of conveying Victor Blancadet's card to his employer.

Almost immediately, a door opened and Maître Des Échinettes in person invited the blind man and his guide to come into his study.

The notary sat Blancadet down in an armchair, indicated a chair to Baillargal, and resumed his place between the two windows, in the shadow projected by two enormous strong-boxes.

"Maître Des Échinettes, you doubtless suspect the motive for my visit…," Blancadet began.

The lawyer approved with one of those engaging smiles habitual to all those who receive numerous visitors in a professional capacity.

"You had an excellent idea in bringing to my attention the existence in Ilderon of a young woman blind since birth; I'm profoundly grateful for that. I've come today to tell you who I am and to ask you for some information regarding Mademoiselle Cécilia de La Moutardie."

"I am at your orders," Maître Des Échinettes consented, generously.

Victor Blancadet gave a full account of his life, explaining how he had lost his father and mother while still young, from whom he had inherited a considerable fortune, represented in part by an entitlement to an income from the State of fifty thousand francs a year. The tragic event of the fifth of May 1885 caused the lawyer to utter sighs and interjections of condolence. Blancadet, of course, made no mention of his revolutionary discovery.

"So, my dear Maître, to sum up, I've been blind since the fifth of May 1885; I'm thirty-five years and three months old; my only family is a single cousin who has been kind enough to accompany me to Ilderon and whose affection will not be affected by seeing me bequeath my income of fifty thousand francs to my wife by way of a marriage contract, in the case that I die first."

Baillargal uttered protestations of devotion to Blancadet, to whom, after some hesitation, he decided to refer as his "dear cousin."

Maître Des Échinettes stood up, but as he had a very long upper body and very short legs, and the chair on which he had been sitting was very high, that movement only elevated his stature some ten centimeters above the table. His robust and thickset hands, distanced from manual labor for too few generations to have acquired aristocratic graces, where white, as if polished by contact with rough stamped paper. His fingers caressing a set of trinkets appended to a prominent abdomen by a red-gold chain, Maître Des Échinettes, with all the solemnity of his thirty years, two of which had already been spent in the notariat, began to speak with great civility.

"'All peoples have known and practiced the healthy institution of marriage. Woe betide those who neglect it or do not treat it with the respect that is owed to it,' wrote one of my masters at the Faculté de Droit de Montpellier, justly. That eminent man, whose speech was replete with abnegation and knowledge, had understood marvelously the relationship of men and women insofar as they are social beings charged with ensuring the perpetuity of the human race. Marriage is not only a right but a duty; I congratulate you, Monsieur Victor Blancadet, on coming to Ilderon-sur-Noizette—which will be proud to give you the title of citizen by adoption—to exercise that right and fulfill that duty."

That ciceronizing exordium had left its author slightly breathless; he paused to get his breath back before resuming, displaying all his eloquence.

"Without any circumlocution or euphemism, with a sobriety of expression worthy of the ancient Spartans, you have laid your life bare before me. I believe, Monsieur Victor Blancadet, that it would be in breach of one of the rules of a ministry that has consented to receive me in its bosom, and which I strive to honor, not to tell you all that I know concerning the young person on whom you have set your sights."

"You're forgetting that I'm blind, my dear Maître," Blancadet corrected him, following the verbose notary's gestures, as ridiculous as they were pretentious, from behind his blue-tinted lenses.

"Mademoiselle Cécilia de La Moutardie belongs to a very old family whom the epithet 'honorable' would be an outrageously derisory proportional recompense for a long past of unalterable fidelity to the holy cause of the legitimate masters of France."

"They are kings, doubtless, of whom you speak?" Blancadet queried.

"My thought might extend, without the most frightful of sacrileges, to others who have an altar in the heart of all good and true Frenchmen, prior to resuming, on the throne, the still-empty place that cannot be filled by a President of the Republic."

"It's said that the Head of State only sits on an armchair—the chair of the Presidency," hazarded Baillargal, whose political convictions were limited to appreciating, without seeking terms of comparison, the government under which he had the pleasure of living.

"Will you permit me, Maître Des Échinettes...?" said Blancadet.

"Please do," the lawyer acquiesced.

"Without being a vigilant Republican or an avant-garde socialist, I am profoundly imbued with liberal and modernist prejudices; do you not fear, my dear Maître, that the traditions of the La Moutardie family might be an insurmountable obstacle to my projects?"

"Those, Monsieur Victor Blancadet, are scruples that honor you, but believe that persons who put their trust in Maître Alcindor Des Échinettes cannot be disappointed. Since you have crossed the threshold of my study, I have not ceased to concentrate all my thought on the means to ensure the success of your affair..."

"One ordinarily commences with a meeting," Baillargal observed.

"What you say, Monsieur, is perfectly exact; I would even say that, in this region, it is an absolute rule to introduce to one another, preferably on neutral ground, young people judged susceptible of being united," Des Échinettes agreed, "but in the present case, I do not know whether it is indispensable to follow the usual protocol."

"I want to confirm strictly to custom," Blancadet declared.

"In my capacity as a notary, profoundly respectful of the customs that my ancestors considered as laws, I can only give you my full and entire approval. Where are you staying, Messieurs?"

"At the Hôtel de l'Esturgeon," replied Blancadet and Baillargal, simultaneously.

"Then it's very simple!" affirmed Maître Des Échinettes, who sat down and took his head in his hands momentarily in order to reassemble this train of thought. "The Hôtel de l'Esturgeon only receives the equivalent of what is known in the City of Light as '*Tout-Paris.*' The La Moutardie family constitutes one of the noblest jewels of *Tout-Ilderon*—that elite which meets at least once a month, on market day, at the *table d'hôte* at l'Esturgeon. Is not that the appropriate place for a meeting? Today is Thursday the fifteenth of April, and as market day is the first Friday following the fifteenth day of the month, it will take place tomorrow. I have just enough time to alert Monsieur and Madame de La Mourtardie. While dining, they will have the all the necessary leisure to examine you; as for Mademoiselle Cécilia, Monsieur your cousin, who must be a connoisseur, since he is a Parisian, will see her and relate to you all the charm that her person exhales."

"With pleasure," Baillargal agreed.

"However," Blancadet objected, "would it not be useful, beforehand, to know the intentions of Mademoiselle Cécilia and her parents? Perhaps a disabled individual such as myself would not seem a possible match?"

"How can you imagine, Monsieur Victor Blancadet, that Maître Des Échinettes, whose prudence is proverbial in Ilderon, could have engaged in operations as serious as the preliminaries to a marriage without having scrupulously investigated the terrain in advance?"

"You've already mentioned me to Monsieur and Madame de La Moutardie?"

"Yes and no—which is to say that I've mentioned you without naming you. discreetly, with the skill that I have acquired in my practice, I have sounded out Monsieur and Madame de La Moutardie to discover whether, in principle, they would accept a blind man for a son-in-law. The mother, who, in bringing her child into the world was unable to give her its light, and the father, who, for twenty-seven years, has been curbed by his grief, after having both expressed their eternal gratitude to me, have told me that their daughter would be perfectly able to find happiness by uniting her destiny with that of a man similarly struck with blindness. I believe it my duty to tell you immediately that the La Moutardie's fortune, once fairly considerable, has somewhat melted away."

"My dear Maître, considerations of that sort cannot have the slightest importance for me; I'm rich enough to be able to offer myself the luxury of setting aside the question of interest; I don't want to hear no more mention of it."

"A marriage contract is indispensable, however," the practitioner of rough paper insinuated.

"Will you please take responsibility for that?" Blancadet conceded.

"I shall put my best efforts into it, and our professional enemy, the Administration d'Enregistrement, des Domaines et du Timbre, will suffer another of the defeats that almost caused me to quarrel with its sub-inspector. Do you want me to sketch a description of Mademoiselle Cécilia? She is a tall brunette with an admirable figure..."

"I shall rely in advance on what my cousin will tell me," said Blancadet, interrupting him rather brutally.

"I've already told you that she's twenty-seven years old," Maître Des Échinettes continued, imperturbably. "As for her curriculum vitae, it is that of a young woman nourished with the most elevated principles by a father and mother who adore her; she is a young woman accomplished in every respect: musically, conversationally, enjoying the most robust health..."

"Thank you, my dear Maître; I'm sufficient edified," Blancadet cut in, irritated by the commercial aspect that the enumeration of Mademoiselle Cécilia's virtues and qualities was taking on in the notary's mouth.

"She's a companion worthy of you!" Maître Des Échinettes concluded, with a grandiose gesture.

"Does the town of Ilderon enclose a few curiosities?" Baillargal asked. "I'm a journalist, and in consequence very fond of historical and artistic matters."

"Monsieur your cousin is a journalist?" Maître Des Échinettes darted at Blancadet, in grandiloquent interrogation.

"Excuse me for not having introduced him to you immediately: Monsieur Alcée Baillargal, a contributor to the *Écho Plaintif*."

"Delighted, Monsieur," the notary declared. "I'm very interested in literature. Your name is certainly not unknown to me, but I ought to tell you that I don't read the *Écho Plaintif*. No one in Ilderon receives it."

"My compliments, my dear Maître," Baillargal replied.

"Everything in our town is worth seeing, from the ramparts, of which only the emplacement remains, to the museum, the chapel consecrated to Saint Ilderon, an unfortunate woodcutter who died the victim of what would nowadays be called a judiciary error, the bridge—oh, Messieurs, I recommend to you the bridge over the Noizette; it's only six meters in breadth, but it was entirely fabricated in Ilderon on the plans of the official engineer of the Ponts-et-Chaussées. It's a very original work and is not the fruit of one of those exalted brains, such as one sees in America. There's also the Mairie, the abattoirs, the animal pound under construction..."

"Thank you, thank you, my dear Maître—we'll visit all of that," said Baillargal, standing up to take his leave.

"It's arranged, then, for tomorrow at eleven o'clock, in the large dining room at l'Esturgeon. I hope that my affairs will permit me to sit down there, as usual, at the table that will, I hope, see the sunrise of your happiness; after lunch, the family La Moutardie will come to my office, where I beg you also to come for the official introduction."

Maître Des Échinettes emerged from the penumbra of his two strong-boxes and took Blancadet by the hand, asking him for permission to lead him to the gate. On the sidewalk, the three men exchanged a series of handshakes, and Blancadet, leaning on Baillargal's arm, drew away. Maître Des Échinettes enveloped his shiny escutcheons with a tender gaze, rubbed his hands and went back into his notarial domain.

XI

As he had gone to bed early, Baillargal found by nine o'clock that he had had his fill of sleep. He got up and, after getting dressed, went into Blancadet's room, where the latter was cleaning his eyes.

"How are you this morning, my dear Baillargal?" Have you slept well?"

"No bad, thanks. And yourself, my dear Blancadet? Have you had any bad dreams?"

"It's you who ought to be asked that, having slept in the executioner's room," Blancadet retorted, parading his powder-puff over the little glass globes. "As good as new! I want to be able to admire Mademoiselle Cécilia at leisure, but I wouldn't want to give rise to the slightest suspicion."

"It's not me who'll give you away."

"Thanks!" Blancadet replaced his eyes and proceeded to dress himself with the utmost care. "I want to make a favorable first impression on Monsieur and Madame La Moutardie..."

"That's perfectly natural," Baillargal approved.

Ten o'clock had jut chimed in the belfry of the Hôtel de Ville when the blind man and his guide quit their rooms. In order to manifest at lunch an appetite worthy of a man of perfect health and conscience, Blancadet contented himself with absorbing a cup of weak tea. Baillargal imitated him and proposed that they take a turn around the Esplanade, which they had neglected the day before. They passed in front of Maître Des Échinettes' office; on the sidewalk outside, a number of peasants, doubtless his clients, were arguing with extremely animated gestures before going in to the notary's house.

At the corner of a street, between an aged lady and a white-haired gentleman to whom she was giving her arm, a young woman appeared, elegantly clad in a somber dress.

"There she is!" whispered Blancadet. "Don't look!"

Blancadet had accentuated the attitude particular to blind people, which causes them to walk with their heads tilted backwards, in order avoid bumping it, the rest of the body comprising an advance guard in order to provide warning. Baillargal, entirely absorbed in his role as guide, only darted an indifferent glance at the group, whose members exchanged a few rapid words.

Madame de La Moutardie had, in fact, detected in the blind stranger the suitor for her daughter's hand, and could not help turning round to dart at the man who might become her son-in-law the first glance of a mother-in-law.

When Blancadet judged that he was far enough away not to be overheard, he asked his companion: "Well, what do you think of her?"

"She's grace and distinction personified."

"It's probable that the La Moutardie family is going to Maître Des Échinettes's house."

"And from there to the Hôtel de l'Esturgeon."

"Tell me, my dear Baillargal…it's a matter of not being late…I'm not at all curious to see the Esplanade."

"Me neither."

"Let's go back to the hotel, then."

"If you wish."

They passed Maître Des Échinettes' office again. On the sidewalk the same peasants were arguing, with the same animated mime.

At the hotel, Blancadet manifested the desire to go up to his room. He rectified the parting that divided his hair into two equal parts, passed a fine brush moistened with brilliantine through his beard, and advised Baillargal to put his less modest academic palms in his buttonhole, which could only make the officer seem more distinguished, for want of a violet ribbon larger than the one he was wearing.

With the vigor of great days, the bell announced the opening of the table d'hôte. Blancadet and Baillargal went downstairs. On the threshold of the dining room, Maître Des Échinettes was waiting for them; not only had he succeeded in escaping from his numerous clients, but he had elected to supervise the setting of the meeting himself. He had therefore asked the amiable owner of l'Esturgeon, who could refuse him nothing, to have two tables set up in a corner of the room; one would seat Blancadet and his cousin, while the members of the La Moutardie family would take their places at the other, along with himself, who had been invited to lunch.

Discreetly, the notary informed "the Messieurs" that things were proceeding admirably. Madame la Comtesse had crossed Monsieur Blancadet's path an hour before and had been very favorably impressed by his "noble and truly virile" appearance.

It was, therefore, with a heart full of hope that the blind man, on Baillargal's arm, went to the small table that a black-clad waiter was defending against all attempts to take possession of it.

"*Tout-Ilderon*" was already assembled. There was "Admiral" Bréchaflot, a worthy mariner who had never married, who was spending his leave as a ship's lieutenant in a château near the town. The mariner had been brilliantly involved in several campaigns, as evidenced by the variously colored ribbons that kept company, on the large lapel of his frock-coat, with the insignia of the Légion d'honneur. To either side of him were Dr. Garbutot, famed for the reliability of his diagnoses; the advocate Platinois, who owed his renown to his indefatigable voice; various local landowners who looked like sportsmen; old soldiers buttering up severe and rebarbative ladies; and earnest young people impressed by the solemnity of conduct in the aristocratic hostelry.

Maître Des Échinettes had made his arrangements cleverly; each of the two tables was, relative to the other, an excellent observation post.

Blancadet applied himself to groping and awkward gestures, and his gaze never quit Mademoiselle Cécilia, who submitted without too much embarrassment to the proof from which she would probably emerge affianced. Madame de La Moutardie, visibly more emotional than her daughter, scarcely touched the dishes that were presented to her. As for the Comte, he strove by means of his detached attitude to deflect the suppositions that the clients of the Hôtel de l'Esturgeon, intrigued by the notary's presence, could not fail to be formulating. In order to avoid any manifestation that might have given rise to a gaffe, Baillargal only raised his eyes from his plate—where he found, thanks to a typically southern liberality of spices, reminders of Virginie—to look at his unfortunate companion.

The lunch came to an end; the desserts were being passed out when Madame Brindolle came to receive the compliments of her clients, who, as usual, declared that the fare had never seemed more exquisite.

The ladies got up in order to proceed, in a room graciously placed at their disposal, with a few adjustments of appearance, leaving the gentlemen the leisure to light a cigar and take coffee. Madame de La Moutardie stared at Blancadet with the expression of resigned tenderness that mothers have for the man who will rob them of a part of their child's heart; then she gave the signal to depart by taking the arm that Maître Des Échinettes offered her. To demonstrate discretion, Baillargal absorbed himself in the choice of a cigar without

206

appearing to notice that Mademoiselle Cécilia was leaving the room, leaning on her father.

As had been agreed, Blancadet and Baillargal went to the notary's house without delay. The young clerk showed them in. Maître Des Échinettes, stationed, as on the previous day, in the penumbra of his two enormous strong-boxes, first complimented his client.

"You have pleased, Monsieur Blancadet; you have pleased beyond all expression; Madame de La Moutardie is literally delighted; it's a double conquest that you've made; I congratulate you officially. It only remains to collect the palm of victory." Addressing himself to the journalist, he said: "Dare I ask you what impression you have formed of Mademoiselle Cécilia?"

"Excellent! Excellent! She's a delightful person," Baillargal hastened to declare.

"And what does Mademoiselle de La Mourtardie think?" asked Blancadet

"But my dear Monsieur, Mademoiselle Cécilia can only see through the eyes of Madame her mother, just as you can only see through the eyes of Monsieur your cousin. She relies on Madame de La Moutardie as you rely on Monsieur Baillargal."

"We're in the same situation!" Blancadet declared, solemnly.

"Monsieur de La Moutardie has raised the question of interests," Maître Des Échinettes, continued, "and..."

"I repeat to you, my dear Maître; I simply intend to leave to my wife, by marriage contract, in the case that she survives me, an annual income of fifty thousand francs."

"I have made Monsieur de La Moutardie party to your project, to which he has no objection in principle. However, his formal intention is to give his daughter, by the same contract, by way of reciprocity, the Château de La Moutardie and its estate, which would revert to you in the case of your remaining a widower."

"There's no need, absolutely no need. If, by misfortune, I were to lose my wife, I do not desire to have any right to the property of the La Moutardie family."

"That is the desire expressed by Monsieur de La Moutardie. I shall introduce you to him, as well as the ladies, if you will permit."

Maître Des Échinettes stood up, caressed one of his strong-boxes in passing, took Blancadet by the hand and introduced him into the drawing room adjacent to his study, in which the La Moutardie family was waiting.

Accustomed to ceremonies of this kind, the notary made the introductions rapidly; Madame de La Moutardie threw herself, sobbing, into the arms of her daughter, who also began to weep. The Comte de La Moutardie addressed himself to Blancadet in a tremulous voice.

"Excuse us, Monsieur; we're provincial, and scarcely know how to dissimulate our sentiments. Pardon the natural emotion that grips us at this moment..."

"That emotion is shared by Monsieur Blancadet," Maître Des Échinettes advanced, desirous of putting an end to the familial scene, whose provincialism seemed to him to be unworthy of the town in which he exercised his ministry.

"Monsieur le Comte," said Blancadet, gripping Monsieur de La Moutardie's hands, which had taken his, "It is me who begs your pardon, if I cannot find the words that can express the immense joy that I experience at this moment; thank you for not having rejected me."

"Why reject you?" exclaimed Madame de La Moutardie. "My child's misfortune is similar to yours. Her eyes have never seen the light, alas!"

"Madame la Comtesse," Maître Des Échinettes interjected, "Monsieur Victor Blancadet will be for you the most respectful and loving of sons, as he will be the model of spouses for Mademoiselle your daughter."

In her mother's arms, Cécilia was sobbing. Blancadet was still gripping Monsieur de La Moutardie's hands. Maître Des Échinettes sought out Baillargal and retired discreetly, immediately after having presented the La Moutardie family with the unique and precious collateral of his unfortunate client. There was a recrudescence of tears and exclamations, in which the names of God and the most influential members of his celestial personnel were invoked.

Monsieur de La Moutardie pulled himself together first and asked "the Messieurs" to be kind enough to go back into the Maître's study, where he would come to join them as soon as he had calmed the ladies' emotion.

The notary had partly disappeared into one of his strong-boxes, inside which he was undertaking a labor of exploration. He freed himself again as soon as he could; the thick steel plate forming the door pivoted of its own accord and blocked the gaping opening. With a solemn voluptuousness Maître Des Échinettes manipulated he multiple locks and complicated combinations, like a man whom no concern can deflect from the most impeccable politeness.

"Excuse me, Messieurs; ministerial officers are obliged to a prudence that the simple mortals whose insouciance and levity I envy do not even suspect. I'm all yours. Would you care to tell me, Monsieur Blancadet, which regime you desire to apply to your conjugal happiness? You have the fish; it's up to you to designate the sauce with which you prefer to eat it..."

"What fish? What sauce?" enquired Blancadet, surprised by these culinary invocations.

"Mademoiselle Cécilia de La Moutardie, of whom you will soon be the husband—which is to say, the master—before God and men! The Civil Code, far-sighted and wise, has not desired to impose on all the spouses that live under its empire a single rule, whose effects, in certain cases, might be fatal to the moral principles inspired by Napoléon..."

"He was a great warrior!" Baillargal granted.

"It's not in my habits to shed the blood of my neighbor, even if that neighbor is born hundreds of leagues from my cradle, but I agree that Napoléon has made war something that astonishes and summons respect and admiration. However, you will permit me to prefer to the most glorious pages of our conquests the less brilliant but more solid and more durable pages of the admirable book that reigns, from our first whimper to our last breath, over all our actions and all our thoughts. Whether you dream of legal community, endowment regime, separation of wealth, or community reduced to acquisitions, you will find them in the three chapters of the fifth part, which deals so eloquently with the marriage contract and the respective rights of the spouses. You have only to make, adopt and assure your choice of the mode of your happiness. Can you extend love further than particularity and fantasy? Notaries, who give engagements a sacred character, are there to sanction the most fugitive of your whims..."

Carried away by the impetuosity of his eloquence, Maître Des Échinettes would have continued for a long time to sing the praises of the Civil Code had not the entrance of Monsieur de La Moutardie stopped him in mid-flow.

"They're crying," said the old man, extending his arm in the direction of the drawing room. "It seems that a great joy hollows out again the abyss of misfortune in which we're accustomed to living."

"Monsieur Baillargal will have the honor of presenting himself tomorrow at the Château de La Moutardie to ask you formally, on behalf of his cousin Victor Blancadet, for the hand of Mademoiselle your daughter," Maître Des Échinettes declared.

On a gesture of protest from Blancadet, the Comte de La Moutardie said: "You have sacrificed yourself for your fellows. I do not understand why the hand of God has struck you so terribly."

"There are secret reasons in the designs of Providence that escape us," opined Blancadet, in a grave voice.

"Could such resignation inhabit a heart less admirably Christian than yours?" exclaimed the Comte de La Moutardie. "Your religion would be one more guarantee if the Comtesse and I were not sure that you would make out dear Cécilia happy. She deserves so much to be happy. To love you like our own child will be a relief to our misfortune. You shall be our son!"

"Yes, you shall be our son!" put in the Comtesse, bringing in Cécilia, whose tear-stained face she was wiping with a damp handkerchief.

Victor Blancadet abandoned to Madame de La Moutardie the hands into which she put her daughter's hands. He raised them respectfully to his lips; then the Comte asked permission for the ladies to retire, desirous as he was of having a conversation with his future son-in-law and his cousin— a conversation to which Maître Des Échinettes was asked to lend his assistance, because it was a matter of settling questions of a material nature.

As he had told the notary, Victor Blancadet, by marriage contract, made a gift to his wife, in the event that he died first, of an annual income of fifty thousand francs, but he struggled in vain against the will of the Comte de La Moutardie, who, by the same contract and by a reciprocal disposition, desired in the case of his son-in-law being left a widower, to leave him the estate of La Moutardie in total property.

All these dispositions were translated into notarial language by Maître Des Échinettes, after which Monsieur de La Moutardie declared that he had something to ask of his future son-in-law.

"I agree to it in advance with the greatest of joy," said Blancadet. "Speak, I beg you."

"It's a duty that I have to fulfill with regard to my race— the race that is concluding in the eternal night of our poor Cécilia's eyes. Many a time, the blood of the La Moutardies has reddened the soil of the Holy Land and that of the most glorious battlefields. It is with an immense dolor that I have seen it wither; I feel profoundly guilty with regard to my ancestors, who had transmitted to me a name that I have stopped in passage to keep it in my possession; it has seemed to me to be abusing a sacred possession. You can render me the honor that the absence of a male posterity has taken from me. Help me, Monsieur Blancadet, not to allow the name of La

211

Moutardie to fall into oblivion. Take it! Be a Comte! Like her mother, Cécilia would be a Comtesse! It's the dearest of my wishes."

"It will be granted," said Blancadet, extending his hand.

"The procedure is rather complicated," Maître Des Échinettes put in. "You're not unaware that it would require a decree by the Head of State; only after its promulgation can the request be presented and a judgment be obtained in the Chambre du Conseil of the tribunal of first recourse of the arrondissement in which the party is domiciled to make have changes and additions made to the registers of Civil Estate..."

"Could you take charge of all that?" Blancadet asked.

"Certainly, certainly! At your orders," acquiesced Maître Des Échinettes, who though it his duty to summarize the conversation. "Monsieur Victor Blancadet, scientist, domiciled in Paris, 140A Rue du Sabre-de-l'Abbé, proposes to become the spouse of Mademoiselle Cécilia de La Moutardie, daughter of Monsieur le Comte de La Moutardie and Madame la Comtesse de La Moutardie, domiciled at the Château de La Moutardie near Ilderon-sur-Noizette. The parties who, let us note for the record, are blind, will reciprocally and simultaneously, by contract of marriage and in the entitlement of survival, the gift of an annual income from the State of fifty thousand francs, and the aforesaid domain of La Moutardie. Monsieur Victor Blancadet engages to add to his patronymic that of La Moutardie with the title of Comte, resigned in his favor by the present and legitimate title-holder; all under the condition, of course, of administrative and judiciary approval, which I, Maître Alcindor Des Échinettes have the mission to pursue and obtain. Is that all?" The lawyer accompanied the final question with a smile of the utmost satisfaction.

"Perfect!" said the Comte de La Moutardie and Victor Blancadet, simultaneously. The latter added: "Monsieur Alcée Baillargal, my cousin, will have the honor of presenting himself tomorrow at La Moutardie to ask you on my behalf for the hand of Mademoiselle your daughter."

Alcée Baillargal rose to his feet and bowed with a reverence whose solemnity appeared adequate to the circumstances. The Comte de La Moutardie shook the journalist's hand effusively. "Thank you, Monsieur, for taking responsibility for that mission. You will be expected tomorrow at La Moutardie. Your time will be ours…"

"Early afternoon is customary," put in Maître Des Échinettes.

"Two o'clock, then?" Baillargal proposed.

"Agreed! Tomorrow at two o'clock; it will be an important date in our lives," said the Comte de La Moutardie, taking his leave.

Victor Blancadet and Alcée Baillargal remained in the notary's study for a few more minutes. The latter took advantage of it to give them some clarifications regarding the protocol customary in Ilderon: the journalist should equip himself with a bouquet, which he must immediately order from the florist whose shop was directly opposite the Hôtel de l'Esturgeon. It would be equally prudent to book the landau at the hotel desk, the only carriage appropriate to the circumstance. By departing at a few minutes to one, Baillargal would be sure of arriving at the Château de La Moutardie at the appointed time.

Maître Alcindor Des Échinettes offered Victor Blancadet his personal congratulations, promising to make his most sincere wishes for happiness at an opportune moment; then he rang for his clerk, who accompanied the Messieurs as ceremoniously as he could to the gate, outside which the group of peasants was still arguing.

XII

Alcée Baillargal took Blancadet back to his room, where he came to join him again after having ordered the bouquet from the florist and retained the landau at the hotel desk, in accordance with the lawyer's instructions.

The two men started chatting; at first alimented by vague matters of an indifferent sort, the conversation gradually took a more intimate turn, settling on a unique subject of perfect relevance: amour.

Without false shame, Victor Blancadet confessed to his companion the profound emotion he felt.

"My unique and dear friend, the poets speak the truth who proclaim the eternal youth of the heart! I'm no longer an impetuous adolescent, and the implacable experience of my thirty-five years would have crushed my Romeoesque shoulders lamentably if I had been gripped by the silly fantasy of still wanting to seek my Juliet down here. For a long time, alas, woman has no longer been for me the mysterious temple in which the unknown flame burns that we approach, after so many sigh and feverish nights, to consume the wings of our dreams at a stroke. I have loved, via the heart and the senses, a number of mistresses; but at this moment I am experiencing something indescribable that I have never felt before. It seems to me that my soul is enlarged, becoming lighter, lighter..."

"Oh, either that's love, or I don't know it!" exclaimed Baillargal, laughing.

"Ah! It had the same effect on you when you saw for the first time the woman who as to become Madame Baillargal?"

"Yes...oh yes, absolutely!" said the journalist, taken back to the first passades graciously offered by the blonde Virginie.

"You felt...?"

"That my soul was enlarged, becoming lighter, lighter...as if it wanted to fly away!" affirmed Alcée Baillargal, lyrically, and concluded: "Anyway, before love, all men, almost without exception, are equal, and experience the same phenomena, with various degrees of difficulty."

"You already loved Madame Baillargal before marrying her?"

"Oh, certainly."

"A childhood amour, perhaps? You grew up side by side, and when age permitted it, your parents united you? The coronation of a long idyll?"

"Exactly...exactly...the coronation of a long idyll," Baillargal repeated, thinking it dangerous to enter into precise explanations about his past and that of Virginie—with which, in any case, he was not very well documented.

"Forgive me, my dear friend; I haven't even asked you whether you've received news of Madame Baillargal."

"Thank you...no, not yet. I telegraphed our address to her yesterday morning. I'm expecting a letter any time now."

At that precise moment, someone knocked on the door. The maid's voice announced: "Monsieur Baillargal, it's a letter!"

The journalist got up, drew the bolt that Blancadet had carefully put in place for fear of some indiscreet interruption, and took a blue envelope from the maid's hands, sealed with a large blob of pink wax.

"With your permission?" he asked Blancadet.

In accordance with custom, the latter replied: "Go ahead, I beg you."

Alcée Baillargal scanned the missive rapidly, transmitted to Blancadet the compliments it contained addressed to him, and added: "My wife will arrive here on Monday morning."

"What joy! She's exquisite, Madame Baillargal."

"Oh...!" said the journalist modestly

"Yes, yes! She's exquisite! I understand why you adore her. Have you been married a long time?"

"Oh no! Only five years," Baillargal threw out, at hazard, his sole preoccupation being to engrave his principal declarations in his memory, in order to impart them to Virginie and thus avoid being contradicted by what she might say to Blancadet in her turn.

"Five years! Five years of happiness! How quickly they must have passed! In five years, I shall be forty. Forty! Forty...," Blancadet repeated, in a melancholy tone.

"Is forty," the journalist affirmed, vigorously, playing his part in the sentimental duet deplorably.

"Frankly, what do you think of Mademoiselle de La Moutardie?" asked Blancadet, heroically launching a question that had been burning his tongue since the beginning of the conversation.

"I think that when you've given her sight she'll be a very accomplished individual," Baillargal replied, with a hint of flattery.

"She had admirable eyes—eyes whose azure is so profound that it gives one vertigo."

"That's true—I've never seen any like them. What a pity they don't work."

"Oh, that's not what worries me, my dear Baillargal; my wife will see as yours does..."

"That's a mercy for which I wish with all my heart."

"Thank you. In spite of everything, though, I'm a little preoccupied. I'd like to know why Mademoiselle Cécilia is blind. She is; that's the essential thing, evidently, but you understand that I'll have to construct an apparatus adequate to her kind of blindness."

"It's complete," Baillargal hazarded.

"Of course—but is it the fault of the eyes themselves or simply that of the optic nerves? That's very important."

"Certainly."

"Yes, because I wouldn't want to have to remove her beautiful blue eyes to have them replaced with globes of glass like mine. If it's a simple paralysis of the optic nerves, a pair of spectacles will suffice to render her the perfect use of sight."

"Any physician in the region can inform you, since you told me that all of them, without exception, have been called to examine Mademoiselle de La Moutardie."

"It's on the representatives of science that I'm counting. Provided that they don't take refuge behind professional secrecy! They're capable of anything, even of not violating, for once, the laws regulating the exercise of their art..."

"You could also interrogate the Comte and Comtesse de La Moutardie..."

"Obviously. But I'm reluctant to have recourse to that means, which couldn't fail to seem inquisitorial. Then again, I want my plans to remain in the most absolute mystery. If you knew, my dear Baillargal, how happy I am!"

"Ah, love is a beautiful thing," granted the journalist.

"And you can't imagine how grateful I am to you! You'll see that I'm not ungrateful. You'll be recompensed for all the trouble you're taking for me."

And as Baillargal dissolved in thanks and warm protestations of devotion, Blancadet announced that he had a surprise in store for him.

Dusk had fallen; Blancadet lit one of the colored candles garnishing the fake bronze candelabras on the mantelpiece, and the virtues and probable merits of Mademoiselle de La Moutardie, whom Blancadet was already calling, familiarly, Cécilia, were exalted until the bell announced that it was time for dinner.

"Your arm, my cousin," said the blind man, resuming his role.

Blancadet wanted, in memory of *her*, to sit in the same place that she had occupied lunch, but a lieutenant of the gendarmerie had just installed himself at the La Moutardies' table, flanked by three individuals whose quasi-criminal appearance needed that prestigious vicinity in order not to appear disquieting.

After dinner, Blancadet and his guide were about to go for a short walk before retiring when they met Maître Des Échinettes in the vestibule, who had come to place himself at the disposal of his clients in case they had any need of his services. He had called in on the florist, who had promised to take every care in making up the bouquet for "the Parisians." With regard to the landau, the owner of the hotel, the widowed Madame Amélie Brindolle, escorted by her two daughters, the elder of which was promised to one of the numerous piano classes at the Conservatoire de Musique de Toulouse, declared that they could count on it for midday tomorrow. She had personally supervised the final preparations; it only remained to decide whether the coachman would wear a frock-coat with golden buttons and a top hat or whether he ought to mount the seat in a simple jacket accompanied by a varnished cloth cap.

Before settling this important question, the notary shook his head several times and asked Madame Brindolle what she thought. She did not want to make a decision. "It depends...either one might..." And she cited examples that formed a kind of jurisprudence on the subject.

Blancadet, interrogated, begged them to ask the advice of Baillargal, who opined sententiously: "Since both systems have merits, one might adopt either. Let the coachman put on the frock-coat and the cap—unless he prefers to ornament himself with the top hat while being content with the simple jacket."

Maître Des Échinettes found that idea very droll and utterly Parisian, but he declared the frock-coat inseparable from the top hat, to which he thought it appropriate to add a "cockade": a sort of tinplate fish like those that serve as a sign for merchants of fishing-tackle.

The windowed Madame Amélie Brindolle, her gaze tender, thanked Maître Alcindor Des Échinettes in the name of the house of l'Esturgeon for being kind enough to remember its evocative but somewhat forgotten arms. The younger of the Demoiselles Brindolle confessed ingenuously that she had never seen Polydore, the old coachman, decorate his hat with the symbolic fish—which earned her a severe reprimand on the part of her mother, who took advantage of the opportunity to send "the children" away.

Madame Brindolle wanted, in fact, to be the first person in Ilderon—after Maître Alcindor Des Échinettes, of course, at whom she was gazing with increasingly humid eyes—to congratulate Monsieur Victor Blancadet. The worthy matron, in extremely well-chosen terms, expressed the most pressing wishes for the happiness of her guest; she permitted herself a few allusions, albeit very discreet, to the future that future that she had seen born and raised, so to speak, the La Moutardie family having traditionally come to sit at table in l'Esturgeon every market day in Ilderon.

Maître Des Échinettes thanked her on Victor Blancadet's behalf, and Madame Brindolle, after having enveloped the lawyer with a long tender gaze, went to reanimate the zeal of her elder daughter, who was studying her piano in the hotel office.

Baillargal proposed that they accompany the notary to the end of the street. Blancadet took his guide's arm, and the three men went out into the Avenue de la Gare, deserted and wanly marked not by a few gas-lamps with dying gleams. When they arrived at the gate of his dwelling, Maître Des Échinettes manifested his confusion at having dragged the Messieurs that far; he indicated a café where they might pause for a while, their quality as Parisians implying a belated bed-time. He yielded to one last protestation of devotion and shook Blancadet's and Baillargal's hands vigorously, saying that before going to bed himself he would "spent two hours with his minutes."

The journalist and his blind man went back to l'Esturgeon without having been tempted to enter the café indicated by the notary. Blancadet stayed up late in the execu-tioner's room talking to his companion about Mademoiselle Cécilia, and the twelve strokes of midnight sounded as he re-moved his glasses, while thinking about *her*.

The next day, the blind man supervised the journalist's costume personally. He rectified the crease of the trousers with an iron, deeming it insufficiently pronounced, and de-plored several times over the excessive modesty of the aca-demic palms scarcely protruding from the silk backcloth of the frock-coat. There was not a single detail that escaped Blancadet; one might have thought that he had served an ap-prenticeship with a great tailor or had been a dresser of juve-nile leads at the Comédie-Française—the arbiters, as everyone knows, of social elegance.

An early lunch had been specially prepared for "the ambassador" and his mandator. At a few minutes to noon, the landau arrived at the sidewalk. Further to increase the majesty of his person, laced up in the frock-coat with golden buttons, Polydore had folded on his seat all the blankets that he had been able to find in the garage; on the left side of the cylindrical beaver-skin hat with the rebellious fur that coiffed him, tail in the air, shone the fish that the widowed Madame Amélie Brindolle had piously polished with her own hands. That fish reminded her of her youth, her marriage, the birth of her children and the death of her husband—her entire life—and on seeing her past reborn in that fish, the worthy lady moistened with a few tears the bouquet that she had insisted on installing herself on the cushions of the vehicle.

Several times, Blancadet, who was very emotional, embraced Baillargal, whom he had escorted back to his room; he told them that henceforth, there was "life and death" between them. As he closed the door again he rectified his emissary's cravat, which had been deranged in the course of their effusions.

Left alone, Blancadet, protected by the thick lace curtains, watched the departure of the rig from his window, and it never entered his head to find it in the least ridiculous. Then, after having circled the table in the middle of the room several times, he made sure that the doors were locked and sat down in an armchair. His thoughts were entirely devoted La Moutardie, but as he was not familiar with the château, he could not specify anything; he only told himself that in the drawing room, which he imagined to be very large and severe in its aspect, with aristocratic wood paneling and ancient portraits, the Comte and Comtesse de La Moutardie were waiting in ceremonial dress, while in her room, *she*, Cécilia, in front of her mirror, was nervously placing and replacing a curl of her hair that was never hanging down over her forehead with sufficient artistry—he completely forgot the blindness of the woman who would be his fiancée, officially, in a matter of hours.

Lost in his dream, he took out his eyes mechanically, wiped them, powdered them and replaced them; then, his hand encountered the small eupantophone on the table, and as the book by his bedside—a collection of poems in prose of which he was particularly fond, and which he always carried with him—was within reach, without thinking overmuch about what he was doing, he opened the little volume at random, and, without looking, slid it into the box. Immediately, the words "The Snow" emerged.

Still absent-mindedly, by simple habit, Blancadet pushed his spectacles over his forehead, leaned back in his chair, very close to the eupantophone, and listened to the story, which he knew almost by heart, certain passages of which he followed with an involuntary movement of his lips.

"With his anguished gaze, Elie Gryll[12] had seen in the panic-stricken darkness white-clad Faith loom up before him.

"In the slow and somber morning of a pale winter day, rising with difficulty like a man curbed beneath a crushing burden, nothing more had remained but the consoling hope of the imminent snow.

"Questioning the gray sky, weighed down by clouds, Elie Gryll, still trembling at his white vision, awaited the arrival of the distant envoy promised by his dream.

"One by one, the mute petals of divine flowers descended slowly, messengers of silence and inviolable peace, and, knees bent, putting his adoring hands together, Elie Gryll murmured piously:

"'Snow, white snow, the color of Faith, as holy and blessed as Faith is to me, to are holy and blessed to me, you in whom its soul lives, clad in your whiteness. Have no fear, light immaculate bird; let your gently palpitating wings settle without fear on the saddened earth, which will resume its mourning when you have flown away...

---

[12] Austruy had previously attributed this name to a "famous novelist" in his story "Ange Devermeil," published in the *Revue Hebdomadaire* in October 1902.

"'Tell me, white snow, do you remember my fiancée? The pale child loved you with a sisterly love, and you loved her too. And on the sad day when her soul was exiled, I believed that it had departed on your white wings toward the starry realms. In my dolorous heart, once illuminated, one of her bright smiles remained to me; of you I have kept a white bouquet collected on the flowers of her grave.

"'The flowers have fled under murderous breaths, and her smile, in the course of time, has turned to bitter tears in which my heart is drowned. White Faith, pure snow, you who render me the soul of my fiancée departed toward the starry realms, be holy and blessed...'

"Elie Gryll enveloped himself with a slow sign of the cross, which he sealed with a kiss, and, quitting the balcony from which his devoted prayer had risen, he went back into his bedroom, where, from the depths of a cupboard, amid blessed box-wood, he took a black canvas bag stiffened by long objects. Then, putting the black canvas bag under his arm, Elie Gryll went out of his house. Bare-headed beneath the snow sowing white flakes in his hair, he walked with a slow stride, as if fearful of troubling the mute intimacy of the somnolent air; he marched straight ahead, toward an invisible goal, toward the high hill that he sensed looming up in the veiled distance.

"It was up there, in a deserted garden enclosed by giant trees, that his blonde fiancée lay, having died in the evening of a winter day.

"One bright morning, on awakening like a joyous bird, the laughing child, almost grave on that occasion, had learned toward him and said:

"'Oh, how happy I am! Oh, let me tell you my dream: I found myself sitting on a soft bed of moss in a vast garden populated with marvelous odorant flowers. One by one, those flowers quit their maternal stems to come to me; there were roses, periwinkles and violets, red roses the color of blood, white roses like flakes of snow; there were a thousand other flowers too, and all of them, offering me their adornment,

222

were inviting me to join their games. The most beautiful of the roses settled in my hair…shivering, languishing tuberoses sought the warmth of my breasts, and a brazen lily, which frightened me a little, brushed my bare feet and caressed my knees…oh, it was delightful!

"'Look here, my friend, I want flowers to cheer up my games! Winter has killed those that were here, but up there, in the distant garden to which you took me once, the flowers are not dead. What do you say, my friend? Would you like to go up there together, to the distant garden, to pick the flowers that are waiting for us?'

"Leaving to his deluded fiancée the virginal softness of her dream, in his most tender voice, he had repeated: 'Yes, my dear soul, we shall go up there together to the distant garden, to pick the flowers that are waiting for us…'

"Under the crepuscular monotony of the gray sky, they had both walked toward the hill where the solitary garden they had once visited was waiting for them. During the long journey, the child had talked joyfully about the beautiful flowers they would find; she would put scarlet roses in her hair and slip languishing tuberoses into her bosom; and with laughter as pearly as birdsong, she had asked him whether he would not be jealous…

"And he said nothing, raising his fiancée's hand to his lips, who shivered under his kiss. Finally, they arrived at the top of the hill, but instead of the garden all in flower, which lived in her puerile hope, a deserted and desolate heath appeared, of which the black skeletons of a few leafless trees seemed to be the chimerical guardians. At that sight, the child had turned toward him, her eyes full of reproaches, and, putting her blonde head upon his breast, had silently begun to weep.

"Sadly, they had both returned to their dwelling. Heedless of words of tenderness and love, she had sat down by a window, and he, in order to distract her, had whispered in her ear the very ancient legend recalled by the snow whose first flakes were beginning to fall.

"'In the heavens, my dear soul, are splendid flower-beds, cradles florid with light and joy. Sometimes, the charitable angels make the earth a gift of a few flowers from those gardens; they spread out over our world in white flakes. Fainting at the cold contact of mortal clouds, those poor flowers settle upon the earth, awaiting the warm breath of spring, whose caress awakens them as human flowers, beautiful and perfumed with the memory of their original abode...

"'Look, my dear soul, at those white exiles; some of them have retained, as their only hope, the implacable goal of their distant voyage, and are settling on the ground, resigned victims; others, rebelling against their fate, which they are cursing, are trying to regain their native land, confiding their frail existence to the caprices of the wind, whose brutal breath bruises them and chases them to rightful places...

"'But sometimes, it happens that the tender-hearted angels weep at the sight of their ravaged divine flower-beds, and, jealous of the earth embellished by their bounty, they recall thereto the departed flowers that are still floating, silently hoping for their celestial pardon; in a white cortege they follow to earth their unfortunate sisters devoted forever to the human realm, and having given them all their perfume, in a farewell kiss, for their earthly adornment, the beautiful absolved flowers, suddenly lightened, fly up again toward the heavens, still shivering from the glimpsed exile...'

"Like a mist fleeing before the bright aurora, the sadness rose from the darkened forehead of the capricious child; at the final words of the legend, with her fervent loving voice, she had slowly implored: 'Oh, beautiful candid flowers, let your pardon fall on me. Do not be jealous if your sisters down here have lent me your forgetfulness; my eyes are opening at this moment to the light! Oh, grant me the mercy of letting me love you!'

"The child had gone out on to the balcony. In a swarm of polar bees, the white flakes came to gather pollen from the golden clouds of her hair, stealing passionate kisses from her

224

neck and hiding in the rapid pleats of lace to linger in the caress of her body.

"He watched the mad girl, whose seductive hands opened joyfully to collect a few light flakes in their gracious calices, which she raised to her lips, tenderly, in order to kiss them.

"Suddenly, the immaculate forehead of the adorable child was circled by a white aureole, covering her luminous face with a supernatural pallor; in a torrent of gold, her unbound hair had flowed over her shoulders, and her two hands had extended their immobile fingers toward the sky; her palpitating eyelids with the long lashes had lowered over the radiant light of her pupils; her lips had stammered distant syllables that he only understood in part: 'White soul...fly to heaven...!' And with a final shudder, she had attempted the supreme caress of a name he knew to be his own.

"Between his arms remained a mute body, which, for atrocious hours of distress he had hugged madly to his bosom; before his eyes, burning with fever, hideous visions surged forth of horrible deaths in the bosom of distant conflagrations, which soon extinguished the gentle soothing tears whose veil enveloped his fiancée, dormant in his arms.

"'She is asleep...she is asleep...her eyes are closed, and her lips, like a flower, are parting to smile at the tender dream she is making...sleep, sleep, and do not wake from the dream that is making your lips flower...'

"And softly, kissing her forehead, he had laid his fiancée down on the silken couch, as white as her soul.

"His tears, exhausted, suddenly stopped, and suddenly, Death appeared, rigid in her glacial triumph.

"Breathlessly, he exhaled the name that he loved to give his modest child; then, suddenly, he cried, in a voice as resonant as thunder in the depths of a bronze vase: 'Hideous sister of men, illusory and vain Death, hear me, you whose ear is deaf only to those who fear you; my fiancée is mine and she shall not go to a cemetery haunted by the spirits of evil! She will be mine until the awaited hour of the eternal communion!'

"And violently, as if to snatch her from some frightful danger, he had seized his mute fiancée from the silken couch into his arms; furtively, like a thief in the black night, he had marched toward the hill, on the summit of which, in the garden enclosed by giant trees, he had dug a deep grave, which the snow had dressed with a bed of fleecy snow. In that cradle, the faithful guardian of his love, he had laid the rigid body; his trembling fingers had taken the blonde hair, which he had extended over the beloved face as a light fabric, and during the long prostrate prayer, the snow had enveloped her entirely with its shroud; and when the last thread of the golden network disappeared, he had gently replaced the earth that he had dug, taking care to efface the every trace of his funeral labor.

"Afterwards, he returned to his despairing dwelling. He had placed the pious tools amid the blessed boxwood in a large cupboard, and had not confessed his secret to anyone in the world. For fear of awakening suspicion, he had never returned to his dear tomb, but every day, at dawn, he took the most beautiful of the flowers of his garden, and let them fall one by one, messengers of his sad thoughts, into the clear stream whose silver thread went to wind around the foot of the hill where his secret slept. For a long time he watched the beautiful flowers glide over the water, which seemed to be glad to offer their perfumed souls to the poor exile.

"Many dolorous days had gone by with the horror of their nights, and always Death had refused the hands that he held out to her. Time, the soother of his pain, had lulled his soul so gently that he was no longer even certain of the reality of the vanished happiness.

"But the one who was dear to him was reborn with the snow; the dead woman loomed up before his eyes, and whispered in his ear the words of the legend he had related to her, and, twin sister of the white flowers of snow, the soul of his fiancée, fled far from the earth toward the starry realms, appeared to him.

"It was the white snow, coming to render the stolen soul of his fiancée, and from the large cupboard, amid the blessed boxwood, he had taken the black canvas bag that enclosed the pious tools; at a hasty pace, he had marched toward the hill, and after having crossed the border of the great trees, he had dug the earth, which resounded lugubriously under the thrusts.

"Finally, in its shroud, the rigid body appeared; on his knees, he had leaned the child's head upon his heart, and had gently removed the veil of spread hair, uncovering the sealed lips, the closed eyes, and the white cheeks and forehead.

"'Forgive me, my sweet fiancée, for the awakening I bring you. As on the ancient mornings, make me the regal offering of your radiant smile…listen, hear your soul, which is knocking at the gates of your body! Open up, open up, my darling, your beautiful soul, which I loved. Why did it flee? Why did my love appear too human to it? Perhaps it was frightened? Oh, deign to accept its return! I will love you in a more serene fashion!

"'And yet, my God, if my amour loved to mirror itself in the azure of your eyes as the day star loves to contemplate itself in springs…if my heart cherished the odorant caress of the gold of your hair as the breeze cherishes that of trembling flowers…I did not know that it was a blasphemy!

"'Softly, in my ear, make the confession for which I am in anguish! Tell me the nature of your secret wound. Tell me why you left me…but no, you haven't gone! Your pious face has delivered me from the frightful dream of your exile. You were asleep, and I watched over your sleep, kneeling, so that when your eyes opened, your gaze would encounter my gaze first of all. But speak, I cannot hear the crystal of your voice; your cheeks are as cold as iced fruits given birth beneath the burning sun; your lips are very pale, like angelic wings…'

"His fingers raised the inert eyelids; his lips placed a kiss on the icy lips, and, anxiously, he watched the snowflakes, celestial messengers of angelic souls; but the eyes did not open; the mouth remained closed...

"Then he took the snow between his clenched fingers, and, recklessly, he plunged it into those eyes and that mouth, whose immobility terrified him. And he stood up, hugging the icy cadaver to his bosom.

"'Snow, white snow, perfidiously clad in the robe of Faith, you have stolen my fiancée from me!'

"In the air, as faint as the song of a distant harp, amid the gathering snow, a voice descended to the earth: 'No perfidy has tarnished my candor! I am always immaculate; but the soul of Faith has never inhabited my whiteness...'"

Noises in the corridor awoke Blancadet from the ecstasy in which he was plunged; with a rapid movement, his right index finger brought his spectacles down from his forehead and pressed the button that stopped the eupantophone. With the habitual gesture of people who have lost track of time, Blancadet took out his watch while Baillargal announced himself through the door. A thrust of the thumb on the bolt, and the journalist came in, hat in hand.

"My dear cousin, I have the honor of bringing you the hand of Mademoiselle Cécilia de La Moutardie, of which you gave me the mission to go in search."

Blancadet threw himself into Baillargal's arms and begged him to recount every detail of the meeting. The narration was interrupted as soon as it was begun, however, by the arrival of Maître Des Échinettes, who had seen the landau returning through the windows of his study. The notary replaced the sincerity of the conversation with his pretentious ostentation.

Blancadet was preoccupied with not giving himself away and Baillargal, judging it unnecessary, if not dangerous, to make the solemn lawyer party to his impressions, allowed himself to be questioned by the latter, replying as far as possible with brief monosyllables, dubious more often than not. Blancadet learned, however, that the Comte and Comtesse both seemed to be very happy, and that Mademoiselle Cécilia had wept a great deal. It had been agreed that the following day, Saturday,[13] Blancadet would go to the château, and that from Sunday onwards, after the mass which he would hear from the bench reserved for the La Moutardie family in the parish church, he would he considered as affianced.

Maître Alcindor Des Échinettes was consulted as to the manner in which the courtship ought to be conducted. Launched into the chapter, which he had at his fingertips by virtue of having recited it to numerous clients, the notary went into a host of details, from the handing over of the ring to the "obol" destined for the poor of the parish, via the quotidian bouquets and the gifts for the domestics.

"Starting from zero, which is today—or, rather, tomorrow, at the precise moment when you make contact with Mademoiselle Cécilia for the first time—I shall guide you, day by day and hour by hour, until your entry into the nuptial chamber, on the threshold of which you will permit me to stop..."

Maître Alcindor Des Échinettes thus followed what he called "the logical development of the flame of love in Ilderon-sur-Noizette." He sketched out the tender dialogues that might he held without any injury to Ilderonian traditions, very rigid in that matter. For instance, a kiss could never be exchanged except in the presence of the young woman's parents.

The notary stressed that it was very difficult for him to regulate the protocol perfectly, in view of the "particular situation" of the future spouses—for he avoided, by virtue of a praiseworthy sentiment of humanity, pronouncing the word "blind." He terminated his lesson by saying that he was sure that whatever he did, a man like Victor Blancadet would always conduct himself as "a perfect and gallant cavalier."

---

[13] The author has lost track of his own timetable; according to previous references, today is Saturday.

XIII

Allowing things to proceed with the most characteristic rapidity, it was necessary to wait for more than two months before the celebration of the marriage. According to Maître Des Échinettes, even that delay would not have been sufficient if the case had been ordinary; only people of the lower classes and the petty bourgeoisie of the Ilderon region contented themselves with a courtship of eight weeks.

Victor Blancadet had no intention of making any protest, but, habituated to more modern comforts that were only distantly recalled by the room of Monsieur l'Inspecteur des Finances, he enquired of Madame Brindolle about a less summary accommodation. As he declared that expense was no object, the owner of l'Esturgeon took him to visit a dependency of the hotel, a long-abandoned cottage that it would be easy to render habitable by equipping it with furniture, which she undertook to supply.

The isolated situation of the building, on the bank of the Noizette, immediately seduced Blancadet; he therefore asked Madame Brindolle to make arrangements for his accommodation that same day. There were two rooms for Baillargal and his wife, and a bedroom and drawing room for him, with a dining room that was sufficient, given that the hotel kitchens remained at their disposal.

The request for a bathroom provoked an astonishment near to bewilderment in the widowed Madame Brindolle.

"When the Messieurs are more familiar with the locale, they will know that there is only one bathroom in the whole of Ilderon, in the Palais of the Sub-Prefecture. A long time ago, a stranger came to found a bath-house in our town; as you can imagine, he soon went bankrupt, and all the materials were sold at public auction. In that era, Monsieur the Sub-Prefect was an old eccentric, and Madame his wife was as eccentric as he was. The Sub-Prefect came to the sale in person along with the rag-pickers and scrap metal dealers; he bought a bath, which he had installed on the ground floor of the Palais. Monsieur the Architect tried to stop him, but Monsieur the Sub-Prefect had friends in Paris; he used their influence with Monsieur the Minister and Monsieur the Architect was forced to concede. Baths are no good in our humid climate; Madame the Sub-Prefect's wife must have abused it, because she died six years later of a malady that the physicians could not understand at all. In spite of that, Monsieur the Sub-Prefect persisted..."

"Perhaps in memory of his wife?" Baillargal hypothesized, amused by this local hydrophobia.

"If he did it with that respectable and pious idea, he was very poorly recompensed, for he soon joined Madame the Sub-Prefect in a cemetery in northern France. Monsieur the present Sub-Prefect, whom we shall soon have had the honor of possessing for five years, is not at all like his predecessor, but one day, a physician from the Faculté de Paris settled in Ilderon; that doctor arrived with a heap of new ideas—as if the old ones weren't good enough—and instead of sending his patients to the pharmacist's, as his colleagues did, he ordered them to take baths. Yes, Messieurs, baths! So, when he was told that there was no such establishment in Ilderon and that his prescriptions were absolutely inapplicable, he manifested such astonishment that Monsieur the Sub-Prefect called an urgent meeting of the Hygiene Committee. There was a long debate; the young physician was summoned to explain his conduct. In order to avoid a scandal, Monsieur the Sub-Prefect offered his bathroom, which he never used, and now baths have become fashionable—there are even people who take them without the physician's prescription!"

"Ours has condemned my cousin and myself to at least two baths a week!" Baillargal declared, with the utmost seriousness.

"What a regime!" said the widowed Madame Amélie Brindolle, pityingly. "You'll have to address yourselves to the concierge at the Sub-Prefectorial Palais. "He's the one who gives the authorizations..."

"Please recommend us to him!" Blancadet implored.

"With great pleasure! All the more so as you need it. My God—two baths a week!" lamented Madame Brindolle, formally belying, by her misaquatism, the protective fish of her house.

The rent was settled immediately, and, while thanking the Messieurs for not arguing about the price—slightly high, but necessary for her to "cover herself"—Madame Brindolle made the observation that, the landau being very solemn for quotidian visits to La Mourtardie; she had at the back of the garage a victoria that she would gladly put at their service. Because of the retractable awning, so useful to shelter from the rain, the owner of l'Esturgeon would accept a monthly fee that she qualified, doubtless ironically, as "very reasonable." It is true that, along with the carriage, she was ceding, at an inclusive price, the coachman Polydore, who would be in the Messieurs' exclusive service, along with his livery, for which Madame Brindolle would not claim anything—except, of course, in the unwonted case of its total or partial destruction, accidental or otherwise.

To seal the bargain, Madame Brindolle drew Baillargal, who had Blancadet in tow, into the hotel office, where she offered them "a drop of Madeira." The journalist accorded more aperitif value to absinthe, but he judged it unwise to exhibit tastes that Ilderonian public opinion might deem crapulous. He ingurgitated the pharmaceutical liquid after having clinked glasses with Madame Brindolle, who drank to the honor of her two guests, especially the one who was about to load himself with the chains of marriage, which she hoped he would find "as sweet as honey and as tender as dew."

Shortly after lunch, the landau appeared, surmounted, as it had been the previous day, by Polydore, whose popularity had increased thanks to the prestige of his outfit; the street-urchins were not the only ones who came to admire him, and several people honorably reputed in Ilderon were recognizable in the circle surrounding the vehicle. No untimely manifestation occurred, however, and it was through a merely curious crowd that Polydore drew away from the Hôtel de l'Esturgeon.

During the journey, which lasted about an hour and a half, the distance separating Ilderon from La Moutardie being about twelve kilometers, Blancadet seemed a trifle nervous, and several times, in trying to stand up, he bumped his top hat on the roof of the vehicle. He spoke a great deal, passing from one subject to another, forming projects and constructing plans, building the edifice of his imminent happiness to a great height. Then he returned to minor details, to the furniture that Madame Brindolle was having transported to the cottage at that very moment.

He hoped that Madame Baillargal would be pleased and that she would consent to spend a few weeks in Ilderon. In that regard he asked Baillargal whether his wife intended to bring her personal maid with her; for his part, he did not want to summon his valet Célestin, on whose discretion it would be unwise to rely. The journalist praised Charlotte's professional qualities, and it was agreed that he would send a telegram to Madame Baillargal that evening asking her to bring the maid with her. Blancadet was having everything that he had already heard about La Moutardie the day before repeated to him when Baillargal observed: "We're here," as the landau turned into a driveway bordered by plane trees with enormous boles.

"My heart is beating, but let's not forget that I can't see a thing," Blancadet replied.

The carriage rolled on for a few more minutes and stopped in front of a rather modest perron, somewhat decrepit in appearance. Baillargal got down with the bouquet and held out his hand to help the blind man down. A domestic, whose costume could have fraternized with Polydore's, asked the Messieurs to follow him, and preceded them through a short vestibule and an interminable corridor.

The lackey opened a door. Baillargal had just enough time to put the bouquet into Blancadet's hands, which could not save him from the impact of the Comtesse falling upon his breast, repeating: "My son, my son..." The Comte de La

Moutardie took his wife's place in Victor Blancadet's arms as soon as she left them free. The bouquet emerged, badly damaged by these embraces; fortunately, Mademoiselle Cécilia, who started o cry in spite of the supplications lavished upon her by her father and mother, could not take account of the ravages of enthusiasm upon the work of Ilderon's florist.

Sheltered behind his tinted lenses, Victor Blancadet contemplated the young woman, and found her even more beautiful than the day before. With the sight that he was going to render to her, she would be a creature endowed with all perfections, and, ceding to an egotistical thought, he told himself, not without pride, that no man in the world possessed a woman as pure.

"Tomorrow, after mass, you'll exchange the betrothal kiss," said Monsieur de La Moutardie.

"Thank you, Monsieur le Comte," Blancadet replied, bowing.

"Oh, no, no, I beg you!" the old man protested. "Is it not as our child that you are entering the house? Call me Father."

"Call me Mother," put in Madame de La Moutardie, brandishing the handkerchief with which she was wiping Cécilia's eyes.

"It will be all the sweeter for me to give you those names, which my lips have, alas, been unable to pronounce for a long time."

"Poor orphan!" cried the Comte and Comtesse, simultaneously.

"You shall find a family and parents here!" added Monsieur de La Moutardie. He turned to Baillargal. "I hope that Monsieur your cousin will not begrudge us stealing you from the tender affection he has for you..."

"Deep in my heart, another love reigns," quoted the journalist, lost in schemes in which metaphysics only occupied a very remote plane.

"My cousin is married, although a poet," Blancadet explained.

"Shall we have the pleasure of seeing Madame your cousin in Ilderon?" asked the Comtesse.

"But of course, of course! My wife is arriving from Paris on Monday," Baillargal put in.

"We shall be very happy to welcome her," said the Comte.

"You're too kind," said the journalist.

As it was not customary to allow two young people to show themselves together before the celebration of the betrothal mass, they remained in the drawing room, where the conversation was not the most animated. The diversion of tea was brief in duration and limited to the noise of little silver spoons colliding with porcelain cups.

Remembering the details imparted to him regarding the first meeting by Maître Des Échinettes, Blancadet stood up to take his leave. He kissed the hand that Mademoiselle Cécilia allowed Madame de La Moutardie to place in his three times. The Comte and Comtesse pressed him to their hearts with equal tenderness before escorting him back to the perron, on the steps of which Polydore was sitting, in the process of admiring the tinplate fish on his hat.

The coachman of l'Esturgeon closed the carriage door on his two clients, replaced his hat on his head and whipped his horses, while Monsieur de La Moutardie called out that mass began at eleven o'clock sharp in the parish church.

XIV

Thanks to the arrondissement's député, whom the games and hazards of politics generally placed in the ranks of the majority, the commune of La Moutardie possessed a brand new church.

The building work had lasted a long time, because it only generated an appreciable activity during the two or three months preceding each legislative election; thus, the candidate could provide timely proof of his solicitude toward local populations, and at every count, with the contribution once obtained from the government for the rebuilding of La Moutardie's church, he obtained a considerable majority in the commune.

There had existed a very ancient Roman chapel, somewhat dilapidated, it is true, but which pious hands and many less respectful of the past could have easily restored. Fortified by official funds, an equally official architect purely and simply razed that "anachronistic construction," as he put it, and in its place he had erected a rectangular building, which, save for the openings intended for stained glass windows, resembled a miniature barracks or covered market. At the height of a two-story bourgeois house he installed, on four solidly-built limestone walls built with blocks of stone taken from a nearby quarry, a roof of bright red flat tiles. On top of one of the four faces of the edifice he had commissioned, from a specialist entrepreneur who guaranteed his work against the effects any construction fault for fifteen years, a bell-tower twenty-five meters high. That was more than adequate to satisfy populations whose pride rose to the height of their bell-tower.

At any rate, the architect, trained in the execution of more modest projects, was an ingenious man; in the construction of La Moutardie's church he gave a further proof of his expertise. Being, naturally, the last person to be unaware that every edifice designed for the Catholic religion has the habit of espousing a vaulted form internally, he arched long laths on foundations of hollow bricks, which joined up at the summit, and which the local plasterer only had to skim lightly to arrive at the constitution of a lovely ogival vault. On the advice of the astute architect, who had not had to take responsibility for the decoration of the monument, the servant of the parish took advantage of this scaffolding to paint the plaster, when scarcely dry, with a bright blue emulsion, which, according to the Maire, a somewhat atheistic individual, and consequently enlightened in all matters, bore a perfect resemblance to the sky of Italy.

During the official inauguration, at which representatives of the civil and religious powers, the Bishop and the Sub-

Prefect, were present, they were unanimous in finding La Moutardie's new church, "due to the benefits of a government as liberal as it was just," simple but in good taste. And over the walls, painted with a local whitewash, the implacable crudity of which nothing could calm, danced the red and green searchlights of blinding windows, beneath the intemperate azure of the fake vault, escaped, it seemed from some excessive laundress.

Introduced by the Comte, who had waited for his future son-in-law on the threshold, on the bench reserved at the back of the church for the La Moutardie family, Victor Blancadet received a veritable shock of light; his ears began to ring and he was obliged to move the branches of his spectacles away from his eardrums. Compliments were exchanged in whispers, out of respect for the sanctity of the location.

Alcée Baillargal sat in a place that had been reserved for him next to the bench, which was too small to contain more than four persons.

The service began amid a great noise of shifted chairs, for the majority of the members of the congregation had turned round to examine Monsieur le Comte's guests. Alcée Baillargal, following multiple images of the stations of the cross in vitrified enamel of the most vulgar aspect, suspended from the walls at a height of between two and three meters, said to himself that God must be very profoundly penetrated with the indignity of his creatures, and also particularly given to indulgence, to tolerate such horrors. He wondered whether the Eternal might not have been better adored in a temple of verdure and flowers than beneath that blue skullcap, a derisory caricature of the sky with which he had endowed the earth.

With an indifferent eye he followed the various phases of the ceremony, of which he did not understand an iota, the gestures of the priest having no significance for one so nearly profane. As he consulted the missal that Madame Brindolle had had the kindness to offer him, he made appeal to what he had found at the hazard of his reading about the celebration of the Mass; his thoughts went back to the Council held in Nicea

237

in the year 325, which had fixed the annual festival celebrating the resurrection of Jesus Christ on the first Sunday after the full moon following the spring equinox. Easter having taken place a fortnight earlier, Baillargal, furnished with that reference-point tried to discover what, in liturgical language, was "proper to the day," the rest of the Mass being absolutely the same in all seasons, and in consequence familiar even to the intermittently faithful.

The experience of a journalist was far from being sufficient, for the introit, swiftly cleared out of the way by the officiant, passed unperceived; with the *kyrie eleison* he believed momentarily that he had found his place, when the orison, the epistle and the gradual threw him off the track again. He made a few more futile efforts and then, battle weary, closed the missal. He watched the priest empty the wine and water into the chalice and prepare the Holy Sacrament, with automatic gestures guided by second nature.

At the moment of the elevation, turning his head, he perceived the Comtesse de La Moutardie taking the hand of her daughter to place it in Blancadet's, which Monsieur de La Moutardie had guided. Although divine protection seemed unnecessary to his own amours, the journalist sensed the essential difference existing between a union so solemnly contracted and a cohabitation cemented solely by sensuality. In spite of the integral skepticism he professed, the journalist had a credulous soul, and the Catholic pomp impressed him. When, after the communion and the reading from the gospel according to St. John, the priest intoned the canticle of the action of grace, Baillargal was on the point of confessing to Blancadet the state of concubinage in which he lived with Virginie, in order not to profane any further the sanctity of marriage, which appeared to him to be an eminently respectable thing.

The officiant prostrated himself one last time before the altar in a triple genuflection, and framed by his choir of children, headed for the sacristy. The crowd of the faithful agitated in a great turmoil in order to flow slowly out of the church, in chattering groups.

Alcée Baillargal was preparing to resume his role as "guide dog" when the Comte de La Moutardie asked him to be kind enough to bring his cousin to the sacristy. The château and the presbytery having a very close relationship, it was quite natural that Mademoiselle Cécilia's fiancé should be immediately introduced to Monsieur le Curé.

Excusing himself, Monsieur de La Moutardie took the head of the cortege; the Comtesse gave her arm to her daughter; Blancadet walked behind her, hand in hand with Baillargal.

The door of the sacristy was ajar. Accustomed to informality, the Comte went in without knocking, and as thrown into confusion, for Monsieur le Curé had taken off his sacerdotal garments and was putting away the sacred vessels clad in a hunting waistcoat. On his back, supporting wide black trousers that were a trifle short, his braces made a large St. Andrew's Cross. Baillargal could not help smiling at the minister of God, nonplussed to be caught in that unecclesiastical garb.

"Oh, forgive me Monsieur le Comte," the priest stammered, seizing his soutane, of which he could not, in his haste, find the second sleeve. It was necessary for Baillargal, charitably, to come to his aid.

Having resumed the decent appearances prescribed by Episcopal authority, Monsieur le Curé rediscovered his aplomb. "The robe does not make the monk, I know," he said, amiably, "but it's a useful coincidence!"

"Excuse us, Monsieur le Curé," Monsieur de La Moutardie interjected. "We should have had ourselves announced."

"No, no, you're at home here," the curé protested, now ornamented by his sash and occupied, while asking for news of the ladies' health, in buttoning his soutane.

"Monsieur le Curé, I have the honor of introducing to you Monsieur Victor Blancadet, Cécilia's fiancé...a good Christian!" said the Comte, solemnly.

"May the blessing of heaven be upon you," said the priest, extending his hand toward Blancadet. "Spiritual vision replaces in Mademoiselle de La Moutardie the material vision of things, which the Lord has not wished to give her, in order that she might remain purer and be more worthy of her spouse. It is by your eyes that she will see!"

"Alas, like my daughter, he's blind," put in the Comtesse.

"Who is?" enquired the servant of the faith.

"Me, Monsieur le Curé," Victor Blancadet declared, simply. "I have been unable to see since 1885."

"Why is that?" the priest persisted.

"An accident—a terrible accident!" Monsieur de La Moutardie explained. "My future son-in-law is a very distinguished scientist. An experiment cost him his sight."

"A sad experiment! But God only strikes judiciously. In taking back the sight that he lent you, has the Eternal not deigned to render more perfect the harmony that he desires to see reigning between Mademoiselle Cécilia de Le Moutardie and yourself? Bless the Lord, without attempting to penetrate his designs!" the curé pontificated.

"We bless him," proclaimed Blancadet and the three representatives of the La Moutardie family, in chorus.

"And you, Monsieur?" asked the priest, turning to Baillargal.

"I bless him in imitation of my cousin," the journalist replied.

"Monsieur Alcée Baillargal, one of the foremost journalists in Paris, cousin of Monsieur Victor Blancadet," the Comte explained.

"May God hold you under his holy protection," replied the priest. Addressing himself to the affianced couple, he apologized for appearing to want to deliver a sermon, and, in not very well-chosen terms, adjured them to give more fervor to their faith, the only thing capable of soothing human misfortune with the hope of another life, which is to the present life what diamond is to carbon, gold to copper and day to night.

Victor Blancadet listened to that sequence of affirmations, inelegant but testifying to a robust and simple faith, without flinching.

Praising the indescribable power of God, the priest observed the derisory pride of human science, which "goes as far as to dare to claim the inanity of miracles."

"If God wanted to restore your sight, a simple gesture would be sufficient for him to do so, but no one in the world can force him to make it! Pray, then, in all the humility of your heart, for is it not written that 'light will be rendered to the blind'?"

The servant of the parish of La Moutardie asked a few question regarding Victor Blancadet's civil and social status and, after having declared that he would pray for the complete happiness of the young couple, he granted a dispensation from vespers "in order that this Sunday might belong entirely to the fiancés."

The Comtesse thanked him emotionally, and everyone quit the sacristy to return to the château, only a few hundred meters distant from the church.

Before lunch, served on a flat tray that was badly dented, but stamped with the La Moutardie arms, the Comtesse had her daughter and the man who was to become her "son" exchange a solemn kiss. She asked Blancadet, on her own behalf and that of the Comte, for permission also to kiss him on the cheeks; the blind man consented with a very good grace, only asking that "his cousin Alcée" should not be forgotten in these demonstrations of tenderness; immediately, the journalist obtained a share, perhaps greater than he would have wished, of the familial effusion.

Blancadet ate as clumsily as possible, and pushed the verity of his acting so far as to tip over one of the glasses set before him. In order not to dishonor the tablecloth in too outrageous a fashion, he had been careful to choose a small Bordeaux glass that the Comte had just filled with a very light

241

white wine. The Comtesse declared that it was nothing, and that similar accidents happened to Cécilia all the time.

In the drawing room, matters were arranged to leave the "young people" slightly isolated in a corner, in order that they might chat more freely. The Comtesse questioned Baillargal about his cousin's way of life. The journalist strove to laud the qualities of his relative's heart, who "had thought of nothing for a long time but lighting a hearth and founding a family." He retold the story, dramatizing it as best he could, of the accident at the Sorbonne, which drew tears from the Comtesse. She enquired about their accommodation at the Hôtel de l'Esturgeon, which, although greatly renowned in the region, perhaps did not "contain all the comforts to which Parisians are accustomed."

Baillargal sang the praises of the widowed Madame Brindolle "so full of attentions and so amiably devoted." He explained how she had consented to have the little cottage on the bank of the Noizette furnished for their benefit; Madame Baillargal would arrive the next day with her maid and would supervise of all the internal details.

"You will not, in any case, have to concern yourselves with nourishment, for although custom does not permit us to lodge Cécilia's fiancé at the château, the Comte and I hope to see all three of you come to our table regularly, morning and evening. I will keep Madame Baillargal company while you make a few excursions with the Comte. There are very curious things to see in the region..."

The main lines of the courtship were settled, and the date was fixed of the first grand dinner that would be offered, in honor of the fiancés, to the family's nearest relatives.

A stroll in the garden and the park preceded the cup of tea that was offered at five o'clock, and, in accordance with local habit, dinner was served as dusk began to fall.

During the evening, by maternal request, supported by Blancadet's plea, Mademoiselle Cécilia sat down at the piano and, excellent musician that she was, played a few pieces by masters that she loved: Beethoven, Schumann and Chopin.

Then, accompanying herself with a strangely-timbred contralto voice, she sang a few melodies.

It seemed to Victor Blancadet that he had never before understood the *Adieu*, so much did the poor blind woman put into that page of Schubert of infinity and serene dolor. It was like a superhuman sob, a reckless aspiration toward an afterlife that might perhaps be a world of radiant light, and like a prayer, winged with hope and faith, living in an indescribable and pure sensuality, sang the exaltation of the unknown: "Death is a friend/Who brings liberty!"

When she fell silent, he would have liked to hear more, but the thought did not occur to him to ask for a supplement to that explosion of the soul. Forgetting his role momentarily he went to the piano and, without saying a word, took Cécilia's hands and raised them to his lips. The young woman's face was bathed with tears. Blancadet remembered just in time that his condition forbade him to perceive anything whatsoever. He complimented Cécilia and took Baillargal as a witness to her ideal interpretation of the *Adieu*. Mademoiselle de La Moutardie, in her somber voice, still veiled by emotion, simply replied that it was one of her favorite pieces.

The Comtesse approached and scolded her daughter, who "was too passionate and was doing herself harm with her music." Cécilia wiped her eyes and begged her mother's pardon. The latter kissed her tenderly.

The time had flown without anyone noticing. They rang for the domestic to have the carriage made ready, but Polydore, a man of initiative, had put it in harness at the time he considered appropriate for the return to Ilderon, and the landau had been stationed at the perron for some time.

Maternally, Madame de La Moutardie advised Blancadet and his companion to wrap themselves warmly because of the chill of the valley, and, after multiple recommendations and oft-renewed embraces, Polydore launched his horses into the darkness of the avenue.

Victor Blancadet confided to Baillargal that he was "absolutely transported" and sensed "the birth of an eternal flame in his heart." He talked about Madame Baillargal, who was due to arrive the following day, Monday, at half past eleven. The journalist, who wanted to have a serious conversation with his mistress before producing her, convinced Blancadet to go to lunch at La Moutardie alone; Polydore would come back to Ilderon with the carriage, which would bring Madame Baillargal and him to the château for dinner.

XV

Before putting Victor Blancadet in the victoria that was replacing the landau, Baillargal took him to visit the cottage that Madame Brindolle had furnished with a very disparate taste, in accordance with the means that were available in Ilderon.

In the drawing room, democratic chairs in bent wood kept company with an Empire side-table and a Louis XV arm-chair. The two bedrooms were provided with old, rather narrow mahogany beds, which the landlady of l'Esturgeon, a docile servant of fashion in matters of furnishing, had had the idea of installing in the middle of the room. A mirrored pitch-pine wardrobe, a night table whose rosewood blushed in being next to a wash-basin in wood reminiscent of white lacquer, along with coat-racks with enormous heads in the guise of household gods, garnished the room destined for Baillargal.

Blancadet's room was more modest in appearance, since its occupant could not taste "the pleasure of the eyes," but the bed was provided with an elastic mattress-base and under the window there was a large elder-tree in which numerous nightingales gave interminable concerts every night.

After having heard a detailed description of the apartment from Baillargal's mouth, Victor Blancadet declared himself delighted and offered all his compliments to Madame Brindolle, who, in order to be sure of not missing her new tenants, was waiting for them, posted a few centimeters from the footplate of the carriage.

Blancadet left for La Moutardie and Baillargal took advantage of the omnibus to go to the railway station.

The train, which had perhaps dawdled in order to admire the countryside, or simply not to cause a disagreeable surprise to the staff, arrived, as was its habit, a good twenty minutes after the appointed time.

Protruding from the window of a first-class compartment, Virginie's head surged forth for fifty centimeters, while Charlotte's emerged much more modestly from an adjacent opening.

With a simultaneous bound, the journalist and his mistress were in one another's arms. Charlotte, very emotional, dropped a parcel in order to shake the hand that Baillargal held out to her in a familiar fashion.

As there were no other travelers, the luggage was loaded up, and the omnibus set off incontinently on the road to l'Esturgeon.

Madame Brindolle welcomed Madame Baillargal, who was "even more beautiful and distinguished than the woman she had expected to greet." She mistook Charlotte for a relative and treated her just as ceremoniously.

The separation of four long days gave some importance to the "alone at last" that followed the census of the parcels taken into the room and the prolix compliments of Madame Brindolle. Virginie, gazing into her lover's eyes, questioned him first about his conduct; he put so much fire into his protestations of complete innocence that the usual scene of jealousy was not even sketched.

"Me, deceive my little Virginie? Never!"

"Monsieur Alcée Baillargal, there is no longer a 'little Virginie'; there is no longer a 'Virginie' at all!" As bewilderment replaced the expression of passionate tenderness in her lover's eyes, she immediately declared, solemnly: "You now have a wife named Valentine!" Full of commiseration, she went on: "You don't understand, my darling? It's quite simple. Your friend Blancadet might perhaps remember Virginie—Virginie Lauria of the Rue des Hautes-Herbes…the letter!"

"Ah! So what?" asked the journalist, still not understanding.

"So what? Well, it would have been necessary to explain to him that I'm not that Virginie, that there's another Virginie in the house…etc., etc. You know very well that I don't like to lie, especially when a simple indiscretion on the part of the concierge might have tipped your friend off."

"So?"

"So? How stupid the province has rendered you, my great fool. I've left the Rue des Hautes-Herbes. We've moved! Since yesterday evening we live in the Rue de la Crémaillère!"

"In Passy?"

"In Passy; yes, my darling, number 20, a second floor apartment overlooking the gardens—a find, you'll see…"

"And Valentine?" Baillargal queried.

"Valentine? You can't guess who that is?"

"It's you!" exclaimed the journalist, radiant with his belated *eureka*.

"In person," said the beauty, with the purest Louis XV-style curtsey. "Since we're married, the apartment is in your name. I paid three months in advance and gave a fifty-franc tip to the concierge, who let me move in without doing the paperwork. You'll regularize the rental agreement next time you're in Paris."

"You're an angel, my Virginie!"

"Call me Valentine! You have to get used to it. Don't you think it's a pretty name?"

"All names go well with you, my darling."

"Especially that one, my darling. Because, you understand, the initial is the same, so it won't be necessary to change anything, with regard to underwear and silverware!"

"You're an admirable little wife! You're not going to go to lunch in that dress?"

"Certainly not," she replied, smiling. "But it's nice, all the same, to have thought about it first!"

Women always take a long time to get dressed, but the presence of a man, especially when that man is their lover and circumstances have kept them apart for a few days, makes them lose the notion of time completely. That is why Baillargal's companion was very astonished to see her watch, deposited on the nightstand, marking two o'clock when the substitution of her costume was still in its initial phase. Charlotte was dispatched to see Madame Brindolle in order to have some food sent over from the hotel kitchens; thus the cottage dining room was inaugurated.

The former Virginie Lauria listened attentively to all the recommendations that her lover made. To the explanation of the religious sentiments of the La Mourtardie family, which it was necessary to be careful to avoid shocking, Valentine replied that she had always been very devout and that, but for opposition from her parents, she would surely have become a nun.

A volley of whip-cracks and the muffled sound of a vehicle announced the return of Polydore, who asked for permission to feed some hay to his horses before departing again for La Moutardie.

A few minutes before five o'clock, the punctilious servant informed them that he was ready. Baillargal came out first, preceding "his lady," who had put on an extremely somber costume in the best and most sober taste. On the ring-finger of her left hand, which she was preparing to cover with a white glove, there was a thick band of yellow gold.

During the journey, Alcée Baillargal reminded his mistress several times over that Blancadet was passing him off as his cousin, and that, in consequence, she was the blind man's cousin by marriage.

' "Understood: I'm cousin Valentine," she said, as Polydore got a grip on his horses, in order to make an arrival worthy of his reputation as an experienced holder of reins.

The introductions were rapidly made. Beginning with cousin Victor, "cousin Valentine" embraced the entire La Moutardie family in succession, on whom she made the best impression. After dinner, the Comtesse told the journalist how glad she was to have made the acquaintance of Madame

Baillargal, "a Parisienne so full of spirit and intelligence that she was so well able to adapt herself to poor provincial people."

Baillargal accepted all these compliments without blinking, and on seeing his mistress play the part of an honest woman with so much perfection he said to himself that in the more-or-less grandiose dramatic performance that is life, the roles are sometimes very poorly distributed; he wondered what the fundamental rules might have been of the pre-established harmony that had spurred the present Valentine into the joyous path of the demi-monde rather than the more serious and more considered road of family and maternity.

Cécilia and Valentine were sitting side by side on a sofa, one as brunette as the other was blonde, and was allowing his philosophical thoughts to run on, trying to grasp the essential differences that might exist between the two young women, when Madame de La Moutardie whispered to him: "One might think they were two sisters, wouldn't one?"

The journalist's mistress took perfect account of the effect that she was producing; from time to time she looked at her lover, and her eyes revealed all the intimate happiness she experienced at receiving marks of deference and respect from the man she loved.

Yielding to the insistent pleas of the Comte and Comtesse, the Baillargal household promised to come to La Moutardie every day with "cousin Victor," and when his clients decided to return to Ilderon, Polydore had been waiting for more than an hour with his whip balanced on his right thigh, ready to depart.

XVI

Victor Blancadet applied himself to paying court according to the most orthodox Ilderonian rituals. Every day, he offered a bouquet to his fiancée, which, according to the perfumes it exhaled, revealed the flowers it contained. On Sundays, the Comtesse also received the homage of "the adornment of renewal," as she referred poetically to the products of the boutique-owner recommended by Maître Des Échinettes.

While Valentine kept company with the Comtesse and Monsieur de La Moutardie confided to Baillargal all the attempts made to cure the strange paralysis of the optic nerves that was the sole cause of Cécilia's blindness, there were, on the afternoons of the already-blossoming spring, long walks in the park, every tree of which was an old friend to the young woman, who introduced them to her fiancé as they passed by.

They stopped at the foot of an oak; Blancadet listened to the description of it that the poor blind woman gave to him, and there was so much fervor and love in her confident admiration of nature that he wondered whether, by rendering sight to her, he might not be taking away the illusion of that external world, which the charitable and pious imagination of her parents made so magnificent and glorious for her.

With regard to the oak of which she said that it "rose up proudly toward the sky," he told her a legend that he had once encountered in the course of his reading.

"One day, the trees took fright at the equality in which they had lived since the commencement of the ages; they made the decision to give themselves a king. One by one, they examined the entitlements of each of them to wear that crown, and it was successively offered to the olive-tree, the fig-tree, the vine and a number of others; all of them, either out of dread or modesty, refused it. It was then that the trees thought of addressing themselves to the oak. He received them when a great wind was blowing, and, after the observation was made that his stature did not bend before the efforts of the tempest, he accepted the title of Majesty. Immediately, the mistletoe attached itself to his body and hoisted itself up to its top. Since then, the oak has nourished that parasite—but the oak would not be a veritable king if he had no courtiers."

Further on, in a grove of secular elms, Blancadet, evoking classical memories, related how, at the first chords of the lyre of Orpheus, mourning the lost Eurydice, a forest of elms had suddenly emerge from the ground; and every evening, as, it appears, the lovers of the land of Plato and Aspasia used to do, the fiancés tore a leaf of a plane-tree, of which each kept half, and the next day, on meeting one another again, they put the two halves together again, to restore the wholeness of the leaf.

On another occasion, before a bush of roses, the degree of expansion of which Cécilia could judge by the scent each one expired, he told her a tale that seemed to have been born for her in the imagination of an old Oriental story-teller.

"A very rich and very powerful king had a son, to whom the fairies, all present at his crib, by a singular caprice, for he received a division of the rarest and most precious gifts, refused that of sight. Ta-Julmuluk, the blind child, grew up in the darkness of his eyes, and all the attempts made to render him sight were futile, even though his father summoned to the Palace the most renowned physicians and magicians in his empire. Ta-Julmuluk was soon a handsome and robust young man, and his infirmity was all the more cruel, for he would have been a worthy successor to his father, whose sole heir he was.

"One day, an old man whom no one knew asked to be received by the prince in order to make a request. Immediately introduced, he asked Ta-Julmuluk to distance himself from everyone else, because he wanted to speak to him in private. Ta-Julmuluk satisfied the old man's desire, who, as soon as they were alone, said: 'Prince, it is up to you alone to dissipate the night that seals your eyelids. Will you have faith in my words if I confide my secret to you?'

"'But who are you, old man?' Ta-Julmuluk asked.

"'What does it matter, Prince? If you want to give me a name, call me Hope; it is the one that my sister Bakawali[14] gave me on the day of our separation, a long time ago. I was your age then, and now, if you were not blind, you would see that my hair is white.'

---

[14] Bakawali is one of the familiar names given to the white night-blooming cactus-flower *Epiphyllum oxypetalum*.

'I will do as you wish. Speak, old man,' said Ta-Julmuluk.

"And the old man said: 'Prince, will you consent to go with me far from the earth? Oh, have no fear; I shall not take you to Hell. It's on high, beyond the clouds, near the sun. But first, Prince, is your heart free of love? For it's necessary that you marry Bakawali. She is blind, like you. She is very beautiful and young, even though she is my sister. I have grown old on the earth; in the land where I left Bakawali, time is immobile and no hours chime. Bakawali is so beautiful that a magician wanted her to become his wife, but Bakawali did not love the magician and she rejected him; then, to avenge himself, the magician took the soul from Bakawali's eyes; immediately, night fell on those eyes, and all the children born at that moment on the earth were condemned to blindness in their eyes and those of their descendants who were born in every corresponding epoch.

"'At the same time, however, the magician said to Bakawali: *Bakawali, He who governs the worlds, while permitting me to punish you for your disdain, has ordered me to tell you that you are free to choose a spouse among the mortals who have been similarly struck by blindness. You may go, hand in hand with him, to find the soul of your eyes, which I have hidden in the mysterious bosom of a flower, in the heart of a rose lost in a field of roses as vast as the immensity. Thus, light will be returned to you, Bakawali, to your spouse and to all the terrestrial victims of the anger you have unleashed.*

"'Then, in order that time should not fade Bakawali's beauty, it was me who came to earth to seek a spouse for her—but not one of the blind men I have encountered thus far has had faith in my words, and not one has wanted to follow me.'

"'I will follow you, old man,' said Ta-Julmuluk.

"'And you will marry Bakawali?'

"'I will marry Bakawali.'

"Immediately, Ta-Julmuluk felt himself lifted through the air, and a few moments later, the old man who was holding him by the hand said: 'This is Bakawali's dwelling.'

"Ta-Julmuluk and Bakawali were married; Bakawali, having become Ta-Julmuluk's wife, found the soul of her eyes asleep in the petals of the rose lost in the field of roses as vast as the immensity, and her husband immediately recovered his sight, as did all the blind people struck by the anger of the evil magician."

"Alas, why are these beautiful legends only legends?" sighed Cécilia, pressing herself to her fiancé's bosom.

"You would be Bakawali and I would be Ta-Julmuluk," Blancadet replied, kissing the young woman's forehead. "Cécilia..." He stopped, and resumed: "Mademoiselle Cécilia..."

"Are you not going to be my husband? Why not call me Cécilia, like my mother and my father?" She added, in a lower voice: "Like all those who love me?"

"I love you, Cécilia!" And Blancadet repeated those words: "I love you...I love you!" in order not to let slip the secret that he had sworn only to confess to his wife. What joy would he not have felt at that moment, however, in crying out to the unfortunate young woman: "It is not in the heart of a rose that the soul of your eyes resides! I have found it in the depths of a crucible, and I shall put it in your wedding-basket!"

The voice of the Comtesse, calling her daughter, dissipated their vertigo, and they slowly made their way back to the château.

Valentine had completely conquered Madame de La Moutardie, who never ceased to question her about the customs honored in Parisian society.

"It's just that here, we're in an almost barbaric land," sighed the Comtesse, whose parents had lived for a long time in the vicinity of Toulouse.

With a very good grace, Baillargal's companion gave the most elaborate details of the society to which she "belonged by birth and by marriage." Boldly, she cited the names collected in the *Guirlandes Aristocratiques* woven on page two of the *Écho Plaintif*, for the vanity of the authentic Greats of the Earth and the bourgeois who had entered into the quarry where ancestors are honorably depicted by large sacks stuffed with coins.

Victor Blancadet, who had observed her very attentively during the first few days, could not believe his ears, for, after all, Baillargal was only a journalist; he remembered his quasi-confession of financial embarrassment and the urgency with which he had made the three thousand-franc bills that he had given him on the eve of their departure disappear into his pocket. The conduct of the young and charming Charlotte, who was brought to La Moutardie almost every day and who seemed more like a confidante than a chambermaid, also surprised him slightly. Then, he told himself that perhaps his present state of mind was making him see things in the wrong light, and he ended up finding cousin Valentine a "very great lady"—which sufficiently explained the familiarity of her relationship with her soubrette.

She it was, at any rate, who was charged with choosing the gifts and instructing the Ilderon jeweler in favor of whom Maître Des Échinettes had recommended "in the name of local commerce," whom it was necessary not to offend by going directly to Paris for the objects of luxury over whose prices it was customary not to haggle.

At the café, Alcée Baillargal had himself introduced by the notary to Dr. Abicolose, one of Ilderon's physicians. That black-clad practitioner, coiffed in an immutable top hat, had a soul less austere than his severe mourning-dress suggested, and it was not without a certain emotion that he found himself in the presence of a man from Paris—the Paris where he had spent his own mad and interminable youth, and where, with a patience that his family had not always shared, he had waited for years and years for his value to be recognized in the form of the parchment thanks to which he could ply the scalpel and order pharmaceutical mortars to triturate the most improbable potions.

Strict justice requires it to be said that Dr. Abicolose did not abuse either the trenchancy of the blade or the heroism of drugs; he was an enthusiast of natural medicine and baths seems to him to be an quasi-universal panacea; he was the man who, three years before, a few days after his installation, had revolutionized Ilderon by specifying biweekly baths in a prescription that the patient had naturally taken to the pharmacist. The laboratory had been so troubled, in the person of its learned tenant, that the stuffed crocodiles had fallen from the ceiling on to the counter and the bottles had changed color in vomiting forth their alcoholic serpents.

That was for Dr. Abicolose immediate celebrity, almost glory, and his colleagues talked scornfully about the "newcomer who did not hesitate to employ the most scandalous means to cultivate renown." The former bohemian of the Latin Quarter, whom the approach of his fortieth year was causing to glimpse the necessities of life, did not stop at that first success, and in spite of the epithet "aquatic" that the envious hurled at him, he made a specialty of all reputedly incurable conditions. The Comte de La Moutardie did not fail to summon him to see his daughter, but in spite of all his effort, corroborated by determined hydrotherapy, he had not achieved any result.

It was in his capacity as Cécilia's physician that Dr. Abicolose interested Baillargal. After a long conversation alimented by the Latin Quarter and its delights, the "fortunate Parisian" and the ex-student were old comrades, and the doctor did not have to be begged to extend himself on Mademoiselle de La Moutardie's case, while opening various parentheses, one of which informed Baillargal that Maître Des Échinettes was the widowed Madame Brindolle's lover.

That same evening, the journalist reported to Blancadet verbatim the words that had emerged from the mouth of the celebrated Abicolose: "I share, in every point, the opinion emitted by the unanimity of the men of the Art who have examined the patient: Mademoiselle de La Moutardie is afflicted by a double paralysis of the optic nerves. Her eyes function marvelously, but, having no communication with the brain, labor entirely in vain. In brief, Mademoiselle de La Moutardie's eyes are total strangers to her; the thread of visual consciousness is severed, and God alone could reconnect it."

"God? Indeed! But me too!" cried Blancadet. "Oh, what joy, my dear friend! What happiness is mine! Just now, I was contemplating Cécilia's eyes, and it was as if a sharp blade entered my heart at the thought that it would be necessary to deliver those blue eyes, of an indescribable azure, to the surgeon's knife: but their heaven is no lie! Cécilia's beautiful eyes are good! My Cécilia…!"

And, allowing himself to be carried away by the Muse, in a lyrical flight that brought Valentine and Charlotte running from the next room, he proclaimed: "I shall give you my heart and render you sight!"

He calmed down and became blind again, in order to talk about a trip to Paris required by the imperious need to see his notary, to put his affairs in order and to obtain the documents indispensable to the celebration of his marriage.

He offered a superb solitaire to "cousin Valentine" and asked permission to take her husband away for two or three days, thinking that such a short absence was not worth the fatigue of a long and taxing journey.

Baillargal's companion readily understood Blancadet's desire to go without her, and she thought it very wise to remain in Ilderon, leaving it until later to go to Paris to buy clothes.

The La Moutardie family, in full dress, augmented by a respectable number of relatives invited to a very ceremonious dinner, watched the departure of Blancadet and his faithful cousin. Also on the platform was Maître Des Échinettes—and, as if by chance, Madame Brindolle came to stand beside him.

From the Gare d'Austerlitz, less elegant and more somber than her younger sister at the Quai d'Orsay, Blancadet had himself taken directly to the Rue du Sabre-de-l'Abbé.

Madame Benoît enquired as to the health of her tenant, whom she was astonished to see escorted by the journalist.

Equipped with his door-key, Victor Blancadet tried in vain to get into his home, the prudent Célestin having obviously forgotten to draw the bolt. He rang, rang again, and provoked a rightful carillon that lasted several minutes, after which Célestin's voice was heard howling: "Will you stop shattering my eardrums? I'll help you—wait!"

He unblocked the door, which he opened wide, and could not suppress a cry of fright on perceiving is master, who questioned him severely regarding his attire, by no means suggestive of an early riser. "What? It's eleven o'clock and you're not up yet?"

"It's just that...when Monsieur isn't here, I take advantage of it to reflect on ameliorations to bring to Monsieur's service..."

"Do you need to be in bed to reflect?"

"I've often heard Monsieur say to Monsieur the optician that the recumbent position is the best one for the functioning of the brain."

That scientific excuse soothed Blancadet's anger. "All right, then! Put your coat on and go fetch me the optician."

Célestin did not need the order to be repeated, and left, agitating his legs to go more rapidly and his arms to introduce them into his coat-sleeves.

It was a matter of constructing a pair of spectacles that would allow Cécilia to see. Blancadet had drawn a plan, which he desired to submit to his optician, a very intelligent man and an excellent adviser. The skillful artisan made a few objections of detail, and then declared the apparatus imagined by Blancadet easy to construct. The principle remained the same, in fact, and it was all the easier to obtain the lightness appropriate to a woman's spectacles because the lenses, only playing a purely decorative role, could be as thin as the rigidity of the crystal permitted.

Blancadet gave the optician a small ingot of assagitator with which to forge two frames, because he wanted to have two pairs of spectacles, one of which would be fitted with a special mechanism permitting contact to be made by a simple pressure at the articulation of the branches. It was necessary, in fact, that Cécilia not attribute the recuperation of sight to some diabolical power—that the operation should be credited to divine intervention.

The nuptial ceremony lent itself admirably to the realization of Blancadet's project, desirous of not troubling the young woman's soul. On a more or less plausible pretext, he would ask Cécilia to make use of the spectacles, and, at the foot of the altar, at the moment when the priest proceeded with the benediction, by means of a simple gesture of the thumb and index finger, he would press the switch, and the established contact would cause the miracle to burst forth, which the priest would hasten to signal to the delighted faithful.

He would, of course, profit from the occasion to render sight to himself, and the La Moutardie church would not take long to become a place of pilgrimage for all blind people desirous of modifying their condition. Miraculous spectacles would be sold there, and the humble servant of the little parish would find himself at the head of a first-rate commercial enterprise.

Blancadet was focusing too much on Cécilia to be able to savor the joy of the situation fully, and he judged it unnecessary to put too much pressure on Baillargal's discretion by explaining in detail the secret reasons for his manner of procedure. The journalist, in any case, was exhibiting an exemplary docility and testified by his services that he was able to render Blancadet an inexhaustible good will. He took charge of all the preliminary measures with regard to the notary, in order to give Blancadet the leisure to supervise the construction of the spectacles and to perfect an improved eupantophone that he wanted to give to his wife.

Twice forty-eight hours was sufficient to conclude both these operations. Alcée Baillargal even had time to go take possession of the apartment chosen by his mistress; he found it admirably distributed and hastened to have some visiting cards printed with mention of his new address.

He called in at the Chancery, where, by the most fortunate of chances, one of his friends was employed in the office responsible for the preparation of decrees regarding changes of name and additions thereto. The friend promised to take violent action against the administrative slowness that is one of the principal guarantees of good social function , and promised to issue with the shortest possible delay the decree authorizing Victor Blancadet to follow his patronymic with that of La Moutardie, along with the title of Comte.

Blancadet was very happy to learn the result of this step—not that he accorded the slightest importance personally to the *particule* and noble titles, but he told himself that, since he was to become a Comte, it was preferable that he figured in that quality on the certificate of marriage, the date of which had been fixed for the twenty-first of June.

The return to Ilderon was completed without the slightest incident. Blancadet resumed his courtship at the exact point at which he had left it four days previously, for Maître Des Échinettes had explained to him many times that protocol would not suffer the slightest solution of continuity.

The fiancé would have enjoyed perfect an unalloyed happiness had he not been preoccupied with the means to employ to convince Cécilia to put on the spectacles that he kept constantly next to his heart, in the interior pocket of his frockcoat; often, to assure him that they were still there, his fingers palpated the copper case covered in morocco leather in which they were contained.

In the course of a dinner at the Château de La Moutardie, there was talk of predictions and fortune-tellers. "Cousin Valentine" confessed that she was a little superstitious and that she had frequently consulted a remarkable somnambulist, whose predictions were always realized with absolute precision.

In spite of the intransigence of her Christian faith, the Comtesse regretted that Ilderon did not possess a pythoness, whom she would have been happy to interrogate about the future of "her children." "What harm is there in that, my friend," she replied to Monsieur de La Moutardie, who offered, in the name of religion, a few timid observations on diviners and sorcerers.

Blancadet sided ardently with his imminent mother-in-law, for the new element of the somnambulist put an end to all the difficulties in the execution of his plans; it was simply a matter of putting the Comtesse in the presence of the somnambulist, whose spirits it would be elementary to ensure, by means of a few louis.

Unfortunately, Madame de La Moutardie did not want to make the journey to Paris, and all attempts made in that direction under various pretexts failed completely. The resource remained of bringing the somnambulist to Ilderon. Baillargal was secretly charge with that mission and left for Paris with that aim. The proposition of a provincial trip with guaranteed minimum receipts was immediately accepted in principle by the seeress; she put the journalist in touch with her husband, who was in sole charge of "the commercial aspect," in order to settle the details of the displacement.

The husband and manager of the placid lady visited by the beyond asked for a week's delay in order to have posters put up in Ilderon and acquaint the public "via the press and other means" of the coming of "Madame Chypra, an extralucid subject accredited by all the sovereign Courts of the entire world."

Three days later, multicolored flyers informed the Ilderonian population of the imminent arrival of "Madame Chypra of Paris." The movement of curiosity was very enthusiastic, and the Comtesse de La Moutardie was not far from seeing the event a something Providential. The somnambulist became the sole topic of her conversations with cousin Valentine, and she was the first person to inscribe her name in the register of consultations deposited at the desk of the Hôtel de l'Esturgeon. Madame Brindolle, out of deference to hr clientele, was content to close the list.

The great day arrived, coinciding with the May fair; an animation bordering on disorder reigned in the Hôtel de l'Esturgeon; Madame Brindolle was so busy that she scarcely lent an ear to the compliments addressed to her, as was his habit, by Maître Alcindor Des Échinettes.

Madame Chypra's husband, in a rutilant Swiss costume with short trousers, bare calves, buckled shoes and a wig powdered with frost, did the honors of the waiting room installed in the executioner's room, the room next door, previously occupied by Blancadet, serving as a consultation room. The Comtesse de La Moutardie, due to open the session by virtue of her order number, had been introduced into the latter, and was waiting for the seeress, who, in the redoubt reserved for amateur photographers, was addressing the final invocations to her familiar spirits. It was there that Baillargal handed her the two pairs of spectacles that the Comtesse would soon carry away.

The interview was quite short, for the spirits spoke with a remarkable precision and clarity.

"You have a daughter who is blind since birth; she is the fiancée of a man still young, very rich, full of qualities and virtues..."

The spirits appeared to make an effort, and Madame Chypra continued: "That man has lost his sight in an accident...he is blind, like his fiancée, whose name in Cécilia..."

The Comtesse trembled in every limb as she listened to the somnambulist, who punctuated her speech with bizarre gestures, undoubtedly cabalistic.

"But sight will be rendered to Monsieur Victor Blancadet, who will be called Monsieur Victor Blancadet, Comte de La Moutardie... Sight will also be rendered to his wife... I see the nuptial ceremony... The priest is blessing them... I see the hand of God touching the spectacles worn by each of the spouses... Cécilia utters a cry: she can see! The husband cries out in his turn: he can see too. The miracle has occurred! The celestial will is manifest!"

Exhausted by emotion, the Comtesse had fallen to her knees, unconscious of her surroundings. Madame Chypra calmly placed the two pairs of spectacles in her hands, and, drawing away after having waited for a few minutes, continued:

"I see an Angel with red, green and yellow wings quitting the heavens... He descends... He approaches a woman at prayer... He says to her: 'Poor mother, God has been touched by your dolor...take these objects...thanks to them, a miracle will be accomplished...' The Angel with the red, green and yellow wings vanishes into the skies. That woman at prayer, that dolorous mother, is Cécilia's mother. It is you, Madame."

"Me? Me?" stammered Madame de La Moutardie.

"In your hands, the Angel has placed two objects," Madame Chypra continued, gradually drawing nearer and multiplying her bizarre gestures, and suddenly crying: "Spectacles! Spectacles! The Angel has put spectacles in your hand!"

As nothing could extract Madame de La Moutardie from the quasi-prostration in which she was plunged, however, the somnambulist thought it desirable to have her husband intervene, and it was that carnivalesque individual who made the Comtesse breathe the smelling salts resuscitative of positive life.

Outside of her ecstasy, Madame Chypra was a woman like any other woman; she therefore found herself obliged to address herself to the spirits again in order to give Madame de La Moutardie an explanation of the presence in hr hands of two pairs of spectacles. With an inexhaustible good will, the spirits put themselves at Madame Chypra's disposal and answered all her questions.

The Comtesse learned that Heaven was disposed to work a miracle in favor of her daughter and son-in-law, but, the Eternal having a horror of preliminary ostentation, it was essential to maintain absolute secrecy regarding what had just occurred. Madame de La Moutardie swore to limit herself to supplying the mysterious spectacles to Cécilia and Victor

Blancadet, without giving either of them the slightest explanation. The Almighty would do the rest.

Cécilia obeyed her mother "blindly." She did not ask for the shadow of an explanation. As for Blancadet, he immediately traded the spectacles offered to him by his imminent mother-in-law for the ones he habitually wore. The Comte de La Moutardie, a model husband, did not exist with regard to his wife; having a chronic approval of her slightest actions, he did not even seek to discover their motives. Among members of the family and friends, no one made the slightest allusion that might draw attention to the unfortunate lot of the fiancés.

The Comtesse attempted to dissimulate her fever, which became increasingly devouring as the date of the marriage approached; in any case, preparations of every kind absorbed the greater part of her activity and she delegated to cousin Valentine the care of installing the bridal chamber in Paris.

While retaining, for the continuation of his work, the apartment in the Rue du Sabre-de-l'Abbé, Blancadet had rented nearby a vast first-floor apartment whose windows overlooked the Luxembourg gardens. He had opened an unlimited credit at his furnisher's, and that businessman, in the name of an art as modern as it was expensive, was in the process of putting his most meritorious efforts into methodically blackening the carte blanche he had been given. A staff not merely independent of the one in the Rue Sabre-de-l'Abbé but completely ignorant of its existence, was ready to enter service.

Everything was going marvelously; nothing had betrayed the imposture of the voluntary blind man; Baillargal's friend had kept his promise, and matters were proceeding at the Chancery with so much rapidity that not only had the decree authorizing the addition of the name and the title of Comte been issued by the time the banns were published, but all the rectifications had been made in the registers of Civil Estate.

It was, therefore, between Victor Blancadet, Comte de La Moutardie, and Cécilia de La Moutardie that there was a promise of marriage, realizable, in accordance with Ilderonian habit, on the third consecutive day of the second dominical publication. Everything was ready; the notaries had drafted the contract for validation by the civil act, considered as an administrative formality that it would have been in rank bad taste to dress with any pomp, the marriage being spiritual in essence and in consequence of purely ecclesiastical jurisdiction.

The holy demands of the priest, and the confession most of all, with its inquisitorial research, had revolted Blancadet at first; then, either by virtue of becoming accustomed or simply out of pity for the soul of the curé of La Moutardie, who merited so completely the forbearance of "forgive them, for they know not what they do," he had become a devotee of such fervent appearance that at the traditional diner offered to the servant of the parish, the curé declared that God would never find a better occasion to work a miracle—which was the unanimous opinion of those present.

XVII

To the great satisfaction of astronomers, who have traced a schedule for the stars from which even comets do not permit themselves to deviate, the sun was kind enough to enter the house of Cancer at the regulation moment, and immediately, the scientist charged with the surveillance of the heavens hoisted a red and green flag over the roof of the Paris Observatoire, which, for that year, authorized in our country the presence of summer from the twenty-first of June to the twenty-third of September.

In the Midi, where nothing is exaggerated, not even the hot season, the sun generally takes advantage of that date to attempt to show its vigor, and, being unable to remain indifferent to an event as important as Victor Blancadet's marriage, it decided to rise over Ilderon magnificent and devoid of veils, leaving to the bell-ringer at La Moutardie church, who had climbed to the top of the bell-tower in order to be the first to perceive it, the care of announcing a radiant day to the château.

In spite of having nothing modern about his ideas, the Comte, as much because of his legendary generosity as the pity inspired by Mademoiselle Cécilia, was greatly loved in the neighborhood, and the population of La Moutardie never missed an opportunity to testify its sympathy to him. For several days, an entirely abnormal animation had reigned in the area, in which everyone—men, women and children—had been laboring either to decorate the church or prepare for the strewing of the flowers.

Everyone who was anyone, the authentic and usurped nobility, which excessive antiquity had caused it to lose its rank, and the overly recent one that had not yet had time to acquire it, Ilderonians and the shifting holders of neighboring fiefs, had been invited to the marriage of the heiress of La Moutardie. During the morning of the twenty-first of June there was, on the not-very-numerous and poorly-maintained roads of the region, a picturesque procession of coaches and berlins, in which the social macadam appeared to be on the move, under the respectful wide eyes of locals in their Sunday best—for, obedient to a very pardonable sentiment of pride, the Administration had given orders for the peaceable functionaries of the Republic to put on a good show before the "*ancien régime*."

As was customary, the signature of the contract had taken place the day before, followed by the civil ceremony, only involving the presence of the witnesses and a few intimates; the civil estate, represented by the Maire in person, in spite of the scorn attached to the status of the lay authority that he represented, appointed himself the spokesman for all the inhabitants in expressing the most ardent wishes for the happiness of Monsieur and Madame Victor Blancadet de La Moutardie, whom he had just united in the name of the Law, while awaiting the religious consecration.

The latter demanded all the pomp that the Catholic church borrows from Satan, with so much success, in solemn circumstances.

The château, naturally, was in revolution, and since dawn, a band of cooks and scullions had take possession of the servants' parlor in order to prepare, under the martial direction of the widowed Madame Brindolle, a lavish lunch, composed according to the most southern traditions of l'Esturgeon.

At nine o'clock, the first rig drew up in front of the perron, and there was an almost uninterrupted succession of vehicles, which seemed a retrospective review of carriage-design, in which the people seemed to be as old as the equipment.

As protocol requited, the groom was one of the last to arrive, and Madame Brindolle saw, perhaps for the last time, the silver fish of l'Esturgeon quivering over Polydore's left ear. Cousin Valentine being Victor Blancadet's only female relative, it was on her arm that he made his entrance to the drawing room where almost all the guests were already gathered.

Conscientiously, Blancadet shook the hands that grasped his own and answered the innumerable compliments lavished upon him with thanks. One of the Comtesse's sisters led him into the room adjacent to the dining room where the wedding basket was displayed; she called him her "dear nephew," and gave him a detailed description of all the gifts, guiding his fingers as far as the "magnificent" gold jewelry that she had offered. Blancadet, his eyes riveted to the manufacturer's hallmark, revealing the eight-four grams of silver that the dozen sets of cutlery contained, showed himself no less grateful to "the most generous of aunts."

With the always-deplored but always carefully-observed belatedness, the bride made her entrance to the drawing room on her father's arm; very upright in her ivory satin dress with sharp pleats, a bouquet of orange-blossom in her hair and another on her corsage, she came forward, veiled in white, smiling, to joining her groom, he kissed her fingertips. Then she received the kisses of a few friends preoccupied with not causing any disarray to their mutual costumes, and the compliments of everyone.

In one corner, a distant relative, who had turned the family spirit of observation to his advantage, remarked the presence of spectacles on Cécilia's nose. He made his neighbors party to the discovery; some criticized the innovation sternly while others approved of it loudly, estimating that Cécilia was right to imitate her husband, who was wearing spectacles.

The Comtesse, naturally, was very emotional, and Alcée Baillargal, her escort, tried in vain to calm her; during the journey from the château to the church, which was made on foot over flowers thickly strewn like a litter, which caught on the trains of dresses, she could not help saying: "I have a presentiment that something is going to happen..."

"And that something will be the best thing in the world, Comtesse," the journalist assured her, determined not to betray his friend Blancadet.

"Yes, yes! But you haven't seen the somnambulist? She hasn't told you that a great event is in preparation?"

"I admit that I have not," confessed Baillargal, without any false shame.

"A heavenly intervention is due to occur..."

"Where?"

"Here, in the church, during the mass..."

"Impossible!" said Blancadet's accomplice, in perfectly acted surprise.

They went into the church. The Comtesse interrupted her confidences in order to plunge her fingers into a rococo font which looked as if it had once been a goldfish tank.

The guests, the first to arrive being the last, as in the kingdom of heaven, gentlemen on one side and ladies on the other, formed a hedge, with their backs to the green shrubs that the Moutardian artists had set up between the door and the railings of the choir. To add to the splendor of that decoration, the Maire's "Demoiselles" had perched in the high branches of juniper-trees a host of blackbirds and thrushes that had been naturalized for too long to be able to mingle their songs with the throbbing chords of the organ played by a blind man, the master of the Chapelle, Diezolotti, brought to Ilderon specially for the occasion.

Cousin Valentine, in a sumptuous brocade dress in which gold was dominant, with a majesty borrowed from the theatrical queens that she had had the opportunity to see, guided the groom, whose impeccable black suit attracted the admiration of local fanatics of tailoring. Immediately afterwards, while the organ exasperated itself in roaring modulations, came Cécilia, on her father's arm, the most beautiful and the most charming of the most beautiful and charming brides.

The bride and groom were installed on the two red velvet armchairs prepared for them; Cousin Valentine and Cousin Baillargal took their place to the right and Cécilia's father and the Comtesse to the left.

As surreptitiously as possible, Blancadet made sure that the flexible extremities of the branches of the spectacles had been properly introduced into his wife's ears, and observed with joy that his mother-in-law had had the delicate attention to fix Cécilia's spectacles as he had done for himself.

The critical moment approached; the priest, a capitulary canon of the diocese of Sarlat, an authentic and decrepit La Moutardie who had claimed the honor of blessing the spouses, emerged from the sacristy amid a cohort of the children of the choir, and, while he proceeded with the preliminary operations, Blancadet took off his gloves in order to have freedom of movement. With a distracted ear he listened to the ancient canon quavering a long sequence of amiable phrases flattering the La Moutardie family and himself. He darted a rapid glance at the Comtesse, sunk in a prayer in which, no doubt, Heaven was adjured to fulfill Madame Chypra's predictions. The Comte was praying with the same fervor as cousin Valentine, and the remainder of the audience ought to be devoted to the habitual and exclusive practice of meditation. There was, therefore, no one but Alcée Baillargal capable of perceiving anything, and there was absolutely no need to conceal anything from him.

The fossilized canon passed the rings and, with his eyes upraised to the heavens, he lifted his arm painfully, pulverizing the ritual words between his gums and the three of four teeth remaining to him. Swiftly, Blancadet slipped the gold circlet on to his wife's ring finger, and his hand rose up; the widely-spaced thumb and index finger squeezed Cécilia's temples simultaneously...

A strident cry cut through the heavy belching of the organ, followed by heart-rending appeals: "Maman! Maman!"

The Comtesse fell to the floor in a faint. Before Monsieur de La Moutardie and the canon had had time to make a movement, Blancadet seized his wife in his arms, crying: "Lord, Lord, you have returned my sight!"

A lighting-flash of mystic madness struck the audience; the green shrubs were overturned; the chairs, dislocated, strewed the ground with their debris, and all the guests, so correct a few moments before, moved like a horde of fanatics, howling at the miracle.

During a moment of calm, Cécilia's voice was heard, continuing to call for her mother. Aided by his mistress, Baillargal had lifted up the Comtesse, who was coming round.

Distraught, Monsieur de La Moutardie was repeating "Lord! Lord!" incessantly, and not budging from his prie-dieu.

The canon remained kneeling in the place where he had fallen; the curé of La Moutardie, clad in his sacerdotal vestments—for he was getting ready to celebrate the mass—ran to the pulpit with such ardor that he stumbled on the steps and had scarcely got up again than he started shouting: "Kneel! Kneel!"

The habit of passivity got the upper hand; the faithful, panicked momentarily, prostrated themselves, and in the silence, Cécilia, now in her mother's arms, was heard saying: "Maman! Maman! There, in my head! A blow...a great blow...Maman! Maman! It seems to me that I'm touching you as I've never touched you before!"

"She can see! She can see" cried the Comtesse, fainting for a second time.

"Lord, Lord! Take my soul for the two miracles that you have just performed!" proposed Victor Blancadet, making his mother-in-law breathe a bottle of salts that a choirboy had gone to fetch from the sacristy.

In his pulpit, which resembled a gigantic font, the curé of La Moutardie was agitating like a man possessed for the greater glory of the striking double miracle that "the ineffable Father of all light" had just provoked. For twelve quarters of an hour, torrents of sacred eloquence poured over the immobile heads; each curbing theirs, Blancadet and Cécilia, their hands united, offered to God the first moments of the sight that he had deigned to give them.

In a final effort, the Curé was exhorting the members of the audience not to hesitate to address themselves to the Lord in case they had need of anything, when, from the height of the organ-loft, a tearful voice descended: "My God, don't forget me! Don't forget me! When there's sufficient for two, there's sufficient for three." It was the unfortunate Diezolotti, demanding his share of divine grace and invoking its distributive elasticity.

In the name of the discretion to which the Creature is bound relative to the Supreme Power, however, the orator pleaded with the organist to leave it to God to choose the opportune moment for a further miracle. Diezolotti murmured a timid protestation, which he doubtless judged blasphemous, for he returned to his keyboard to unleash a formidable Canticle of Actions and Graces, which voices formulate in a sequence of screeches free of any harmonious intention.

Breathless, his forehead and temples soaked with sweat, the curé of La Moutardie allowed the arms that had been furiously beating the measure of the thanks barked toward the fragile vault representative of Heaven to fall back again. With difficulty, he descended one by one the steps that linked him to firm ground, and, either out of forgetfulness or fatigue, went back to the sacristy without saying mass, which was, in any case, unnecessary to the sacrament administered to the spouses Blancadet de La Moutardie.

All the guests were due to partake of the lunch serve at the château; the wedding party had, however, to pass through the sacristy to complete the formalities of inscriptions and signatures.

Blancadet put his wife's arm beneath his own; with a simultaneous movement of impulsive affection, Madame de La Moutardie abandoned her cavalier to seize the left hand of her daughter while the Comte took possession of his son-in-law's right hand. That violation of protocol forced cousin Valentine to take Baillargal's arm. Like a flock of sheep momentarily dispersed by lightning, the audience grouped behind them.

The verger presented the register to the spouses and the witnesses, which he qualified as *ad hoc* with a solemn insistence, and, after a plea for the souls in Purgatory, the cortege, preceded by the curé of La Moutardie, headed for the château, to the frenetic acclamations of the population, who could not be distracted from ritual demonstrations of sympathy by the news of a double miracle.

On the threshold of the courtyard, three-quarters occupied by the large horseshoe of numerous tables carefully juxtaposed, Madame Brindolle prostrated herself before the "sacred witnesses of celestial intervention" and solicited the broadest indulgence for the meal, victim of the long delay and surely unworthy of the reputation of l'Esturgeon. In the midst of the general approval, Maître Alcindor Des Échinettes declared that miracles had to come before gastronomic enjoyment. Everyone sat down, at random, without paying any heed to the names written on the little cards placed on the artistically-folded napkins.

The first dishes circulated; the sight of the nourishment reawoke the sentiment of hunger and all the guests appeared to have forgotten the extraordinary event that had just occurred. Without even manifesting the slightest curiosity with regard to the "miraculized" couple, everyone began eating and drinking with the ardor that was the pride of every nuptial feast in Ilderonian territory.

As the emptiness of stomachs diminished, the action of jaws slowed down; a few words were exchanged to begin with, precursors of conversations that did not take long to turn to the strictly relevant subject of miracles.

A humanist who was something of a theologian made his neighbors party to various Latin names—*mirabilia, portenta, signa, prodigi, miracula*—all signifying miracles, which he defined as "works accomplished independently of the laws of nature." He spoke about the best-known miracles and observed that, since apostolic times, they had completely ceased to burst forth unexpectedly in the humble church of La Moutardie.

With an unaccustomed insistence, all gazes were fixed upon the couple incessantly invited to the work of the flesh, so shameful and so criminal when the civil and religious authorities have not regulated and sanctified its consummation.

Contrary to the habit of brides who have not benefited from a miracle on their wedding day, Cécilia was not blushing. She often raised her hands to her face and then, as if fearful of touching the frail spectacles, lowered them again to grope for the hands of her husband, and both of them, without exchanging a word, gazed at one another, sunk in a mutual contemplation of indefinable tenderness.

Suddenly, there was a great tumult outside, and Polydore, who was preparing for the honor of guiding the newlyweds' carriage while doubling in the servants' parlor, as Madame Brindolle's lookout, launched himself between the two rows of tables crying: "It's Monseigneur! It's Monseigneur!"

From a kind of diligence that had stopped outside the arch of the entrance, several priests labored to unpack, as carefully as possible, a violet mass in which the Bishop of Sarlat was recognized. A telegram had notified him of the double miracle that had occurred in his diocese, the most holy and the richest diocese in France, and he had hastened to come, resigning himself to allowing himself to be hoisted into the prehistoric vehicle charged with ensuring administrative transport from Ilderon railway station to La Moutardie.

The prelate's short legs ended up contriving a base adequate to sustain his immeasurably developed paunch and Monseigneur de Sarlat blinked his little eyes, which had remained singularly keen and malicious in a visage in which fat had abolished all shape.

Respectful of the letter of the hierarchical scale, the curé of La Moutardie folded his tall frame into a very low genuflection in order to hold out the aspergillum to his spiritual and temporal superior, which the latter agitated three times in a gesture of Episcopal blessing.

At the moment when Monseigneur penetrated into the courtyard, a strong odor of truffles arrived from the door leading to the kitchen, and it seemed for a moment that the perfume of the much-vaunted fungus was emanating from the very person of the dignitary of the Church.

Followed by his general staff of curates and abbes, the bishop advanced, brushing with his ring the lips of the guests who had left their places to come and form a double hedge for this passage. The majority, out of respect for their festival clothing, had spread their napkins on the ground in order to kneel down. Imitating the vulgar faithful, Blancadet and his wife had knelt down, and, as at the exit from the church, the Comtesse took her daughter's hand and Monsieur de La Moutardie took Blancadet's.

Monseigneur de Sarlat paused momentarily; several times he measured he distance separating the ground from his kneecaps; it must have appeared to him to be unbridgeable, for his lips had a slight pleat of bitterness at the corners; his little eyes trembled with malicious gleams, and, with an unctuous and hieratical gesture, he ordered "those whom he Lord had elected" to get up. In a slow, voluntarily monotonous and blank voice, he narrated the adventure of the "two blind men of Jericho," which was marvelously appropriate to the situation.

"Jesus came out of the city of Jericho, followed, as always by a large crowd; two blind men were sitting by the roadside in order to beg. At the noise in their vicinity they enquired as to its cause, and received the reply that it was Jesus of Nazareth passing by. Immediately they began crying with all their might: 'Jesus, son of David, have pity on us!' All the crowd heard them, and everyone expressed the desire, out of respect for the august person who was the their object, to put a stop to their reiterated clamors of 'Son of David, have pity on us!' When he condition and the plea of the mendicants had been observed by everyone, the Savior finally stopped and enquired in his turn what was happening, as if to prepare the crowd more fully for the double miracle that he was about to accomplish, to awaken its curiosity further and render it more attentive. Then he had them brought forth in order that each member of the audience had time to get into a good position to observe what was about to happen. Then he asked them what they wanted. Finally, everything being disposed, and on the response that they desired that sight be given to them, Jesus touched them, saying to them: 'See, your faith his saved you.' Immediately, they saw, and joined the crowd that was following him."

To the spouses Blancadet de La Moutardie who were the only ones standing in front of him, Monseigneur de Sarlat said: "Like the blind men of Jericho, your faith has saved you! You have asked the Lord for sight, and he has given you sight!"

From the crowd that was crammed beneath the coaching entrance and overflowing into the courtyard, a vice shouted: "Monseigneur! Monseigneur, have pity on me!" It was the organist Diezolotti again, who could not renounce his inclusion in the present miraculous promotion.

One of the priests, who had heard the musician's first request in the church, went to calm him down and make him hear the voice of reason.

The bishop resumed the exegesis of St. Matthew's gospel, to which he added the episode of the blind man of Jerusalem related by his evangelical colleague St. John, and was saying a few words about the "blind man of Bethsaida" when

Dr. Abicolose, cleaving through the crowd, arrived beside him.

The prelate drilled his blinking eyes into those of the representative of science, who immediately knelt down in order to have himself blessed.

"Monseigneur, I've been informed that God has just rendered sight to two blind persons; I want to place myself entirely at your disposal for all the medical and scientific observations useful to this celestial intervention, destined to be the glory and the wealth of the region..."

A handshake provoked by the bishop sealed the alliance of the two men, who scarcely knew one another.

"In the name of the Faith and the Church, I thank you, Monsieur le Docteur. I would indeed be grateful to you if you would draw up a rigorously exact sworn statement of the miraculous facts of which you are the enlightened and impartial witness. I suspend for you the sacred character of the man and the woman whom God had just touched with His own hand. Approach them, examine them. Far from committing a sacrilege, you will be agreeable to the Lord."

The ecclesiastical personnel present isolated the young couple as best they could from the crowd, behind whom Monsieur and Madame de La Moutardie remained. With Monseigneur's assent, Dr. Abicolose asked Baillargal, an expert in reportage, to take notes, and commenced his examination.

To the numerous questions asked by the man of the Art, Blancadet replied with a firm voice, while his young wife was only able to stammer monosyllables of affirmation or negation.

The physician called attention to the essential difference there was between "seeing" and "seeing again"; he remarked that a person blind from birth to whom sight has just been given had no notion of space, but when he asked Blancadet, only deprived of sight for eleven years, to make evaluations of the distance between objects he indicated to him, the latter took a malign pleasure in offering improbable figures—which caused

Dr. Abicolose to say that "everything is magnified in memory."

The spectacles adorning the noses of the miraculized individuals had, naturally, been noticed by the practitioner; he wanted to take account of the role they played. Blancadet took off his first, and, uttering a cry of alarm full of justice, replaced them precipitately before declaring that he could not see without them. The same experiment produced a similar result with Cécilia. "In my head everything has gone to sleep!" she stammered, while Dr. Abicolose turned the spectacles with the unusual branches over and over in his hairy hands. He asked the name of the optician who had supplied them.

Moved by piety, the Comtesse de La Moutardie was on the point of mentioning Madame Chypra, but as she had faith in the power of the somnambulist who had sworn her to secrecy, while reserving the confession of the sin of deceit to her deathbed, she gave the fictitious name of an optician whom she domiciled, at hazard, in the Rue de la Paix in Paris. Blancadet had no trouble providing a fictitious address for the manufacturer, whom he invented completely.

Very perplexed, Dr. Abicolose looked at Monseigneur de Sarlat, whose eyes shrank as they blinked more rapidly than usual. Blancadet, feigning a poignant emotion, took the spectacles from the physician's hand and replaced them on his wife's nose. Cécilia trembled in every limb, and to Dr. Abicolose, who interrogated her as to what she felt, she replied that she seemed to be waking up from a profound sleep.

"Why, since he wanted Cécilia to see, did the Good Lord impose these spectacles upon her? It's ugly for a woman!" murmured a voice behind Monseigneur's back.

Glad of the diversion, the bishop turned round and looked the author of the observation up and down severely. "Shut up, Mademoiselle!"

Cousin Valentine, the individual addressed, blushed deeply at that title, which the prelate had only applied to her out of gallantry, by virtue of her young and elegant appearance. Baillargal hid his face behind the sheets of paper on which he was scribbling his notes and Blancadet summoned up all his strength in order to remain impassive.

Monseigneur addressed Dr. Abicolose: "It is futile, Doctor, to try to penetrate the secrets of the Most High. God wanted to accomplish a miracle by means of spectacles; that was right. Let us bless him and thank him. Let us pray with all the fervor of our faith and our hearts. As for you, neophytes of sight, depart immediately for the Eternal City! The Holy Father, to whom I shall telephone, will receive you. In kissing his slipper, you will offer to God the most ardent testimony of our gratitude. Leave this very day! Leave without losing an hour!"

"Oh, my children, my children!" wailed the Comtesse.

"Mother, it will be our honeymoon voyage," Blancadet interceded. "I've already visited Italy. It's the most beautiful country in the world, and it will be more beautiful still when Cécilia has seen it."

Familial effusions of an indescribable tenderness followed, after which the bride withdrew, accompanied by her mother, who gave her the usual advice while helping her to change her dress. In his turn, Blancadet went to exchange his formal suit for a traveling costume.

It was nearly five o'clock when the two spouses were ready to leave. They had just enough time to get to Ilderon to take the express to Toulouse, from where they would set off for Rome.

The farewells were touching, and might even have been heart-rending without the presence of Monseigneur de Sarlat, who preached a sermon to the Comtesse on the resignation that a Christian mother ought to show on such an occasion.

After a final series of multiple kisses and hugs involving the young and old La Moutardies, cousin Baillargal, cousin Valentine, Madame Brindolle—who had insisted on closing the door of the coupé driven by Polydore herself—and little Charlotte, for whose curiosity her mistress reproached her in vain, the young couple received the Monseigneur's final benediction through the carriage window as he ordered the coachman to get to Ilderon station as quickly as possible.

The departure was effected without the slightest incident, as news of the miracle had not yet reached the station.

As Blancadet was congratulating himself on that, in Polydore's presence, the domestic said, in a tone of intense veneration: "Ah, one can say that Monsieur le Comte was lucky there—but we did, however, get past the drunkard."

"What drunkard?"

"Trinquebord, the correspondent of the *Gazette de Toulouse*. That individual divines what is happening for ten leagues around. He's come to La Moutardie to recount the glorious miracle in his own fashion. Oh, if Monsieur le Comte knew how they talk about God in that paper! The government ought not to permit such things. If Trinquebord had seen the carriage it would have been necessary to stop. Oh, it's not good not to be amiable with him! But he was drunk, as usual, and had gone to sleep in his cabriolet. Monsieur le Comte will understand that I didn't wake him up!"

"Thank you, my friend, thank you," said Blancadet, placing a few gold coins in Polydore's hand.

"May God conserve the sight of Monsieur le Comte, as well as Madame la Comtesse," said l'Esturgeon's coachman, gratefully. He asked for permission to kiss the hands of the newlyweds as he assisted them to climb into the compartment, of whose exclusive use they were assured all the way to Toulouse, as testified by the copper plaque hung up by the conductor of the train.

XVIII

The newlyweds' honeymoon rose into a cloudless sky, to remain there for an incalculable number of quarters. The next day, the Toulousian sun, filtering through the shutters of their room, had saluted them as man and wife, and during the day a telegram had taken the best of news to La Moutardie.

The journey to Rome, composed of short days and long nights, was a sequence of intoxications too intense to be mad. Cécilia only had eyes for her husband, and scarcely consented to dart a few glances at the world, which had, in any case, only existed for her for such a brief time.

In Marseilles, she reproached herself for not having given sufficient thought to Heaven, and expressed a desire to go to church. Blancadet, kneeling beside his wife, watched her pray, telling himself that he was the unknown but true object of veneration.

Before arriving in the Eternal City, Cécilia, by way of contrition, deprived herself of the sight of her spouse for an entire hour, and when she put the miraculous spectacles back on her nose it was to address a further explosion of gratitude to the Lord.

Their meeting with the Holy Father went very well.

When they presented themselves at the door of the Vatican, the concierge, who had not been alerted, thought he was dealing with two ordinary mystical lunatics and replied dryly that His Holiness was out. Blancadet laid siege to the holder of the pontifical cordon in order to get him to inform the competent authorities of the presence in Rome of the miraculized of La Moutardie announced by Monseigneur de Sarlat. A young pupil cardinal approached, exhibiting his exit pass; doubtless to make him laugh, the incredulous doorman told him the names and titles of the two visitors—but to the great astonishment of the guardian of the threshold, the young hopeful of the eminent purple raced away in quest of his superior, the curator of miracles and graces.

"My God, it's a gaffe! It's a gaffe! May God, forgive me!" moaned the concierge, desperately striking his head on Blancadet's feet, whose toes suffered considerably from that penitent demonstration.

The curator of miracles and graces arrived with the principal employees of his service; with all due regard to the beneficiaries of divine bounty, Blancadet and his companion were introduced into a vast study, the administrative severity of which was attenuated by the palliative discretion that envelops all things in elevated ecclesiastical circles.

From a mahogany sideboard, surmounted by a silver cross, the young secretary took a thin dossier, which he placed on his chief's desk. The curator of miracles and graces began by complimenting the objects of celestial distinction, and then read the report transmitted by Monseigneur de Sarlat, the certificates delivered by Dr. Abicolose and the depositions of the principal eye-witnesses. He drew up an official record of the subsequent interrogation, which Blancadet was required to sign twice, once for his wife, who was not yet able to write, and once for himself.

The miracle of La Moutardie was henceforth a historic fact, the slightest details of which were fixed with clarity and precision. The next day the Vicar of Christ gave it the sovereign consecration of a Mass, followed by a solemn audience in which the holy slipper received the labial affections of the Moutardian heroes. The Pope deigned to exhort the miraculized couple to persevere in the path of Faith whose light had just struck them; he pronounced a few words in praise of Monseigneur de Sarlat, an exemplary member of the clergy of France, ever worthy of the envied title of the eldest daughter of the Church, and concluded by instructing the sacred couple not to miss any opportunity to offer themselves as living testimony to celestial clemency.

Cécilia's grateful piety would easily have devoted itself to the work of Christian diffusion, but Blancadet, who did not find the role at all to his taste, obtained by means of conjugal love a respite from any manifestation.

In order to escape the importunities inherent in their condition, immediately known to Roman journalists and photographers, they quit the Eternal City by the first available train and, after many detours to elude the curiosity-seekers hot on their heels, they arrived in Venice, where all the gondoliers considered them as vulgar and ardent lovers.

One evening, as the moon was weaving its delicate silver web on the surface of the water, they disappeared completely into the communion of their bewildered souls; softly, close by, a voice rose up, which told them a dreamlike story of love, and so harmonious were the syllables designed by the voice that they seemed to be born from the voluptuous languor of the song itself. Like the moonlight, which was drowning in the bosom of the profound darkness of the waters, the voice died away into silence, and Cécilia asked her husband why the waves were no longer speaking. Blancadet did not have the heart to reveal the prosaic presence of the eupantophone; without a word, he took his wife's hand, and their entwined fingers abandoned themselves to the living warmth of the water.

The following day, however, he decided to acquaint Cécilia with the eupantophone. He had found an account of the event at La Moutardie in a French newspaper, and he had it read by the instrument—which, he said, was on sale in several shops in Paris.

In a quarter of an hour, the young woman had learned to make use of it, and, without manifesting the slightest astonishment, she agreed to the perfect convenience of the eupantophone, which scarcely knew any repose for the remainder of the voyage. Cécilia's sight was, so to speak, still theoretical, for, deprived of education, her eyes could not give her even a relative knowledge of things whose exterior aspects alone appeared to her. The eupantophone, on the contrary, addressing itself to her hearing, refined by her very blindness, would have procured her many joys had not her one and only thought being for her husband.

Every day, a new tenderness, the unprecedented communion of some virgin cell of their souls, affirmed the consciousness of their love, and, but for the secret of the spectacles, which Blancadet kept to himself, the ideal couple would have found its absolute terrestrial realization.

At the beginning of September, after a sojourn in Switzerland, they returned to Paris, where Baillargal and cousin Valentine were waiting for them.

The journalist, to whom Blancadet had, on the occasion of his marriage, made a donation of a very round sum, considered as a forever-inexhaustible treasure, had shown an exemplary discretion. Even his mistress had not received the slightest confidence, and the double miracle of La Moutardie had thrown her into full devotion. Her piety was remarked in all the churches in Passy, which she frequented assiduously.

Alcée Baillargal recounted in detail to his friend Blancadet everything that had happened in La Moutardie, where his "wife" and he had remained until the Sunday after the marriage. Several times, the Comtesse had manifested the intention of going to kneel in penitence to ask her confessor what she ought to think about the intervention of Madame Chypra; he had had a great deal of difficulty persuading her that her silence was indispensable to the continuation of the miracle, but she had sworn to keep quiet, as much out of affection for her son-in-law as for her daughter, confirming by that exceptional tenderness the character of the classic mother-in-law.

The Comte de La Moutardie had asked Monseigneur de Sarlat whether Cécilia and her husband would be beatified and figure in the calendar; the bishop had replied that many of the saints inscribed in the roll of honor had less eminent entitlements than theirs, but that His Holiness was the sovereign authority in such matters.

The entire world had been excited by the miracle, which had revolutionized the whole Ilderonian region. Madame Brindolle had obtained the concession for a hotel-restaurant patronized by the ecclesiastical authorities, and had she did not have the capital to construct the premises she had gone into partnership with Maître Des Échinettes, who had found a financial backer.

While cousin Valentine helped Cécilia to install herself in the apartment in the Rue du Luxembourg, Blancadet went to visit the Rue du Sabre-de-l'Abbé. Madame Benoît, who had been kept up to date with events by the newspapers, was so impressed by the appearance of her tenant that she fell to her knees before him without conserving the presence of mind to reproach him for his marriage, which she had not even known to be in prospect.

Célestin, whom several miracles would not have been sufficient to impress, was more severe on what he described as his master's "secrecies."

"I have not addressed my good wishes and felicitations to Monsieur, since Monsieur did not see fit to inform me of his marriage."

Blancadet, amused by the discovery of the previously unsuspected man of the world in his valet, asked Célestin to be kind enough to forgive his involuntary forgetfulness.

The domestic was deigning to condescend to forgiveness when a young woman of rather elegant appearance came into the drawing room without warning and threw her arms around his neck. "This is my fiancée," he told his master. "I was obliged to rid Monsieur of the cook, who was completely neglecting her service; I replaced her with this person; I hope Monsieur will be content with her. We are soon to be married."

Happiness is, it seems, the elder brother of generosity; Blancadet did not even think of becoming annoyed by Célestin's presumption, and promised him a regal gratification on the day of his wedding.

The letters from the Comte and Comtesse de La Moutardie begging Blancadet to come with Cécilia to La Moutardie became increasingly pressing. Anticipating the horrors of celebrity, Blancadet persuaded his wife, this time, only to pay a flying visit to the Ilderonian region. An automobile more diligent than the most renowned of express trains thus transported them to La Moutardie, where they were not expected.

The Comte and Comtesse saw their daughter again with an indescribable emotion. The tenderness of mothers is infallible and they can read the secret hearts of their children like an open book; Madame de La Moutardie saw nothing but felicity in Cécilia's; with large tears pearling on her cheeks, she threw herself upon her son-in-laws hands—hands, she said, that had brought happiness into the house—and covered them with humble kisses of gratitude.

To interrupt such a joy with an immediate departure would have been a sacrilege. Blancadet asked his father-in-law to tell the innumerable pilgrims who had come running from twenty leagues around that he and Cécilia had left La Moutardie; the automobile was hidden in an old garage, and in the delights of the most complete mystery, an entire week went by, after which the Comtesse, silencing her affection, begged her children not to renounce their numerous plans for voyages and excursions. After having obtained from their parents the promise to come to Paris before New Year's Day, Blancadet and his wife consented to depart.

Successively, they were guests of the mountains and the sea. Cécilia waxed ecstatic over the height of the most famous peaks, and the Ocean introduced her to immensity.

On one of the most fashionable beaches, Cécilia asked her husband where all those people came from, who were wearing identical garments and making the same gestures.

"They come from everywhere," Blancadet replied, "but particularly from Paris, where a race of men and women lives who are to the human species what migratory birds are to the animal realm. As soon as summer arrives, those men and women pile a part of their worldly belongings into huge trunks and race to the railway stations in search of the train that will carry them far away from Paris as rapidly as possible, to which they return with the same haste when autumn arrives. They form what is known as the holiday nobility, which counts its quarters according to the number of its displacements."

"Will we be among them?" Cécilia acquired, naively.

"If it pleases you, my Cécilia, we will be," Blancadet granted, gallantly.

The chill came early that year; the young couple went back to Paris in the early days of November, and lived almost in common with the Baillargal household. Cécilia and Valentine were the best of friends and Baillargal had already obtained from Blancadet the promise of financial support for a newspaper he was planning to create.

Cécilia had received the present of a marvelous eupantophone; she was literally delighted with it, and as she thought about her father and mother, whose eyes were very weary, she asked her husband to buy one of the convenient instruments for the dear old parents. Naturally, Blancadet did not have to be asked twice, and he immediately set about constructing a new eupantophone.

Every day, he spent an hour or two in the Rue du Sabre-de-l'Abbé, where Célestin reigned as master. The cook Athénaïde must have been supplying him with fine dishes, for he never ceased singing her praises. When Blancadet questioned him about the date of their marriage, Célestin replied that Athénaïde was content, for the moment, with his word, and that he would be able to keep her "a child of the people conscious of her duties" if circumstances required it.

Blancadet would have shown a somewhat tyrannical inclination by insisting, and his own happiness rendered him profoundly respectful of others' pleasures; returning to Cécilia his egotism was limited to thinking there was no one else in the world who loved as he did. It was a love of infinite delicacy, a paradise in which every tenderness faded away softly to give way to another, and, in the stammering fervor of her soul, Cécilia confused in the same adoration the Lord and her husband.

One delight after another, Blancadet discovered an unsuspected treasure every day in the heart of his ignorant and simple wife, and with an almost holy emotion he listened beside the bright fire of the hearth every evening to his dear Cécilia giving him a naïve account of her impressions. She asked him questions about what she had seen, and he replied as to a curious child.

Once, she wanted to know whether it was really true that there were only forty Academicians. Blancadet explained how Cardinal Richelieu had instituted the Académie Française with its forty members, whose number had remained the same for nearly three centuries in spite of the multiplication of everything. When he manifested some astonishment at the question, Cécilia explained that in the afternoon, an Academician, the youngest of them all, had strolled with her in the Jardin du Luxembourg.

"There were five of them dressed in black coats with shiny top hats; on the left side of their breasts all five wore a silver plaque, probably the insignia of their dignity. They were chatting by the fountain, and I had been looking at them for a moment when one of them came over to me, hat in hand, as gallantly as could be, and offered me his arm to make a tour of the garden. I didn't know whether I ought to refuse, but he'd already put my arm under his, and his friends, who surrounded me immediately, paid me compliments. They were all very well brought-up and full of gaiety..."

Victor Blancadet, Comte de La Moutardie, had immediately recognized in the gallant and joyful cavaliers five employees of a funeral parlor; without any anxiety, he wondered how far his wife had taken the innocent adventure, and, in order to let her go on to the end, he refrained from interrupting her with any observation.

"The one who offered me his arm asked me whether I knew the works of art exhibited in the garden, and when I confessed that I had never seen them, he offered to show them to me..."

"And what did you see, my dear Cécilia?" asked Blancadet, curious about the undertaker's esthetics.

"Oh, I don't remember very clearly. We climbed a staircase...oh yes! At the top, on the edge of the terrace, there were large statues on stone pedestals. My guide told me that they were queens of France and he added, laughing, that none of them had been as beautiful as me. Then we went past a tall woman with angel's wings, protecting a bald man whose legs couldn't be seen. My guide took his hat off respectfully and said that he was a member of the Académie. It was the monument of a Comte who wrote verses...the Comte de...de..."

"De Lisle. Leconte de Lisle!" Blancadet whispered.

"That's it! Yes—it appears that he was a great poet and wrote beautiful verses. My cavalier recited a few of them. In the eupantophone, they'd be admirable. Could the eupantophone do that?"

"Oh, certainly. That poet's works are on the bookshelves. You only have to take down the volumes. But Cécilia, how did you find out that the man who so gallantly offered you his arm was a member of the Académie?"

"Oh, I suspected as much. Firstly, there was that ceremonial dress in the middle of the day. The language he employed: well-chosen words, always so apt. Then, he invited me to go with him to the Académie..."

"To the Académie?" asked Blancadet, with a certain bewilderment.

"Yes, the Académie. It's very close to the garden and poets meet up there every evening..."

Blancadet realized that it was a matter of a wine-shop in the Rue Saint-Jacques, near the Panthéon. Verlaine and his friends, who had frequented the establishment, had given it the pompous nickname of "the Académie." Cécilia's explanations proved that he was not mistaken.

"I thanked my guide very much and told him that I would be very happy to go to the Académie with my husband. Then all five of them started laughing like madmen. Why were they laughing, my Victor?"

"Probably because they were in a joyful mood," Blancadet replied, kissing his wife. "Academicians are always very cheerful."

"Oh, so much the better. I was afraid that they were making fun of me. It was getting late; I wanted to come home. My guide said that he wanted to accompany me. His friends bowed very politely, shook his hand and went away, still laughing madly. We went back through the garden; he told me again, as we went past the queens of France, that none of them had been as beautiful as me and told me stories to make me laugh. He forced me to stop in front of a thin column terminated by the head of a bearded and unkempt man, and said: 'That thick cane with the badly-sculpted pommel represented a poet who went to the Académie every day; you can see that he has no feet—he put them all into his verses.'"

Blancadet, completely reassured as to the conclusion of the undertaker's flirtation, laughed wholeheartedly, and scarcely reminded himself to advise his wife to show less enthusiasm to the kind attentions of strangers.

"My cavalier asked me my name and when I told him that I was Madame Victor Blancadet, Comtesse de La Moutardie, he wanted to know how long I had been married, and...." Softly and hesitantly, in a low voice, she added: "...And if I loved you..."

"And what did you reply?" Blancadet interrogated, with the utmost gravity.

A long kiss was the response; Blancadet was content with it—without, however, completely disinteresting himself in the fate of the "Academician," for he did not think there was any need to unmask the man from the funeral parlor.

"So, he accompanied me to the door; he told me that it was very painful to separate from me, and that he would like very much to see me again. I invited him to come here. Oh! I haven't told you that he's the fortieth, which is to say the youngest, of the Academicians; the number 40 was on the silver plaque fixed on his coat. Won't you be glad to receive him?"

"Certainly!" Blancadet exclaimed, kissing his wife.

Thanks to the devotion of cousin Valentine, however, Cécilia made rapid progress in all things, and when, toward the middle of December, Monsieur and Madame de La Moutardie arrived from the depths of their province, they experienced a new joy in finding, instead of their simple and slightly rustic child, an elegant and utterly precious Parisienne.

The Comte congratulated his son-on-law on that metamorphosis, which had "made an admirable butterfly of the poor caterpillar."

The eupantophone requested by Cécilia for her aged parents was ready, but it was agreed that they would wait for New Year's Day to present it to them, and Blancadet made arrangements to be in a position to make a similar gift to cousin Valentine.

The Comtesse de La Moutardie asked Baillargal for the address of Madame Chypra, whom she desired to see again. At Blancadet's request, the journalist made a preliminary visit to the somnambulist to bring hr up to date with what had happened; the poor woman was so impressed by the realization of her prediction that she suffered a cerebral fever and scarcely had the strength to grant Madame de La Moutardie an audience.

The interview was, in any case, merely an ordinary consultation and was limited to a tearful duet, for Madame Chypra was even more emotional than her client. The spirits stammered a few incomprehensible phrases, which affirmed perfect happiness for the miraculized couple.

If the goddess Felicity had returned to the Earth, she would doubtless have selected for her temple the apartment in the Rue du Luxembourg.

Within its serenity, however, the azure of that heaven hid the invisible fluid that unleashes the lightning; a volcano was slumbering in those waves of tenderness and infinite love.

On New Year's Eve, Blancadet went to his laboratory in the Rue du Sabre-de-l'Abbé to give the order for the two eupantophones destined got Madame de La Moutardie and cousin Valentine to be transported to the Rue du Luxembourg.

When he got home, as he had the habit of doing, he wanted to kiss his dear Cécilia and headed for the drawing room where she was. Scarcely had he turned the door handle when a lightning-flash sprang from the eupantophone, and zigzagged toward the back of Cécilia's neck.

He threw himself on the body of his wife, who had collapsed on the floor in a brief convulsion.

XIX

"Then you deny it?"

"Let me weep" Let me weep!"

"Then you confess?"

"Let me weep! I beg you, let me weep!"

"In a game of chess, blowing is not making a move. Before the law, weeping is not answering. You've wept enough. Answer."

"My wife! My wife!"

"You'd have done better not to kill your wife! Anyway, you're all the same; according to you, it isn't the victims that ought to be mourned by the murderers! And then, you, you're a criminal, how should I put it? Interesting! No doubt the jury will take account of this detail: your wife deceived you..."

"Oh, not that! No...no! I beg you! Not that! No...no! Cécilia! My Cécilia!"

Victor Blancadet collapsed on the carpet. The examining magistrate turned to the advocate, a very young man already perfectly indifferent to the spectacle of grief, for, with a smile on his lips, he let a vague gaze wander over the human form lying at his feet.

"Maître, the attitude of the accused is strange. I'll say more than that: it's abnormal. What? This is a man who has killed his wife? Let's understand one another; it's not a matter of the *flagrante delicto* for which the legislator anticipates the blood of the guilty party or parties. In the absence of *flagrante delicto*, however, every time adultery is proven, the clemency of the jury routinely acquits a husband who punishes his companion's fault; we are establishing the proof of that circumstance, the most fortunate of all for the accused, and he is the one that protests against the eloquence of the facts! This attitude, Maître, is absolutely abnormal and corroborates my opinion. Victor Blancadet is mad!"

"My reason! Oh, they're attacking my reason now!" Blancadet groaned.

The examining magistrate shrugged his shoulders and continued. "In my opinion, the accused is manifestly insane; he's afflicted with mystical madness, the most dangerous of all. He thinks he's God! Is that madness, yes or no? But I'm not qualified to make a pronouncement as to his condition; that's up to the men of the Art. Since you are not addressing any request to me with that objective, I shall therefore appoint three alienist physicians to the task, who will examine him. We can, however, that measure notwithstanding, proceed inconstantly with our investigation."

"I'm at your orders, Monsieur le Juge," stammered the young Maître, whose eyes, overflowing with tears, betrayed the emotion that his perpetual smile strove in vain to disguise.

"Monsieur John Plum, would you be good enough to re-read the official statement?"

The clerk John Plum nodded his head as a sign of assent; the magistrate, with a similar movement, seemed to thank him. Ordinarily, the examining magistrate Marius Bouïgri and his clerk were inseparable instruments of the Law. At the Palais, they were known as Castor and Pollux, and stories of which they were the heroes served the advocates to kill time during the suspension of hearings. The younger members of the bar could not imagine Bouïgri without John Plum or John Plum without Bouïgri, and yet the old togas affirmed that the two individuals had once existed separately.

Having come from Marseilles, where he had been the public prosecutor, Marius Bouïgri had found the clerk John Plum in the examiner's office, vacant for several months, his irritable humor having been the despair of all the examining magistrates attached to the Court of the Seine. To the great surprise of his colleagues, Bouïgri declared himself delighted with John Plum; at their first contact, the two men had sensed that they were made for one another. A similar comprehension of the law, a philosophy similarly limited to elementary religious beliefs, and tastes sufficiently satisfied by the reasonable usage of the pleasures of the mind and the body, along with a common bachelorhood, had made each of them the complement, initially precious and soon indispensable, of the other.

What united John Plum, who belied his Anglo-Saxon name by the perpetual agitation of his thin and stiff person, and the corpulent and placid Marius Bouïgri was more than friendship; it was an imperious need to live the same life and share the same thoughts. To avoid, not only any argument, but the mere observation of any difference of opinion, the two companions were obedient to the "Zanzibar."[15]

They admitted as many combinations of numbers as there were possible opinions on the question to be settled; the leather cup was shaken and the indication given by the dice was adopted without the slightest reflection. In the majority of cases, odd and even, representing the affirmative and the negative, were sufficient.

Thus, when the sensational Blancadet de La Moutardie affair landed in Bouïgri's office, it was necessary for the judge and his clerk to adopt an identical conviction. One of the even numbers indicating guilt had emerged from the cup, and a second cast of the dice had revealed the irresponsibility of the murderer.

"Guilty and insane!" John Plum had proclaimed.

"Guilty and insane!" Bouïgri had repeated faithfully.

"That's right!" the magistrate and his clerk had confided to one another after that first interrogation to which Blancadet was subjected, witnessed by a young trainee clerk, in conformity with the law, and by a representative of the order of advocates, since the accused had stubbornly refused to choose a defender—whom he would have be able to select from the most aquiline of the Paris bar, his case exciting opinion to the

---

[15] Zanzibar, in this meaning, is a very simple game played with dice—usually, but not necessarily three of them. In competitive play the competition is simply to score the highest points total, but the version played by the two men of law is even simpler, the equivalent of tossing of a coin.

highest degree by virtue of its passionate and mysterious aspects.

Prostrate in his grief, Blancadet did not hear the voice of John Plum, who seemed to be clearing up some trivial news-item by the most brilliant specialist of that so little-esteemed but commercially-invaluable genre of letters.

There were the initial observations: Blancadet found unconscious on the body of his wife, still holding in his clenched hand the minuscule stiletto with which he had struck her. Then came the confessions of the accused, who, on coming to his senses, had repeated several times: "My Cécilia! My Cécilia! It's me who has killed her!"

Bouïgri advanced a "Permit me, Monsieur John Plum" so amenable that the clerk stopped reading instantly. The magistrate addressed himself to Blancadet.

"'My Cécilia, it's me who has killed her!' Do you hear that, accused? Those are the words that emerged from your mouth! It was only later, obedient to some unknown desire to lead the law astray that, having taken account of your frankness, you retracted your confession. You have invented an accident provoked by the bizarre apparatus that you call a eupantophone, about which we shall talk again in due course..."

"It's horrible! It's horrible! The truth! The truth!" Blancadet croaked.

"The truth? It emerged stark naked from the profound well of your denials and reticences! Who could possibly believe that an electric spark could have struck the stiletto that your wife was using instead of a pin to sustain the edifice of her coiffure and caused her to plunge it into the nape of her neck between two cervical vertebrae? And if we admit, momentarily, the existence and the role of that extraordinary spark, how do you explain the presence of the poison that made, of a seemingly inoffensive item of jewelry, a weapon so terrible that the medical examiner was able to kill an ox of considerable size simply by pricking it lightly?"

"Monsieur le Juge, my client has declared that he bought the stiletto in Venice during his honeymoon voyage," the advocate observed timidly.

"And has the accused proved that it was not him who dipped the point of the stiletto in curare? Let us not forget, in fact, that Monsieur Blancadet is a chemist of the most dangerous sort. In any case, in addition to his formal and peremptory confessions, we have discovered the motives that drove Blancadet to kill his wife. Is it necessary to reconstitute the scene? It is simple and banal. The unfaithful spouse receives a letter from her lover. And what a lover! An employee of a funeral parlor!"

"The undertaker! The undertaker!" croaked Blancadet, whose teeth were chattering.

"Ah! You're here now?" the magistrate Bouïgri observed, triumphantly, continuing his argument. "She takes imprudence and immodesty so far as to have her amorous correspondence read by that eupantophone, whose ingenuity is, I admit, very remarkable. The husband is behind the door; he listens; he listens, like the tiger crouching in the jungle, preparing to pounce; abruptly, like a released spring, he opens the door; he enters; he strikes. What is more natural, more logical and more banal? No need for the spark. The hand of the husband, armed by the anger boiling in his veins—that's the spark!

"Now, was jealousy the only motive that caused Victor Blancadet to act? That is the question! *Is fecit cui prodest*,[16] the sage maxim, the veritable skeleton key of troubled consciences, has served us in this affair. We know that Victor Blancadet has forced his father-in-law to cede to him, with his name, his title of Comte, and in his marriage contract, he stipulated that in the case of survival on his part, he would inherit the château and estate of Le Moutardie. Is not foreseeing the

---

[16] An abbreviated form of a dictum suggesting that the person who benefits from a crime is likely to be the one who committed it.

death of his wife, in making provision for it in his marriage contract, for a husband, to have a secret desire to see his wife dead? Does she persist in living? One kills her!"

"You're mad! You're mad!" howled Blancadet, straightening up in sudden wrath.

"Hold him! Hold him!" the magistrate cried to the two Republican guards, whose heavy hands had already weighed upon the accused, immediately fallen to his knees.

A man came in, after having knocked lightly on the door.

"Look, here's the doctor now. Are you well, Doctor?"

"Not bad, thanks. You?"

"Very well—but it's our man who isn't," Bouïgri replied, pointing at Blancadet. "He's just had a terrible crisis."

"The reaction!" the doctor approved, tranquilly. "All the guilty experience that psychic shock. And the confessions?"

"Nothing at all. He persists in denial!"

"I've advised you to confront the accused with the body of his victim. That's excellent!"

"Indeed! But it's a brutal means and you know that I take a certain pride in conducting an investigation elegantly, like a man of the world. The methods which the majority of my colleagues employ are repugnant to me. It's only in the last extremity that I'll have recourse to a confrontation. The victim's body…?"

"Is still at the Morgue, and will remain in the refrigerant apparatus until you give permission for the burial," the doctor replied, smiling.

"Good. Apart from that, anything new?"

"Nothing. I was passing your door and came in to shake your hand."

"Thank you! And all my compliments on your report on this affair. The terms are absolutely precise. Oh, Doctor, you're a precious man for the Law!"

"My God yes," the doctor accorded, modestly. "But if there were no cases more confused than the Blancadet affair, I wouldn't have any great merit. Which of my colleagues would not have reached the same conclusion? Blancadet's guilt is blindingly obvious! Let's see—the stiletto! And the poison? Let's not forget the poison! The most concentrated curare, which does great honor to Blancadet as a toxicologist!"

"And with regard to his mental faculties?"

"Oh, as to that, my dear magistrate, you will have to interrogate my alienist colleagues. *A priori*, however, one can say that Blancadet is..."

"Guilty and insane!" muttered John Plum, remembering the oracle rendered by the dice.

"Guilty and insane," echoed Bouïgri, faithfully. "Anyway, you can judge for yourself." He addressed the accused, now perfectly calm: "Victor Blancadet, Comte de La Moutardie, are you the inventor of the extraordinary reading machine that you call a eupantophone?"

"Yes," Blancadet replied.

"I've examined the instrument," the doctor put in. "It's truly admirable, and leaves phonographs and gramophones of all types and all brands far behind."

"Victor Blancadet, are you blind?"

"I've already told you when and how I lost my sight."

"According to the information I've obtained, that seems to me to be accurate. As for the miracle of the twenty-first of June..."

"There was no miracle of the twenty first of June," Blancadet interjected, dryly.

"There!" cried Bouïgri, holding out his arms. "And it was you who rendered sight to yourself, as it was you who rendered sight to your wife, during the marriage ceremony!" mocked the judge.

Blancadet stood up, but his attitude was so calm that the Republican guards thought it unnecessary to intervene. "Monsieur le Juge," he said, without the slightest apparent emotion, as if he had made a grave resolution, in a strange voice, "twenty years ago, my eyes were destroyed by an accident; I replaced them with the eyes I presently wear, which are made of glass; thanks to them and these special spectacles, I continue to see as before. I have tried to help my fellows profit from my invention; no one wanted to listen to me, and scientists treated me as a madman. That was the first blow struck by the unknown you call God and others call Fatality. Then, obedient to the common law, I searched for happiness; I found it, as perfect as one can dream. Spectacles like those I wear myself rendered sight to the young woman I loved, and I staged the miracle whose success was universal, as much to avoid importing a disturbance in the soul of my companion as to disarm God-Fatality by attributing the glorious paternity of the transformation to him."

Blancadet had raised his voice; at a sign from Bouïgri the two Republican guards had drawn nearer in order to stifle the slightest amplification of gesture with their solid grip.

"Oh, no—God-Fatality you were not disarmed! It was my happiness that it was necessary to hate, and you have strangled it! You have taken my dear wife, Cécilia, from me. She's dead. To kill her, you extracted the fatal spark from the eupantophone that my hands had created. Cease to be invisible, O God-Fatality! Stand face to face with me! Don't tremble! Take my life—I give it to you—but I want to spit in the face of your imposture! I want your vilest and most abject slaves to hold you in disgust, O God-Fatality! Lie! Lie!"

"Hold him! Hold him!" cried Bouïgri, who had stopped smiling. But before the Republican guards had exerted the vigor of their biceps upon Blancadet's shoulder, the latter, his hands pressed together, sobbing, addressed a prayer to the magistrate: "I beg you, I beg you, respect Cécilia's soul! My Cécilia, so pure, so pure!"

"Take him away," Bouïgri ordered.

The guards took hold of Blancadet; while they were putting on the handcuffs he was heard to murmur: "It's over now! Do with me as you will! They won't get another word out of me. It's over…it's over!"

The guards took the accused away.

"Well, my lads, what do you think of that citizen?" Bouïgri sniggered.

What the doctor and John Plum thought could not have been too sad, because those two individuals rivaled one another in hilarity while Bouïgri sent away the young defender, whose nerves had definitely betrayed him, and who was weeping without making any attempt to hide the fact.

"Have the witnesses been summoned for today, Monsieur John Plum?" asked Bouïgri.

"Indeed, Monsieur le Juge; all the witnesses, as usual."

"Good! Very good. It's getting late. Anyway, we've done enough work for one day. Monsieur John Plum, will you please tell the witnesses that we'll hear them tomorrow? Tell them all to come, as usual. One never knows with whom to begin."

An office boy for whom John Plum rang was sent to fetch the citations to appear from the witnesses. The clerk inscribed the next day's date on each of them, after which the office boy put them back in the relevant hands. One witness asked to speak to the magistrate, who gave the order to send him in immediately.

"I am Maître Alcindor Des Échinettes, notary of Ilderon-sur-Noizette, Monsieur le Juge."

"All my felicitations, Monsieur le Notaire! What do you desire?"

"I'd like to be heard as soon as possible, Monsieur le Juge. I left important business in Ilderon, in abeyance..."

"Affairs in abeyance are the best ones for a notary as conscientious as you appear to be..."

"It's evident that an affair not definitively regulated always repays the interest and embarrassment that it causes to a notary's studio; however, life in Paris is expensive and the indemnities we're allowed..."

"Of course. If you had planned to entertain dancers from the Académie Nationale with the franc and a quarter with which the Administration indemnifies you daily, you would certainly be disappointed..."

"I am cited for tomorrow. You will hear me tomorrow, Monsieur le Juge?"

"I will hear you if you depose. Will you depose? That is the nub. And I can tell you nothing, as the will of a magistrate is subordinate to the unpredictable phases of the investigation."

"That's very annoying."

"To whom are you talking? Hold yourself at the disposal of the law before which you have been duly summoned. That is the only advice I am permitted to give you. Until one of these days, Monsieur le Notaire!"

Maître Alcindor Des Échinettes bowed and went out to rejoin the widowed Madame Brindolle, who had not thought it prudent to allow her lover to go alone to the modern Babylon

The doctor took his leave of the magistrate and the clerk, and a few minutes later, Bouïgri, accompanied by his faithful John Plum, left the Palais de Justice.

The following day, at one o'clock in the afternoon, the magistrate Bouïgri consulted the list of witnesses, and John Plum, dice-cup in hand, was about to ask the dice for the name of the one that would be called first when Bouïgri cried: "Oh, John Plum! My dear John Plum! You can't think so! A journalist, Baillargal...Alcée Baillargal has been cited, and we're making him wait! In our profession, you see, my dear John Plum, it's necessary to be extremely careful with anything concerning the Press, immediately or distantly. The Press is Opinion, and Opinion is our sovereign—everyone's tyrannical and capricious sovereign! In secret, we scorn the old prostitute, but let us not attract the anger of her lovers of the heart. Have Alcée Baillargal introduced; we'll hear his wife immediately afterwards. Let's be men of the world—that's my specialty!

Bouïgri got up to welcome Alcée Baillargal, under whom John Plum slid the best armchair in the study.

"Monsieur Alcée Baillargal, the Law expresses via my mouth all its regrets for the disturbance it is occasioning you. To drag a man of letters away from his work-desk is a crime that only the gravity of the facts and the solemnity of the circumstances can excuse. Your family relationship with the accused Blancadet has made it a strict duty for me to ask you to appear before us; I will permit myself, if you will be kind enough to authorize it, to ask you a few questions..."

"I must first declare to you, Monsieur le Juge, that no family relationship links me to poor Victor Blancadet."

"What? Let's see...but you're his cousin..." Bouïgri insinuated.

"Monsieur le Juge, a few words will suffice to clarify the matter..."

"Speak, speak, I beg you. I make no insistence on that collaterality!"

"Thank you, Monsieur le Juge. If I were Blancadet's cousin, I would not seek to hide it..."

"You have more courage than me! There are moments in life when one has the right, and even the duty to desolidarize oneself with relatives who have become compromising. It's not funny to wake up one morning as the relative of a murderer!"

"There are family embarrassments," Baillargal agreed, "but those considerations have nothing to do with the one responsible for my action. I only know that I owe the Law the truth, the whole truth..."

"I will go as far as to ask you to swear an oath to that effect."

"I'm ready to swear!" said Baillargal.

"Raise your hand! That's done. Thank you. A slightly ridiculous formality, I confess, is the word 'journalist' not synonymous with honor and probity? You were saying, then, Monsieur Baillargal, that Victor Blancadet was wrong to claim you as his cousin?"

"Absolutely. I can give you a brief account of the history of our relationship."

"I'm listening. Would you be so kind as to take a few notes, Monsieur John Plum?"

"Of course, Monsieur le Juge—with pleasure!" the clerk consented.

"A little over a year ago, hazard, or, if you prefer, professional flair, permitted me to discover Victor Blancadet in his retreat in the Rue du Sabre-de-l'Abbé. Oh, that first meeting! It seems like only yesterday, do deeply has it remained engraved in my memory—and I can assure you that there was reason, Monsieur le Juge, Blancadet told me about the accident that had destroyed his eyes, and he held them out to me in his fingertips—without, however abolishing his sight, since he was able to decipher before my eyes a few words that he had asked me to write on a piece of paper, which happened to consist of a harmonious alexandrine..."

"Aha! He was already mad!" Bouïgri put in.

"Aha! He was already mad" repeated John Plum, consigning the words that had emerged from the mouth of his friend the magistrate to the piece of paper on which he was scribbling energetically.

"Why mad?" asked Baillargal, wondering whether the Law was not lacking respect in the person of its most distinguished instruments.

"Why? You find that normal: a man, a Frenchman, who juggles with his eyes, who says to them 'hey presto!' while spelling out the syllables of your writing, which is in verse? Come on, Monsieur Alcée Baillargal, we're not in the concierge's lodge and the *roman feuilleton* is not our pastime!"

"They're the facts!" protested Baillargal.

"They're jokes!" snapped Bouïgri. "But continue I beg you, without losing sight of the majesty of the Law."

"Very well," Baillargal concluded, a trifle vexed. "I ask no more than to resume, while simplifying. So, Victor Blancadet was blind, and he could see; but in order to marry, he wanted to be blind and not to be able to see..."

"Let's see! Let's see!"[17]

---

[17] The exclamation "*Voyons!*" [Let's see] is used in French as an exclamation of incredulity, where an English person might say "Come on!" or something similar. I have usually substituted some such phrase, but as it is part of a play on words

"I can no longer see anything at all!" said the clerk putting down his pen.

"I can't be any clearer, though!" Baillargal excused himself. "A real and reciprocal sympathy was thus established between Victor Blancadet and myself. He asked me to assist him in his matrimonial project; I thought it my duty not to refuse him my collaboration, all the more so as he seemed to be alone in the world, without any relatives..."

"And that's why you passed yourself off as his cousin!" Bouïgri discovered.

"Exactly, Monsieur le Juge!"

"The end justifies the means," Bouïgri approved.

"As Ignatius Loyola said," added John Plum.

"Don't write that down, Monsieur John Plum; there's no need," the magistrate advised.

"There's no need," the docile clerk acquiesced.

"Let's arrive at the marriage, if you don't see any inconvenience in that, Monsieur Alcée Baillargal."

"I can't see any, alas. On the twenty-first of June..."

"The day of the miracle!" Bouïgri interjected.

"Monsieur le Juge, I have an important declaration to make to you: there was no miracle."

"Ah! You too are going to deny the work of God?" the magistrate deplored.

"Victor Blancadet has talked?"

"What do you expect him to do? No later than yesterday, in this very room, he launched a long series of imprecations against Heaven. It was terrible—isn't that so, Monsieur John Plum?"

"It was terrible!" approved John Plum.

"I believe that the poor fellow is mad," Bouïgri concluded.

"I'm profoundly respectful of your opinion, Monsieur le Juge," Baillargal went on, "but you'll permit me to affirm to

---

here, it is necessary to retain the literal translation, even though it sounds a trifle odd.

.

you that Victor Blancadet could see before the twenty-first of June. I swear to you on all that I hold most sacred that Blancadet has advantageously replaced his eyes by glass eyes and spectacles of his own invention; he enjoys an artificial sight as good and perhaps better than his natural sight..."

"Thank you, Monsieur Baillargal," the magistrate interrupted, who had begun to get annoyed as soon as the journalist began speaking. "Tell me what you know about the crime and I'll return your liberty. The scientists commissioned to examine Victor Blancadet will fathom the mysterious aspects of the case. Had the accused made you party to his conjugal unhappiness? Had he ever manifested before you the desire to kill his wife to bring her back to the path of duty?"

"Monsieur le Juge, Cécilia de La Moutardie was the model of wives, her virtue..."

"And the employee of the funeral parlor?" Bouïgri objected, sarcastically. "The letter found in the eupantophone?"

"That happens every day in Paris; one meets a woman in the street, one follows her, and, if one happens to discover her name, one writes to her..."

"Sad mores!" Bouïgri put in.

"I don't disagree; but it's certain that the idyll sketched in the Jardin du Luxembourg only had that wretched note as a consequence..."

"Let's assume that he accused had exaggerated the range of that flirtation; he could have believed that he had been deceived, and when one believes that one is deceived, one acts as if one really has been."

"Believe me, Monsieur le Juge, Victor Blancadet had not and could not have had the slightest suspicion of his wife; was it not Cécilia herself who told him about the stroll with the undertaker?"

"A refinement of perversity, perhaps; with women, it's necessary to expect anything!"

"Absolutely anything," corroborated John Plum.

"Victor Blancadet adored his wife, and he would not have obeyed an abrupt impulse of jealousy, even if..."

"Which is to say that, according to you, the accused would willingly have been a complaisant husband!"

"No, Monsieur le Juge, but when one is in love, believe me, one suffers and one does not kill..."

"That's literature, that! Me, I'd kill..."

"I'd kill too," John Plum thought aloud.

"In sum, it appears to you that Victor Blancadet has not killed his wife, who did not deceive him?"

"Absolutely, Monsieur le Juge. With regard to the scene itself, I can't tell you anything. I learned everything from the newspapers. I haven't seen Victor Blancadet since his arrest..."

"He's still in isolation. But you'll see him soon, for I have the intention of confronting you with him..."

"At your disposal, Monsieur le Juge."

"If you'd be kind enough to go into my back room while we interrogate Madame Baillargal...you can read the newspapers while you wait..."

Bouïgri installed the journalist personally on the green velvet sofa that occupied more than half the minuscule room, and went back into the study, being careful to close the communicating door.

"My dear John Plum, go fetch Madame Baillargal. It's necessary to be gallant with ladies, especially those of journalism!"

John Plum pulled his waistcoat down over the concavity of his stomach and went out, only to return precipitately, slamming the door behind him.

"Marius! Marius!" he cried collapsing in his armchair. "It's the beauty!"

An indescribable scene unfolded. The clerk had just recognized in Madame Baillargal a person whose conquest he and Bouïgri had made three years before, in one of those establishments in which the principal virtue is rapid service. The verve of John Plum and the good manners of his companion had quickly reasoned with the professional scruples of "the beauty," who had declared that she answered to the name of Yseult.

A fine supper brought the preliminaries to a close and when Yseult enquired as to the flame that was reserved to crown her that night, the dice-cups had emerged of their own accord from the pockets of the candidates; the lot had favored John Plum; Yseult had consoled the unlucky player with a kiss and, as she had lamented the distance between Montmartre and Montparnasse, she had offered him the arms of an excellent armchair in which to await the dawn.

The beauty's lodgings were comfortable, and as his heart was vast and inexhaustible, on the prayer of the victor at Zanzibar himself, the vanquished had not been exclusively reduced to the embraces of the Louis XV armchair that served him as a bed.

That very Parisian idyll had had numerous sequels; "Marius and John," always in convoy, presented themselves so frequently at the blonde Yseult's domicile that the concierge no longer stopped them. Bouïgri had passed himself off as a manufacturer of bathing-suits and Plum for a teacher of languages.

One evening, they had arrived as usual, John furnished a superb bouquet and Marius carrying the comestibles necessary for the intimate supper that Yseult liked on returning home from the theater. The concierge had called out to hem and handed them, on behalf of his tenant, a letter and a package. In the letter, Yseult announced that, to hr great regret and for important reasons, it was impossible for her to see them again. In the package they found nightshirts, slippers and petty items of toilette that belonged to them.

"But I thought she loved me!" John Plum had sighed.

"I thought so too," Marius Bouïgri had exhaled, with a similar sigh, putting the gallant material under his arm.

Neither of them had ever seen Yseult again, and now here she was, reappearing as the legitimate wife of the journalist Alcée Baillargal."

"It's the beauty! Marius, it's the beauty!" John Plum repeated.

"What are we going to do? She'll recognize us!" observed the magistrate.

"Probably," opined the clerk.

"And then?"

"Then? Nothing. Don't flinch! I know women. She won't give herself away! It's the beauty! Marius, it's..."

"Come on, John! Hold steady, my dear John! Send her in!"

"Madame Baillargal...Madame Alcée Baillargal, will you please come in!" said John Plum solemnly, opening the door.

With his nose in his dossiers, the magistrate invited Madame Baillargal to sit down. The journalist's companion had started with surprise on rediscovering her language teacher and bathing-suit manufacturer as an examining magistrate and his clerk, but she immediately understood that neither of them intended to recognize her.

"Madame Alcée Baillargal," Bouïgri began, without daring to raise his eyes to the witness, "you know the accused Blancadet; tell us what you know about him. You're not his cousin, since Monsieur your husband is not his cousin; he has confessed his innocent subterfuge to us. Tell us what you know about Blancadet."

"I don't know anything, Monsieur le Juge."

"You witnessed his marriage."

"Yes, Monsieur le Juge, I witnessed the miracle. Alcée...that is to say, Monsieur Baillargal... says that it wasn't a miracle...but I saw it."

"Indeed!" said Bouïgri, encouragingly. "How did it happen?"

"Well, that poor Monsieur Blancadet and his future wife were blind, and the Good God rendered them sight on the twenty-first of June; it was in the middle of the Mass that it happened: Cécilia first, Monsieur Victor immediately afterwards. Oh, I can still hear Monsieur Victor crying: "Lord!

305

Lord! You have give me back my sight!' The Good God must be very powerful to do such things."

"Yes, Madame, that is an entirely just observation!" Marius Bouïgri observed. "In sum, according to you, the miracle is indisputable?"

"I don't dispute it…," the former Yseult excused herself. The judiciary apparatus, even seen through two lovers once subject to regular appointments, impressed to the point of anxiety.

"And about the crime, Madame, what do you know?" the magistrate interrogated.

"I don't know anything, Monsieur le Juge. It was an accident! Monsieur Victor adored his wife, who certainly merited it…"

"Being adored?" articulated John Plum, while writing.

"Yes, Monsieur John," the present Madame Baillargal could not help replying.

"Thank you…thank you, Madame!" Bouïgri interjected, swiftly. "We'll return you to Monsieur our husband, and one day soon we'll summon you again if we have need of you for a confrontation."

Marcus Bouïgri went to fetch Alcée Baillargal from the annex to his study, reiterated his apologies and those of the Law, which had found it necessary to disturb him and Madame Baillargal, and, escorted by John Plum, he accompanied the sympathetic journalistic couple as far as the staircase of the gallery.

The magistrate and his clerk had not yet had time to congratulate one another on the fortunate outcome of that unexpected encounter when Maître Alcindor Des Échinettes demanded to know whether the Law was disposed to hear him. Marius Bouïgri decided to authorize the notary to return to Ilderon, where he would have him interrogated by rogatory commission, and that same evening, the express bore Maître Des Échinettes and Madame Brindolle away.

The investigation followed its course slowly and surely. Victor Blancadet was extracted from his cell two or three times a week to be brought before the examining magistrate, who deemed it necessary to confront him with his parents-in-law.

The interview was painfully tragic, but the immensity of their dolor could not extract from the old couple the slightest expression of hatred or anger against the man they continued to call their son. When the magistrate insinuated that Victor Blancadet might well have wanted to get rid of his wife in order to enter into possession of the reciprocal donation stipulated in the marriage contract, the Comte de La Moutardie made a gesture of negation so haughty and so disgusted that Bouïgri did not even dare to mention the undertaker and Cécilia's infidelity. In their distress, the Comte and Comtesse begged the magistrate to return their child to them, since death had taken the other. Blancadet had a crisis of despair so violent that he was carried away unconscious.

In spite of the most scrupulous research, it was impossible to discover the undertaker, who must, according to Bouïgri, have "buried himself."

Célestin responded with the greatest alacrity to the invitations of the Law and had no hesitation in declaring that the accused had "a sly and somewhat hypocritical character"—which was not astonishing, for "there are people from whom it's necessary to expect anything," and, in his opinion, an individual like Blancadet, who, although blind, could see with an apparatus of glass eyes and spectacles, didn't inspire the slightest confidence.

He wanted to go into detailed explanations, but Bouïgri would not hear any attempt to criticize the miracle of La Moutardie and the unfortunate valet was roundly abused, as was Madame Benoît, whose deposition also tended to establish that Victor Blancadet could see with the aid of his glass eyes and spectacles long before the twenty-first of June.

The optician was summoned in his turn and, taking the letter of the oath to tell the truth, the whole truth and nothing but the truth, tried hard to prove the virtue of the spectacles constructed by him in accordance with Victor Blancadet's plans. The name "assagitator," the metal amplifying vibrations, provoked a veritable fit of rage in Bouïgri, and he threatened the overly conscientious optician with a mental examination, like Blancadet himself. The worthy and placid spectacle-maker, struck by the discredit that that measure would bring upon his house, immediately thought of his wife and children, and approved and signed everything that the examining magistrate desired.

What Bouïgri desired, as he often confided to his friend John Plum—which was, in principle, a sufficiently legitimate desire—was "not to be taken for an imbecile," and he estimated that "one could not be anything but an imbecile to believe in the possibility of blind man seeing without the most direct celestial intervention."

The most categorical witness statements and the most peremptory evidence could not erode his conviction, and when the physicians he had commissioned to examine Victor Blancadet deposed their report he wondered whether "alienist" and "alienated" were not two rigorous synonyms, in the French language that was not supposed to contain any.

Had not one of the three princes of medico-legal science summarized and endorsed Blancadet's assertions? It was the complete theory of sight without eyes, the globes of glass serving as recording apparatus and the auditory nerves taking the place of the optic nerves via the intermediary of a metal amplifying the vibrations. The physician admitted the perfect possibility of the phenomenon and considered the accused as "a genius worthy of being classed in the rank of the most glorious sons of humankind." And he added that "his prescience of the infinite rendered him absolutely irresponsible for his actions."

Of his two colleagues, one was of the opinion that "the Blancadet case" was the most striking example of demonic possession that he had ever encountered. Did not Satan reign as master over that soul dazzled by the ineffable contact of God? He concluded, in consequence, the spiritual irresponsibility of Blancadet, while affirming his full and entire responsibility before human justice.

The third expert belonged to the young school of integral eclecticism. In his understanding, the most entire mysticism copulated with the most ardent positivist doctrines, and the result was an absolute scorn for every kind of affirmation or negation. As a "glorious son of humanity" Blancadet seemed to him to be irresponsible, but as a "subject of the infernal powers" the same Blancadet had without restriction to answer for his actions. That breadth of views, embracing the entire panorama of possible conclusions, merited the triumph; it was translated into "limited responsibility," and it was with that metal reference-point that Victor Blancadet, after a preliminary summons to the general court, was transferred to the Court of Assizes of the Seine under an accusation of murder committed on the person off Cécilia Blancadet, Comtesse de La Moutardie, his wife.

XX

In all places that are centers of authority, the Court of Assizes is the legal and gratuitous representation of a drama in which all the scenes have been carefully rehearsed behind closed doors during the investigation. At the heart of certain provinces, the Palais de Justice holds, successfully, often without being exposed to any competition, the part of the program advertised as *circenses* in the most thoughtful Roman histories, the *panem* being assured by social fringe specified under the rubrics "rentiers, functionaries and assimilates, manufacturers and merchants."[18] In Paris, where the spectacles in question have an exceptional frequency and diversity, the clientele flocks willingly to Themis; the modest and reserved

---

[18] The reference is to the *panem* [bread] and *circenses* [circuses] by which Roman emperors proverbially kept the city's population sufficiently satisfied not to revolt.

goddess receives with infinite grace, and only her Roman toga prevents her from practicing a broader hospitality.

Major trials generate "takings," as they say at the Society of Authors and Dramatists, and at the administration of the Assurance Publique, where a legal project is under consideration permitting the installation of poor-boxes at the entrance doors of the most sought-after courtrooms.

The Blancadet trial was inscribed in the first pages of contemporary judiciary magnificence; thus, several weeks before the date marked for the hearings, everyone in Paris who was anyone wanted to have a seat at the Court of Assizes.

Counselor Le Chatouillard, whose colleagues called him "the pianist," as much because of the delicacy of his touch as his hair, still Absalomian in spite of his forty-five years, experienced a very legitimate joy on learning that the Blancadet trial would fall within his fortnightly rotation.

The number of applicants was comparable to the sands of the sea, whose immensity the courtroom as far from matching. With an angelic patience Counselor Le Chatouillard received everyone, and for everyone he found a phrase that rendered his refusals delightful. To pretty women he expressed his keen regret at being unable to place them on his knees, and to men he revealed the names of important individuals that had solicited him in vain. The misfortune of others helps one to support one's own; without unleashing too much anger, Counselor Le Chatouillard, by skillfully distributing his favors, contrived an audience exclusively composed of the most stellar Parisian society.

On the very morning when the trial was to open, Alcée Baillargal was authorized to visit the accused in his cell at the Conciergerie. Victor Blancadet seemed indifferent and insensible to everything that was happening. As the journalist exhorted him to defend himself energetically, he made an imperceptible shrug of the shoulders, which translated his complete renunciation of the slightest effort.

310

"What's the point?" he concluded, with a resigned gesture. "My advocate can say what he pleases. Let them do with me as they wish. It's not of the slightest importance."

"It's necessary that you emerge from the courtroom with your head high, acquitted. You're innocent!"

"I'm unfortunate! I'm unfortunate!" And he put so much anguish into the word "unfortunate" that he did not seem to have anything left of that which attached him to life.

Alcée Baillargal having pronounced the names of the Comte and Comtesse de La Moutardie, he was gripped by a tremor and murmured: "Poor souls! Poor souls! They too are unfortunate. Their child! My Cécilia! Ah…!"

After a long silence, the journalist embraced Blancadet and, having begged him not to let himself be overwhelmed by despair, left him to go to the courtroom, already invaded by a crowd as elegant as it was compact.

At noon precisely, the jurors came to take their places on their bench. The twelve citizens who combine the plenitude of their civil and political rights with the enviable prerogative of passing judgment on their contemporaries are at the Court of Assizes what the musicians of the orchestra are at a lyrical performance; their presence is essential, but the ignorant public does not pay the slightest attention to them, all its favor being reserved for the artistes whose role, often easier, is more plastically personal.

The installation at the bar of the young trainee, whom Victor Blancadet had not bothered to dispossess of his defense to the profit of the principal subjects of the List, who had asked him repeatedly for the honor of pleading his case, only aroused a mediocre curiosity.

The "star"—the person whose name would have taken up three quarters of the poster on its own, had it been a matter of the theater—was indisputably the accused; all eyes were, therefore, hypnotically fixed on the little door through which he would enter the stage. The door opened, but it was only a sergeant-major in the Republican guard—but a man in a black

311

frock-coat, in full mourning-dress, was on his heels: that was him, Blancadet, Victor Blancadet, the accused!

There was a long ripple of movement in the audience, which was not completely calmed by the three raps announcing the Court energetically struck by the usher on the door of the Council Chamber.

President Le Chatouillard came forward, escorted by his two colleagues, with Advocate-General Procivet, charged with sustaining the accusation, bringing up the rear. He sat down and surveyed the audience with a long satisfied glance. He creased his clean-shaven lips into a smile, which each of his invited guests attributed to their own destination, and pronounced the sacramental: "The hearing is open!" The jurors took the oath, and after the reading of the charge sheet by the clerk, the usher proceeded with the roll-call of the witnesses, who were relegated to the location reserved for them.

The interrogation commenced. The Absalomian President La Chatouillard dispensed a great deal of wit, but, doing honor to his soubriquet "the pianist," gave proof of an exquisite dexterity in not abusing the superiority of his situation relative to the accused. Victor Blancadet responded to each question with a slow downward movement of the head, which the President translated for the jurors with a uniform: "The accused agrees! No dispute on that point."

That monologue, which did not permit the organ of the public ministry the slightest intervention, was closed by the honorable Monsieur Procivet, with the reflection that: "The accused does not appear to be combative. He denies nothing, but denying nothing strongly resembles confessing nothing."

"We shall hear the witnesses," said Monsieur Le Chatouillard.

"Bibi! Jocaste Bibi!" called the usher, opening the door to the room reserved for the witnesses.

An aged woman, whose red and green floral-patterned dress resembled the plumage of some exotic bird was guided to the bar by the usher, who stimulated her with reiterated: "Come on, go forward, Madame Bibi!"

In spite of President Le Chatouillard's most meritorious efforts, it was impossible to extract from the witness her name, forenames, age, profession, domicile or any of the other more or less indiscreet items of information of which the law is fond.

Monsieur Procivet came to the rescue and, in elegant and florid terms, explained how the present Madame Bibi, formerly the maiden Jocaste, not followed by any patronymic by virtue of her status as an unrecognized natural child, had been a cook in the house of the long-deceased father and mother of the accused. Subsequently, the maiden Jocaste, having come to Paris, had married the chemist Lehargnol, and had been rendered a widow by the catastrophe of the fifth of May 1885. It was thanks to her that the accused had entered Lehargnol's laboratory, where he had escaped the accident—"to your misfortune, for you would not be on the bench of infamy today," Monsieur Procivet graciously parenthesized, turning toward Blancadet.

The widow Lehargnol had legitimately remarried a certain Bibi, a veterinarian in the vicinity of Fontainebleau. "It is for that reason, Messieurs the jurors, that the woman is now called Madame Bibi, Jocaste Bibi," the honorable Monsieur Procivet concluded.

The account of her biography had had an effect on the worthy Madame Bibi's lachrymal glands; she was weeping copiously, and was only just able, between two hiccups, to make President le Chatouillard understand that "she knew absolutely nothing about Victor Blancadet, whose parents were very worthy people."

"Go sit down," concluded Monsieur Le Chatouillard.

The usher called: "Alcée Baillargal."

The journalist came to the stand, submitted to the standard questionnaire, and raised his ungloved right hand without hesitation in order to swear to tell "the truth, the whole truth and nothing but the truth."

He recommenced the story of his first visit to the Rue du Sabre-de-l'Abbé and solemnly affirmed that Victor Blancadet

313

definitely enjoyed the faculty of sight without eyes long before the twenty-first of June. He entered into explanations so confused that the President interrupted him with the traditional "Messieurs the jurors will decide," and asked him to provide enlightenments regarding the crime itself. Baillargal replied that he knew absolutely nothing about it, but he considered Victor Blancadet absolutely incapable of having killed his wife, whom he adored. The President returned to the refrain: "Messieurs the jurors will decide," and thanked the journalist, who was replaced on the stand by his mistress.

"Madame Baillargal," said Le Chatouillard, full of urbanity, "you knew the victim. In your opinion, did she deceive the accused?"

"Never! Never!" cried the pseudo-cousin Valentine, fervently. "Cécilia was an honest woman."

"Messieurs the jurors will decide. You were not present at the scene of the murder?"

"I was at home in Paris, Monsieur le President, when the terrible accident occurred."

"That's all, thank you!"

The procession of witnesses continued; there was Maître Des Échinettes, who came to affirm the resistance he had had to vanquish in order to make Victor Blancadet accept the clause of contractual and reciprocal donation to the survivor. The widowed Madame Brindolle declared that she had never had anything for which to reproach her temporary client.

"You keep, in Ilderon, the Hôtel de l'Esturgeon Miraculeux, do you not?" asked President Le Chatouillard, and, after an affirmative response from Madame Brindolle: "Are you unaware that the accused claims that there was no miracle at La Moutardie?"

"But that's not possible! Do you want to ruin me, Monsieur Blancadet de La Moutardie?" squealed the widow, consoled by Maître Des Échinettes.

"Calm down, I beg you, Madame," said Monsieur Le Chatouillard. "The commercial enterprise with which you have had the fortunate idea of endowing your region is legitimate and respectable. Thank God, the miracle of the twenty-first of June cannot be called into question; the medical certificates are there to establish it. It is not the allegations of..." Monsieur Le Chatouillard hesitated. "...The law does not permit me to say 'a murderer,' that can destroy the edifice of which God has placed the first stone. The pilgrimage of La Moutardie will be the rendezvous of all the blind people of the earth. The Holy Eye will be the feast whose glare will radiate over the first Wednesday of every summer denoted in the pages of the Gregorian calendar."

Monsieur Le Chatouillard concluded his peroration with a very dignified: "May your efforts be rewarded, witness! Go sit down."

Célestin appeared, his upper lip augmented by a superb moustache symbolizing his human dignity, because, for the moment, he was completely unemployed. He offered appreciations of his former master qualified personally as "severe, but just."

Madame Benoît and the optician, one out of timidity and the other by prudence, did not make their voices audible. After the passage of witnesses of "morality" who, for the most part, did not know who or what they were talking about, Monsieur Le Chatouillard announced that, by virtue of his discretionary power, he had authorized the Comte and Comtesse de La Moutardie not to appear at the hearing. He had acted with a simple humanitarian motive and out of respect for the grief of the father and mother of the victim. Nevertheless, he was ready, if the public minister or the defense thought it useful, to order their immediate summoning. The honorable Monsieur Procivet, who knew that Monsieur and Madame de La Moutardie were sympathetic to the accused, remained mute, and the defender, for his part, refrained from raising the slightest objection.

It was the turn of the practitioner who had examined the body of the victim; he deposed with a luxury of magisterially methodical detail. He explained the accused thesis. He operated various eupantophones seized in the course of searches before the eyes of the jurors, explaining their mechanism. Then he reconstituted the scene of the crime; with the poisoned stiletto in his hand he demonstrated how a simple prick had occasioned the sudden death. The jurors learned that *Strychnos toxifera* is a plant that climbs along trees in America as *Hedera helix*, commonly called ivy, does in Europe; that the savages procure an aqueous extract from it the scientists call curare; that it was to that all-powerful drug that the victim had succumbed. He had, in fact, found in Cécilia Blancadet all the symptoms of death by suppression of the contractility of the motor nerves.

The doctor became so absorbed by his subject that he forgot that he was holding the stiletto steeped in the redoubtable curare; an oratorical gesture more ample than the others caused him to brush his epidermis with the redoubtable point. He uttered a scream and, after having observed that there was no flow of blood, declared dramatically that: "A thousandth of a millimeter more and I was dead. I have nothing to add, Monsieur le Président."

Everything directly relating to the facts was exhausted. The three alienist physicians filed through in their turn, each bringing a different appreciation of the mental state of the accused. Under diametrically opposite considerations, the trio arrived at the same scarcely-compromising conclusion: "Victor Blancadet is an abnormal individual, in whom an accident occurring in extraordinarily exceptional conditions has caused a partial loss of the notion of good and evil."

A suspension of the hearing permitted the Court and the jurors a brief period of rest before the speeches for the prosecution and the defense.

Monsieur Procivet, after an exordium in which he exposed the duties of the Law in general and his own in particular, went over the arguments of the accusation one by one. In an almost thunderous voice he repeated the confession of the accused: "My Cécilia, it's me who has killed her!" adding: "Those words, accused Blancadet, sprang from your conscience, driven by an invincible force comparable to the pressure of powder exploding in the breech of a firearm and expelling the projectile."

He flagellated in advance the excuse of Fatality that the defense bench would not fail to invoke. "Fatality, Messieurs the Jurors, is the modern scapegoat that is no longer content merely to take on the sins of Israel!"

He accused "sieur Blancadet" of having "wanted to live the Shakespearean dream of simultaneously realizing and inheritance, satisfying a jealousy and avenging his honor."

He read the love letter written by the employee of the funeral parlor. The style had a sentimental lyricism of the most beautiful effect. "We have been unable to discover its author," explained Monsieur Procivet. "The suspicions of the law were directed at an employee whose education in letters rendered him capable of such gallant phraseology, but he denied it so forcefully that the Law was unable to shake him." Monsieur Procivet criticized the conduct of the undertaker, whose shame rebounded on the entire corporation, although exclusively composed of "dutiful and conscientious individuals."

He brandished at the end of his arm the blade of the law over the nape of the man who, his crime accomplished, had fled the responsibility. "Why not proudly proclaim the justification of your act? Your rights as an offended spouse and betrayed husband were respectable! It was legitimate for you to make the creature capable of forfeiture toward conjugal faith expiate her sin! You could have said to us: 'I loved my Cécilia; she betrayed me; I killed her.' No man would have found it in him to condemn you; you would have emerged free from this courtroom and your head would not have bumped into the lintels of the doors because the horns with which your wife had ornamented your forehead would have been severed at the root by your bloody hand."

The honorable Monsieur Procivet continued, showering redoubtable blows upon Victor Blancadet and the beauty of the French language, every word of which, in his mouth, took on the consistency of a heavy cobblestone. He begged the jurors to give him the head of the accused, not for himself—who had no use for it—but for Society, whose destiny he bore in the pleats of his red robe.

The young trainee's speech was skeletal in its sobriety and totally deprived of the images, as bold as they are unexpected, that are the honor and joy of courtroom orators.

With a simplicity of soul that made Monsieur Procivet, the President and his colleagues smile, he declared that he had come "solely to defend the honor of the victim, for the accident of the eupantophone was so indisputable that anyone endowed with any common sense would seek no further for the key to the dramatic mystery..."

"You're insulting Messieurs the jurors," Monsieur Procivet interjected.

"Why?" the defender replied. "Messieurs the jurors are men of common sense. They will acquit!" In his juvenile confidences, he repeated: "Isn't it true, Messieurs the jurors, who are men of common sense, that what I am asking of you is a word of justice. Proclaim it! Humanity will be grateful to you for it."

When the defender sat down, Preside Le Chatouillard addressed the accused.

"Victor Blancadet, do you have anything to add in your defense?"

By a negative moment of his head Blancadet testified that what would happen at the end of the hearing was of no more interest to him than what had preceded it.

The jury went out to deliberate; during the suspension of the hearing the usual bets were laid for and against the condemnation. The habitual audience of the Court of Assizes was unanimous in finding Victor Blancadet uninteresting and unworthy of the manifest interest in his case.

The negative verdict read out by the foreman of the jury caused a disappointment all the more veritable because Blancadet manifested not the slightest emotion, allowing himself to be meekly led away by the Republican guards after the verdict of acquittal, after which President Le Chatouillard ordered that he be "immediately set at liberty, if not retained for any other cause."

XXI

Blancadet did not recover from the frightful crisis he had traversed. Like a wounded man who does not know whether he has veritably escaped death, and who still doubts the possibility of life, he remained for long hours in complete hebetude, motionless, with his spectacles on his knees.

He had given his friend Baillargal a power of attorney to proceed with the immediate sale of all the movable possessions in his apartments in the Rue du Sabre-de-l'Abbé and the Rue du Luxembourg. The unfortunate individual tried to avoid anything that could remind him of the past and give substance to the atrocious nightmare with which his eyes were still filled.

Often, in the course of the somber reveries that overwhelmed him, a hoarse cry caught in his throat: "Cécilia! My Cécilia!"

And that was his entrance into the room, the spark flashing from the eupantophone, the horrible specter of his wife lying on the floor; and then the pursuit, the arrest, the accusation of murder, the maddening investigation in which, step by step, bruise by bruise, sob by sob, he had reclimbed the calvary of the frightful adventure, harassed by the magistrate, who, at each of his weaknesses born of the excess of his grief, found in his shredded being another fiber still sufficiently alive not to remain dead to suffering.

He took his head in his hands, and there was an abrupt release that brought out the full ludicrousness of things: the silhouettes of the examining magistrate Marius Bouïgri and his acolyte John Plum loomed up again; the melodramatic thundering of Advocate General Procivet, whose official virtue was mounted on the pedestal of all the human and social flaws contained in the voluptuously-explored mire of police dossiers, sounding even more ridiculously than in the lamentable tally-ho of his condemnation; the frightful and macabre irony of the law exhausting itself in superhuman efforts to extract from the letter written by the employee of the funeral parlor evidence of the dead woman's infidelity; the professional aberration of the accusing magistrate rejecting the evidence of facts because of their overly perfect simplicity and using his genius to stand up phantoms hatched by a delirious imagination; the procession of witnesses of so-called morality, dressing up the truth as best they could in favor of or to the detriment of the accused, according to whether they were called by the defense or the public ministry.

And those alternations resulted, for Blancadet, in an inexpressible lassitude, an insurmountable disgust for everything, a total paralysis of the self that rendered him incapable of the most futile of thoughts. He had not yet asked himself why he had followed Baillargal to the Rue de la Crémaillère, and, like a child who never has the slightest caprice, without a wrinkle on the surface of his inalterable passivity, he lived vegetatively, like a body devoid of a soul.

Very charitably, the journalist's companion tried to find him a few distractions. The evenings, until late into the night, were spent in endless games of manille[19] in which Charlotte was given to him as a partner. Meekly, he allowed himself to be guided by the young maid, whose fervor for the game often went so far as to treat him as an imbecile with regard to a card inopportunely played. The pseudo-Madame Baillargal called her to order, although Blancadet made no protest. One evening, he committed so many errors, and so massive were his blunders, that Charlotte, exasperated by a fatal revoke, had thrown the cards at his head shouting that she no longer wanted to play with someone who was incapable of distinguishing the trumps.

Valentine sent Charlotte to bed, and, in the course of the conversation that followed, Blancadet agreed that Charlotte was right and that he was, indeed, seeing rather poorly.

---

[19] A card game that has some similarity to whist, played with a piquet deck.

Baillargal begged him to take more care of his eyes; meekly, he took them out and, after having examined them attentively, said: "They need cleaning. My powder is like people; as it works, it becomes black, and, like servants, appreciates idleness so much that it's incapable of the slightest effort..."

He guided Valentine in the scrupulous work of toilette, and his artificial eyes, caressed at length by the powder-puff laden with virgin sensitive powder, recovered all their means.

The next day, he played manille brilliantly, and after a successful finesse, Charlotte could not prevent herself from throwing her arms around his neck and kissing him on both cheeks.

Valentine proposed that they celebrate the victory with a supper in which truffled *foie gras*, washed down by a generous bottle, would accompany the cheese soup that Charlotte hastened to make.

While the cook was weeping onion tears, Valentine confided to Blancadet that young Charlotte thought him charming.

"And what do you think of her?"

"Charming, obviously," Blancadet acquiesced.

"You know, Monsieur Victor, she likes you very much, and I believe that she has a weakness for you..."

And, as Blancadet remained mute, Valentine continued: "You ought to like her too, and you ought, for your part, to have a weakness for her."

"I'd like nothing better," the Baillargals' lodger had said, obediently.

The cheese soup flowed, that evening, in honor of Charlotte, who did not return to her room on the sixth-floor.

A maid sent by an employment agency occupied it henceforth, and the following spring, the registrar of the arrondissement received a touching declaration of the birth of a male child, the son of Sieur Victor Blancadet and the demoiselle Charlotte, domiciled together in the Rue de la Crémaillère. Blancadet had to produce identity documents in which mention was made of his title of Comte de La

Moutardie; the employee, posted behind his grille, pronounced it several times in a loud voice, concluding:

"It isn't because you bear a ridiculous name that you have to blush at being noble."[20]

---

[20] In fact, Moutardie is not so very rare as a French surname in more than one province, and only sounds slightly silly to Parisian ears because "moutardier" means "mustard-pot."

SF & FANTASY

Adolphe Alhaiza. *Cybele*
Alphonse Allais. *The Adventures of Captain Cap*
Henri Allorge. *The Great Cataclysm*
Guy d'Armen. *Doc Ardan: The City of Gold and Lepers*
G.-J. Arnaud. *The Ice Company*
Charles Asselineau. *The Double Life*
Cyprien Bérard. *The Vampire Lord Ruthwen*
S. Henry Berthoud. *Martyrs of Science*
Aloysius Bertrand. *Gaspard de la Nuit*
Richard Bessière. *The Gardens of the Apocalypse*
Albert Bleunard. *Ever Smaller*
Félix Bodin. *The Novel of the Future*
Louis Boussenard. *Monsieur Synthesis*
Alphonse Brown. *City of Glass; The Conquest of the Air*
Emile Calvet. *In a Thousand Years*
André Caroff. *The Terror of Madame Atomos; Miss Atomos; The Return of Madame Atomos; The Mistake of Madame Atomos; The Monsters of Madame Atomos; The Revenge of Madame Atomos; The Resurrection of Madame Atomos; The Mark of Madame Atomos; The Spheres of Madame Atomos*
Félicien Champsaur. *The Human Arrow; Ouha, King of the Apes; Pharaoh's Wife*
Didier de Chousy. *Ignis*
Jules Clarétie. *Obsession*
Michel Corday. *The Eternal Flame*
André Couvreur. *The Necessary Evil; Caresco, Superman; The Exploits of Professor Tornada* (3 vols.)
Captain Danrit. *Undersea Odyssey*
C. I. Defontenay. *Star (Psi Cassiopeia)*
Charles Derennes. *The People of the Pole*
Georges Dodds (anthologist). *The Missing Link*
Harry Dickson. *The Heir of Dracula*
Jules Dornay. *Lord Ruthven Begins*
Alfred Driou. *The Adventures of a Parisian Aeronaut*
Sâr Dubnotal *vs. Jack the Ripper*
Alexandre Dumas. *The Return of Lord Ruthven*
Renée Dunan. *Baal*
J.-C. Dunyach. *The Night Orchid; The Thieves of Silence*

Henri Duvernois. *The Man Who Found Himself*
Achille Eyraud. *Voyage to Venus*
Henri Falk. *The Age of Lead*
Paul Féval. *Anne of the Isles; Knightshade; Revenants; Vampire City; The Vampire Countess; The Wandering Jew's Daughter*
Paul Féval, *fils. Felifax, the Tiger-Man*
Charles de Fieux. *Lamékis*
Louis Forest. *Someone is Stealing Children in Paris*
Arnould Galopin. *Doctor Omega; Doctor Omega and the Shadowmen* (anthology)
Judith Gautier. *Isoline and the Serpent-Flower*
H. Gayar. *The Marvelous Adventures of Serge Myrandhal on Mars*
Léon Gozlan. *The Vampire of the Val-de-Grâce*
G.L. Gick. *Harry Dickson and the Werewolf of Rutherford Grange*
Edmond Haraucourt. *Illusions of Immortality*
Nathalie Henneberg. *The Green Gods*
V. Hugo, P. Foucher & P. Meurice. *The Hunchback of Notre-Dame*
Romain d'Huissier. *Hexagon: Dark Matter*
Jules Janin. *The Magnetized Corpse*
Michel Jeury. *Chronolysis*
Gustave Kahn. *The Tale of Gold and Silence*
Gérard Klein. *The Mote in Time's Eye*
Fernand Kolney. *Love in 5000 Years*
Paul Lacroix. *Danse Macabre*
Louis-Guillaume de La Follie. *The Unpretentious Philosopher*
Jean de La Hire. *Enter the Nyctalope; The Nyctalope on Mars; The Nyctalope vs. Lucifer; The Nyctalope Steps In; Night of the Nyctalope; Return of the Nyctalope; The Fiery Wheel*
Etienne-Léon de Lamothe-Langon. *The Virgin Vampire*
André Laurie. *Spiridon*
Gabriel de Lautrec. *The Vengeance of the Oval Portrait*
Alain le Drimeur. *The Future City*
Georges Le Faure & Henri de Graffigny. *The Extraordinary Adventures of a Russian Scientist Across the Solar System* (2 vols.)
Gustave Le Rouge. *The Mysterious Doctor Cornelius* (3 vols.); *The Vampires of Mars; The Dominion of the World* (w/Gustave Guitton) (4 vols.)
Jules Lermina. *Mysteryville; Panic in Paris; To-Ho and the Gold Destroyers; The Secret of Zippelius*
André Lichtenberger. *The Centaurs; The Children of the Crab*

Kurt Steiner. *Ortog*
Eugène Thébault. *Radio-Terror*
C.-F. Tiphaigne de La Roche. *Amilec*
Louis Ulbach. *Prince Bonifacio*
Théo Varlet. *The Golden Rock. The Xenobiotic Invasion; The Casta-
ways of Eros; Timeslip Troopers* (w/André Blandin); *The Martian
Epic* (w/Octave Joncquel)
Paul Vibert. *The Mysterious Fluid*
Villiers de l'Isle-Adam. *The Scaffold; The Vampire Soul*
Philippe Ward. *Artahe*
Philippe Ward & Sylvie Miller. *The Song of Montségur*

MYSTERIES & THRILLERS

M. Allain & P. Souvestre. *The Daughter of Fantômas*
A. Anicet-Bourgeois, Lucien Dabril. *Rocambole*
A. Bernède. *Belphegor*; *Judex* (w/Louis Feuillade); *The Return of
Judex* (w/Louis Feuillade); *The Shadow of Judex*
A. Bisson & G. Livet. *Nick Carter vs. Fantômas*
V. Darlay & H. de Gorsse. *Arsène Lupin vs. Sherlock Holmes: The
Stage Play*
Séamas Duffy. *Sherlock Holmes in Paris*
Paul Féval. *Gentlemen of the Night; John Devil; The Black Coats
('Salem Street; The Invisible Weapon; The Parisian Jungle; The
Companions of the Treasure; Heart of Steel; The Cadet Gang; The
Sword-Swallower)*
Emile Gaboriau. *Monsieur Lecoq*
Goron & Emile Gautier. *Spawn of the Penitentiary*
Rick Lai. *Shadows of the Opera: Retribution in Blood; Sisters of the
Shadows: The Curse of Cagliostro*
Steve Leadley. *Sherlock Holmes: The Circle of Blood*
Maurice Leblanc. *Arsène Lupin vs. Countess Cagliostro; Arsène
Lupin vs. Sherlock Holmes (The Blonde Phantom; The Hollow Nee-
dle); The Many Faces of Arsène Lupin*
Gaston Leroux. *Chéri-Bibi; The Phantom of the Opera; Rouletabille
& the Mystery of the Yellow Room; Rouletabille at Krupp's*
Richard Marsh. *The Complete Adventures of Judith Lee*
William Patrick Maynard. *The Terror of Fu Manchu; The Destiny of
Fu Manchu*
Frank J. Morlock. *Sherlock Holmes: The Grand Horizontals; Sher-
lock Holmes vs Jack the Ripper*

Jean Petithuguenin. *The Adventures of Ethel King*
Antonin Reschal. *The Adventures of Miss Boston*
P. de Wattyne & Y. Walter. *Sherlock Holmes vs. Fantômas*
David White. *Fantômas in America*
Pierre Yrondy. *The Adventures of Thérèse Arnaud*

SCREENPLAYS

Mike Baron. *The Iron Triangle*
Emma Bull & Will Shetterly. *Nightspeeder; War for the Oaks*
Gerry Conway & Roy Thomas. *Doc Dynamo*
Steve Englehart. *Majorca*
James Hudnall. *The Devastator*
Jean-Marc & Randy Lofficier. *Royal Flush*
J.-M. & R. Lofficier & Marc Agapit. *Despair*
J.-M. & R. Lofficier & Joël Houssin. *City*
Andrew Paquette. *Peripheral Vision*
Robert L. Robinson, Jr. *Judex*
R. Thomas, J. Hendler & L. Sprague de Camp. *Rivers of Time*

NON-FICTION

Stephen R. Bissette. *Blur 1-5. Green Mountain Cinema 1; Teen Angels*
Win Scott Eckert. *Crossovers* (2 vols.)
Jean-Marc & Randy Lofficier. *Shadowmen* (2 vols.)
Randy Lofficier. *Over Here*

ART BOOKS

J.-M. Lofficier & D. Taylor. *Tongue Lash*
Jean-Pierre Normand. *Science Fiction Illustrations*
Raven Okeefe. *Raven's L'il Critters; Rave's Faves*
Randy Lofficier & Raven Okeefe. *If Your Possum Go Daylight...*
Daniele Serra. *Illusions*

www.ingramcontent.com/pod-product-compliance
Lightning Source LLC
Chambersburg PA
CBHW022221010726
47493CB00002B/545